A Super Duper Adventure Against Nightmares
E David Seibert

Co-Pilot's (Pro)Log:

Space
Somewhere Diagonal to the Constellation of Taurus
Aboard the Ship of no Determinate Name
Co-Pilot's Quarters (Well, one of them)
Olivia Jones turns on the recording device and speaks:

"So. Umm. Yes. Olivia Jones here… God this feels dumb. Whatever. I just thought- like, it's been like six months since we left Earth. Well, I mean I think it's been six months. Alibaster gave Penelope and me these like calendar things that keep in sync with time on Earth, to help us stay orientated despite the fact that time and all of its measurements are in fact a lie. At least, it's a lie in any way that can be understood by anyone other than Penelope, and other temporally sensitive folks.

"Off track. Focus, Jones.

"So, let's say it's been six months. Half a year out here with two people who drive me absolutely bat crap at times, but I also could not imagine my life without. And it's been good. We've been good. We've done some good, which was the whole point of this… excursion.

"Just last week we rescued the three Hexagonal Queens of the great city-state of 'Slide-Eyes-Way'. What did we save them from, you ask? Only a hive of thrice-undead ninja monks who wanted to topple the empire of said great city state and start, and I quote: 'A nine billion year feast on the souls of all your innocent.'

"I know, right? What jerk-holes. Luckily, we were able to seal them into this ancient obelisk thing that sits just outside of our collective understanding, and save the day.

"Oh, and a month before that we exposed a used space car dealership that had been using bootleg time travel to save money by selling just one car to multiple people, multiple times, along multiple timelines. Causing what Penelope had deemed 'a massive chronal cluster-flek'.

"And before that we went to this planet that was all one big restaurant. Each continent specialized in a different delicacy. We stayed for three weeks- probably- and ate more Korean barbecue than should ever be consumed in one lifetime. Don't ask me how a planet that's never heard of Earth had Korean barbecue. I'm just grateful it did.

"So yeah, it's been great. And it's been terrifying. And it's been gratifying. And I wouldn't have missed it for anything. It's just…We've been out here for as long as we've been out here, and I felt like I should star keeping some sort of journal or something. Some way to articulate things. Some kind of, I don't know, catharsis for my very- for lack of a better word- *peculiar* life. So these may get ramble-y. Sorry. (Well, if anyone else ever hears these then I'm sorry.) I'm not a great story teller. Sometimes I like to start with the most exciting parts and work my way out. Like being dropped into a maze from above. I always hated books that started in the middle, but I can't help doing it myself… Sometimes my thoughts are a jungle I have to hack my way out of.

"Anyhoo, what else is new with me? I haven't talked to my family in half a year, because Earth isn't very advanced when it comes to interstellar communication, and I'm currently a bajillion light years away from it. I miss my family, but ever since that fateful day when I was sixteen and got called into the universe, I knew I had been drifting away from them.

"As for the Fate Makers… Oh, haha. I just said 'fateful', didn't I? How punny of me. Anyway, I haven't heard much from the Fates either. We have a weird ambivalent relationship, and we pretty much keep out of each other's ways. But they also gave us free reign to help or interfere wherever we feel like it. That privilege opens a lot of doors, and makes our work a lot easier on some occasions… and a lot more difficult on others.

"For this privilege, the Tribunal gave us certain guidelines that we more or less try to follow. The situations we find ourselves in don't always allow for strict adherence to the rules. But there is one rule, the main rule, which I won't let any of us break: No killing.

"After… Ophelia… After I had to… I just. I just wanted. I can't. I know she had to- but I never want to… Not again. Never again. And I won't let my friends live with the same… It's like a hole. Or an emptiness. It sits right in the heart of my soul and if I focus on it too long I just want to lie down and never get back up. I can't let my friends do what I did. I can't let them live with this… pit.

"…

"I guess the real reason I started this one-sided podcast now instead of months ago is because it's hard to find a therapist that would get it; that would understand my- *our*- peculiar life, and I just needed to talk to someone- to something- about the…

"It's the nightmares.

"They keep getting worse."

Chapter 1: Exemplary Essential Exposition

Two Space Weeks Later (which are like regular weeks, but in space)
Outer Edge of the Terminal Clusters of the Infallible Magi
Last Few Sections of the Eternal Gold Storms
Control Bridge of Team Dumb Luck's Space Ship (which was not their official team name, just used for space tax purposes)

While still living on Earth, Olivia Jones had once watched a documentary about the tropes often used in science fiction shows and movies; which bits used were practical, and which weren't. And she remembered some smart science-y dude talking about asteroids, and how- unlike in movies- asteroids were actually usually pretty far apart from each other, and the odds of having to bob and weave left and right like an old arcade game was not very realistic.

And right now- as Olivia and her friends ran around their ship's control console, frantically pressing buttons and typing commands that forced the ship to narrowly avoid each hurtling asteroid (which were all made entirely of gold, making the "Eternal Gold Storms" very aptly named)- she really, really wanted to punch that smart science-y dude right in his bespectacled face.

"Three more layers and we're through," Alibaster said as the outer hull bucked against something that- if weighed and sold- would have helped a moderately sized Earth country retire early. Alibaster was the leather-jacket-wearing-antiauthoritarian-alien-genius captain of the ship. He was only the captain by default, since it was his ship to begin with, and he was the one who taught the others how to fly it. (In Alibaster's personal dictionary, the word "fly" seemed to be defined as, "to slingshot from one planet to the next with hapless abandon, and crash with consistency".)

He fell sideways into Penelope, who immediately pushed him away with a grunt. "I doubt there's any chance we can get those warlock guys to turn the tractor-beam bridge back on and let us pass out of here safely, is there?" she asked as the full force of her- admittedly petite- body struggled against a stuck lever.

Penelope Brownstein-McClain was one of the ship's co-pilots: a multiversal anomaly acutely attuned to the dimension of Time. She was born from the tipping over of certain temporal dominoes by an evil god who wanted to use her to escape their prison, and keep her body and powers for their own horrendous usage. Loves included buttered noodles and sarcasm. Hates included the exact situation she was in currently, and sports talk radio.

Even though there was quite a lot going on at the moment- with death coming at them from all sides and all- Alibaster and Olivia still found a moment to stare at Penelope and blink several knowing blinks.

"What?" Penelope asked over the several alarms going off. "All I said was that it was stupid that the dude knights in their video games wear armor and shields stuff and that the chick ones only wore chain-mail bikinis."

The Infallible Magi- for those who were unaware (which included everyone except the members of the Infallible Magi, said member's mothers, and several wayward travelers)- were a group of men...

Well, a group of boys...

A group of males. The Infallible Magi were a group of males who were never wrong about anything, so there's really no point trying to have any sort of civil discussion. Because any participant of any discussion that was not a Magi will be automatically wrong; regardless of topic, or how educated the participant is on said topic, or how many PHDs said participant has acquired during many years of hard work and study on said topic.

They will be wrong.

Everyone has met someone that could qualify to become a member of the Infallible Magi. But these particular males from one particular planet decided that they just couldn't take "the ignorance of the plebeian masses" any longer, and decided to set up shop in the middle of the Terminal Clusters. Truth be told, they were only deemed "terminal" by Planetary Board of Health and Safety officials after several years of habitation by the aforementioned males, none of whom could ever be bothered to learn how to clean up after themselves or bathe regularly. For who could maintain good hygiene techniques with so many grand ideas just at the fingertips? ("Grand ideas" was the colloquial name for a popular recreational substance that those of the Magi were often found partaking in.)

Why were they called "Magi", one might ask?

Because they thought it sounded cool.

So with all this in mind, one could easily imagine such a group. (And if one cannot, it might mean that one is in fact eligible for entry into "Infallible Magi" society, and should immediately enroll themselves in the nearest gender studies class available.) And if one could easily imagine such a group, then they could also easily understand why- when heinously offended and disrespected by a well traveled and surefooted eighteen year old female-type- they immediately banished said female-type and her friends from their planet, and turned off the one device that would assure their safe passage out.

Hence the looks Penelope just received from her friends.

Luckily (or unluckily, as the case may be), this was not their first game of dodge ball with asteroids, and over the last few months, the team had had some precautions implemented, foreseeing that such events would not stop anytime soon... no matter how hard they wished or prayed. These precautions mostly included denser alloy hull plating for the ship; stuff that no ordinary space rock could make much of a dent in.

Though it was starting to sweat a bit at the constant barrage of giant chunks of solid gold. (If hull plating were inclined to sweat, that is.)

"Why did we come here again?" Olivia asked as she typed something that a passing observer might take as a rather shaky rendition of "Chopsticks" on the nearest control panel. Olivia was the other co-pilot. She was picked at the age of sixteen to choose whether the people of Earth should learn about life elsewhere in the universe. A lot has happened since then.

"One of them had a limited edition, signed, perfectly minted twelve volume set of-" Alibaster started.

"We're about to die because he wanted to see a nerdy thing," Penelope interceded. "Again," she added with a sigh.

"Which I didn't even get to see!" Alibaster rebutted.

"So we're about to die for nothing!" Penelope shot back. *"Again!"*

"We're in the last level of the storm," Olivia said after checking some environment readings. "Focus, people."

Alibaster and Penelope stopped bickering. Impending death and the hope of preventing it was always a good motivator to pause petty arguments. There was plenty of time to yell at each other later, assuming they survived. And Team Dumb Luck always had to assume their survival. Honestly, their unfounded self belief was the cornerstone of their entire operation.

But inflated self confidence was only to be expected. They *had* saved the universe after all.

Twice.

The trio operated the controls like a… Well, not a well oiled machine, so much as a machine that desperately needed oiling, but still was grinding along despite itself. And as this wheezing, straining machine, they managed to just barely get their ship out of the path of a golden lump roughly the size of Liechtenstein.

"Aaannd, we're out," Alibaster said, the view screen (or space screen, as Olivia had once referred to it) no longer showing any asteroids- golden, silver, bronze, or otherwise- anywhere in the vicinity.

The three exhaled a collective sigh of relief, and slumped into their chairs with various groans, quiet swears, and grateful acknowledgments to one deity or another.

After a quiet minute, Alibaster stood back up, flipped a switch on the controls, and a projection screen unfolded from a latch in the ceiling. On the screen were various star charts. He pulled a big red marker from his pocket and put a large X through one small cluster of stars. This was not the only red X that had been drawn on the screen.

"Well that's one more place we can't go back to," he said with a hint of satisfaction, before putting the cap on the marker with a satisfying snap, and flipping the switch again to make the screen roll back into the ceiling. Alibaster liked getting kicked out of places. It was a sense of pride for him to see just how many people he could tick off.

In total, Olivia had counted about fourteen red X's. All the places they had been banned from for various "misunderstandings". Some were bigger than others. The bans varied in area, and ranged from as small as a collection of islands on one tiny planet, to as large as entire arms of certain spiral galaxies. They'd been traveling a little over six months, which meant they had managed- on average- to get banned from two places a month. And some change.

Not everybody wanted their help.

Which was, of course, their choice. Olivia never wanted to inflict herself or her views on anyone the way her misguided doppelganger Ophelia had. But still, they had definitely been making a name for themselves the past half year.

Hadn't someone once said something like "If you're making enemies, that means you're doing something right"? Olivia wondered. She didn't know if she believed that entirely. Life was never as simple as the quotes posted on her mother's social media pages suggested.

Either way, she really didn't care to make enemies. It's not like she stayed in one place long enough for any convoluted revenge plots to be enacted upon her and her friends. All that mattered were those they had helped, and those they had brought to justice.

"So where to now?" Alibaster asked as they all stared into space beyond.

"Pull up the requests," Olivia told him.

Yeah, that's right. They had requests. Like they were private eyes or something. People from all over submitted entries for certain things they needed help with. The scale of the requests varied. Anything from "Please help, my twelfth-cycle hatchling Sky Ravager escaped its embryonic cradle and is now rampaging through the nearest populated city. And they are ever so fussy at that age," to, "the brood mother of the previously mentioned Sky Ravager escaped its habitat in the Voided Epiphany, and is now trying to digest several impressively sized star systems."

And yes, those were both real examples. That had been a particularly busy week for the trio. They actually almost had to call for assistance from the Fates. But it turned out the brood mother was just looking for its baby, and as soon as the hatchling was recaptured and put in back in its incubator, the mother disappeared back into its own dimension, without any stars or planets more than twenty percent digested.

Alibaster pulled up their inbox on a holo-screen. It wasn't full (the team wasn't *that* well known yet), but there were a decent amount of requests. The three took turns scrolling through them on their own tablets.

"How about this one?" Penelope asked. "This guy's aunt is apparently an evil empress. She killed his dad- the rightful emperor- and he wants us to help dethrone her and her regime, so he can take his claim as next in line. He wants to, quote: 'Slit that ungodly trollop's throat from ear to ear, and give my people the stern hand and unyielding leadership they deserve.'" Penelope paused for a few seconds. "Unquote."

"Sounds kind of Medieval," Olivia said with her head resting on her fist. "Also: yikes. Is it just me or does he sound kind of..." She struggled for the right word.

"Dictator-ish?" Penelope suggested. "Yeah, I'm seeing it too, now that I said it out loud."

"No politics," Alibaster said. "We need to keep Kertsraw off our backs."

That was true, Olivia knew. It was one of the rules laid out by the Fates. They couldn't involve themselves in anything political. No government coups, no taking sides in disputes or wars, no helping unstable would-be emperors slit their aunt's throats.

They kept looking.

"Telepathic serial killer?" Alibaster suggested. "Apparently this guy's claiming his body was taken over by an outside influence and he went on somewhat of a spree before being caught and 'casting the demon' from his mind."

"Might be real," Olivia allowed. "Telepaths aren't exactly rare."

"Might just be a guy trying to plea insanity to reduce sentencing," Penelope said, ever the devil's advocate.

Alibaster considered. "Let's put that in the 'maybe' pile. I'll look at the case evidence; see if there are any inconsistencies and whatnot. See if it's worth looking into further."

It went on like this for a while. Sorting requests into viable, nonviable, or possibly viable. In the end they finally decided on one: a city on a planet not too far away was being haunted by future ghosts. These were ghosts of people who had not been born yet; the descendants of the population from generations down the line. The problem was that it was proving tricky for the local priests to banish from existence spirits that had yet to exist.

"Then that's settled," Alibaster said, setting their flight path. "From here it should take us until about tomorrow afternoon to get there." Since they were now all living on the ship full time, they had needed to implement an automated day and night cycle to keep their internal clocks from losing their minds. A twenty-four hour Earth routine for the two Earthlings, and the Illetican who had lived a fair amount of time on the planet himself. Right now, according to the ship, it was 5:32 PM.

Penelope stretched in her chair. A long, arduous sort of stretch that lifted the shirt above the navel and was accompanied by a pitiful half groan half cry. When she finally settled back down, she breathed deeply and stood up. "Food," she said simply, and walked out of the control room.

"I don't suppose she'll bring us any?" Alibaster said without turning around in his seat.

Olivia did turn around, towards the empty threshold into the corridors beyond. The chances of Penelope coming back anytime soon seemed slim. Olivia wasn't hungry anyway.

"You good here?" she asked, standing up herself.

Alibaster nodded, staring out at the stars. "Probably going to draw up some specs on those future ghosts; see if I can rig up something to communicate with and/or banish them."

"Sounds fun." Olivia rubbed her eyes. "You want me to bring you something to eat?"

Alibaster shook his head. "Nah." He opened a compartment under his seat, and pulled out a family sized bag of honey mustard flavored pretzels. He had stocked up before leaving Earth.

"Dinner of champions," Olivia said under her breath before walking out of the control room.

Olivia showered. She spent a while showering, not stepping out of the stall until she was that healthy grandma-in-a-sauna level of pruned. Until there was so much steam that it might as well have been fog. She wiped the steam off the mirror and stared at herself. She looked about as boiled as a lobster at a hot tub party in July.

But she still looked like her.

Like Ophelia.

And it was getting harder and harder to look in the mirror.

How many people had that problem? How many people couldn't even look at themselves, because if they did they would also see the person they had murdered?

Who else had ever witnessed (caused) their own death, in the third person?

She sniffed, trying to redirect her train of thought, and focused on her eyes. They had tired lines under them. Not surprising. When was the last time she had a good night's sleep? Months ago. Before leaving Earth.

No, that wasn't quite right. There was that time about two months ago. Olivia had met up with DF, an old friend from her first voyage into space. Her first alien friend. Well besides Alibaster, but Alibaster was basically human. He just aged slower than the humans on Earth. DF- with her giant black pools of eyes, cloud white skin, and pin-like teeth- was definitely not human. She was a part of a species quaintly known as the noid.

She had been just as Olivia had remembered her. Still been bubbly and kind and genuinely interested in everything Olivia told her. (Even though Olivia didn't tell her everything.) She hadn't realized how much she had missed DF's wonderment at anything and everything.

It had been a good day.

It had been a good night.

It had been a long night.

But at the end of it, Olivia had slept like a basket of kittens. But of course DF had a life of her own; they couldn't stay together. Ships in the night, and all that. Well, spaceships in the night.

Olivia smiled at the memory, and saw that her reflection was blushing. She sniffed again and applied a generous amount of lotion to herself, seeing as her lengthy shower probably hadn't done much good for her skin. When she was as slick as a seal, she went to her room.

Her room was fairly spacious. All that memory tech junk had been dismantled forever ago, so the rooms no longer took the form of a room from her childhood. This one had a large circular bed that could have fitted five of her comfortably. There were adjustable light marbles lining the walls, several holo-screens that could move around to suit her needs. Recently, a wall of books had been added. A literal wall. They had gone to this star system that was one big library. She had stocked up. Especially now that she had translating contact lenses that were able to rewire her brain into understanding any written language.

There was also a desk, where she sat now. She streamed the Withive (the universal equivalent of the internet) on one of the screens. She read some of the books on her wall. She swiveled in her swivel chair. She stole Alibaster's yo-yo from his room. She practiced said yo-yo.

Olivia did everything she could to keep from going to sleep.

For a while it worked.

Until it didn't.

And eventually, after scrolling through all the pan-galactic celebrity gossip, reading three novellas about "a Grout named Grite who liked to Bite", and giving up trying to learn how to walk the sploorperflet (an Illetican house pet that vaguely resembled a schnauzer), Olivia Jones could not fight the sandman off any longer. She had thrown the last punch though.

Now Olivia slept.

Now Olivia dreamed.

Chapter 2: Nightmarish Memories

Running. She's running. From what? What's behind her? She can't remember. Though she knows she knew a moment ago.

No. Nothing's behind her. It's ahead of her. Tracey, her brother. He looks different than she knows him. He's shorter, his legs stubbier. His cheeks are chubby with baby fat that jiggles as he makes his waddling run through the backyard.

He's three years old again.

Again? What did that mean? Olivia wondered. He had been three this whole time.

"I'm gonna get you!" she heard herself say to him as she tried to slow her own running so as not to catch him too easily. Her voice was higher pitched and just a tad bit nasally. She was…

How old was she?

Seven? Eight? She felt like that was something she ought to know.

Tracey giggled that cute toddler giggle. One which made it sound like every funny thing he heard was some sort of inside joke too complicated for adults to understand.

The grass at Olivia's ankles was higher than she recalled. Or maybe she was shorter.

Shorter than what? What odd thoughts she was having.

She glanced behind her, expecting to see Morgan (had she been born yet?) trotting along with them. Instead she saw that something was in fact chasing her. It looked like an angel with wings on its hips and shoulders, four spindly arms, with a thin humorless mouth, and a body that had been cut directly from the cloth of Time.

Krah. (Who was Krah? Where did that name come from?)

He… They… It. It was following her. And even though she didn't know what this thing was (or at least she didn't think she knew), she knew it meant her harm. She turned back towards her brother.

"Ru-" but she stopped when she saw Tracy was no longer there. And the land had changed. She was no longer at home. She was in the Land of the Lasting, on Kertsraw. And she wasn't standing in ankle high grass, but in the center of a pool of black slime that was dragging her into the Nothing at the center of all creation.

She wasn't just sinking. Branches of the inky darkness were clawing at her like fingers, digging into her skin and pulling her down. When she screamed, there was no sound.

Because now she was in space. Deep space. She had just been ejected from a freighter sized ship hauling a cell of mercs-for-hire. And there was no noise. And there was no warmth. Space was amazing to look at, but without any protection all it provided was pain and fear. But at least they never lasted long.

Olivia worked her way through these various memories- some of the scenarios distorted the truths of the actual events; a horrible kind of hindsight to show her a more dramatic retelling of the terrors she had endured.

But these dreams- for she realized them to be dreams by now- were not the worst. Because the thing about recurring dreams was that there was a rhythm to be worked out. Eventually the dreamer catches on to the patterns and stories they're put through every night, and learn to just ride the wave.

And as she felt each nightmare sweep past her, as her mind dropped her into terror after terror, Olivia knew that the worst was yet to come.

And then it did.

There she was.

Ophelia Jones, destroyer of worlds.

And there Olivia was, watching the twisted version of herself writhe on the floor of her patchwork spaceship. As one third of the triad Fate Maker, Olivia had willed herself to die. And the multiversal connection between Ophelia and herself had caused her double to die too.

The actual event of dying had taken no more than ten seconds, Olivia's unconscious mind vaguely recalled. But there, in this looping nightmare, the death throes of Ophelia lasted for what seemed like hours. And try as she might, Olivia couldn't look away. As if someone had grabbed her head and was holding it steady at the image before her. Telling her, "Look at it. You did this. You don't get to look away. Claim responsibility."

The scene kept going and going, for so long that it might have been comical, if each new second hadn't pulled Olivia's heart further and further down, causing her to sink as if guilt were made of lead.

Then, suddenly, unexpectedly, thankfully, something new appeared. Something which had never been there before in any of the retellings of Olivia's worst memory.

Looking down at the pained ghost of Ophelia, in half invested curiosity was a… fox.

Olivia was so shocked, the troubled mess of emotions swirling through her abated for the moment.

What's a fox doing here? she wondered. It hadn't been there before. It had simply materialized; inserted itself into being, as if it had always been there. As if there was no more natural thing in the world than a fox in a spaceship in a nightmare.

It looked at Olivia. Its eyes were ghost white, but other than that it looked like any ordinary red fox.

"Don't fight it," the fox said without moving its mouth. "Let it happen. Stay until it's over."

Though she didn't know why, Olivia listened to the creature. She turned her gaze back towards Ophelia, and watched the agony she had inflicted.

And as she watched Ophelia, the fox watched her.

And she waited, forcing herself not to look away.

And finally, Ophelia stopped moving.

Olivia didn't feel better, but she was very relieved it was finally over. *At least until I'm forced to relive it all again,* she thought bitterly.

The fox turned to leave, and she watched it walk away from her. The scene of the ship fell away back into space, and the fox walked out into the stars. Intrigued, Olivia followed it. Eventually they both stopped. In front of them was a planet Olivia vaguely recognized. It was just a large body of water, save for the one continent cut in half by the planet's equator. The fox and she both looked at it for a moment.

"I need your help," the fox said. "This seems like as good a place as any to start. You have a connection to this planet, and those you need to find."

"What?" was all Olivia could manage.

"Not yet," it said. "No answers. You have to start asking questions first. Curiosity, decision, quest, searching… There's a formula to these things, you know."

Olivia did not know. "What?" she asked again.

"Start here," it said, and nodded towards the planet. "Take the rebel genius and the anomalous child. Pique their intrigue and your own. I'll return when you reach your destination."

The fox flicked its tail, the planet shrank to the size of a robin's egg, it flew into Olivia's head, and the fox disappeared.

She stood amongst the stars for a while, before she found herself on the swing set at the park by her middle school. She pumped her legs, and on the swing next to her so did DF. They smiled at each other.

Olivia continued to dream.

Chapter 3: Placed on a Do Not Call (to Action) List

A gentle touch on the shoulder was all it took to shock Olivia back to the world. She woke up with a start and a sharp inhale, and blinked several times. Alibaster was standing next to her. Alibaster never came into her room. *Oh,* she thought as she got her bearings.

"You're in my chair," he said.

They were in the control room. How had she gotten there? Had she fallen asleep there? No, she definitely remembered being in her room.

Groggily she stood up, swaying at the attempt. She took the two steps to where her own chair would be, and as she plopped back down, the chair morphed into existence and rose up to greet her.

"Sleep well?" Alibaster asked.

She grunted, closing her eyes again. Had she slept well? What time was it? How long had she been asleep? She had a loose memory of a dream, but it was sand already slipping through the fingers of her mind.

"What'd you do?" Alibaster asked.

Olivia didn't understand the question. She opened her eyes once more and saw him looking from one screen to another, tapping things and then dismissing them.

"We're on a new flight path," he said. "Why are we on a new flight path? We're nowhere near where we're supposed to be." He looked to Olivia, expectantly. Accusingly.

She just shook her head. She didn't know anymore about it than he did. Also, it was very rude of him to expect her to start speaking in anything other than grunts and throaty coughs less than twenty minutes after waking up.

He checked some more things. "We're heading home," he said incredulously. "Why did you set the coordinates for Illetica?"

Once more, Olivia failed to have an answer.

Alibaster pulled up the control deck's security footage from last "night". He fast-forwarded until the screen, very clearly, showed Olivia walking into view. She was manipulating the controls with confidence and precision, like an old pro. After a minute or so of fiddling, she fell into the captain's chair, where she stayed until just now, apparently. The footage ended.

"I-" Olivia started, staring at the screen. "I don't remember doing that."

Alibaster hmmed. "So you somehow found your way from your bedroom to here, in the middle of the ship's night-mode? Then preceded to expertly- *perfectly*- reprogram the flight path to take us to Illetica's exact galactic coordinates- which I was not aware you knew- all while sleep walking?"

Olivia blinked. Alibaster hmmed again.

Penelope chose then to walk in. She was wearing basketball shorts and a T-shirt which was three sizes too large, with some anime character on it. Her neck-length hair was completely cow-licked and tangled on the left side, and she was eating diabetes inducing sugar cereal straight from the box. She fell into the spot her own chair was situated and it morphed into being to catch her. Like a parent catching a toddler that was trying to jump down the last three steps instead of scooting down on their bottom.

"What's up?" she asked through a mouthful of cereal, as she flung both her feet over the side of the chair's right armrest. Something seemed… off about her, Olivia noticed. Like she was trying too hard to seem nonchalant. It was there in her eyes. Just the tiniest hint of… what was that? Trepidation? Anxiety? Olivia didn't know, but she also didn't ask.

"Olivia can apparently pilot the ship in her sleep," Alibaster said.

Penelope nodded. "Nice."

"I mean literally."

"Then it's even more impressive."

"But why Illetica?" Alibaster pondered, more to himself than anyone else. He turned to Olivia. "You have absolutely no recollection of doing this?"

Olivia shook her head.

"Or why you did this? Or how?"

She repeated the previous motion.

Alibaster pinched the bridge of his nose. "I really hate mysteries this early in the relative morning. Especially ones that might be indicative of outside influences leading us into a trap."

This may have seemed a bit paranoid to some. Indeed, Alibaster did seem to be jumping to conclusions; one may even say pole vaulting to them. But living the life the three of them did- seeing the wonders and the dangers of creation as they all have- it was only expected to become a tad overcautious to anything that couldn't be easily explained. Who knew when an evil god or an immoral alternate reality doppelganger might be herding them towards destruction? It was frustrating, having to anticipate all improbabilities.

"Hold still," he said to Olivia. He pressed a switch on the console that she had never seen him use, and a small death ray looking device morphed from nothing out of the ceiling. Alibaster manipulated a screen, and the thing shifted its focus to Olivia.

"So you're killing her?" Penelope asked as if she had just walked into the movie theater a half hour late and was trying to piece together the plot. "Is that what's happening now?"

"I'm not even going to dignify that question with a response," Alibaster said without looking up.

"That was a response."

He ignored her and spoke to Olivia. "I'm scanning you for unusual energy signatures. Have to make sure you aren't possessed or being driven by a long range psychic or anything."

A strobing silver light- the likes of which would not seem beneficial for small fish or people prone to seizure- emitted from the head of the not-death ray, and looked Olivia up and down. After a minute it beeped, and folded itself back into the ceiling.

"Nothing," Alibaster said, reading the screen. "I can't decide if that's good or bad."

"So what should we do?" Olivia wondered. "Should we just ignore whatever this was? Should we just turn around and go deal with those future ghosts like we were going to?"

Alibaster didn't answer; his fingers were steepled in front of his face.

The worry that had been on Penelope's face was more obvious now. She was struggling to keep the mask on.

"What is it?" Olivia asked her.

Penelope made eye contact with her, but took a moment before answering. "I think-" she started, setting the cereal box down on the floor and wiping crumbs from her shirt- "I think we need to go to Illetica."

"You want us to go?" Alibaster asked.

"That's not what I said."

"But you feel that we should."

"Should? Probably not."

Alibaster seemed exasperated. "My time on Kertsraw did nothing to lessen my hatred for cryptic speak. Do you know something we don't about all this? If so, please share."

Penelope sucked in a cheek, as if swallowing some sort of comeback. Then she exhaled. "It's not something I know. It's something I feel."

"What do you feel?" Olivia asked.

"I feel like this at… Well, I think of them as tipping points."

Olivia and Alibaster looked at her.

"It's what I call spots in time that feel… important. Things- lives, realities- hinge on decisions made during them. Like when you-" she looked at Olivia- "invited Earth into the universe. It affected so many, that it couldn't help but… *happen*. Like the current of a river. It's harder to row against it than with it. It's hard to explain. It's just an instinct. But I think we need to go to Illetica. We need to go because it's what happens next. It's where the river is flowing. Does that make any kind of sense?"

Alibaster and Olivia shook their heads.

"Yeah, I thought not. It's all very… wavy. I don't know. I only partially understand it myself. I've been feeling this one since I woke up. Thought I was just hungry, but the more I think about, the more I feel in my gut that what happens next needs to happen. For some reason or another, we have to go to Illetica."

"You've felt things like this before?" Alibaster asked.

"Before my abilities grew, no, I don't think so. But since Krah… yeah, in small ways. Usually only in things that involve me directly. History is being made constantly, all around the universe. I can't feel all that all the time. I'd go insane."

"And you never told us about these 'feelings'?"

"Here I thought we were all entitled to our secrets," she shot back. "Or maybe you want to explain to us just everything you went through when the Fates imprisoned you?"

He was silent, but his face was furious.

"Besides, it never really came up," Penelope continued, ignoring his glare.

"But this thing you feel now," Olivia said, "it feels… important?"

Penelope's face was pale. "I haven't felt it this strongly since before…" She trailed off. But she didn't have to finish. Olivia could guess. *Since before Ophelia cut a swath through reality like a hot scythe through a stick of butter.*

"So whatever's happening is big," Olivia inferred.

"Could be."

"And it's happening on Illetica."

"At least in part, sure."

"That means it's probably some kind of trap," Alibaster said, regaining his cool.

"Then it's our normal nine to five," Penelope shrugged.

"Fates?" Olivia wondered.

"If they're involved, they either would have told us about it or told us to keep out of it," Alibaster said. "And if it's something big and they aren't involved, I don't want to alert them before we have any facts. All we have to go on right now is a sleep walking coincidence and a gut feeling that might just be indigestion."

"I was really looking forward to future ghosts," Olivia said with genuine disappointment. "But I'd like to know how I did what I did," she conceded. "Flying the ship in my sleep. Suddenly knowing complex interstellar coordinates… Something must have happened to me. Maybe we'll find answers on Illetica."

Alibaster sighed. His curiosity always got the better of him in the end. "Fine. Let's go see my brother."

Chapter 4: We've all got Issues

The trip would take most of the day. They had been on the other side of creation when Olivia had decided to do her midnight snooze-and-drive, and even with faster than faster than light technology, space was still fairly large.

Alibaster spent a while fidgeting with the controls, but there wasn't anything for him to do really, other than check diagnostic readings and make sure they stayed on the path Olivia had programmed. He didn't speak much during this time, and Olivia got the feeling he was jealous that whatever had happened to her to make her able to fly the ship so perfectly hadn't happened to him. Which meant he was probably mad at himself for feeling this way, because it was quite frankly a stupid thing to be jealous of. After a while he decided to go to one of his workshops to tinker.

Olivia checked the Withive, to see if there was any sort of buzz about something or another happening on Illetica, but there was nothing. That wasn't completely unexpected, she had to admit. Illetica was a bit of a backwater; not a planet prone to deal in the juicy gossip that kept subscribers hooked. The last galactic news story about the planet had been seven cycles ago. (A cycle was some really complex way to mark the passage of time as a whole universe, instead of using the orbital paths of individual celestial entities. It involved long, complex, four dimensional equations that started to melt Olivia's brain after the third division sign.) It had to deal with a new sort of medicinal fungus discovered there that had been the talk of the town. Nothing dangerous, though.

She used the ship's tachyonic communications relays to try and contact Musty, Alibaster's surrogate brother. He didn't answer. That wasn't very surprising either. Who answered phone calls anymore? Eventually she gave up, and spent the time skimming through three more novellas in the *Grout Named Grite* ennealogy. She appreciated the artwork, but a dude that liked to bite people simply was not a good enough basis for a character to successfully sustain nine stories.

Penelope spent this time pacing, clenching her jaw, and becoming increasingly anxious. "It's like a stomachache that gets worse and worse with each passing minute," she tried to explain. "But like, in my head."

"So like a headache?" Olivia asked.

"No."

And that was the end of that discussion.

Penelope was a difficult person to understand sometimes. She never seemed quite sure what she meant by anything, and if she did, she could never find the right words to articulate them. Olivia knew that this bothered Penelope. She barely understood herself, so how could she ever expect anyone else to understand her? For one glorious (and exceptionally odd) instant, she had understood herself, and her friends had understood her. When the trio had been briefly transformed into the triad Fate Maker, and their souls had all been connected and interchangeable. It had been like the upside-down puzzle piece the universe had given her was finally turned the right way, to fit in its slot.

But Olivia knew she didn't want to be a Fate Maker, not really. None of them did. Godhood was a burden that nobody ever seemed to grasp. And so when Olivia had- temporarily- died, and the transformation had been reversed, they were all relieved. They had all been reset, and none of them had remembered any secrets; be that of the universe, or one another. But there had been a lingering remembering of remembrance. And knowing that Penelope once had understanding, even for a minute, made living without it that much more infuriating. She had voiced this opinion numerous times over the past few months.

"It's like my head's at half mast," she had told them once. "It sails fine, but not as well as it did. Not as well as I know it could."

Olivia sympathized. A fourth dimensional existence placed in a limited human mind had to be frustrating. All these feelings and instincts she couldn't rationally explain or understand. It seemed like every day she had knew abilities emerging. It was as if she couldn't keep up with her own evolution. Not even the Fates knew how far her powers would grow or what shape they might take. Penelope was the ultimate variable in an already flexible universe.

"I'm something that was never meant to happen, being forced to happen again and again each day," she had said on one of her less lucid days. Those days happened rarely. But whenever they did, Olivia wished she knew how to help ease Penelope's confusion.

"You said the last time you felt this way was before Ophelia?" Olivia asked now.

"Yeah," Penelope nodded. "It was the first time I'd felt it like that. It was like my soul had gone quiet. An open field before the tornado touched down. And then when it did- I assume this was the act of Ophelia actually entering this universe- it was so much… disarray. I thought going into the universe of Time would help."

Olivia remembered Penelope's parents taking her to the hospital, because she had fallen unconscious and they hadn't known what else to do. "Did it?" Olivia asked. "Does going there help?" She herself had only visited the universe's underbelly once, but she was never meant to have gone there in the first place. Penelope, though, was designed for it.

"Eh," Penelope pulled a face and gave a so-so gesture. "It didn't help that specific situation, since the damage being done was collapsing timelines and pulling out the basic root structure of everything." She paused. "But sometimes… I've said before that I try not to go there too often. Things don't line up quite the same as they do here. I could be there for only a moment from my perspective, and it could be hours here."

"But sometimes?" Olivia said.

"Sometimes it feels like the place I'm meant to be. There, all alone, keeping watch on things. An aspect of existence with a population of one."

"I'm sure that would be lonely."

"I like my own company, sure. But I don't think I'd want to be trapped with it."

Olivia thought about that. This girl- this eighteen year old misfit- could have the power of a god if she wanted. More so than if they had all stayed together as the triad Fate. She could keep watch on the universe from just beyond its normal boundaries. All she had to do was choose to be alone forever.

"Your thoughts have gone mauve," Penelope said, looking slightly above Olivia's head. "What're you thinking about?"

Olivia blinked. "Please stop looking at my thought processes."

"You're worried about something."

Olivia gave one dry laugh. "I'm worried about everything."

"Well, yes. Of course you are. You'd be stupid not to be. But specifically..." Penelope finally sat back down. "Are you worried about me?"

"A bit," Olivia admitted.

"What a coincidence. I'm worried about you too." She spoke quickly, as if embarrassed at what she was saying.

Olivia knit her brow. "Why are you worried about me?"

"Well for one, you're the only friend I have that I'm not constantly angry with. I suppose that's cause enough to- what's that word? 'Care'?" She gave a weak smile. "And also our rooms are down the hall from each other, and the walls are thick."

"Why's that matter?"

"I probably shouldn't be able to hear you screaming at night."

There was a silence. Olivia sighed, and put her head in her hands. "What good friends we are to one another. Constantly fraught with worry for the other's well being and not being able to do jack or squat about it."

"I think that's what caring is." Penelope scrunched her nose. "Personally I don't care for it. It's exhausting. Nice use of 'fraught', by the way." She paused for a second. "Want to talk about it?"

"Talk about what?"

"Your nightmares."

"No," Olivia said, before starting to talk anyway. "It's just everything. All the stuff we've seen and done. All those times we've cheated death. Don't get me wrong, I love what we do, I love living this life where we're free to help people and do things by our own rules."

"*Mostly* by our own rules," Penelope interjected with a mumble.

"But it's starting to take a bit of a toll. Like my mind can't shut down and rest properly. Like it's perpetually in panic mode or something. I'm fine when I'm awake- for the most part. But when I go to sleep..."

"The floodgates open," Penelope said.

Olivia nodded. "I've started keeping a log- an audio diary- to try and talk myself through things. It helps a bit. And sometimes the nightmares don't even bother me. I just wake up in a cold sweat and forget the details of them."

Penelope waited for her to continue.

"But there's one that stays with me, whether I'm awake or asleep. I can't get away from it, because I see it- I see *her*- every time I look at my reflection." Olivia could see that Penelope understood what she meant. And Olivia hated dumping all this on her friend, but the thread had been pulled, and the tapestry was unraveling whether she wanted it to or not. She looked at Penelope with all the seriousness she contained. "How do I cope- how do I live day to day- after killing myself?"

Olivia wiped an errant tear from her cheek, and Penelope had no answer, other than to sit next to her friend and hold her for a while.

Later, Penelope went to go make something for them all to eat. A "last meal", she called it. She always called it that whenever they were about to walk into certain danger. The team had an average of three last meals every week. Olivia offered to help, but Penelope hated people messing with things when she was in the kitchen. She said it was like a parent offering to help their honor student with their homework. The offer was sweet, but it always hindered more than helped, because the whole process inevitably became the parent standing over their kid while the kid explained all the ins and outs of calculus to the parent, and basically doing little more than being in the way, and can they take a step back, and yes letters *are* used in math, and no it didn't matter what the book said this was the right way to do it.

So Olivia left Penelope to her devices (and utensils), and set off to see what Alibaster was up to.

She found him exactly where he said he was going to be: in his workshop. To the untrained eye the untidy area was indistinguishable from an auto body shop that had been ransacked by a petulant tornado. She stepped over and around the clutter of scraps and discarded projects, down the rows of shelves like a library of metal, until she found him at one of his workbenches. He was floating upside-down in the air about seven feet above it. He had something in his hands that he was fiddling with; poking and prodding the circuitry with small, precise tools.

"What're you working on?" Olivia asked.

Alibaster looked down at her (or up at her, depending on one's view), and shrugged. "Who knows? We'll see what it does when it's done."

"How will you know when it's done?"

"When it starts doing something."

"Why are you floating?"

He pointed down/up to a gadget on the workbench. It looked unremarkable, like so many of his creations. It was the size and shape of a Bundt cake, and had something that slid up and down measurements on the side, like the way to adjust old thermostats. Or maybe like a slide ruler. Then he pointed to a circle on the ground beneath/above him. It looked like a hula-hoop. Actually, Olivia was fairly certain it *was* a hula hoop. It had been cut open around the circumference, infected with all sorts of odds and ends, then patched back up with duct tape crudely placed in six places.

"Gravity nullification field," Alibaster said. "Wanted to see if I could suspend the ship's artificial gravity in one fixed location."

"And now you can."

"Looks like it." He didn't seem impressed with himself. "Can you get me down? Just move the thing on the thing slowly down to the one."

Olivia went to the cake looking device, and slowly "moved the thing" from the zero it was on to the number one marked next to the slide. Alibaster drifted back to the floor, in the center of the hula-hoop, landing on his head a delicately as a figure skating feather. He stood up, and threw the thing he had been working on onto the bench.

"Well?" he asked.

"Well what?"

"What can I do for you?"

Olivia didn't have an answer. "Penelope's making our last meal," was what she found herself saying.

Alibaster nodded. "Oh, good. Another one. Not morbid at all, our Brownstein-McClain."

He spoke quickly, kept working, and refused to meet her eye. He wanted the conversation to be over and for Olivia to leave. But she wasn't putting up with his brooding, and she wouldn't give him the satisfaction. Even if she knew what had brought on his attitude in the first place.

"When's the last time you went home?" she asked.

He pretended not to have heard.

Olivia leaned against the bench and crossed her arms. She wasn't going anywhere.

Finally Alibaster spoke. He put his palms on the bench and looked down at nothing. "Remember when I took you? After we first met? And we watched my father's Last Goodbye?"

Olivia nodded, before realizing what he was saying. "You haven't been to Illetica in five years? When we were on Earth, you told me you tried to visit regularly."

"'Tried' being the operative word. Could never bring myself to go. Ever since dad… There's really nothing there for me anymore."

"What about Musty?"

He cringed. "We talk sometimes. Rarely. We aren't children anymore. We each had different paths. He works at a hospital. Wants to be a doctor. He had always been dad's apprentice in pathology, but he needed more professional training."

"Good for him. You must be proud."

"Absurdly. I'm glad someone followed in dad's footsteps. I know he would have loved it to be Musty."

Olivia grinned.

"What?" Alibaster asked.

"Paging Doctor Musty. We have a code eleven. Doctor Musty needed in surgery. Stat!"

He gave a glimmer of a smile. "I'm pretty sure he'd go by Doctor Musscivite."

She ignored him. "Musty, MD. Pleasure to meet you."

"I'm literally the only one who calls him Musty."

Olivia chuckled to herself. "How much does he know?" she asked after a moment. "About your- our- life?"

"Not much." His face fell again. "I don't want to worry him. He still thinks I'm one of Kertsraw's exceptional."

"So that's why you don't keep in touch?" Olivia asked. "So you don't have to lie?"

"Yeah. It is."

That was all he said before he closed back up and went back to work on the trinket he had been floating with; pulling a magnifying lamp close to him, turning the light on, and putting the mess of circuitry underneath.

Alibaster had never been good with people. On the surface level, sure. He could talk anyone's ear off about this, that, or the other until the stars went out. But for the serious things- the important things… It was frustrating for him. To talk like that. To slow down and focus inward and give the vulnerable pieces of himself away. Even with those he cared about. He would rather face life threatening danger every day than have to deal with his emotions, share them, or have serious discussions. He would rather ignore the only family he had left than sit down with him and go over the last epoch of his life and everything he'd been through. The only reason he talked to Olivia about anything was because she had experienced most of it with him.

Olivia wasn't his mother. She wasn't going to lecture him about what he should do. Because she knew *he* knew that if he really cared about Musty, he'd come clean. But it was his life. His choice.

A while later, the intercom on the wall behind the workbench crackled, and Penelope's voice came out. "Soup's on if anyone's eating."

Olivia pushed the talk button. "We'll be right there."

Alibaster stood up straight and turned the light of his magnifying lamp off. He produced a- presumably completed- clockwork pyramid. "Ok," he said, "let's see what it can do." He turned a dial under the square base, the four triangle sides unfolded, the whole shape hummed…

And then the whole thing burst into flames.

Alibaster quickly dropped it into the perimeter of the gravity defying hula-hoop, and jumped to the Bundt-y control mechanism, forcing the slide thing up to the number ten.

The pyramid crunched into the floor as if stepped on an invisible elephant. The fire engulfing it shrunk until it was the size of a candle flame, where it quickly went out. He breathed a relieved sigh and moved the slide back to one.

"Congrats," Olivia said, nonplussed, "you've invented fire. Go back in time, sell it to the human race, patent it, claim ten cents in royalties anytime someone lights their cigarettes."

Alibaster didn't seem to have heard her. "Lucky that worked. I wasn't sure how fire would react in an increased gravity. Dumb luck it didn't just compress downwards and expand out."

"Dumb luck?" Olivia asked, looping her arm through his and dragging him through the workshop towards the door. "Why Prometheus, you're singing our song."

They passed a small chalkboard hanging next to the door, which read "63 Days since last crash landing", and made their way towards food.

Chapter 5: The Domestic Scene

Their last meal was veggie pizza: Broccoli florets, chopped olives, sun-dried tomatoes, microgreens, thinly sliced lemon, and crumbled feta cheese. Or at least some varying form on all those ingredients, since the trio rarely stocked their cabinets at Earth grocery stores. As Penelope unveiled it on the table, she smiled at her creation.

"That looks awesome," Olivia said.

Penelope's smile dropped. "Yeah well, don't get used to it." This is what she always said whenever someone complimented her culinary work. "I'm not your personal chef."

Olivia said nothing, though she shared a knowing look with Alibaster. Of course Penelope wasn't their personal chef. But she kind of was, all the same. Neither Olivia nor Alibaster had ever asked Penelope to cook for them, and Penelope never cooked for them other than last meals. Part of the reason they had so many was because Penelope would never admit that she actually liked cooking, or doing nice things for others.

They each pulled a couple pieces onto their plates. It obviously tasted great. Penelope had a knack for picking up new ingredients and finding gastronomic homes for them. If she ever got tired of the cosmic vigilante life, she could definitely open a restaurant.

Penelope used a fork and knife to eat her share. Alibaster picked each individual ingredient from his slices, popping them into his mouth one at a time. Olivia ate hers like a normal person.

"How are you doing?" Olivia asked Penelope after she inhaled her first piece. "Still have that 'stomachache in your head' feel?"

"No," Penelope said. "I think my chronal instincts started to understand that we're heading in the direction they want us to go. It's like when you think you're about to slip on a patch of ice and your brain goes into panic mode, but then you catch yourself and your brain just goes, 'Oh, good. Carry on.'"

"Good." Olivia nodded. *I think.*

Alibaster chewed an olive with concentration. Well, he was probably concentrating on something else, but it bled into his chewing so it looked like he was trying to break down and catalog each of the olive's individual elements with his tongue.

"Squidlark for your thoughts," Olivia said to him. Squidlark were like pennies, but also like birds with tentacles. On a casino world, one of the patrons told her it was a very popular saying, and while she had since realized that the stranger had just told her this for a laugh, she still tried to pepper it in whenever she could because it was so much more fun to say than "penny".

"I just hate not knowing what we're doing," Alibaster said. "We usually get to choose our own... adventures. Excursions. Missions. Whatever we call them. But this one's apparently been chosen for us. And I really hate not knowing what's going on. I hate not being able to plan in any way."

"Probably doesn't help that your whole home planet might be in danger," Penelope said, before realizing she had said it. Alibaster and Olivia looked at her. "Right," she said, "shutting up forever now." She stabbed a section of vivisected pizza with her fork and shoved it into her mouth.

"What do you think the odds are I actually was just sleepwalking, and somehow managed to accidentally reprogram our flight?" Olivia asked rhetorically, though still somehow knowing an answer was coming.

"You know, I've actually been doing some probability calculations," Alibaster said as he pulled out a pocket abacus. He was obviously glad for the change of direction in the conversation. He liked having things he could quantify. It helped him feel at least a little bit in control. "And I think the odds of you doing all that without any prompting, mind altering, or outside persuasion are about..." He made a few more corrections to his computations. "About seventy four billion three hundred eighty four thousand three hundred thirty eight to one..." He looked up and saw Penelope and Olivia's faces. "Give or take." He quickly pocketed his outdated calculator.

"So not very likely," Olivia inferred.

"And as I said, there was no trace of outside energy- telepathic or otherwise- manipulating you." Alibaster ate a piece of broccoli.

"Maybe it's not her that was being manipulated," Penelope said. "Maybe it's the timelines. Someone powerful pulling at that strand of probability, forcing it to occur for some reason or another."

That suggestion might have sounded fairly ludicrous to outside listeners, but the trio had seen that exact thing happen before. The Fate Maker Mawteze had been trapped and weakened, and needed rescuing. So he used what little power he had left to override Penelope's freewill by throwing her soul to Time, hijacking her body so that the team would find and save him.

"They wouldn't have even had to do anything to your soul to control you," Penelope said. "You were already asleep; your motor functions were up for grab."

Olivia really hated that idea; that anyone could puppeteer her like that.

"But who are 'they'?" Alibaster asked, once more frustrated. "If you're right, the power to do that would have to be Fate level. I feel like the Fates would just tell us to go to Illetica if they needed us there. I don't often follow orders, but they would know I wouldn't leave my home in the lurch."

"A powerful time sensitive?" Penelope suggested.

Alibaster scoffed. "Yeah, because the universe is teeming with those. And even so: To what end? What's the point of all this?"

A holo-screen on the wall behind him blinked a soft blue. Alibaster turned around and slid his finger across it. A message appeared; the ship telling its crew that they had just entered Illetica's star system.

"Well," Olivia said, "I guess we're about to find out."

They all finished their meals (Alibaster having left his two slices perfectly clean and devoid of toppings), and made their way back to the bridge. Everyone took their seats, and waited as the other planets in the system flew past.

"Hull shields on maximum," Alibaster said, manipulating the console. "Better safe than sorry," he mumbled to himself. "Assuming we survive to be sorry," he added.

Soon enough, there they were, hovering right above the limits of Illetica's atmosphere. They all looked ahead at the predominantly white and blue sphere, until the one slice of land- imaginatively named "the Continent"- swam into focus.

The ship sat still. "Your program stopped," Alibaster said to Olivia whilst checking a screen. "The ship's in manual control again." It was implied what he was trying to say. *We could leave now.*

Just turn around and go. Not let ourselves be sucked into someone else's trap or game. Go back where we came from and fight ghosts that don't exist yet.

No one wanted to be the first to voice it, but they all knew this was probably the best thing to do. But before anyone built up the courage, the ship lurched.

"The planet's gravity just caught us," Penelope said, checking the readings on her own screen. And in that instant, the choice had been decided for them.

"Wait," Alibaster said, "that doesn't make any sense. Where we are right now... If we were caught in its gravity, we should have just gone into geostationary orbit. Why are we descending?"

Olivia got a bad- but oh so familiar- feeling. She was pretty sure she knew what was happening, but didn't want to say in fear of jinxing the situation. That was when all the lights went off, and all the gentle hums of machinery running throughout the ship could no longer be felt or heard, and she half wondered if just thinking something was enough to make it happen.

"We're crashing," she said. She didn't need to check any of the readout screens, she just knew. (Which was just as well, since they were all turned off too.) It had happened so often, she could almost set her clock by it. Part of her wanted to go to Alibaster's workshop, erase the number sixty-three on the chalkboard, and replace it with a big fat zero.

The three had to harness themselves into their seats by hand, since all the power was off. This was very difficult since the G-force was picking up, and the ship's own artificial gravity was kaput. The planet came closer to them by the second, like an accelerating face unable to deflect from a raised fist.

"EMP?" Olivia asked.

Alibaster shook his head as he desperately tried to restart literally anything at all. "I don't know. How could I know? Everything's off. Gone. Life support, engines, water heater..." He blew a quick raspberry. "Dead."

It was tough, straining against the increasing force of gravity, but the three tried everything they could think of to restart the ship after they strapped in. It all proved about as effective as Caligula's campaign against the Atlantic. The ship was Poseidon, and the three of them were the military, fruitlessly stabbing the English Channel.

"Hang on!" was all that Alibaster said. Though with his cheeks almost behind his ears at this point, it sounded more like, "Haag udd!"

A combination of the increasing pressure trying to steamroll their bones, the increasing heat leaking in from the outside (the hull shields were obviously no longer at maximum), and the increasing lack of recycled oxygen... Well, they all took their toll. There was nothing they could do to fight it.

First went Alibaster. Then Penelope. Then finally Olivia.

As the ship plummeted towards Illetica, the three of them promptly passed the flek out.

Chapter 6: Dream a Dream of Fiends

She was at her grandma's house. That much was obvious to Olivia. The one her grandmother had lived in until Olivia had started high school. She was in the TV room, sitting in the leather recliner that she distantly recalled should itself be sitting in a storage unit. Staring at a blank television, her fingers stroked the arms of the chair. *How long have I been sitting here?*

No one else was around. Usually when she ended up there, she wasn't alone. Her grandmother or other relatives were usually there with her to fill the space; to fill the emptiness that otherwise lounged around the place like a lethargic cat refusing to give up its spot in the sun. It was not a house that thrived on being vacant.

But there is no one but me.

So Olivia sat, and she stayed, and she stared.

Am I supposed to be doing something? she wondered. *I can't remember.* Her mind was muddled, her reflexes nonexistent, her synapses firing at the speed of cold molasses. This wasn't new. These situations have often been like this for as long as she could remember.

What situations?

What was I thinking about?

I don't…

Through the muddle of her mind, she has a strange feeling that something should have happened by now. Something should have… started. Something should have begun. She wasn't sure what she meant by that, but she couldn't help but feel like she waiting for a play to start.

She got tired of waiting, and started exploring the house.

Nothing seemed out of place as she passed through the TV room, into the kitchen, and past the dining and living rooms. But as she took a step into the hallway which led to the bed and bathrooms, she heard something.

"Sshhh," something hissed urgently and icily. It sounded like pages being ripped out of books.

Curiosity propelled Olivia forward.

She turned her head into the first door on the left. The old computer room/guestroom. Sitting in the chair in front of the computer was a writhing mass of flesh and fabric.

No, wait.

She blinked, and realized that her first impression must have only been a trick of the light. Now she could see that sitting in the chair was in fact a man, and on the man's lap sat a woman. And crawling all over the couple were at least three children. Small girls who were scuttling around the pair, like disturbed spiders that had just been shaken in a jar.

Olivia was standing nearer to them now, though she couldn't recall stepping into the room.

The man looked at her. Olivia could not describe his features. Nor could she describe those of the woman or the girls. She tried studying each of their faces. She looked at every wrinkle, and crease, and twitch. But no image would stick in her head. Every time she tried looking away, all that remained was a palpable feeling of revulsion. Of wrongness. It was the eyes, that was it. The only detail that hung in her mind was the eyes. All of them were pure black with nothing but copper pinpricks of light for pupils. And there was something else… Their eyes didn't look as if they were part of their faces, so much as underneath them. Like their faces were just masks, obscuring something terrible.

"Hello there," the man spoke, shocking her out of her trance. It was a harsh and strained sound. He coughed, and spoke again. "We needed to use the computer." Now the voice was starkly different. Friendly; reassuring, even. As if the simple act of coughing had allowed him to adjust his voice as easily as one adjusted a crooked tie.

"Who are you?" Olivia asked once she found her own voice. Even though no definite image could stick in her head, she got the faint impression that those before her were meant to be her grandma's old neighbors, the children carbon copies of the couple's one daughter. But maybe she attributed this too them just to have something familiar to grasp to.

From the man's lap, the woman studied Olivia like a fasting man might study a menu, and the doll-like children stopped their crawling for a moment.

The man answered. "We just needed to use the computer."

"Does my grandma know you're here?"

"Oh, I doubt it. No one does but you. And even you will soon forget about us. Everyone does. But don't worry. I plan to fix that."

At that point Olivia considered calling the police.

As if reading her thoughts, the man gave a short burst of laughter. A bark of dangerous glee. "You go ahead and try that Miss Jones. See if it helps. Go on."

So she did. She quickly backpedaled until she was back in the kitchen. She picked the familiar white phone off the wall; it's cord drooping to the floor from years of being stretched. Olivia tried to dial, but the numbers on the buttons were little more than gray smudges.

"What is the nature of you emergency?" a calm feminine voice asked on the other end of the line, even though Olivia had yet to dial.

"There's a…" she started, not really knowing how to explain. "There are people in my grandma's house. I-"

She felt a chill on her neck and turned around to see two more children standing in the kitchen with her. *Where did they come from? How did they get past me without me seeing them?*

"Olivia Jones," a new voice spoke from the receiver in her ear. It seemed distantly familiar.

"Yes?" It didn't occur to her to think it odd that so many strangers seemed to know her today.

"You need to listen to everything I say if you are to survive the next few minutes with your soul intact," the voice said as she stared at the two mannequin-like girls.

"Ok," she said, still in a daze.

"Good," continued the voice. "Alright firstly: you're dreaming right now."

Olivia nodded sagely. "That makes sense."

The two girls in front of her tilted their heads, as if a switch inside them had just been thrown, and they were starting to wake up. A low clicking sound started bubbling up from their throats.

"Secondly," continued the voice, "you are in as much danger as you have ever been in your whole life."

She blinked, and almost scoffed at the audacity of that statement, but the two girls looked like they were about to leap, and she wasn't about to insult anybody that seemed to want to help her.

"So you're telling me I should wake up?" She tried slapping herself in the face. *Ow.*

"No! Stop! I am absolutely not telling you that. Waking up is the last thing you want to do right now."

"Not loving my options."

"But there is good news: this is *your* dream. So you can fight against it." There was a pause. "For the time being."

Right, of course, Olivia thought. *It's so obvious.* And since it was so obvious, she did the obvious thing when facing monsters in dreams, and tried to think the girls away, or think herself somewhere else entirely. None of it did any good.

"I need you to focus," phone voice said, "and I need you to take control. You did it before. Take a breath. Try and calm down."

It was all kind of surreal. And even though Olivia still didn't quite feel the danger of the situation, she inhaled deeply. It was difficult to breathe. Why was that? She could have sworn for half a second she could feel her chest- her physical chest- rise, a universe away. But it felt like something was pushing against it. The feeling dissipated, and she pulled her focus back to the now. Trying once more, she moved a hand over the girls, like wiping marker off a dry erase board.

For a second nothing happened. Then they the girls started losing their definition, becoming translucent. Then they became transparent, like glass sculptures. Then they were gone entirely.

"Good job," said the voice.

Can he-it- see me? Olivia wondered. *Where are they? Who are they? And what were those girls, and those… people in the computer room?*

"That won't hold them for long," the voice continued. "Their curiosity at how you dispatched their agents will soon be replaced with rage."

"The people in the computer room, you mean?" Olivia looked back down the hallway, but now it seemed to be elongating, pulling at itself. Like in movies when a camera zoomed in while also pulling away. The action caused a pained sound, like a strangled fiddle.

"You need to get out of there." The voice sounded worried now. "It delights in distress, but it has a very short attention span when it comes to messing with dreamers. Right now, you're just a small nuisance to it. Get out of its path, and it should forget about you."

"What is 'it'? Who are you?" Olivia asked.

"Questions later. What exits do you see?"

She scanned the kitchen. "The door leading to the garage and the door leading to the back porch."

"No. To obvious."

"Ceiling vent?"

"The vents this close to… No. I wouldn't risk it. It wouldn't lead out. It would lead behind. It won't take you where you need to go."

"What's that supposed to me-" Olivia stopped herself. *Questions later.* The threshold to the TV room was gone now, only a dense gray fog in its place. The hallway leading to the bedrooms was done stretching and distorting, and now looked like the maw of some twisted nightmare.

"Your foundation is collapsing," urged the voice. "You have no time left."

"The only other way out is the window above the sink," Olivia said quickly. "But that just leads to the back porch too." Then she noticed it. "Oh. Wait. Huh, that's weird. Outside that window, it seems to be night. But outside the window on the door, it's day. How's that work?"

"Perfect," the voice said. "This is not your grandmother's house, Olivia Jones. Every exit here may lead somewhere different. It could work. Go through the window. Now."

She climbed up on the sink, phone receiver still in one hand. She forced the small window open, tore at the bug screen, which came away like so much cobweb, and awkwardly shimmied- legs first- out of the house.

Chapter 7: A Place in Between

She fell. She hit the ground. And she kept going as the ground broke away beneath her.

Now she was right side up again, falling-

No: flying.

No… swimming?

Floating perhaps. Or levitating.

It was quiet, and there was nothing to see, except herself. Though no light source could be seen, so how could she see herself? Her skin felt like it was being caressed by feathers. Goose flesh appeared all over her to accommodate the sensation.

A string was now in front of her. Just an ordinary white string one might use to tease a cat with. It rose farther than her eyes could strain. Before she could reach out to touch it, it came to life as if suddenly possessed. It wrapped itself around her body, slithering its way from her torso to her toes in a lazy attempt at mummification.

Then it pulled, and she rose.

At least it felt like she was rising, for there was still nothing to see other than the nothingness, herself, and the string. Either way, she imagined that this must be what unassuming fish felt like after being hooked.

Finally, she stopped rising. The string unwound itself from her and started to… Shrink? Disappear? It was hard to make sense of. As if it was vanishing out of existence bit by bit. Inch by inch.

Once her arms were free she reached above her, where the string was dematerializing into. She hit a wall. Or perhaps it was the ceiling. Like being stuck under a lake, but the surface was frozen. She pounded on it, hoping what lay beyond would yield… something.

Nearly all the string was gone now. It was reeling itself back through a small hole in the ceiling, and leaving her behind. A foot of string was left before she noticed something tied to the end of it.

A piece of chalk. Had that been there before?

She snatched it in her hand, but had no need to act so swiftly, for the string was apparently done reeling itself in. What else was there to do, but the only thing to do when given chalk?

She drew.

On the ceiling, she used the chalk to draw a large square.

The nothingness disintegrated within the square's perimeter, and she could see a world beyond. She floated up towards it, and she had an uneasy feeling that the curtains were being drawn.

Chapter 8: Space Squids and Studio Apartments

The voice on the phone had been right. This was definitely not her grandma's back porch. From the looks of things, it was, in fact, outer space. There was a brilliant green nebula on the horizon. (Did space have horizons? And if not, what would the equivalent be considered?) And radiant bring-tears-to-the-eye stars of every conceivable color scattered across her vision.

This was not the most amazing thing though. Olivia twisted around and saw several skyscraper sized buildings floating along with her. In fact, the window she had just climbed out of was a window of one of these buildings. And while seeing normal brick and mortar buildings drifting in the void was an interesting sight, it still was not the most amazing thing she could see.

For each of the mountainous buildings (there were probably around ten) had a large tentacle coiled around them. At first Olivia thought they were vines, but the appearance of the giant squid in her vision gave the truth away quickly enough.

Even for a giant squid, it was massive. Olivia reckoned about thirty-five of her lined up head to toe could be made to create the diameter of one of its eyes. She stared in awe, not sure what to do. The creature was looking in her direction, but blinked slowly and indifferently. As if she were nothing more than a mote of dust that had wandered into view.

She could have stared and studied the creature forever, but she heard a faint noise that seemed to be coming from her hand.

The phone! She had it in her hand once more. The coil was stretching out from the window she had escaped from, even though from the window now she could only see darkness. She put the old receiver to her ear.

"Yeah?" she asked, absently; still staring at the squid and the buildings in its grip.

"Where are you?" the voice asked. "I can't tell where the window sent you."

"Space," she said simply. "Green nebula behind me. In front of me there're a bunch of buildings, and a big squid." A thought occurred to her. "Are you that fox? The one from my dreams before?"

"That is how you perceived me, yes," the voice said. "Now hang on, I'm trying to discern where you are."

"Where are *you* now? Why talk to me on the phone?"

"The thing you just ran from can't be allowed to see me. It can't know I'm helping you." There was a pause. "The colony squid! Of course. That could actually be useful in helping you find your companions."

Gears turned in her head as she realized what he meant. "Alibaster and Penelope are here too?"

"Like you, they are probably in their own dreams right now. But once they find their way, you can make contact." There was another pause. "I need you to find the largest building. It should stand apart from the rest."

Olivia found it easily enough; it dwarfed the other skyscrapers by comparison. The squid actually had to keep two tentacles on it instead of just one. It also looked slightly askew. Like a puzzle cube with a million sides, each of which had been turned a fraction of a degree away from the others.

"Go to it," said the voice of the fox.

Olivia pressed the speaker button on the phone, tied the cord around her waist like a belt, and started swimming towards the colossus. The stars that she thought were far away swept through her fingers as she made her wide strokes. The small but intense heat of the sand sized stars tickled.

"So what's a colony squid?" she asked, ever the pro at small talk.

"Celestial squids are deeply empathic creatures. Sometimes, when planets are dying, they hear the cries through the deepest of space, and they try to help the ones left alive."

"Really?" Olivia asked. "So they just rip buildings from their foundations, load up the survivors, and away they go?"

"I think it's a nice story," the fox said. "A dream of last minute salvation from the stars. I believe it's called hope."

"So they aren't real," Olivia inferred. "It's just a dream. Like everything else here."

"I do not see why the two must be mutually exclusive. The realest things in creations begin as dreams. Reality is not limited to the literal or tangible."

Olivia didn't know how to respond to that.

"Are you close?" the fox asked after a few minutes.

"Yeah. But this place is big. Where exactly am I going?" Her attention was drawn to a battered tavern sign that jutted from one of the windows nearest her. It said "The Swan and Swine".

"Go in," the fox said. "I think the coast is clear for now. I will meet you inside presently."

"And then?" Olivia asked. "Are we supposed to find my friends in this place?"

"What we are intending to find-" the fox said in a chin raised sort of way- "are angels."

Chapter 9: Are IDs Needed to Drink in Dreams?

While from the outside it might have seemed like a hole-in-the-wall tavern awkwardly attached to the massive floating building- like a suspicious looking mole that would invoke a trip to the dermatologist- from the inside it was quickly made clear that The Swan and Swine was actually more of a nightclub.

It was dark, save for the numerous moving searchlights and strobe lights wafting across a sea of partiers of every size and species. The music that boomed from every possible nook was loud and mentally intrusive, and the bass was turned up so high that the genre of the music could not be determined.

After untying the cord from her waist (which had yet to reach its limit) Olivia pressed the phone to her ear as hard as she could, hoping to hear the fox's voice for guidance. It was no use. Between the music, and the noise of the many club goers, the phone was rendered useless. She sighed, let go of it, and it shot back out the window she had entered like a taut rubber band let loose. Finding the bar, Olivia decided that it was as good a place as any to stay out of the way and figure out what to do.

Find angels? What does that mean? Are there angels here? How does that help me find Penelope and Alibaster?

The bartender crossed over to her as she found a stool at the end of the bar. He looked human enough, but had a weird orange monster hovering around him. It was small and squirrelly looking, but flashed her a sharp-toothed smile which oozed malevolence. After Olivia ordered something "super fruity and umbrella-y", and the bartender turned to make her drink, the monster bobbed after him like a balloon on a string.

Looking around, she noticed that many of the people in the place had a similar looking creature hovering above them. Each monster looked different, and they varied in size, color, and demeanor. Some were little more than rats, others were large and dragon-like. But no matter the size, none of them seemed to take up any space. As if these things- whatever they were- were light constructs only. Ghosts following around clubbers for some reason.

"It's kind of neat, isn't it?" asked a voice to Olivia's left. She looked over and saw a (humanoid) girl- anywhere between Penelope's age and her own- taking a spot on the stool next to her. She had had to yell to be heard over the din of the place.

"I'm sorry?" Olivia asked at an equal volume.

She had dark olive colored skin and a shaved head. She was wearing black leggings, a slim gray sweater dress with a faded jean jacket over it, large hoop earrings, some brilliant gold mascara, and holographic blue rimmed octagonal glasses with lenses about the size of Olivia's palm. There was also an ugly puce flower behind her ear. The petals were wilting and the stigma was brittle, like it could just snap off at any time.

Olivia looked down at herself for the first time and saw that she was wearing baby blue pajamas covered in pictures of yellow ducks wearing nightcaps. The pajamas that her grandmother used to keep at her house for whenever Olivia spent the night there as a kid. Her wearing them now must have been left over from the start of her dream. She suddenly felt underdressed.

"The Drift Back," the pretty stranger said.

Olivia shook her head to indicate she didn't understand.

"The… recreational substance?" the girl tried again. "That's what the monsters are."

"The monsters are… drugs?" Even if this was a dream, Olivia didn't get it.

The girl laughed. "No, no. Ok, so, you take it- this one's a nasal spray- and for a bit of time depending on the dose, all of your negativity forms into a semi-physical being, and just… drifts back. Lets you get on with your life for a bit without dragging yourself down."

The bartender dropped a drink in front of Olivia, and it was indeed easily identifiable as "super fruity and umbrella-y". She had to take several umbrellas out just to find a place to find the straw. The bartender's monster gave her a rude gesture as he turned to help other patrons.

"What do you mean negativity?" Olivia asked her new friend.

"Anything really. Self loathing, jealousy, greed. Any internal junk that holds you back. The things we'd all be better off without. The more negativity you have, the bigger the creature that forms. Drift Back can be addictive because of that. Who can say no to instantly becoming their best self?"

Olivia considered this. "You don't have one of those monsters."

The girl smiled. "Never touch the stuff."

"You sound like you're advocating for it."

"I don't mean to. It's just… I understand why people take it. I know that people don't always like being constrained by who they are."

That sounded like something Penelope would say.

"I'm Olivia," she said, raising her hand.

The girl took it. "Kozmoklor. Koz. First time in the S&S?"

Olivia nodded. "Waiting for a… a friend, I guess." She threw a look that she hoped indicated that the situation was complicated, but she didn't feel like going through all that with someone she just met, and quite frankly, might not even be real.

Koz nodded. "Me too. He's always late. All work, no play." She caught Olivia staring at the flower again. "A little inside joke between us." She didn't explain further, but she took the pathetic looking flower out from behind her ear and set it on the bar.

As Koz scanned the room for whomever she was meeting, Olivia scanned the room for the fox. Neither of them found who they were looking for. *This is ridiculous,* she thought. *I can't just wait for a mysterious forest creature- who probably has ulterior motives for helping me (because they* always *have ulterior motives)- to help me find my friends.* Olivia decided to take some initiative.

"You don't know where I could find any angels, do you?" she asked Koz.

Koz gave a smirk. "I just told you I'm meeting someone, and here you are trying to flirt?"

Olivia felt her face go red. "No, no. I just-"

Koz laughed. "I kid, I kid. I'm guessing you mean the Scripts?"

"The…?" Olivia's voice trailed off.

"You really are new here, aren't you? The Script Angels. The messengers of love. The winged and inked. Whatever they like to be called this week."

"Oh. Um. I guess so."

"Well, where else does one expect to find angels, but on high?" Koz gestured upwards towards the balconies. They were harder to see, darker than the dance floor and the bar. But every now and then a spotlight would pass over them, and the outlines of what could only be large wings could be seen. Koz sipped at her own drink. "What do you need to talk to those self righteous birds for?"

"I need to find my friends. I was told that the… *angels* might be able to help."

"You said you were meeting them here."

"Other friends. I don't know where they are, and I need to make sure they're ok."

Koz pulled a face. "Are they in some sort of danger?"

Olivia sighed. "I would be very surprised if they weren't. Danger has a way of always finding them. Finding us."

Koz stood up. "Well let's go then."

"You don't have to come with me," Olivia said. Though truth be told, she would really appreciate the company of someone who seemed to know how this place worked.

"Of course I do. You've piqued my interest. And if I don't, I'll just keep waiting here, bored out of my skull, waiting for my boyfriend to show up. Not that I blame him for running late. He still hasn't quite gotten the hang of this place yet. He's been practicing though, bless him."

Olivia stood up from her own stool, deciding now was not the right moment to try and decipher what that all meant.

Koz led the way, and they wove themselves through the many bodies on the dance floor. Olivia muttered half-hearted apologies left and right as she bumped into people and people bumped into her, though she knew that nobody could hear them anyway. The Drift Back monsters clung to the air around their hosts, and eyed one another in many different but equally nasty ways.

They passed the DJ- a rambunctious looking emu headed lad with six talon-like fingers on each hand- and found the stairs leading to the balconies.

A bouncer stopped them when they reached the top, totally eclipsing the door. As if someone had bricked up the door entirely, and painted a black shirt and sunglasses on the wall.

"We need to talk to the angels," Koz said. The music wasn't nearly as loud now, so there was no need for her to shout.

The wall of a man looked the two of them over. "Got an appointment?"

"Only for the dentist next month," Olivia said nervously. Koz and the bouncer both looked at her. "Sorry."

"No appointment," Koz said.

"Buying or selling?" the bouncer asked.

"Neither. My friend here needs a messenger."

"They aren't in the habit of making house calls anymore."

Koz shrugged. "Maybe they should get back in the habit."

Bouncer boy inhaled. "Wait here." He opened the door, and had to walk through sideways in order to fit his massive bulk through.

"I've got to say-" Olivia said when he was gone- "this is definitely one of the oddest dreams I've had."

Koz looked confused. "This isn't your dream."

Olivia scoffed. "Then whose is it? Are you going to tell me that I'm just a figment of your subconscious, and not the other way around?"

"I'm as real as you are." Koz looked worried now. "Do you really not know where you are? What this is? How did you even get here? Nobody can get here without knowing."

Before Olivia had a chance to order her list of questions, the bouncer came back. "You get three," was all he said, before stepping aside (with considerable difficulty) and letting them pass.

"Three what?" Olivia asked. "Seconds? Minutes? Days?"

The bouncer just nodded. "Depending on their mood."

"Time means nothing here," Koz whispered to her as they went through the door. "Seriously, how are you here? Nobody gets here on accident."

"Get where?" Olivia asked as they walked. Even though they were out in the open again, the music was still dimmed. Dream logic, she supposed. "This club? I just came in through the window. I was at my grandma's, then I was in space with a squid, and now I'm here." She thought it was all pretty straight forward. For a dream.

"No, not the club," Koz said, audibly frustrated now. *"Here."*

As much as Olivia wished for an elaboration, there were more pressing things to worry about. Finding her friends was about the top twenty things on that list. Though, wherever *here* was, her being there probably had something to do with that fox, she reasoned.

They reached the part of the balcony that overlooked the club, and sitting on a giant plush couch, looking away from the dance floor were four honest to god angels.

Chapter 10: Even Angels have Demons

They all looked human enough. Save for the telltale wings, which were white and fluffy and relaxing in between the backs of the couch and the backs of the angels. Unfurled to their full length, Olivia had no doubt that the wingspan would be very impressive. They were all incredibly muscular, and looked like Greek sculptures. They wore no shirts or shoes, and had no discernible facial features that could identify them easily as male or female. And though Olivia had a nagging hunch that they had nothing to cover up, they wore black ankle length slacks. Their entire bodies were covered in tattoos. It was a mess of script and symbols that she didn't recognize.

One of them spoke as Koz and Olivia approached them. "Look, my others. Guests."

"Indeed?" said another tiredly. "How wonderful."

"How exciting," said a third without excitement.

"What can I do for you?" asked the fourth.

"Don't you recall?" asked the first. "Our servant just informed us. These two literals wish to use our services of old."

"Oh, yes," the fourth nodded. "I do recall that. Vaguely. Seems like ages ago. I cannot be expected to remember all that happens. I am not father."

"It couldn't have been more than a minute," Olivia broke in, starting to get annoyed at them for talking like she and Koz weren't there.

"Really?" asked the third angel. "So long ago."

Koz nudged her. "What did I just say? Ever heard the phrase 'time is relative'?"

"Constantly," Olivia admitted.

"Well that's for the waking world. Here, time is irrelevant. Especially to the native inhabitants. You have to let the concept go to maneuver with any success here."

That bit of information only made Olivia worry more about Penelope. She was connected so deeply to the concept of Time… The poor girl must be lost at sea. Wherever she was.

"So this creature you wish us to find-" the first angel said- "do you wish us to kill them, or would one of you rather do the honors?"

"What?" Olivia asked, horrified. "No, no, no. No killing. I need to find my friends. Not for killing reasons, just for like- you know- normal reasons."

The angel shrugged. "Have it your own way. You wish us to send a message to these 'friends'?"

The third lifted their right arm. "I seem to have a vacant space under my deltoid that could be used for this occasion."

"What are you willing to offer in this transaction?" the second asked Olivia.

"What? You mean like money?" Olivia asked. She patted herself down. Her ducky pajamas didn't have pockets.

"There is no such thing as money," said angel one. "It is simply a construct."

"The same could be said of all things," rebutted angel four.

"That is an excellent point," added angel three.

"So how can I pay?" Olivia asked, cutting off their repartee.

"With the only currency that matters in this- or any- life," said angel two.

"The soul," said angel one.

"My soul?" Olivia was incredulous. "You want my soul just to send a message?" She didn't even know if she strictly believed in the soul, but she suddenly felt very protective of it regardless.

"Just a small piece," angel three explained. "A hair follicle, nothing more."

"Though if you are prepared to pay more-" angel four added- "my others and I will indeed make it worth your while." They plucked one of the feathers from their wings and dropped it into a small container in their hand. The feather melted like ice and filled the container with a glowing liquid. The angel put a nozzle cap on top of the container, and it suddenly looked like nasal spray.

Drift Back, Olivia realized. Koz had said it was a nasal spray. This was where it came from? Angellic drug dealers? Divinity repurposed as euphoric narcotics.

"For as little as a finger of your soul, we are prepared to give you seven bottles," angel two said.

"She doesn't accept," Koz said.

"No, she does not," said a new voice from behind Olivia.

She turned and saw the familiar outline of the fox.

The creature walked up to them. "I told you to wait for me," he said to Olivia.

"No you didn't."

"Well I shouldn't have had to."

Koz eyed the fox with uncertainty. "I take it this is the friend you were waiting for."

Olivia nodded. "Koz, this is the mysterious fox. Mysterious fox, this is Koz. She's-"

"They," Koz corrected.

"Oh, sorry. They've been helping me. What took you so long?"

The fox swished his tail. "The expanse of the Paracosm is always increasing. It is not always quick or easy to traverse."

"Right," said Olivia, not really trying to follow any of this anymore.

They all turned back to the angels, who now seemed slightly peeved that they had to go any amount of time without being paid attention to.

"Look who it is, my others," said angel four, looking down (in more ways than one) at the fox. "It is the lost pup. The stray, come to barter, perhaps."

"You know each other?" Olivia asked.

"All here know of the stray," angel one smiled. "By reputation if nothing else."

"The creature's essence reeks of rebellion and the fight against its other."

Olivia blinked. "Care to explain that?"

"Not at the moment," the fox said. "I'll explain everything. Once you find your friends. You need to be reunited. That's what needs to happen next."

"I'm not arguing the point," Olivia crossed her arms. "But apparently to find them, I need to sell a piece of my soul. Can they do that?"

The fox gave the canine equivalent of a shrug. "What's in a soul?"

"Don't you start getting philosophical on me. I'm confused enough with all this already."

"Memories," Koz said. "That's the payment here. When they say 'soul' they mean parts of you that make you *you*. Memories, pieces of your personality, hopes, loves. All the things that make up your dreams."

"They do taste delicious," angel two said.

"You eat them?" Olivia asked.

"They can't feel the way Literals can," the fox said. "Ingesting the emotions of others is the closest they can get."

And as she looked past them, down to the forgotten dancers below, and all the Drift Back monsters above them, a picture started to paint itself in her head.

"You sell Drift Back in return for bits of your customers' 'souls'. Each time, they lose a piece of themselves, forcing them to want more Drift Back to feel whole- to feel good- again. You take the good pieces of them to eat, leaving only the bad pieces. You also use small pieces of yourself to make the drug. And the more you take from them, the more they need what you're offering. So the more you lose of yourselves in turn. Souls sold for drugs and used as drugs." She was starting to feel nauseous. "As a friend of mine might say, it's all a negative feedback loop."

"Aptly put," the fox said. He turned towards the angels who seemed not to pay Olivia's accusations any heed. "You will find the people we are looking for, and you will do it without touching a single cell of her soul."

"Why would we do that, little aberration?" angel two asked.

"If you know what I am, then you know what is hunting me. Hunting us all. I've been hiding myself, but I could call it here right now if I so choose. The damage it might cause… I could burn down your entire pitiful operation with no effort at all."

"You wouldn't dare," said angel one. They all suddenly looked worried.

The fox pulled his lips into a snarl. "I know the stakes of my mission. I know the limits I will go to secure victory. But you do not. Just because you know of me, do not assume you know me."

There was silence between the angelic junkies.

"Fine," angel one said finally. "What is the message?"

"You misunderstand," the fox shook his head. "You're going to do better than simply send a message."

Chapter 11: Getting in my Own Head

Of all the things Olivia had experienced in her life, being carried and flown by an angel was definitely one of the most surreal.

"Picture those you wish to find," angel one had told her. Olivia did as instructed, holding the images of Alibaster and Penelope in her head. After a moment the angels started moving their heads in different directions; like needles on a compass attempting to find north, or a bloodhound trying to pick up a scent.

"We have located one of them," they said at last.

"We believe this one is called 'male'," said angel two.

Alibaster. Olivia gave a sigh of relief.

"Where is he?" the fox asked.

"At a partition," said angel four. "He is not stationary. He tries to cross over."

"He won't get very far without an invitation," Koz chimed in. Olivia had been so focused on her friends, she had forgotten about Koz.

"I gifted Olivia and her two companions with invitations the moment they entered their domains," the fox said. "They are all needed, and they cannot help if they are trapped in their own dreams."

"Help with what?" Koz asked. "What are you? A Native? A Fathom?"

The fox didn't answer.

There was always a part in every major adventure in which Olivia Jones had taken part where the number of questions she had accumulated for what was going on was so great, that she didn't even know where to begin in asking them. A point where her mind just reshaped itself into a single exasperated question mark.

Such a point had just been reached. Since no one seemed to want to explain anything to her right now, she focused on the one thing she actually cared about. "What about my friends? This 'partition', is it dangerous?"

"Not generally," the fox said. "Just disorienting. You passed through one. The place between your grandmother's house and here. The trouble is one never knows where the partition will drop you."

"Then we need to go get him." Olivia couldn't imagine that Alibaster knew any more about this place and what was going on than she did. Even if this was all a dream, she couldn't risk having her friends get lost or hurt.

So now they were all flying high in the sky with angels. All in all, the sensation wasn't nearly as off putting as teleportation had always been to her. She likened the experience to hang gliding, which she had done once while escaping the Creeping Carbuncle of Crawldoor.

At their own insistence, Koz joined them. They seemed very intrigued by whatever was going on, and said they wanted to follow it through to the end. That was fine by Olivia. She knew when she was out of her depth, and could use all the help she could get right now.

"What about your date?" Olivia had asked.

They'd just shrugged. "Like I said, he's not great at navigating yet. If he was going to show up, he probably would have by now."

They had exited The Swan & Swine through a glass ceiling. In real life, it would have probably just led to the next floor up in the ginormous building. Or back into space with the colony squid. But as the fox had told her, every exit could lead somewhere different. So instead of flying through the minuscule stars she had swam through, they were now …

It was like a tunnel of light. Not like hyperspace, though. Hyperspace was mostly blues drifting in and out of vision. Where they were now looked more solid. And there was a greater spectrum of color to see. As if someone had rolled up a rainbow like a newspaper, and they were all falling through the center. If nothing else, it was pretty.

As they traveled- each of them gripped tightly to the chest of one of the angels while the fourth angel led the way- Olivia tried to think about everything that had been happening. She had to try and piece it together. She was starting to get the feeling that this wasn't just an ordinary dream. There had been everything Koz and the fox had said, for one thing. But also, it didn't feel like a dream anymore. Not since she climbed out the window at her grandma's house. She didn't feel sluggish and vague and incomprehensible like she usually did in dreams. If anything she felt alert, and everything felt and looked real. Not grainy and shifty and obscure, but as matter-of-fact as if it were really happening.

What was it the fox had said? Dreams and reality don't have to be mutually exclusive? What did that imply? That some dreams were as real as the waking world? That she, Alibaster, and Penelope really were in danger, and were summoned to this dream world (a realm in its own right?) to help the fox with… something or another? That made sense on some absurd level. If the fox really was real, he could have indeed been the one to have her reset the ship's coordinates in her sleep to take them to Illetica. But why Illetica?

And if this place were real, that might mean that the people and creatures were too. Such as Koz, the people in the club, the squid, and the things that looked like people but weren't people that had almost attacked her before.

Koz had said that they were as real as she was. Could it be possible? Could people actually share dreams? But this wasn't her dream. Koz had said that too. Then what? Some kind of shared space where the minds of dreamers coalesced? It was a nice though, but if true it just opened up a whole new avenue of questions. She was racking her brain trying to grasp what was happening. But without any facts, all she could do was guess.

"Approaching wyrmhole exit," said the head angel.

"Wormhole?" Olivia asked warily. She and wormholes did not have a copacetic relationship.

"*Wyrm*hole," Koz corrected, enunciating. "Do you have wyrms where you come from?"

Olivia tried to remember what a wyrm was. They were like dragons, right? There was a monster on her brother's favorite video game. It was called the Ulti-wyrm or something. It was the boss battle. Tracey never swore unless he was on that level, trying to beat the creature.

"Only in a fictional sense," she finally answered.

Koz gave a short laugh, as if she had said something funny.

The tunnel of colors fell away to reveal a nondescript desert. There was nothing but heat and sand in all directions. Three blistering suns sat in the center of the sky, and the angels had exited the wyrmhole so far up that Olivia quickly acquired a fear she was certain Icarus had felt a few seconds before his destiny with gravity.

"Has the boy crossed the partition?" the fox asked.

"Yes," said the angel holding Koz. "His essence is distinct. He has been here for an age."

"Here where?" Olivia asked. "This desert?" Had Alibaster just been wandering? It could take forever to find him in this still sea of sand.

"Behold," angel one said, pointing to the horizon.

Olivia squinted, and would have shielded her eyes had she not been too terrified to loosen her grip on her transport's mighty muscles. There was something in the distance. It was difficult to make out at first other than an indistinguishable shape made visible by its juxtaposition to the flat land around it. Like a beauty mark on otherwise clear skin. As they got closer, it became more vivid. It was a building- maybe a spaceship. Its shape was a flat wide dome, maybe a mile in diameter, connected by millions of dark polygonal plates. The plates appeared to be made of glass, but instead of refracting the intense light from above, they seemed to absorb and disperse it.

"What is it?" Olivia asked, as they landed right next to the structure. She was sweating and her throat was parched. Visible waves of heat could be seen rising from the ground, and since she was barefoot, it didn't feel too good. When she hazarded putting her hand to one of the glass plates, she expected it to be burning, but it felt more like it'd been sitting at the bottom of an arctic tundra instead of this dead and dry expanse.

"A prison," the fox said, hopping from two of his padded feet to the others.

Olivia wondered what dreams needed prisons for, but didn't voice the question.

She looked over to Koz, who now looked completely different than they had in the club. Now they wore a tartan T-shirt of different pinks, straight fitting red jeans, and black hiking boots. Their hoop earrings had been replaced by small white gauges, and their mascara was gone. The only thing they had from before were their large blue glasses.

"You changed," Olivia said with surprise.

Koz looked down at themself. "My clothes? Oh yeah, that just kind of happens for me. I hardly notice anymore. More of a force of habit."

Dream rules, right. "Why'd you change?"

"It's daytime here," Koz explained. "I feel more masculine during the day."

They did look more masculine than they had at the club, Olivia realized as she studied them. They even carried themself differently. "But I thought you told me time was meaningless here," she argued. "That it was irrelevant. A construct."

Koz shrugged. "Well so is gender."

Olivia couldn't argue with that. She looked down at her own pajamas, and wished she knew how to magically change her own clothes.

Koz focused their attention to the dome, and frowned. "There's a lot of anger and despair here."

It might have been an odd thing to say, but Olivia had met telepaths before. Perhaps Koz had similar abilities, and could sense what the others were feeling inside. Or it was just a good guess. Of course there would be anger and despair in a prison.

A prison.

Oh…

"We need to get in there," Olivia said urgently.

Two of the angels stepped forward and grabbed opposite ends of the nearest glass plate. As they pulled, the glass cracked and shifted until it was a wonder it hadn't shattered entirely.

"Enter," the angels ushered them in.

Olivia was wary, but felt more at ease when Koz went ahead of her, fading into and then through the broken glass.

"Wait here," the fox told the angels as Olivia stepped through.

"And find out where Penelope is," she added.

"My others and I will attempt to find your third to the best of our abilities," one of them said with what might have been snark. Then their voices and the heat fell away in an instant.

The contrast between the scalding temperatures outside and the meat locker vibe inside was sudden and dramatic. It only felt pleasant for a moment, before Olivia and Koz started shivering. Olivia wished she at least had socks. Frost even formed on the walls. The fox was nonplussed.

It was obvious at once that this place was a prison. It was also obvious that whoever designed the prison had been out of their mind. There was no point of reference for... anything. When Olivia tried to look at one single point for too long, she found she was suddenly looking somewhere else.

There was a word for all this, she knew there was. There were old paintings that dealt with it. When things just looped back in on themselves, or seemed different from another angle or perspective.

Recursion. That was it. It was troubling to conceptualize anything she was seeing because it could easily become another form of itself when viewed at a different vantage point.

"Give it a moment," the fox said. "You need to relax. Allow yourself to adjust. To become in sync with what surrounds you."

Olivia blinked. Even Koz, who obviously knew more about this dream stuff than her, seemed to be having a difficult time too.

Eventually- thankfully- they both adjusted to the craziness. Olivia found it strange, looking for the right words to describe the feeling. The closest she could get to analogizing was to say the experience was like turning on a lamp after waking up in the middle of the night, and waiting for her eyes- which have to start off closed- to slowly align to the light. It was still nonsensical, but in a way that could be navigated.

They all looked around once more. A number of cells littered the place, lining the towering walls at all points. They all differed in size to appropriately house the creatures kept inside, but they were all cubical in dimension. A big hologram jutting from a wall told them they were walking down floor 45, cell block 6353323. They walked past a cube as large as a house. Inside, it held a creature a story and a half high that looked like a big boil that was about to burst. As they passed, it hit at the space between its cell and them, but a curtain of energy rippled and held it back.

"There can't really be more than six million cell blocks here, can there?" Olivia asked. Even if the dome they were in was a mile across, and the space inside was all twisty-turvy, there was still no way it could house so many creatures. Unless maybe most of the prison was underground. Like back on that hollowed out moon that refined Equip's Liquid Solar Energy.

"How many sentient creatures exist that feel trapped inside themselves?" the fox asked. "This prison could be nigh infinite."

"The Natives call people like us Literals for a reason," Koz said to Olivia. "You can't let this place be confined your own prism of understanding. This is not a realm you can wrestle into a box."

Olivia tried to extrapolate meaning from that.

They passed a cell no larger than a hatbox. Inside was a sleeping frog. When the fox passed it, the animal woke with a start, and suddenly was transformed into a small, scared, naked man, who scuttled to the back of the cell.

"So this isn't a real prison for actual criminals," Olivia scratched her head. "It's more of a… state of mind. A place of mentality, in which people trap themselves?"

Koz smiled, and nudged her with an elbow. "She can be taught."

"Though you do need to quit describing things here as not real," the fox said. "If this place were not real, I would not have had to enlist your help in the first place."

"Help with what?" she asked. "You still haven't told me anything. And, if I'm being honest, I think I'm taking this all pretty well considering I have absolutely no clue what is happening."

"Explanations once we find the other two," the fox said. "I don't want to have to repeat myself."

She was about to argue, but the frustration died in her throat as they passed more and more cells. Koz had been right. Every creature they walked by seemed filled with rage; hammering against their cages, or filled with terror; clawing at the walls or themselves, or just hiding in a corner.

And Alibaster was somewhere here. He always acted like nothing fazed him, but sometimes there were moments- flickering instances- where the look in his eye was far off, his face was grave, and his posture was slouched and protective. He would quickly snap out of them though, and get on with whatever it was he was doing. Neither Olivia nor Penelope ever called him out on those moments, but Olivia had the feeling that in those instances his mind was being drawn back to his time as a prisoner of the Fate Makers. On the rare instances he talked about that time, he had tried to explain it as being trapped within himself. He hadn't known where his mind ended and his body began. Olivia tried to understand what that meant, but she knew he could tell that she couldn't fully comprehend what he meant. Even when she and Penelope had visited the universe of Time and had found him alone in that black box, she still didn't really know what to make of it. All she knew was that it had been the worst time of his life.

And now he was here somewhere. In a whole new prison of the mind. She didn't know how long he could hold on.

"You're worried about your friend," Koz said.

Olivia nodded. "He shouldn't be in this place."

"Well that was up to him," the fox said. "It can be difficult for newcomers here. Especially if they don't have the proper control over themselves. As your friend entered, the domain probably latched on to the dark corners of his mind. They ate at him, and he ended up here."

"Why did you let him come here?" Olivia asked. "You've been helping me. Why not him? Why not Penelope? How come you could find me, but you couldn't find them."

"What do you think I am?" the fox asked. "I have influence here, but I am not omnipresent. I could only pick one of you to guide. I chose you. You were the least difficult of the three."

They had been walking for some time, and they had yet to turn a corner, or climb any of the many sets of stairs they had seen. Somehow though, the hologram on the wall told them they were now on floor 8, in cell block 234. Looking up, Olivia could just barely make out the cell of the boil shaped creature that had lashed out at them. It and its cell were upside down now from her perspective, and seemed to be about eight stories away. There was really no rhyme or reason to this place. "Just keep going," the fox said. "And keep your eyes open. We will find the boy eventually. Your connection will guide us."

I sure hope so, Olivia thought. *Or else we could be trapped in this surrealist maze forever.*

It was so sad. All the creatures being kept there. Keeping themselves there. She could hardly look at them after a while. She shivered, half from the presence the prison gave off and half from the cold.

Koz draped a heavy serape shawl over her. They pulled it out of thin air, and when Olivia looked down, she found a giant duck just like the ones on her pajamas smack in the center of the shawl. Olivia laughed. She appreciated the gesture too much to feel ridiculous. Koz themself had traded their checkered T-shirt for a warm looking flannel.

"You've got to teach me how to do that," she told them.

Koz smiled kindly.

As Olivia tried to return the smile, she caught a glimpse past Koz, into a cell beyond.

"What the..." she said, stepping around Koz and looking into the twenty by twenty concrete cube.

The inhabitant was one of the fearful ones. Its face was hidden as it clutched at itself, but Olivia still recognized the familiar figure.

"Ophelia?" she whispered.

The girl in the cell raised her head to look at her, and her eyes were instantly filled with pure terror. She screamed. And suddenly Olivia was screaming, for she was in the cell now, on the floor looking at the mad god woman who had murdered her. *Mustn't let her near. Mustn't let here in! She'll kill us again! She will never stop. Why won't she stop? Why does she seek me only to watch me take my final breath?*

Over and over and over again.

Get out! Get out!

Get me out...

Please...

Why can't she just leave me alone?

Why can't I live?

Tears were falling hard and fast, blurring her vision. She was on her knees sobbing, and she didn't know if she was in the cell, outside of it, or both.

Until she felt someone grab her, and pull her into an embrace.

"Hey, hey. Olivia, hey. Look at me. Look at me. You need to calm down, girl. Slow breaths now. Come on, you can do it... That's it. In and out. It's ok. You're ok."

Olivia did as the voice told her, calming down enough to wipe the tears from her eyes. She found Koz holding her, cradling her on the floor like Olivia used to do with her sisters when they got hurt.

"What did...?" Olivia started, looking back into the cell. It was no longer herself staring back at her, but a lumpy creature the colors of a bad bruise. It seemed curious as to what was happening outside its cell.

"As I said," the fox said gently, "this place can be difficult to newcomers."

After a moment, Koz helped Olivia to her feet, and after asking twenty times if she was sure she was ok, they kept walking.

They really had to find Alibaster.

Chapter 12: Pull Yourself Together

Floor 0, cell block null. This was where Olivia and her new team finally ended up after walking for a timeless epoch. It didn't look any different than the other hundreds of hallways they had been down, except the other levels and cells all looked very far off in the distance now. As if they had been walking inside a deflated beach ball, and it suddenly expanded and pushed outwards around them.

"What is this?" Olivia asked.

"Special cases," the fox replied. "The ones that are so locked within themselves that they refuse to acknowledge anything outside their own mind. The ones that push back against any kind of familiarity or companionship. Even the meager offerings the prison could provide."

Olivia's heart felt like it was going to jump out of her throat. "This is the mental equivalent of solitary confinement."

"Indeed."

Koz could obviously read the worry on Olivia's face. They tried to put a comforting hand on her arm. "We don't know your friend is here."

"He's here," she said. "He spent a good part of his life trapped in a prison of his own mind. He spent years with no company but the voices in his head. A box of himself that he couldn't escape. It almost broke him. He was kept from going insane by the Fa- by his jailers, but only just. If this place feeds on fears, then this would be it for him. The absolute last place in all the multiverse that he would ever want to be again."

Koz looked stunned. Olivia knew they were wondering just who she and her friends were, and what they had wandered into by tagging along with this stranger from the club.

Olivia tried to ignore the look, and carried on into the darkening corridor. She never thought about it too much, but she really hated the Fate Makers sometimes. For all the good and help they had offered the universe, they could still be capricious and unsympathetic. It was a wonder Alibaster didn't hate and disrespect them a million times more than he already did. If they had been regular flesh and blood mortals, Olivia was sure that he would have sought revenge at some point.

Part of her knew that was one of the reasons he had gone so fiercely after Andize Equip when they had first met. Yes, the man had had Alibaster's father murdered, but the method of investigation and pursuit that her friend had taken… It was all indicative of someone who had nothing to do for years except ponder their own feelings and anger, suddenly being set free to seek retribution and revenge. And since he couldn't go after his captors, he had found someone else to face his wrath. If Equip hadn't done what he did, Alibaster would have just found someone else to pursue, of that Olivia had no doubt.

It was a true testament to him as a person that, when it came down to it, he didn't end up pulling the trigger. He could have ignored Olivia's plea. He could have gone down another path and been thrown right back into the hole he had just been pulled out of. But he rose above his rage, and had been able to let at least some of his anger and resentment go. And now, with Olivia and Penelope, he was refocusing his genius and drive into something more productive: helping others.

And still, after all that pain and suffering and trying to move on, he had found himself there again. He had been pulled back into the hole, because the isolation that had found its way into his mind and soul- the crippling loneliness that he tried to keep pushed to the depths of his heart every second of his life- called out louder than the innocence he had lost.

She would get him out of here.

She wasn't about to let the person she loved most in this universe go through his hell again.

She would walk however far she had to walk. She would fight whatever she had to fight.

But she would get him out.

They came to the end of the hallway. By now the light had faded away entirely, and they had walked the last bit of distance through a tunnel of darkness. There was only one cell, there where the hallway ended. Inside was illuminated by a small hanging light bulb, by which the three could barely see inside the cubicle.

"He must have pushed even the other solitary prisoners away," the fox said in a hushed awe. "His repressed pain and fear must be tremendous."

Koz looked on the verge of tears. They were hugging themself and shifting from foot to foot. "I- I feel it," they said. "Oh, how he tries to push beyond it. How much he relies on his own intellect to banish the dark. To use his own mental capacities and means of logic to sweep it all away. An objective and rational approach to meditation. But it's still there. It's always still there."

"Not if I have anything to say about it," Olivia said. She balled her hands into fists and took one final step, to see clearly into the cell.

He wasn't there. It was just an empty cement block. How could he not be there? She felt him reach out to her. Koz could feel him right now too. Where the hell was he?

She studied the cell for any clue, but she couldn't step inside. The same energy barrier shielding all the cells stopped her from entering. The sheet of light rippled as she knocked against it, and the air inside the cell seemed to become disturbed. No, not the air. What was that? Smoke? Mist? Fog?

It swirled around the space, filling every square inch.

Why was the cell filled with smoke?

"Interesting," the fox said to himself. "Complete mental disassociation. He was so unwilling to find himself in the place he feared most, that he cast himself apart entirely so as not to deal with it. Piece by piece. A state of non-being."

Koz sniffled to themself and shivered.

"Oh my god," Olivia said as she realized what was being said. She put her hand up to the barrier of light. "Alibaster?"

The wispy outline of a hand formed out of the smoke on the other side. It pressed itself briefly on that side of the barrier, before dissipating once more into the rest of the mist.

Alibaster had become a ghost of his former self.

And he was starting to fade away.

"We have to help him," she said urgently. "How do we help him?"

"He is ignoring the reality of this place," the fox said. "He refuses the situation in which he has found himself, and in doing so has separated from himself to block any outside stimuli. A child holding his hands to his ears and closing his eyes when someone tries telling him something he does not want to hear. The only way to help him is to get him to face the truth of where he is. He needs to accept what is happening now, and what has happened in his past. If he continues this denial, the damage to his psyche could be irreparable."

"Like when you first showed up in my dreams," Olivia remembered. "When I was reliving that nightmare, you told me not to look away, to face what had happened with Ophel-" She stopped herself and looked at Koz, but they were not paying attention. They barely even noticed Olivia or the fox anymore. Whatever emotions they were getting off of Alibaster were starting to take their toll.

The fox inclined his head. "You can regret your past. You can hate it and rage against it. But you cannot deny it entirely. To do so harms only yourself, not those whom you have wronged or who might have wronged you. Acceptance and ownership of one's life is the first step to gaining control over it."

Olivia thought about how she could help Alibaster do that. How could she reach him when he was like this? Nothing more than atoms and smoke, desperately seeking release.

She took Koz's hands in her own. At her touch, Koz was momentarily stirred out of their stupor. "You're some sort of telepath, right?"

They shook their head slowly. "Empath. Read emotions, not thoughts. When emotions are extraordinarily powerful or absent... they affect me... Forced to feel what they do."

"But that has to work two ways, right?" Olivia guessed, even though she really had no clue. "Like, if you latch onto someone's emotions, it's like you tie a string around you and them. There's a connection, right? One that can probably be broken at differing difficulties depending on the strength of the person emoting."

Koz lifted one shoulder. They were still dazed and talked with slow and broken sentences. "Guess so... This one not a string... More like chains. He's forcing himself not to feel. Weighing us down. It doesn't work... it can't. Repressed pain always rises."

"Either way, a connection extends to both sides. Those you find yourself bound to can use the string- chain, whatever- to pull you, but you can pull back. You don't have to just be along for the ride."

Koz squinted in the dim light, trying to assimilate this information. "Maybe."

"I know you can. You have to. You have to distance yourself from my friend. Untangle your emotions from his. I'll help. Focus on me. What am I feeling right now?"

Koz tried to concentrate. "Fear. Panic. Anxiety. Confusion."

"Or as I call it: my brain's standby mode," she said, trying to lighten the situation. "I need you to concentrate. Feel what I feel. It's all so much isn't it? All these thousands of things flying through me right now. What else is there? Look further down. Is there anything else?"

Koz opened their mouth, but let it hang open for a moment before saying anything. "Intrigue. Resolve. Determination."

"My mother would call that last one stubbornness, but yes. Because while I might feel fear and panic and the others, I know there are things that need doing. I can worry about what's about to happen later. I can worry about the danger and the worst case scenarios some other time. Right now, in this moment, I know I just need to help my friend. There is nothing more than this. This minute. This instant. I thought this was all a dream before, but I now know that it has to be something more. This is happening. This is real. I accept that."

"Acceptance."

"Exactly. Now I need you to take what you're feeling from me, and I need you to use it to pull against the chains holding you and Alibaster together. I need you to help me use them to pull him out of the hole this place has cast him into. Can you do that, Koz? Can you help me do that?"

"I don't... I can't..." They took a breath, and looked Olivia in the eye. "Yes. Yes, I can do that."

They turned to face the cell, closed their eyes, and concentrated.

Olivia watched as the smoke in the cell began to swirl. At first it dispersed from itself further, as if a swath had been cut through it. Then, it pooled and funneled, and started reshaping itself. All the smoke came together, and coalesced into the vague outline of a man. The features became more refined and vivid, and Olivia held her breath as hope found its way into her. Koz gasped as they felt the new emotion, and then fed it into the cell. The last ingredient needed to bring him back fully.

Finally, there he was. Kneeling on the floor, with his scene kid haircut and his battered leather jacket, two sizes too small. He inhaled, blinked, groaned as he made the perilous journey to his feet, and as his eyes adjusted they found Olivia. He gave one of his tired grins.

"Hey Jones," Alibaster said. He looked her up and done. "Nice outfit." Then he looked to the fox and Koz. "So, um. What'd I miss?"

Olivia flung herself forward, the barrier separating them was now gone. She hugged him so tight, she was sure that if these were their actual bodies and not just some weird metaphorical manifestations, she would have been giving some of his ribs a trying time.

"Let's get you out of here," she said.

Chapter 13: One Friend Down, One to Go

"What exactly is going on?" Alibaster asked as the four made their way out of the prison. Like with Koz and Olivia, it had taken him a minute to become "in sync" with the strange recursive nature of the place.

"Long version or short version?" Olivia asked.

"Hmm. Short."

She took a breath. "So. As far as I understand it, we're asleep. But we aren't dreaming. Or if we are, it isn't our dreams that are being dreamed. This is all really happening on some level. We might be in some weird sleep realm or something. This fox brought us here, but lost sight of where you and Penelope ended up because he could only watch one of us at a time: me. He seems to have some sort of status here because the angels who brought us to you were scared when he threatened them. I don't know why he brought us here in the first place. He refuses to tell us anything until we find Penelope, but I'm guessing it's to defeat some sort of great monster or something that threatens this realm. You know, the usual stuff." Olivia paused for breath and looked to her right. "And this is Koz. They've been helping me since I got here, and I honestly couldn't be more grateful. Koz, Alibaster. Alibaster, Koz."

"That was the short version?" Alibaster asked. "What's the long version?"

Olivia rolled her eyes. "Like I said, I don't know. The fox won't tell me."

Alibaster eyed the creature, unsure what to make of him. Then he turned his gaze to Koz. "Koz?" he asked.

"Short for Kozmoklor," they replied.

Alibaster's head rose slightly. "You're Illetican."

They nodded. "You must be too. It's the only planet I know of which names its people the way we do."

Ah, Olivia realized. *Minerals, but spelled different.* She should have known. But how was she supposed to know all the different mineral names? She wasn't a geologist.

"Koz is an empath," Olivia said, happy to show off her impressive new friend. "They're the one you should thank for the rescue."

Alibaster nodded his appreciation. He seemed impressed. "Empathic abilities are rare on Illetica."

"Yeah I've heard the statistics," Koz said. "Like one in three hundred thousand."

"Three hundred fifty three thousand, nine hundred twelve," Alibaster corrected.

"Well aren't you just a walking Withive," Koz laughed.

The hologram on the wall told them they were on floor 636, cell block 123111. There was no way to know for sure if that indicated progress, but the fox was leading them all pretty self assuredly, so hopefully his confidence in his sense of direction was justified.

"So I've got to ask-" Koz started, adopting a more serious tone- "who are you people? At first I thought Olivia was just lost, and I wanted to help, but now..."

"Do you want to leave?" Olivia asked. She tried to hide the disappointment in her voice. She really liked Koz. But after what they had just been through- what she had asked of them to rescue Alibaster- it was understandable that could have been too much.

"No!" said Koz quickly. "Qlarn, no. I'm sticking by you closer than ever now."

Olivia smiled.

"You said you wanted to help Olivia," Alibaster said. "Well then you'll fit right in with us."

"We try to help people too," Olivia explained. "It's kind of our thing. Our 'calling' or whatever. I know it sounds cheesy, and makes us sound super self-important, but it is what it is."

"Help people," Koz said. "How do you mean?"

They passed a cell which held four thousand and five screeching bats. Olivia couldn't explain where that number had come from, but she knew it to be true nonetheless. When their eardrums were no longer being assaulted by the din, she tried to explain.

"We're kind of like… consultants for really weird things. Help for hire. We go to different places where a situation is too extreme or odd for typical people to deal with it, and we do what we can."

Alibaster put up his index finger, in that professorial manner of his. "For instance, before we were… diverted, we were heading to Vogaridusykem, where ghosts from about five generations in the future were harassing people in the capital city."

"And what makes you so specifically qualified to deal with these things?" Koz asked.

Alibaster got defensive. "After you've saved the universe once or twice, you learn how to think on your feet, and turn extraordinary problems on their heads to find equally extraordinary solutions."

Olivia elbowed him in the side. "We're also very lucky. Like, stupid lucky. But that doesn't convince people when you're handing out business cards."

Koz considered all they had heard. "Saved the universe?"

Olivia cringed. "Long story."

"Twice?"

She shrugged. "I try not to think about it."

"You're not joking are you?"

The fox suddenly snarled into a cell the size of a spacious wardrobe, which held a two foot tall clown, manically kicking the ground in shoes twice his size. The clown backed away, and the fox carried on as if nothing had happened.

The Earthling and the two Illeticans looked at each other in astonishment and bemusement.

"Anyway," Koz continued, "I guess I can see why this fox, whatever it really is, wants your help. If you really are who you claim. But still, it's a pretty incredible story. Are you sure you're not Natives here? I'd believe it more if you were. There are loads of those epic types around."

Alibaster raised an eyebrow at Olivia, but she just shook her head.

"But I have to know-" Koz went on, looking at Alibaster- "I felt so much of the things you try to stave off. I'm sorry if it makes you uncomfortable, and I don't mean to pry-"

"But you're about to anyway," he said.

Olivia was two seconds away from elbowing him again.

"Yes," said Koz. "You feared it so much. It still haunts you; though I can sense that time has passed. What did you do? What were you imprisoned for? I wouldn't ask something so personal usually, but I like to know what sort of company I'm keeping."

At first it looked like Alibaster wasn't going to answer at all. This was a very sore subject for him, and he almost never discussed his life before being released. But after a time he inhaled, and looked straight ahead. "I fell in love with the wrong person."

All the air seemed to be let out of Koz's balloon. "That's it?"

"That was enough."

"Was there an inappropriate age difference?"

Alibaster wrinkled his nose. "Not in the way you mean."

"Was it on a planet that frowned on different species… mingling?"

"You could say that."

"Did this person love you back?"

"I honestly don't know."

"Where are they now?"

"Dead. She died saving our lives. Saving everyone's life."

"I'm… I'm sorry."

For a second Olivia was worried he would say something snarky, but he surprised her. "Thank you."

They continued in silence for the rest of the way. Olivia wondered if Alibaster's willingness to open up so easily had anything to do with what Koz had done down in his cell. Was he really starting to accept his past now, or did he just instinctively trust Koz the way he did when he had first met Olivia? Or did empaths just bring that side out in people? With someone that could read emotions, it must have been easier to let one's guard down around them. When they said "I know how you feel," that was literally true. She continued to ponder the exact nature of Koz's abilities the rest of the way. She wondered what Penelope would make of them.

At last they made it out of the prison, stepping through the plate of broken glass they had entered. The desert was much cooler than it had been. Probably because the suns were setting. It was still a lot hotter than inside the prison though, and Olivia ditched her shawl.

A slew of stars could be seen in the dusk sky. But they seemed to be the normal, far away kind. She couldn't tickle her fingers with them like she could with the ones around the colony squid.

The angels were still there, they hadn't seemed to have moved at all.

"Thanks for waiting," Olivia said.

"We had no choice in the matter," said one of them. (She had forgotten which was which, so now she would have to number them all over again.)

"No," the fox said, "you did not."

"Wow, you weren't kidding when you said angels, were you?" Alibaster said. He walked around them, studying them. "How interesting. Even with wings, the humanoid form should not be able to fly. It's not an efficient enough shape. What else makes you stand apart? Hollow bones perhaps? Maybe you don't fly at all, and it's more of a controlled glide…"

Koz leaned over to Olivia. "He's going to have a hard time here, isn't he?"

"If you thought *I* was literal minded…" she started before trailing off. She walked up towards the nearest angel. "Please tell me you found Penelope."

"Yes. It took more mental acuity to locate the female designate than it did the male, but we did indeed locate her."

"Why did it take more effort?" the fox asked worriedly.

"This is unknown. Perhaps for a time she was not fully here. Still floating in the place between her dreams and our sphere."

"Where is she?" Olivia asked.

The angel pointed straight up and then lowered his arm about twenty degrees. "Not far at all. In the grand scheme of things. Only ten stars hence. On the shrunken world."

The fox calmed noticeably. "Good. Good. That is a relatively safe place for her to be until we can collect her. She should stay out of trouble there."

"I don't recognize any of these star patterns," Alibaster said with his eyes to the sky and his hands on his hips. "But if you're right, and Penelope is on a planet orbiting the tenth nearest star..." He muttered some calculations to himself. "If we had a ship with decent enough tachyon burst sequences, we could be there in a couple of hours."

Olivia patted his shoulder. "Oh my sweet deluded alien genius. Dream realm, remember?"

"Well whatever realm it is, it still has to have rules. Even different dimensions adhere to fundamental laws."

"We are beyond your scope of reference and understanding," the fox said as one of the angels scooped him up. "Learn this quickly or perish."

The remaining three angels each took Olivia, Koz, and- to some resistance- Alibaster. And in less time than it took Olivia to count to ten, they had sped high above the desert, past two moons, and out of the trinary star system entirely.

Chapter 14: Welcome to (What's Left of) Our World

It's no secret that Olivia hated teleporting. It was disorienting, being one place, and then within an eye blink being in another. She never knew whether she was coming or going, and no matter how many times her atoms dispersed then reassembled, she just couldn't get used to the sensation. She was always left with a sour stomach and the distinct feeling that she had just kicked the laws of physics in a tender place.

It now appeared that Alibaster had just discovered a mode of transportation that he abhorred just as much as Olivia did teleportation.

He didn't scream as the group was flung through the heavens by four jacked and angelic junkies. But there was a stillness about him as they shot past stars so quickly that the lights they gave off became stretched lines in their vision. His eyes were wide, and he dared not even breathe. His face was paler than usual. Or was that green? He just hung rigidly as the angel grasped him, like a baby cat when the mother picks it up by the scruff.

It could be suggested that it wasn't terror lining his face, but confusion. He might have been racking his brain trying to figure out how they all weren't suffocating or freezing to death. Or how these angels could fly faster than most space ships, or how the force of their speed wasn't causing anyone's skin to fly off like a fat pair of pants on a malnourished man in a slapstick routine.

Alibaster was- without a doubt- wondering all these things and more, but these questions were all just background noise to him at the moment. The whispered impossibilities that were stoking the flames of his already vomit inducing fear.

It was odd, because Olivia felt like she probably should have been scared too. But for some reason the journey was more exhilarating than anything. Like a roller coaster, but instead of safety harnesses she was gripped by large unyielding biceps.

To each their own, she supposed.

Soon they started slowing down.

When the angels had said "shrunken planet", Olivia half expected a tiny little world the size of a bouncy ball. And that upon reaching the world, they would have to somehow shrink down to an appropriate size in order to land on it.

This did not seem to be the case. Because it turned out the shrunken planet wasn't a planet at all. It was… What was it? An island? An island unattached from a planet, simply floating in the void. That's what it looked like. A mass of green and a few pools of blue could be seen from above, with blips of light coming from and around a number of homely looking buildings. They landed on the outskirts of what was probably a town or village.

The angels let their passengers go, and Alibaster turned, ran twenty yards in the opposite direction, and started retching right off the edge of this world. A minute passed before he collected himself and returned. Everyone politely ignored the incident, even when he spit into the grass and wiped his mouth with his sleeve.

"So," he started with a haggard breath, as if nothing had happened. "This is where Penelope is?"

"This is where my others and I last sensed her before her signature faded like a dying candle flame."

"That doesn't sound good," Olivia said.

"Let's go into town and see if anyone's seen your friend," Koz said. It felt pleasantly warm now, like a relaxing summer evening. Koz had changed their clothes accordingly, into a loose fitting blouse, Capri pants, and ankle strap sandals.

As they all made their way towards the lights, the fox explained where they were. "This was once part of a peaceful planet, full of non-hostiles and pacifists. They left everyone else alone, hoping to be left alone themselves. But things rarely work out that easily. An invasion fleet threatened to wipe them out, so the planet decided to shrink itself to hide from the invaders. It worked. The entire planet was miniaturized, except for this one village. For reasons unknown, this place didn't shrink with the rest of the planet, which started shrinking and never stopped, lost forever in subatomic oceans. Only six hundred survivors left of the whole world. The invaders ultimately left the people alone. They were all bluster, it turned out. Besides, what was the point of invasion if there was nothing left to invade?"

They all thought about this as they reached the first street. The town looked like it was built in eighteenth century Earth. All brownstone buildings and candle lanterns lining the cobblestone streets. Several people were milling around, and paid them no mind.

"That makes absolutely no sense," Alibaster finally said.

"Indeed?" the fox asked, feigning interest.

"First off, when a civilization sees alien invaders approaching, whose first thought would be, 'Hey guys, I think we should just shrink ourselves and hope the bad guys go away'?" Alibaster asked. He didn't expect an answer, so he didn't wait for one. "And if they had that kind of technology- which, by the way, the power needed to shrink a whole planet would be enough to force a main sequence star into a red giant several million years earlier than intended..." He seemed to forget what he was saying, before continuing with previous fervor. "If they had that kind of technology just lying about, why not use it on the invaders? And why did this one village survive? How are they- how are we- surviving now? There is no atmosphere here. This place has no world, no sun, no protection. It's just drifting."

"Aren't we all?" Koz asked.

Alibaster thought about the question for a second, before realizing that it was rhetorical, and he deflated.

"The places of this realm are the consequences of those who dreamed them," the fox said. "They do not always align with meanings or scenarios that would make sense to you."

They neared what must have been the town square. Larger groups of people were gathered there, enjoying what looked like a festival. There were many paper lanterns lit, hanging on lines between buildings and streetlamps. Children held balloons or hot sweets. Some families sat on small patches of grass that circled the area, sitting on blankets like they were having a picnic or waiting for a fireworks show. And the sound of soft music was buzzing from the distance, but it could not have been said where exactly it was coming from.

"Wonder what the occasion is," Olivia said as they wove their way into the crowd. The residents of the town didn't seem to notice or acknowledge any of them, even the four shirtless winged hunks covered in ink, or the talking fox. They simply stepped out of the group's path when nudged away. Alibaster even tripped at one point and bumped into a jovial looking old man quite harshly. Alibaster profusely apologized, but the old man just looked right past him, his eyes glazing over until Alibaster finally gave up and moved on. The second he was out of the man's line of sight, the jolliness returned to the old timer's face as if nothing had happened.

"Are we ghosts?" Alibaster asked. "What's going on here?"

The fox looked up to Olivia. "Well?" he asked, expectantly. "What do you think?"

Olivia looked to Koz, who just shrugged. She thought about all she had just been told about this place, and what she had just learned about the nature of the places of this... *domain*, and what that indicated about the person who had dreamed this particular dream.

"Maybe the dreamer was not one to draw attention to themself," Olivia started. "They hated conflict, and when it arose they would rather hide than run or fight. They drew into themself, choosing to stay alone in their own little world than have to deal with anything outside of it that could be considered threatening. This town is what is left of that mindset. The people here are programmed to ignore any outsiders."

Foxes couldn't smile. To think a fox was smiling would be simply a mistake of an anthropomorphic nature. Olivia was pretty sure she was making that mistake now.

"There is hope for you yet, Olivia Jones."

Alibaster blew raspberries obstinately. "Neophytic psychobabble."

Olivia blew raspberries back. "Says the king of *Techno*babble."

She thought some more. "So in this realm there are real people, like in the prison and in the club. But there are also dream people? Like the people here? Just remnants of someone's sleeping mind."

This time Koz answered. "There are the sleepers and the dream-folk, yes. There're also the Natives. Like our esteemed friends here." They motioned to the angels who looked increasingly bored with each passing second. "And I'm guessing..." their eyes fell to the fox, who said nothing. Koz continued. "The Natives were here first. Well, obviously. That's what 'Natives' means, isn't it?"

How could there be natives in a place of dreams? Olivia wondered. *Dreams are created by sleepers, right? So how could anything or anyone exist before there were sleepers to dream them into existence?* Every question she had answered about this place just ignited fifty more questions. *Which came first, the dreamer, or the dreams?*

"But the dream-folk- or Fathoms- are more than just products of some unassuming sleeper's unconscious," the fox added. "When left to their own devices, away from the mind of the one who thought them into being, they start to evolve; to become full entities in their own right, breaking free of their 'programming'. But it can take a while, and in the early stages of their disillusion, it can take effort to reach them in ways beyond what they were designed to be."

"I about fell on top of that old guy, and he didn't even flinch," Alibaster said. "How much effort could it take?"

The proverbial light bulb flashed on over Olivia's head. She grimaced at what she was about to do, but needs must. Picking her target- a sturdy looking man a head taller than herself- she reeled back and struck him on the chin as hard as she could. She ignored the crack of pain that his jaw bone left on her knuckles, and really hoped that once would be enough.

Her companions just stared at her in disbelief. Even the angels were momentarily pulled from their self-pitying tedium. None of the Fathoms stirred from their festivities, not that she had expected them to. The man she had punched, on the other hand… He blinked several times, as if waking up, then looked down at Olivia.

"Oh," he said, nonplussed, "hello there. Sorry, I almost bumped into you."

"Not a problem," Olivia sighed. Yes! She knew it would work. Or, she had hoped anyway. She was used to having to wake up heavy sleepers, after all. Not that she had ever punched Alibaster in the face while he was sleeping, she wasn't a monster. But some degree of physical discomfort was often involved. She continued, not knowing how long the shock of the blow would last until the man's eyes glazed over and he reverted back to his factory settings. "Real quick, have you seen a girl? Young, about my age. Surly, sarcastic, takes no guff from anyone." Was she describing Penelope, or her uncle's old gumshoe novels? "She might have arrived here out of nowhere, and seemed kind of out of it."

The man considered. She knew it was a shot in the dark. If the people here hadn't noticed them, why would they have noticed Penelope?

"No," he said finally. "I can't say that I have."

"Oh," Olivia said, not bothering to hide her disappointment. "Thanks anyway."

The man nodded politely, and started to turn away, massaging his chin as if he had hurt it somewhere.

"Wait," Olivia caught his attention once more. "What is this?" she motioned to all that was happening around them. "Why are all you here? Is it a holiday or something?"

The man laughed. "Surely you know what day it is? Where have you been?"

Olivia shrugged noncommittally.

"It's the anniversary!" the man said, spreading his arms.

"Anniversary?"

"A year to the day, it is. A year to the day since the young goddess crawled forth from the earth below us, and gifted us humble folk with her majesty."

Olivia looked to Alibaster, and she knew the look he had on his face was mirroring her own. Worshiped as a god. That was a new one.

"And where is she, your goddess?"

The man pointed. "In her sacred spot for all to behold for eternity."

That didn't sound great.

She thanked him again, and the gang took off in the direction indicated.

They pushed their way past everyone, a little ruder than before. Not that any of the dream-folk noticed. The crowd got thicker and more congested the further into it they ventured. Until at last, they reached the last layer of people, all of whom were circled around something. Olivia shoved and pushed people aside, until she breached the ring of onlookers.

Right there, in the center, standing on some sort of dais, was Penelope. Fear lined her face, though from another angle it could have been mistaken for rage. The two could often be interchangeable for her.

She was wearing a slightly tight polo shirt, slightly long khaki pants, and a name tag on the right side of her chest that said "Hello, my name is: Penelope".

She was also, currently, made completely of stone.

Chapter 15: Penelope, our Lord and Savior

"Man, the people here must have really taken to her," Alibaster said, studying the statue. "To sculpt an image in her likeness like this. Some sort of icon through which to worship her."

"No," Olivia shook her head. "It's more than that. I can feel it. This isn't just a sculpture of her, it is her." She looked at the fox. "Isn't it?"

"I'm afraid so," the fox said.

"What?" Alibaster asked, incredulously. "No way."

"Look at the way she's positioned," Olivia said, pointing. "That guy said that she burst from the earth when she first arrived. That would make sense, since she looks like she's trying to stand up. See how she's sort of crouching? And her body's slightly contorted, as if she suddenly found herself in a strange place and was looking around frantically. She's also looking intensely at her hand. I think she saw herself turning to stone, little by little, and that's why she has that look on her face." She was pleased with her deductions, but sadly, nobody took time to admire her Holmes-ian moment.

"How could such a thing happen?" Alibaster asked.

"It no doubt had to do with her mental state when she arrived here," Koz said. "Like when we found you transformed into smoke."

Alibaster raised an eyebrow. "When you found me *what*?"

Before anyone could explain to him the precise means of his self imprisonment, the fox interjected. "Actually, I believe it is something else entirely. This one is an anomaly in the universe. She feels the ebb and flow of Time more acutely than maybe any other living thing. She must have more power and knowledge than she even knows how to access or comprehend."

Alibaster and Olivia both acknowledged the truth in this.

"So how-" the fox went on- "would such a child react when suddenly finding herself in a realm where the laws of Time are mooted, and taken as suggestion only? How would she respond to finding herself in a place no longer tied down by the fourth dimension, but in a higher plane of existence entirely? Well, the answer is right in front of you. This stone form she has taken is representational of her body and mind rejecting the Paracosm, and trying to root itself back into something it can understand. 'Time means nothing here?' her instincts asked. 'So that means there is no past, present, or future. That concept cannot be coped with, so I must also become something that has no past, present, or future. Something fixed within this nonsensical place.' And fix herself she did. It was her mind's defensive mechanism, trying to force her into a constant within a place or no constants. She anchored herself in the storm. In doing so she ended up as part of the very foundation of this town, which is more than likely why the Fathoms here can perceive her, and why they might worship her."

There was a brief pause as they all processed this. Then Alibaster asked. "You said this place, the 'Paracosm', was a higher plane of existence. So high that time couldn't even affect it. For that to be true it would have to be a universal dimension in its own right."

"For once, you are correct," the fox said. "I think you would consider this to be the fifth dimension."

"Dreams?" Olivia asked.

The fox shrugged. "Dreams, ideas, stories, belief. All these are ingredients that make up the Paracosm."

"That's incredible," Alibaster said. "There's always been conjecture that there were more than four dimensions, but nothing ever proven. If this is true, then it turns everything about the universe on its head. The implications-"

Olivia cut him off. "This is all very informative. But I think we should focus on getting Penelope de-statued."

"I don't think I can be of much help this time," Koz said. "There are no emotions for me to latch onto. There's just nothing. And not the kind of forced nothing he was giving off before." They nodded to Alibaster. "What's happening to your friend isn't repression. The fox is right, she's shut off completely. Trying to home in on her mental state is like… Well, it's like trying to bleed a stone."

Olivia bit her inner cheek. "The key?" she asked Alibaster.

He shrugged. "Maybe. I don't really know if that kind of mojo is connected to our physical bodies, because we left those back in our resident reality. And if this is a higher plane of being, where the usual rules don't apply, we might be cut off from our abilities entirely."

They were talking about the Key of Three. A special sort of power gifted to them and Penelope by the Fate Makers. A failsafe, should their own power ever waver. When the three came together in a certain way, they had abilities similar to the universe's custodians. They hadn't tried to use the power since the brief moment they had been the Triad Fate, all those months ago. They hadn't needed to. And though none of them had said it, they had all been slightly afraid to.

"Worth a try, at any rate," Alibaster said.

Olivia took one of his hands in her own, then they both climbed the three stone steps of the dais on which Penelope had been placed. This act prodded some of the townsfolk to finally start noticing them.

"Who are they?" one voice asked.

"What are they doing?"

"They can't be-"

"Not allowed to touch her holiness-"

"Someone stop them before-"

"Wreak vengeance upon us all-"

"Uh, guys?" Koz's voice drifted towards them from amid the rising tension of the crowd. "These people are starting to wake up. Whatever you're about to do you might want to hurry. I'm allergic to being sacrificed."

Olivia took her free hand and placed it on top of one of Penelope's, and Alibaster did likewise.

They focused, and almost immediately felt the surge flow through them as they always did when they closed the circuit of dormant power between them. It started from the right, at the tips of the fingers, then moved like static through the body, and then passed through the finger tips of the left hand, and into the next of the three. The energy cycled through them, getting quicker and increasing in power with each loop made.

It felt slightly different than it usually did. Alibaster and Olivia could feel how lethargic it became when trying to course through Penelope. It was like blood in an artery, trying to squeeze its way past a clot. It still flowed, but not as efficiently as it should have. The power felt sluggish, which meant that this could take longer than expected.

Unfortunately, the townsfolk didn't seem to have patience for that. Their murmuring was getting louder and more agitated every second.

"Guys?" Koz's voice was tinged with worry now.

"Hold them back," the fox commanded. "Do not let any of them interfere."

"Why does it matter to us what happens to these Literals?" one of the angels asked.

"Just do it!" the fox snarled.

The angels must have listened, because there came no further protests.

Back on the dais, the power kept flowing heavily and awkwardly between the three. Penelope was quite literally the stone in the stream, stopping the water from moving freely. Olivia thought about what else to do, and her mind kept going back to her blood clot analogy. The more she felt the power flow and considered, the more it seemed like Penelope's condition was causing the energy to slow and congeal.

During her teenage years, Olivia loved hospital drama shows. And due to her fixation on them, she learned a thing or two. For instance, there was this thing called hypercoagulation, when a person's blood clotted excessively. It could cause pulmonary embolisms or heart attacks.

The syrup-like nature of the force which should have been moving through them like electricity was starting to become uncomfortable. Down to her very bones Olivia started feeling very weak. As if she had been swimming laps for several hours. It was obvious Alibaster felt it too. They were both shaking, and their legs were wobbling as if large toothpicks were buckling under the weight of watermelons.

This was it. Her analogy had been apt. The power was turning against them. An energy embolism brought on by the curdling that the stone Penelope was causing. How to stop it before it killed them?

"We have to… let go," Alibaster said, starting to loosen his grip on Olivia's hand.

"No!" With great effort, Olivia squeezed his tighter. "We don't know… what that will do." Their voices were slurring. Even their tongues were going slack. "Could make it… worse."

"S-suggestions?"

As a matter of fact, she did have an inkling of an idea.

Giving blood helped prevent embolisms and heart attacks. It forced the body to create new blood that wasn't so congealed. (*Was that right?* Olivia wondered. *That sounds right. Let's hope it's right.*) So maybe if they could somehow expel a portion of the energy…

But they had never done that before. Their power wasn't of the superhero-shoots-bolts-of-energy-out-of-extremities variety. Their power was mainly about manipulating events to a negligible degree, to pull an outcome more favorable into being. They had only ever used it to help them stay alive in dire situations, and even then they used it sparingly.

But they had to try. If she and Alibaster could force the power down, squeeze it into a concentrated form, then they should be able to change the nature of it so it could be expelled. Because as everyone knew, energy couldn't be destroyed, but it could change state.

In theory, anyway.

To be completely honest, Olivia was pretty sure she was talking out of her rear as she tried to explain the idea to herself. She had also once heard that energy couldn't leave an isolated system. What exactly did that mean? Did it apply here? If the three of them counted as an isolated system, then that rule would only hinder their situation further. So she chose to ignore it, hoping that her sheer denial of the laws of thermodynamics would be enough to dissuade them from appearing. Hopefully she was misinterpreting what it meant.

She had never been stellar at this kind of stuff. In school, her science classes were the ones that kept her GPA lower than her parents would have liked. It had all been proven kind of academic anyway; her life was often much more science fiction than what the people on Earth would have considered science fact. For instance, two months ago she and Penelope had been chased off a planet by a nest of spiders the size of station wagons. On Earth it was still generally agreed that spiders could not reach such a size because they'd be crushed by their own weight. It went to show just how little anybody actually knew about anything.

Oh my god, focus.

They had to try something, and they didn't have any other ideas. If the power was left as it was, it would continue poisoning them.

"Follow… my lead," Olivia strained to say. Every inch of her felt clumsy and alien now, like how her mouth had been numbed when her wisdom teeth had been taken out, but on a bodily scale.

Everything pertaining to the Key of Three was more of an art than a science. They didn't control the Key, they were the Key. So when using the Key's power, they always had to just trust their instincts. Even in the uncharted waters of what she was about to attempt, Olivia still felt certain inclinations about how she should go about what she intended.

What she was doing- forcing the energy into a more refined form to be disposed of- it was like tensing a muscle. It was like tensing every muscle. It was like she was forcing the very essence of her being into a patient but taut crouch. An animal poising itself before a pounce or sprint.

The connection between them allowed Alibaster to feel what she was doing, and he started- with trepidation- to do the same himself. Once they both felt like their auras were in the positions they needed to be in to correctly harness the compacted energy, they tried to shift it. They had to move it from wherever it was coming from and nudge it somewhere else entirely to be expelled. They were trying to wrestle lightning into a sack to be hurled away.

It was difficult.

"Wait for it…" Olivia slurred, though she didn't need to talk. Alibaster and she were literally on the same wavelength at the moment. It made her feel better though. It made her feel a little bit more in control of the insanity that was her life.

They just about had the energy positioned…

"Now!"

A halo of light appeared above each of their heads. The halos grew and expanded until the three merged into one. There was a moment of pause as the anger of the townsfolk died into hushed amazement.

And then the energy blast to end all energy blasts shot forth from the unified halo, and into the eternal night above.

Everyone that could be seen was shielding their eyes. The village NPCs couldn't ignore the power released on such a scale. In the corner of her eye, Olivia saw her traveling companions. Koz had a look of wonder and uncertainty on their face. The fox... Well, it was hard to read a fox's facial expressions. But Olivia could have sworn he looked afraid. Deeply, properly afraid.

Even the angels, who had blocked the crowd into four different sectors using their full wingspans to hold them back, even they looked- if not impressed, than at least intrigued.

Olivia and Alibaster instantly felt better. Letting go of all that compromised power, it was a great relief. Unfortunately, the only analogy Olivia could think of to describe it was that of a good belch relieving an upset stomach.

They had to stop soon, though. They couldn't let all the power escape. Who knew what the consequences of that could be? There needed to be some left to create more. They just had to make sure they cut off the dead branches. Man, she was really mixing her metaphors here.

They started relaxing themselves slowly; bottle necking the power shooting into the sky until it was nothing more but a pitiful stream of light, and them nothing at all. Both Olivia and Alibaster breathed a sigh of relief. A hand suddenly squeezed Olivia's, and it wasn't the hand Alibaster was holding.

Penelope coughed and spluttered, as if she'd held her breath for too long. She blinked several times, before noticing her friends' hands in her own. "Oh," she said hoarsely. "Again?"

Alibaster smiled tiredly, and nodded.

"You really should not have done that," the fox said in almost a whisper. Olivia would have asked what he meant, but she was more focused on Penelope.

They all let go of one another, and Penelope tried getting her bearings. She looked past her friends and into a sea of people. Any Fathoms in the village that had not been in the square were certainly making their way now. Those that had already been there were all on their knees, prostrating themselves before their stone goddess turned flesh.

"Um," Penelope blinked again, and looked back to her friends. "Anyone want to fill me in on just what the hell is happening here? Bullet points, please."

Alibaster crossed his arms. "Dreaming but not really. Brought here by woodland creature. I was in prison and made of smoke. You were here but made of stone. Now you're a living god to people that were just starting to understand the concept of free will." He put up another finger with each item he listed. "Oh, and Olivia made a new friend."

Koz waved awkwardly.

Penelope gave a deep frown. "I changed my mind. I'm going to need the unabridged version."

Alibaster ushered for Olivia to "take the stage". She scratched her head, feeling astonishingly drained, and tried to explain.

Chapter 16: Learning to Count

Once Olivia had done her best at explaining the situation, Penelope still didn't look any less at ease. "I don't like it here. This 'Paracosm', it feels… gross. It feels like ants are crawling all over me."

"I'm guessing that has something to do with your sensitivity to Time," Alibaster said. "Which is why you were stone in the first place."

"Time is fluid usually; water rushing in an ever branching and diverging river," Penelope said. "But now- here- it's as if it's… gaseous. It has no real form and takes no set paths. It's only here as an afterthought. It's all very wrong."

Olivia put a hand on her shoulder. "We'll figure it out. But we have other things to deal with right now."

"I think the top of the list is your new subjects," Koz said, gesturing to the hundreds of people bowing and silent. The angels still had their wings unfurled to block any of them front breaching the small circle of safety the team had for themselves, though they needn't have bothered. None of the dream people would dream of getting too close to their goddess now, not after that display of her awesome power which woke her from what they had assumed to be her eternal sleep. The ones nearer the group strained to hear what was being said. What ancient secrets were being whispered just out of earshot?

"What do you want me to do?" Penelope asked. "Lead them in a round of hymns? Turn water to grape juice?"

"Well you need to do something," Koz urged. "I don't know how long they'll stay pacified. That display of power- however you all did that- put them in a trance. I can feel it; their minds are filled only with devotion. I've seen it before with Fathoms recently cut off from the ones who dreamed them up. They don't yet know how to act without direction. So they find it wherever it may present itself. They've latched onto you. So, direct them."

Penelope blanched at the idea, but relented. "Fine." She cleared her throat and stepped away from the others. "Hello, my… people."

A few voices stirred in the crowd.

"You need to project," Alibaster said.

Penelope gave him an eye so full of stink it could down a skunk. "If you don't like having all your teeth in your mouth, do please keep talking."

Alibaster put his hands up in a faux surrender.

She turned back to the crowd, this time speaking louder. "Everyone, go home."

The dream-folk started looking at each other in confusion. What had she just said?

"And stand up," Penelope said. "This is really flattering, but trust me; I'd make a very bad god. I don't even check my email, so it's guaranteed that I would forget to check my incoming prayers. I also hate hospitals, so I wouldn't be making any visits to perform miracles. Not that I can do that kind of thing to begin with. Also the idea of kissing random babies makes me very uncomfortable."

"I think that last one's for politicians," Olivia said.

"Whatever," Penelope sighed, then raised her voice again. "So please go home."

"But-" one of the people started to ask as they all slowly got to their feet.

"Are you questioning me?" Penelope asked with all the command she could muster.

They all shook their heads in frightened unison. After a second they decided that their deity had spoken, and started shuffling away from the square.

"Who are we to question her wisdom?" someone mumbled.

"Such humility. How truly honored we are to have such a humble goddess," said another.

"She must be an impostor," a third grumbled. "The *true* goddess wouldn't have forgotten to wish me a happy birthday."

They all ambled away in different directions slowly- almost cautiously. As if this were all some sort of test and any second now Penelope would shout, "Psych! Come on back everyone! Where are those babies at? I got foreheads to kiss." But no such things came from their lady's lips, and soon enough the streets were clear.

A breeze blew litter around the cobblestones and grass.

Olivia turned to the fox. "Gang's all here now. So will you finally explain the details of what exactly this is, who you are, and why you brought us here?"

The fox wasn't listening. His legs were shaking as he paced back and forth, to and fro. His head turned in one direction, then another, as he strained his ears and nose, trying to hear or smell something.

"I really wish you had not done that," he said. "That display of power that you released. It might as well have been a flare. We need to get out of this town. We need to find somewhere safe."

"What do you mean a flare?" Alibaster asked.

"There is a certain thing waiting in the dark," the fox said. "All it needs is a light to follow. Let's go. Explanations will have to wait."

"Typical," Olivia muttered.

"Let's go back to the Swan & Swine," Koz suggested.

"A good a place as any, I suppose," the fox conceded. He turned to the angels. "Prepare to open another wyrmhole."

None of the love messengers showed signs of having heard him. They seemed off somehow. Two were holding their heads as if trying to stop their brains from leaking out their ears. One clutched his stomach and was hunched over, as if about to vomit. The fourth one swayed unsteadily, as if drunk.

Koz sighed. "I think they're in withdrawal."

"Is that what you're feeling off them?" Olivia asked.

Koz shook their head. "Call it an educated guess. Probably left all their tasty morsels of souls back at the club."

"Pull yourselves together," the fox commanded. "You were once the warriors of the Breathless Voice, and now you fall to substance abuse."

"We were never warriors," one angel said, slurred. "We were never privy to the Presence, or Her council."

"And it is not our lack of souls that is causing my others and I distress," said another. "Something is wrong. Something is interfering."

"Interfering?" Penelope asked, still getting used to the concept of angels in the first place. "Interfering with what?"

"With us," a third angel said simply, before retching in a rhododendron bush.

Olivia never thought she'd learn if angelic sick looked just like normal human sick. She never thought she'd be in a position to find out. But she was, and she did. And it did. Except maybe with a bit more star dust sprinkled throughout.

"All the more reason for us to leave," the fox said. "Now."

Nobody argued. The fox's fear was enough to silence any more questions or debate for the moment. The angels did their best to steady themselves, and each one found a passenger. The one that had just thrown up chose Alibaster, who clearly did not like the pairing. Considering he had thrown up a short while ago himself, it was sure to be an eventful journey.

"Anyone have any travel size mouthwash?" he asked.

Another angel picked up Koz, and another the fox. A fourth picked up Penelope, who liked the experience about as much as a rabid raccoon would. It was clear from the look on her face that she would much rather have tried crafting her own wings out of pipe cleaners and construction paper and having a go at it herself.

A fifth angel wrapped Olivia in their toned and tattooed arms. A thought tugged at her mind; an itch that she couldn't quite scratch.

"Forming wyrmhole access point now," the angel holding the fox said. The swirl of rainbow light started forming into existence a hundred meters above them all.

They all started to lift off the ground, and that was when Olivia's thought came close enough to scratch. She shifted in her angel's arms, until she turned around and saw its face clearly. Because the thought had been this: *Weren't there only four angels?*

The face that greeted her own was like the other angels in the most basic of ways. But upon studying the eyes- deep black spheres with copper irises- it became clear that the face was too malleable looking. Too rubbery. As if it could stretch and form and droop. In short, it looked like a mask. This became more prominent when the eyes beneath locked with Olivia's own stare, and the face was forced into a hideous, wax-sculpture-in-a-lit-candle-store grin.

Olivia had two consecutive thoughts then, as she realized just what was carrying her.

The first was: *Hoo-boy.*

The second was: *I could probably survive a fall from this height.*

And she wriggled out of the creature's grasp, and plummeted to the ground.

Chapter 17: The Dumbest Plan Olivia has Ever Had (so Far)

Luckily, they hadn't raised that high up; maybe fifteen feet maximum. Also luckily, they had been hovering over a patch of grass instead of over the cobblestones. Unluckily, the patch of grass Olivia landed in was the same one that one of the soul snuffing angels had just spewed in.

Ugh. Still, two out of three ain't bad.

Olivia always tried to look on the bright side of things. Even if rhododendron branches poked at her flesh, and several of the yellow ducks on her jammies were now a different shade of yellow entirely. She had just enough time to be disgusted before the thing which wasn't an angel was swooping back down after her.

"Something's happening!" she heard Koz yell from above. A quick glance told her that the other four and their angels were nearing the wyrmhole. But at Koz's words, they turned their collective gaze back to the ground, and saw Olivia running.

"No," the fox's voice was hardly a whisper. Full of terror and incredulity. "We are not yet ready for this fight."

"Get us back down there!" Penelope's voice demanded.

"We have to help her!" agreed Alibaster.

Back on the ground, Olivia was zigzagging through buildings, throwing small stones at doors and windows, and yelling. She wasn't quite sure what she hoped to accomplish by this, but maybe if enough people came outside to check out what was happening it would be enough to distract the creature following her. Or maybe she could hide in one of the brownstones. She didn't know. She also didn't know if her knocking and yelling would even be heard by the dream-folk. Was she going to have to start punching people again? What she did know was that with the amount of running she did on a daily basis, she should really invest in a treadmill for the ship. If there was one thing she hated about this life she had chosen (other than the fear of imminent death at every turn) it was sheer mountainous amounts of cardio. Some corner of her mind cursed this dimension for not letting this manifestation of her body be in better shape than her physical one.

She hazarded a look back, and saw creature was taking its sweet time. It was hanging back in the air, never getting closer than a dozen yards. This worried Olivia more than anything, because she had seen enough horror movies in her life to know that if the monster wasn't chasing its victim, it was because it didn't need to.

Finally, a door opened, and an old lady- hair full of curlers- poked her head out. Yes! Good. Maybe the Key of Three's light show had been enough to ground Olivia into this village; sync her to its spectrum. Or maybe she just got lucky, and happened to be passing as the old lady was coming out for her after dinner smoke. Either way, gift horses and all that.

Olivia ran up the stone steps to the lady's door, shoved past her with several breathless rapid-fire apologies, and closed and locked the door behind her. Locking an old lady out of her own house while being chased by a monster was not the most heroic thing Olivia had ever done.

"Sorrysorrysorrysorry," she continued even after the door was closed. She hoped the door would hold for at least a moment, but she knew the creature had seen her go in, so there was no point hoping she had lost it entirely. She was sure the thing would leave the old lady alone. Pretty sure.

A plan was starting to take shape in her mind. It was still cooking at the moment, roasting at a simmer. Slow and steady, but it was coming all the same. After quickly opening every drawer, door, and looking out every window, she flew to the stairs. The only thing Olivia hated more than running for her life, was running for her life up steps, but it had to be done. What she needed wasn't on the first floor.

She was starting to sweat, and the sweat was starting to mix with the vomit on her clothes, and it was all a very horrible and grotesque feeling. If her mind wasn't already buzzing with several fears and instincts and complaints, all fighting for Olivia's attention, she might have been disgusted.

Five storys. Five flights of steps. Five! Five Qlarn-damned stupid son of an ill tempered brood queen… And they weren't cute little one-two steps either. This house must have been taller on the inside than the outside, for they were five (five!) fully awful flights of steps. And as Olivia stopped on each floor, hurriedly tearing open anything that could open, she didn't see anyone else hanging out on the floors as she passed.

Why did one little old lady need five floors to herself? There was no way that was a good idea. It was just an injury waiting to happen. Also, where Olivia came from, these kinds of homes were expensive. This lady must be loaded. Maybe she was like, the mayor or something. Or maybe she inherited from an oil baron uncle when the rest of the planet shrunk itself. Or maybe she just made a lot of good investments. Or this community had put aside the use of monetary currency, realizing that the only commodity worth anything was the love they held for each other.

Olivia was distracting herself from the many, many steps (did she mention there were five flights of them?) she was being forced to climb.

But she had to climb all those steps, because none of the first four levels of the home revealed what she needed. Her heart started sinking the higher she climbed, because there was a very real possibility that what she needed could not be found in the first random house she flung herself into. And if it didn't appear by the time she reached the top floor, then all she would have done is succeeded in backing herself into a corner.

She reached the fifth floor, and Olivia felt like she had been running up the down escalator since the early days of the Pleistocene epoch. But she didn't have time for fatigue (what else was new?). She searched the open concept living area frantically. As with each previous floor, she looked out the windows. But just like the others, they led to the street below. More people were milling about outside again, but she didn't stop to look for her friends. All she could do was hope that they had been able to persuade the angels to land, and that they hadn't gone through the wyrmhole without her. Then, even if she miraculously deterred the creature in the angel mask, she would be stuck forever in this town without a home.

Still, there were worst places to be stranded. A nice throw rug right there, a bookshelf on that wall… The whole place would need to be painted. Blood orange walls with oak wood flooring? What was that old lady thinking?

Not the time, Jones, she scolded herself.

There were a few closet spaces and cupboards. She searched through them, but found nothing that one wouldn't expect to find in such places. Except for a black cat that hissed at her upon swinging open a weathered bread box. The box had been locked by ways of a little metal latch at the bottom. She didn't even know bread boxes could lock. And who would lock a cat in a bread box? The cat didn't seem to mind, but still. It was angry at her for having its nap disturbed, and she quickly closed the lid again, but didn't lock it back; adding another "sorry" for good measure.

"Please, please, please," she murmured to herself as she ran out of places to check. She found a large vent grate on the floor, but remembered the fox saying something about vents, and decided to make that a last resort.

She wondered if the creature was even still following her. Back in her grandma's house, the fox had said that whatever it was, it had a short attention span. Maybe it had forgotten about her, and went away.

Yeah right, she scoffed. *I'm lucky, but not* that *lucky.* It was probably just taking its sweet time, because it knew it had her cornered. A cat toying with a mouse. She knew it too, honestly, but she refused to be backed up against a wall. Especially one she had backed herself against.

Looking up, she saw one final possibility. The ceiling was high, and a table had to be moved, which only exhausted her more. But once it was situated where she needed it, she lifted one of the adjoining chairs on top of it, and then climbed on top the table and the chair. Standing on her toes, she was just able to reach the pull cord attached to the panel in the ceiling. Having the cord so far out of reach didn't make any sense, but neither did much else in the Paracosm, so…

With her middle and ring fingers she pulled on the cord, and the hatch to the attic swung open, revealing an attic ladder. (Yet more stairs for her to climb.)

She looked up into the attic, and her fear (at least some of it) dissolved, as her hopes became well warranted. Because the attic was not an attic at all. For not all doors in this strange place led to where they were supposed to.

She poked a finger gently past the threshold, and water rippled as it connected. The attic led to the floor of some body of water. She pushed her whole hand into the water, yet none of it fell onto her. As if some invisible membrane was keeping the liquid from adhering to gravity. Minnows nipped at her fingers. She smiled, but her face faded into seriousness in an instant. She didn't have long.

Climbing back down the ladder, and off the table, she found a closet on the far end of the room to hide in. It had that familiar old lady smell. That of an old wooden chest filled with quilts that hadn't been opened in years. It also had a mop sitting against the wall and a host of cleaning supplies. All of which were coated in a very distinct layer of dust. How ironic.

Olivia wondered if the person who dreamed this village originally had really been so detailed in their unconscious architecture, or if once in the Paracosm, the dreams- now adrift from the dreamers- just started becoming more refined, and filled in their own blanks. The Fathoms might not be the only ones to become free entities, but the worlds they inhabited as well.

She closed the closet door just as she heard the creaking of heavy footfalls come from the staircase. What she was about to attempt was probably the oldest trick in the book, and all she could do was pray that it was a book her pursuer hadn't read.

Doing all she could not to make noise, Olivia crouched down, and put her eye to the closet door's keyhole. It was one of those old fashioned ones that could be seen through. For a moment she wondered if she had just hidden from the old lady, who had found a way back into her house. But in an instant, the thing that was not an angel stepped into view. Its head spun around in an animalistic manner, a hunter trying to regain a scent. Immediately, its false face found the attic ladder. It took a step closer. Then it sniffed the air, and turned towards the pseudo-kitchen area.

Come on, come on, come on… Olivia pleaded, not even daring to breathe.

From her position, she couldn't quite see what it was doing, but she heard something snap open, and then a violent hiss. The cat in the box. Olivia was wondering if it was going to do something to the cat, but she heard the box shut once more, and the thing stepped back into view. The cat was nowhere to be seen. As Olivia hoped that it didn't kill the kitty, it made its way back towards the hatch.

It studied the water flowing in the square in the ceiling, before floating up to it as easily as a balloon. It stuck its head into the "attic", then its shoulders. The tips of the wings joined it, then the chest, and more and more, until soon enough none of the creature could be seen any more.

Olivia didn't have time to waste. She flung open the door to her hiding spot and raced back across the room. In one nearly graceful hop, she was back on the table, and looked up into the impossible lake. There it was. Hovering about a foot above the bottom of the waterbed, shimmering and distorting in view, still searching for its prey.

Olivia got to work folding the ladder back onto itself, before pushing it back into the ceiling. Before the hatch closed entirely, she saw the creature look down, obviously seeing what she was doing. It was difficult to tell by the water, but the creature didn't look angered, it just stared at her in what might have been mild curiosity as the door swung closed.

She breathed a sigh of relief. She didn't know how she knew, but she had a feeling that once closed, the door that had lead to that body of water would be closed of entirely to that side. The doors that led other places were one way trips only. It couldn't come back after her that way.

Unless she was wrong, of course. In which case the thing would simply open the hatch back up, leaving the whole ordeal of stairs and vomit covered pjs all very pointless.

She didn't wait around to find out.

But she did take a quick peak in the bread box to make sure the cat was ok. Satisfied that it was, when its claws tried to slice at her in a small arc, she headed back to the ground level.

Chapter 18: The United Notions

Nearly the entire population of the town was back outside. Penelope's decree hadn't taken. Nobody seemed to know why they were outside though, and everyone was just milling around aimlessly. The old lady was not on her front step where Olivia had left her, and she hoped it was because she had decided to join the gathering crowd, and not because the creature had done something horrific to her.

Looking down into the masses, Olivia found her friends. She whistled and waved, and they all made their way to her. Minus the angels.

"They dropped us off and took off into the wyrmhole," Koz said after Olivia had explained what she had done. "They said the fox broke his promise."

"I did not summon that thing," the fox said. "You three did."

"Yeah, well we needed to wake Penelope up," Olivia said. "And since you haven't told us anything useful, we don't have a nice handy dos-and-don'ts list, telling us helpful things, like how to not summon monsters that wear fake faces."

There was a pause. "You are right," the fox conceded. "You- all of you- deserve to know why I brought you here, and what we are fighting."

One of the dream-folk down on the street pointed up at them. "Look! It is our once stoned goddess!"

Penelope winced. "Terrible title." As the others started to redirect their attention, Penelope gave Olivia a look. "Way to go. With all your yelling and rock throwing, you brought them all back out. A god needs her privacy, you know."

Olivia didn't dispute her, but she had a feeling that the people outside were not entirely her doing. "Let's go inside," she said. "Hopefully an 'out of sight out of mind' approach works on these people." She opened the door to the house back up, and invited everyone in as if it were her own home.

"We should not linger," the fox said. "The beast could find its way back here."

"Our way off this rock just left without us," Alibaster said with his hands behind his head. "We can do a quick Q and A before figuring out what to do next."

Olivia went to the nearest sink, and did her best to clean her shirt. Then they went into the living room, and all fell into various chairs or couches.

"The floor's all yours," Olivia said to the fox.

He was quiet for a time, pacing the length of the floor as he collected his thoughts. If he had had hands to wring, he would have. His white eyes found their way to his audience. "Let me begin with a story..."

In the beginning there was Nothing. And that was good.

Actually, this was false. There was darkness. This darkness was everything. But since there was not yet light to differentiate darkness from something else, the fact that it was everything also meant that it was nothing. One absolute is in turn also its opposite. This was just one of many true contradictions which hold things together.

So in the beginning, there was Nothing.

But not really.

And from this Nothing, there was potential. And from that potential, universes were spawned, expanding outwards from the darkness that would serve as the heart and template for all realities. Something was always created from Nothing.

Then, in one such something... Ka-blam! The main Event. This was how the worlds began, not with a whimper, but a bang. The universe before died out, the wheel of creation kept turning, and a new existence was forged atop the dying embers of the last. Existence was breathed anew.

Laws had to be made so this new existence could make sense, so that it could be perceived and understood. Some of these laws took the form of dimensions; ways to measure or quantify the aspects of all that now was. As this bubble of creation started expanding, the concept of space was implemented. Space was made up of three of these new laws, or dimensions. The first dimension was the still point, something that was rare in this maelstrom of new birth, but existed nonetheless. The second dimensions were the lines- the contacts- which connected these still points; reaching out, touching and linking to one another. The third and last of the spacial dimensions elaborated upon the first two; forming things from conceptual into tangible.

As the universe expanded and heated, celestial bodies were forged by a law that would come to be known as gravity, and started an endless dance around one another. Thus the concept of Time was added to the mix. The fourth dimension. A way to measure and mark how things came to pass. And as this new thing called Time went boldly forward in all directions, meaning was injected into the expanse. This meaning would come to be known as life.

During this age of new laws, guardians imbued with the heat and energy of this new life rose up to quash the would-be conquerors of the old existence. A battle that- if lost- would have cost the guardians all the potential yet to be seen by the new and mewling universe. After the endless bloodshed of the first war, the guardians had little time for reprieve. For one of their own then tried to take the reins of everything for themself; using their aptitude towards the fourth dimension to harness the direction in which the universe would find itself. For their transgressions, their siblings trapped them within the very Nothing which started it all; isolating the ally-turned-enemy within the only place where their affinity for Time could not be misused. The guardians settled on a world of their own, and watched from their perch as life took a foothold on so many new worlds.

Single cells split, forming simple complex creatures of instinct. (Another one of those true contradictions.) Creatures which knew no more than what existed right in front of them. A time of truths, and truths only.

Over several supereons, the simplicities evolved, and the complexities grew, forming many beings of higher intelligence. Creatures with critical thinking skills and new yearnings to understand the things around them. With these new thoughts and desires, came unprecedented things.

The truth of one's senses was not the only thing now, giving away to something opposite.

Lies. Non-truths told or accepted for personal gain or amusement.

Lies took many forms. The most interesting, the most influential, and the most important of which became known as stories. Educational or enjoyable tales told for a variety of reasons. And with stories, many new things were birthed.

Imagination at what could lie beyond the immediate senses.

Faith and Belief in things that couldn't be quantified or qualified.

Symbolism; comparing and connecting one thing to another by the thread of fantasy.

And these in turn created even more aspects of sentience, like roots of a tree forever branching off and out.

Confusion.

Division.

Disdain.

Discord.

Motivation.

Drive.

Longing.

Hope.

Love.

So many new things for life to add to its arsenal. These things were not good or bad in themselves, only in the sense and purpose of any given creature who wielded them. It was a wonderful time, these early days of story. These beautiful or horrible lies had so much power then. They could reshape reality itself. Creating more new things, which were never meant to have physical form. Legends were forged, myths were fact, wars were waged. Wars over stories. It became too much. These things could not be contained within the constraints of this infinite yet limited universe.

So a new law was quickly built into the framework of everything, as an addendum.

A fifth dimension.

One where the excess power of these stories- for words had more power than any other force in creation- could be contained; could pool together in a place that was not held back by the four previous dimensions. A place where these stories could exist unconstrained; without harming- or being harmed by- the outside universe. (Though their influence and memory still could.) A place that could not be visited in the physical, but could exist only on an ascendant plane.

One that could only be properly accessed when the floodgates of the mind were open; when the chance of inspiration and all other emotions were heightened. To enter this realm, one had to be asleep.

It gained many names over the years, but the most prevailing was the Paracosm.

The Paracosm was not a dream, though dreams were the quickest route to it. And dreams could easily drift into its borders. New islands wading in seas of truthful lies. Not everyone could visit the Paracosm. An invitation was needed, preferably by a Native; one of the story creatures who were written into the fifth dimension when it was created. Upon waking or returning, the visitors rarely ever remembered they had been there at all. Forgotten as quickly as the dreams used to enter and exit.

Along with the Natives and visitors (sometimes referred to as Literals), there were the Dream-folk, or Fathoms. Beings from dreams who drifted into the Paracosm, and became more self aware and cognizant the longer they were apart from the mind that dreamed them.

Life was approached differently there, and so was death. Natives lived for as long as their stories were told and remembered. Once the last person who knew their tale died, the old story fell away. Yet if their story was ever recovered or retold, they were reborn and granted a new term of existence. After all, it was very difficult to kill an idea altogether. The Fathoms- the background characters, created without intent- stayed alive as long as they stayed within the confines of their dreams or stories. To venture beyond was to be erased.

As for the visitors… One may think that because the body is not physically present, there was no danger to be found. This was false. There was an old adage that if someone died in their dream, they died in real life. This was also false. (For how would anyone know?) But for all their similarities and connections, the Paracosm was different than dreams, so any danger found within it would prove very real to any visitor's mortal well being. The question had often arisen if visitors could find their way to the Paracosm's shore after they died. And while the idea was not unheard of, the occurrence was extremely rare. And in any case, any version of a visitor found within the walls of the Paracosm after death, could not truly be said to be that person. The same way the android duplicates on the dead world Pryvid could not be said to be the originals of the departed they resembled.

Time passed. Or the closest approximation that could be identified in that plane. And as is the way with all good things, eventually a shadow must fall over it. This particular shadow was forged by nightmares; an amalgamation of every negative impulse from every dream that had found its way to the Paracosm. Each time a scenario entered the realm which invoked fear or hatred or pain, a new drop of malevolence was collected, and the creature would draw strength, willing itself into existence. A gestalt entity of numerous forms, but one controlling mind. No one knew what it truly looked like, for its true form was always concealed behind false faces or the faces of others. Hidden by lies. Its purpose was never clear, though its actions spoke for themselves. Wherever any aspect of the monster tread, the place and its inhabitants were corrupted; infected with the nightmare's influence. This would add to the total number of appendages the creature had to reach with, and soon enough the whole dimension would be poisoned and turn into a sick parody of what it was meant to be.

This in turn would bleed into the first four dimensions. There would be no more dreams, only nightmares. And all the dreamers in the universe would soon be nothing but frightened husks, too empty to hope or strive or create. Filled instead with whatever fears of hatreds the nightmare fueled them with. And life- the universe's great meaning- would then become meaningless.

That could not be allowed to happen. So as the universe's guardians had once joined forces to battle back monsters, so did the Natives of the Paracosm rise up to take on this ultimate foe. A trillion stories from a billion worlds united against one enemy. Heroes, villains, gods, myths, and fables all came together. It took everything they had and more to fight the creature and its army of itself. The battle was so devastating its effects were felt by countless dreamers around creation, for it was a thin membrane which divided dreams from the Paracosm. Many wars on multiple worlds were fought during these times, though it was doubtful anyone could truly say what they were fighting for. The most destructive of these wars were those of Tycophant and the Sin Cells. But that was another story altogether.

In the end, the beast was corralled and beaten; the creature condensed back into a single form, and the Natives' power all but depleted by the effort. But the creature couldn't be killed entirely, no more than bad thoughts could be. So it had to be imprisoned. But where? They could not keep it anywhere within the fifth dimension, where it could still access nightmares and gain its strength back to escape.

There was only one option.

It had to be imprisoned somewhere wholly alien to it. Somewhere its influence would be dampened, and its perception muddled. It had to be kept in plain sight, in the physical universe. But how to take it there? No Native or Fathom could leave the Paracosm. It had to be a visitor; someone with a foot in each lane of reality. The visitor was picked; a young man from a planet of no consequence with a particular penchant for navigating the Paracosm. Each night when he was asleep, he would be given instructions, and each morning when he woke he would set to fulfilling those instructions, with only a foggy remembrance of why he was doing so.

He had a simple life, a farmer and his newly pregnant wife. He was kind and responsible and down to earth, which was why his wife started getting worried as he became increasingly irresponsible in regards to his duties. When he was supposed to be seeding the land, he was instead scavenging the town junk heap for metal. When he was meant to be feeding the animals he was at the smithery, melting down and recasting the metal into new shapes. When it was time for supper, he was outside, fitting all the new pieces together, and installing compatible software. He was even writing his own codes now. To make the integration process smoother, he said. His wife never knew he had such an ability.

Whenever she asked what he was building, what he was spending so much time on, her husband became glassy eyes and distant, mumbling something incoherent, as if talking in his sleep. Then he would turn back around and go right back to work.

After a few months, the work was done. Something told the farmer that the time was now. While his wife was asleep, he snuck out behind the barn, and pulled aside the tarpaulin that had been hiding his creation. It was not large. It could fit no more than one person within it, but one person was all that was needed. He dragged it to the open field, and crawled inside. The hatch closed as he lied down, leaving only an airtight window in front of his face. Screens lit up on the window, and he initiated the proper launch sequences.

He read the diagnostics once more, and saw that there was only enough air for one journey. He would be in stasis for the trip though, so he wouldn't need as much. But deep down he knew that it didn't matter. He wouldn't be coming back.

The small shuttle rose. The anesthetic gas was released. The man slept. The craft flew.

The next day the wife would find her husband and his machine gone, and the only clue to where he had gone and what he had done would be the blueprints he had drawn for his creation, left on his workbench in the barn. The wife would think that the machine looked like a coffin. A coffin that could fly. She believed that he had taken his life- and his death- into his own hands. He had been sick for months. A mutated type of cancer had been eating away at his heart. None of the doctors they had been to could gain any information about the tumor, only able to speculate on how little time he had left.

So he must have chosen how much time he had. He must have built that machine as some sort of message. The coffin represented the death, of course. But the augmentation- making it able to fly like that- must have represented hope. That perhaps death wasn't the end after all. That there was more to the story beyond what they could see.

The wife would later tell the story to her daughter, and the others of the town. The tale would spread all over the world, and using those original designs, would eventually become a part of the planet's heritage. The dead would no longer be put in the ground, but shot into the sky.

It was so typical, wasn't it? So wonderful. Taking something without context and forging it into a grand story to be shared, until it became part of the very culture itself.

Because that was not what the farmer had intended when he built his coffin shaped ship. It was to be his final resting place, but not in the conventional sense. He had built it as a container. As a prison.

To hold him, as the Natives of the Paracosm pushed the beast they had been battling into his mind, allowing it to get as close as it was allowed into the literal universe. It nagged at him, pushing and screaming in the back of his mind like a slew of intrusive thoughts. The beast was weak though, and the farmer was strong willed, and he pushed through the noise to do what needed to be done.

The small ship was flown into an error in reality. A stillborn nebula, which sanctioned no light or life. Space there was not open, it was thick and slurry; condensed and dead. It was thousands of light years across on all sides (if light could navigate through it), and completely impassible to any and all that tried to venture through. Once entered, nothing could exit. Not the fastest or most powerful vessels. Not hope or thought. As with black holes, entering this place was a one way trip. But the farmer did not plan to ever exit.

And trapped he did become.

Once the coffin reached the dark heart of the stain, it came to a halt with a grateful wheeze. Even though it was impossible to navigate through, the farmer somehow instinctively knew when he had reached the end of his journey.

It had to be this way. It had to be there. There was nowhere else in the physical universe which was so cut off, and out of reach from any life. There, within the stain, the creature would have no influence. It couldn't interact with literal life the way that stories did before the Paracosm's inception.

Without air, the farmer soon died. It was a peaceful death. He just fell asleep and didn't wake.

The creature, however, was still trapped in the mind of the corpse. Trapped forever. The dead don't dream, so there was no way for it to find its way back to the dimension that spawned it.

In the mind of a corpse in a coffin at the center of a never born nebula. Trapped in a box in a box in a box.

In the Paracosm, the Natives and Fathoms spread the tale to the visitors: Do not try and traverse that abysmal place. There was nothing to be found there but death and nightmares.

And upon waking, the dreamers did remember the warning, though they knew not where it came from. Those warned passed it along to those that did not visit the higher realms when they slept, and in no time at all, the stain- this newly named "Abysmal"- was quarantined from the rest of the universe. The legends formed over the ages, and the superstition of the Abysmal- a place where nightmares collected- kept any curious travelers away... for the most part.

All was well. The evil was defeated and imprisoned. Creation spun on.

Until recently, when another evil from another creation found her way to this universe. Her intent was to destroy this reality just as she had done with a number of others, and fashion what remained into something else.

This, obviously, frightened the guardians of this universe. For she had already killed many of their counterparts, and they themselves had not seen battle for many millions of years. They were no longer the warriors forged by the power of the beginning. They had regressed, and become little more than cowardly bureaucrats. So they did what any powerful cowards would do.

They hid.

They took their planet, and moved it across the void, to the one place where it would not be found. Letting those who they claimed to protect suffer while they held on to their illusion of safety.

The guardians knew nothing of the fifth dimension. They had no idea the Paracosm existed. How could they? They were the first Literals that came to be in this universe. They may have powers of abstract and consequence- of fate- but they never held the power of stories. They had never dreamed. So when they picked up their planet and dropped it smack down in the center of the Abysmal, how were they to know? How were they to know what was there? What had been there for many, many centuries. Waiting.

The coffin was dislodged from its eternal resting place. It fell into a loose orbit around the displaced planet. As much as the sludgy space of the Abysmal would allow for such a thing. When the planet was put back in its proper place, the coffin went along for the ride.

The hibernating beast woke, tasting the strangeness of the literal universe for the first time in oh so long. So improbable was this occurrence, that the sheer irony of the events being caused accidentally by those who called themselves "Fate Makers" was insurmountably staggering.

But it happened, nonetheless. The evil was free.

Soon enough, one of the many ships that were shrouding the planet for protection noticed the strange, ancient casket drifting along. They brought it aboard, filled with the possibility of monetary gain. Instead they found only the frozen remains of the farmer, never able to guess what was living just beneath the surface.

The crew of the ship was trying to decide what to do with the coffin they had brought aboard. One of the pilots remembered a tale she had been told. One of a planet of people that shot their dead into space, towards their sun, and maybe this was from that world, and had somehow found its way woefully off course.

The captain asked where she had heard this tale, and the pilot said that one of the engineers had told her. That his home planet was the one that did this. The engineer was called up to the airlock in which the casket had been brought. The captain asked if it looked familiar to him. The engineer said that the design was older than any he had ever seen, but it was without a doubt from his world. He theorized that it must have been one of the earliest coffin rockets, before they had gotten the automatic navigation down to a science. It must have missed its mark when shooting towards their sun, Yon, and had just been floating out in space for hundreds- maybe thousands- of years. They needed to put this man- whoever he was- to rest. Properly.

The captain agreed, realizing that there was no pecuniary reward to be had, and ordered the coffin to be released back into space, on a trajectory course to the nearest sun. And so it was. The unknown man who sacrificed himself to save the dreams and stories of the universe was finally at rest.

But not before his prisoner escaped.

For the first time in eons, the beast flexed its muscles, using what little strength it had to reach the mind of the engineer; infecting it, as the man looked down at the corpse, whispering an ancient prayer often spoken on behalf of the deceased as part of their final goodbye.

And as the coffin was shot back into the void, the poor engineer felt a small tickle at the back of his mind. But he ignored it, chalking it up to the emotions raised by this strange, impossible, situation.

It had been so long since the creature had touched a living mind. They were so… much. Even from a rather left-brained child such as this. There was so much going on, that after so long being isolated and alone, the beast was almost worried it would drown in the man's fears and anxieties and aspirations and all the rest.

No. It would not be drowned. Not now, not after all it had endured. It would simply drink the ocean. And so it did. Gaining strength with every passing breath. The engineer did not notice his soul being devoured. And the more it consumed and corrupted, the more its hunger grew. It wanted to take everyone on this ship, and the ships beyond, and the planet below. It wanted to surge through every Literal mind across the cosmos. But it couldn't. Not yet. Its will was not strong enough. So for the moment, it would have to be content with the engineer.

The engineer- oblivious to all that was happening inside his head- simply went back to work. And when his shift was over, he went back to his cabin to sleep. It was the most beautiful thing the beast had seen in a long, long time. All those thoughts and worries given free range, not held back by the waking hindrances of logic and structured thought. It took everything the beast had not to feed on it all right there and then; not to turn everything in the man's mind blank and black and hellish, leaving only the husk of the engineer in its wake.

It had self control, though. It still needed its host for the time being. For he was not one of the invited. He could not reach the Paracosm. Which meant that the beast was still stuck half in and half out of the Literal plane. So it needed to find someone who could take it home. But that wasn't all. There was also the certain matter of the being who had kept it prisoner within his dead mind for all that time. Such injustices could not go unpunished. The farmer was gone though, so the beast would have to claim its vengeance in the form of the planet from which its captor had hailed. The same world which the engineer it was now slithering its way through was from.

So while the engineer slept, the beast took control. Directing him in his sleep. Nudging him with thoughts and directions the same way the Natives of the Paracosm had directed the farmer to his doom. The man was directed to one of the long range escape pods. He overrode the security codes (he had installed half of the systems himself, after all). He initiated the unlatching sequence, separating the pod from the main ship. And before anyone even knew he was gone, he was on his way back home.

Back to Illetica.

Chapter 19: Olivia's Dumbest Idea Since the Last One

The white eyes of the fox burrowed into each of them as he finished his tale. Somehow, they had been able to see everything he had been describing in real time, like a narrated movie. Now though, the walls of the house came back into view. The group of four looked at each other.

"Hmm," pondered Alibaster.

"So..." said Penelope.

"Huh," added Koz.

It had been some tale. There was a lot to unpack, and everyone was just trying to wrap their heads around the scope of it all. There were questions. Of course there were. But where to start? It was like staring at a sandwich too large to hold or fit the mouth around. They were trying to figure out the way to best approach the goliath plate of knowledge they had just been served.

Olivia was glad to have some pieces to fit together, though. "I guess that's how- and why- you directed us to Illetica initially."

The fox nodded. "It swept through numerous minds on the planet, one by one, until it found someone that could piggyback it into the Paracosm. From here it was able to extend its reach further, and could reach the dreams of anyone in close proximity to Illetica. In time, its influence will grow stronger."

Eyes shifted to Koz. "What?" they asked defensively. "I can't be the only one on Illetica that's been invited here. Don't blame me."

"No one's blaming you," Olivia said. "Or accusing you. It really doesn't matter how the thing got back here." She sat back in her chair and crossed her arms. "Ok, no. Sorry. This thing needs a name. We can't just call it 'the beast' or whatever."

Penelope chuckled. "If we're ranking our list of priorities, naming the ancient tulpa of nightmares and bad thoughts is probably only about fifth on that list."

"I'm guessing you already have ideas?" Alibaster said.

Olivia leaned forward, and conjured a spooky-story-around-the-campfire voice. "I'm thinking 'The Dream Reaver'."

"Clever," Penelope said with a sigh.

"I can't believe the Fates were the ones that caused this," Alibaster said. "Actually, yes I can."

"At least it's not completely our fault this time," Olivia said. Sure, the Fates had moved Kertsraw into the Abysmal to get away from her double, but that had been their choice. Their fear.

"So what's this thing- this 'Reaver'- been doing?" Alibaster asked.

"Since reaching Illetica it hasn't made any overly aggressive moves," the fox said. "It has stayed hidden for the most part, only reaching out to grab the occasional mind before letting it go, like a fisherman releasing his catch. For now it seems content to just toy with minds, and possibly explore and chart all the aspects of the Paracosm that hadn't been here when it was imprisoned. It is testing the waters, but there is no doubt that it will eventually mount a full scale attack."

"You beat it once," Koz said.

"Not me," said the fox. "But yes. It was beaten back before. Just barely. A lot of the stories and dreams that fought it the first time around no longer exist; forgotten and lost to time. Or they have been reformed- retold- many times over, and have forgotten who they had been or what they originally stood for. In any event, maybe enough forces could be rallied once more, and maybe it could be enough to push it back into its box. But I am hoping that things won't escalate that far. Another battle like that would leave both the Paracosm and the literal plane scarred and broken just as before. It would take too long for them to heal. I would prefer if this was handled with the least amount of bloodshed and damage done."

"Which is why you enlisted us," Alibaster said. "I'm wondering something though. Once this thing was imprisoned, why wasn't another one created? You said it came to life as a conglomeration of nightmares. Well, it's not as if people stopped having bad dreams the second this thing was gone. Why didn't another one come along?"

"It was formed in the earlier days of the Paracosm," the fox said. "Back when the realm was new, and not fully formed. There was not yet structure. Leaving an opportunity for something like this to force itself into existence. Since then, many safeguards have been put into effect. The creature is the only one of its kind that can ever be."

"Well that's something at least," Penelope said. "Even if it can make an army of itself, hey, at least it's still an army of one." Nobody could tell if she was being sarcastic or not. Penelope was really good at that. Occasionally, she would scratch herself in random places, as if riddled with chickenpox. The timelessness of this dimension was really getting to her.

"This has all been very informative," Olivia said. "And while I really don't care for my body being hijacked while I'm asleep to take us places we didn't agree to go… Well, we're here now. So I guess we'll help if we can." She looked to her friends for confirmation. Penelope shrugged in an "I don't want to, but I will" sort of way.

Alibaster nodded.

Koz looked down at the floor. Olivia felt bad. Koz hadn't signed up for all of this. Well, none of them had. But at least Olivia, Alibaster, and Penelope were somewhat used to this sort of thing. Koz's night (or its closest approximation) had started with them waiting for their date at a club. They had just wanted to help Olivia, who had been completely ignorant of the Paracosm until now. Now they were kind of stuck in this mess.

Olivia reached over and put her hand on Koz's. "Sorry you got dragged into this."

Koz shook their head. "It isn't that. It just started feeling very weird all the sudden."

"It?" Penelope asked.

"I can't really explain. Something at the back of my mind… Like a calm that wasn't there a moment ago."

"Calm is nice," Alibaster said. "I'm all for calm. Got any more? I'd love some myself."

Koz almost chuckled. "You know what calms are usually proceeded by, don't you?"

Penelope was looking out the nearest window. "Guys? My disciples are acting weird."

"Weird how?" Alibaster asked, getting up to look for himself.

"Weird like, 'controlling AI just shut off every robot, and is rebooting them all for the uprising'."

"That's very specific," Koz said.

"It happens quite often," Alibaster said, half distracted by whatever he saw outside. "We've stopped several of such uprisings. Helped win a few too. It's all a matter of perspective."

Olivia, Koz, and the fox were all at the windows now too. The fox's eyes were just barely high enough to reach over the sill to see out. And Penelope had been right. Dozens- hundreds- of people were now lining the street. Perhaps the whole town. All of them were standing stock still, facing the house their goddess was in. None of them spoke. None of them seemed to breathe. Olivia wondered if Fathoms needed to breathe. They were like robots awaiting new commands. Soldiers awaiting orders.

The fox started whimpering.

"Oh," Koz said. "I get it." Nobody asked what they understood, but they explained anyway. "My abilities. It's like… it's like listening to a radio. A radio of emotion. Always. But most of time everything gets drowned out. Like the radio's turned down almost all the way and placed in another room. Background noise. Which is fine, especially when I'm around a lot of people. I'd go crazy if I was always absorbing the emotions of everyone I happened to pass or be near. I can even get readings off Fathoms if they have enough autonomy. But all the sudden, it's like the radio just got switched off. Except for you guys. I didn't notice what the feeling was. This has never happened before."

"You don't notice your nose until it's cut off," Alibaster said.

"It's found its way back," the fox said. "The false flesh you tricked must have just been a scout. The very basic of the beast's selves. There aren't many of them. They're difficult to make. Follows simple orders only. No higher thought function."

"You're making my victory seem very hollow," Olivia muttered.

"Its consciousness is snaking its way through the villagers. When it's captured them all entirely, it'll have a host of six hundred to fall upon us. We need to leave this dream."

"It may have escaped your attention-" Alibaster said with his forehead to the glass- "but our escape angels left us. Can you open up one of those wyrmholes yourself?"

"No," the fox admitted.

"The attic?" Olivia suggested. The scout creature had to be gone from that river or whatever by now.

"That would be the first place it'd expect us to go," the fox was pacing. "It could have another army waiting for us on the other side of that portal."

"We need to find another portal then," Alibaster said.

"There aren't any more in the house," Olivia said. "I checked everywhere."

"And it's not like the neighbors are going to let us out to check around," Penelope said.

"Options?" Alibaster asked.

"We could stay and fight it," Koz suggested. Everyone looked at them with different faces of incredulity. "What? That was why you three were brought here anyway, right? How are you planning to beat it if you just keep running from it?"

"That's a fair point," Alibaster said. "But we usually like to come up with a plan before it all turns to shype and gets us killed."

Olivia snapped her fingers, suddenly remembering. "There's a vent. A big one. On the top floor." She looked at the fox. "You said vents lead 'behind'. Whatever that means, would it give us some breathing space?"

The fox looked unsure. "It may."

"Come on," Olivia said, and they all made their way to the stairs.

"Behind?" Penelope asked. "Behind what? What does that mean?"

"And what's to stop the beast- the Reaver- from just following us through?" Alibaster asked.

The fox looked as though he were about to answer. But before he could the front door burst in, all but shattering the top hinge, and leaving the whole door askew on its axis. There had been no reason to do that. The door hadn't even been locked. But as far as intimidation games went, it was getting the job done. The group stopped in their tracks, and looked outside at the mob clustered at and near the door. They couldn't be classified as an *angry* mob (which made a nice- if somewhat lateral- change of pace); for their expressions were all vacant. Only the occasional eye twitch or muscle contractions indicated that the people weren't just wax mannequins put on display in a really intrusive manner. At the front of the gathering was the old lady whose house Olivia had… borrowed.

"Oh," Olivia said with a start, as they all looked into a sea of tense placidity; twelve hundred eyes staring in their direction. "Um. Sorry I kicked you out of your house," she went on, specifically to the old lady. She was talking softly, almost whispering. But she couldn't have said why. "Very rude of me. You can have it back now. My friends and I just need to use something upstairs…"

She motioned for her friends to follow, and took a tentative step forward. The stairs were right across from the front door, so they had to go a little further towards the danger before they had a chance of escaping it. The instant her foot left the ground, all the mild and uniform faces turned furious. Hissing ensued. Teeth turned to fangs, and eyes into black orbs with copper pinpricks.

Olivia quickly put her foot back down.

The faces of the dream-folk returned to their calmed state, though their eyes were still black.

"Well, this is going to be an issue," Penelope muttered.

"Why doesn't it- they- attack?" Alibaster asked.

"I think it's pondering what to do," the fox said. "As long as we are trapped, it has no need to harm us. No need to exert energy it may not have."

"Which I guess is why we've been able to talk for so long," Koz said.

"An ancient evil with concerns for privacy," Alibaster said. "How novel."

"So we can just stay here?" Penelope said.

"I'd really rather not give it time to 'ponder'," Olivia said. "It could decide we're just better off dead than trapped."

"Ha," said Penelope. "So our options are stay in the living room indefinitely and wait for the monster to decide to kill us, or try to make it to the top floor of this place, which will make up the monster's mind about killing us, causing several hundred angry vessels to come after us before we can hopefully escape into an air vent." She looked around. "Have I missed anything? Did we leave the stove on or something too?"

There was a sullen pause, before Alibaster spoke up. "Actually, I think you did."

"Did what?"

"Leave the stove on. Or the oven at least. When you made those pizzas. I dread to see the energy bill."

"Take it out of my rent."

"You don't pay rent."

"We don't get an energy bill. It's a spaceship, not a condo."

"Guys!" Olivia interrupted. "As much as I love your super witty banter, there really are better times for that sort of thing."

"We need to do something soon," Koz said, their face twisted in discomfort. "It's hard to translate the feelings I'm getting off of them now. The closest I can relate it to is 'enraged anxiety'."

Olivia looked to the fox. "Before I got here, when I was still dreaming, the Reaver took the form of my grandma's neighbors, and spoke to me. Can it use the people it's taken over here to communicate with us?"

The fox nodded. "It can. It does not tend to though. Speaking through the constructs it is granted in dreams is a different process than speaking through the inhabitants it takes over in the Paracosm. Besides, it has never been one for words."

"A super villain that doesn't give evil monologues about how great he is," Alibaster said. "What a nice change of pace today is."

Olivia had another one of her almost plans. She turned around to her friends and lowered her voice. Hopefully the Reaver was still busy uploading itself into all the Fathoms, and wasn't actively listening to them. "You all get to the top floor- disclaimer there are more stairs than there has any right to be. Find the vent. You'll know it when you see it. It's on the floor, and large enough to get in. I won't tell you not to wait for me, because I know you will. So wait for as long as you can, but if any of the zombiefied villagers come after you, go in."

"What will you be doing?" Penelope asked.

"I'm going to step outside and try to have a chat with the night terror. I need to know what it wants; why it's doing what it's doing. With any luck, I can keep it busy enough for you all to escape. Maybe I can talk it down."

"Since when do the bad guys ever get talked down?" Alibaster asked in a loud whisper.

"I just… I have to try." Olivia ran a hand through her hair. "If there's even a sliver of a chance that things could turn out better than… I have to try." Nobody pressed her further. Penelope and Alibaster understood, as much as they could, but Koz probably thought she was just overly optimistic.

"I'll stay with you," the fox said.

"No. Go with them. You know the most about the Paracosm. They'll need you to navigate this place."

Reluctantly, the fox agreed.

Everyone else took turns volunteering to stay behind with her, but she refused their offers. "Just trust me. Please. I'll be fine. Wait until I close the door."

And that was the end of that discussion. She turned back around; the dead eyed townsfolk still waiting outside with their eternal patience. "I'd like to talk," she said, taking a step closer. The people had a flickering moment of rage, but when they saw she was heading for them and not the stairs it quickly subsided. None of them answered her outright, though. She tried again. "Parley?" She wasn't entirely sure what that meant, but she had seen it in a pirate movie, and liked the sound of it. Still, there was no real response, and she took the omission of negatives as a positive. She reached the front porch/stoop area, and did all she could to casually close the busted door behind her.

The old lady looked like a fresh corpse standing upright. They all did.

The lady's jaw ticked and her tongue clicked, but eventually words formed in a horrible parody of speech, which bubbled up from the throat but couldn't quite make it out of the mouth unscathed. "Therrre isss n-nooo eescape."

Olivia forced a smile. "Lovely. Let's discuss that, shall we?"

Chapter 20: Attempting to Find Sympathy for the Devil

"Do you have a name?" Olivia asked. "Something you prefer to be called?"

The old lady tilted her head in four jerky movements, then the shoulders spasmed in what could- in certain circles- be considered a shrug. "Ieeeee am-am leeegioonn. Iee ammm mee."

That's probably a no, Olivia interpreted. "Well that's ok. Names are overrated. Everyone's got one these days. I'm-"

"Iee-weee- knoww h-whooo youuu arrrrrrre."

"Oh?"

"Weee-meeee-Ieee haaavve seeen y-y-youuu thhhhhroough thheee meeeess ooof maanny llliteerrals."

"Through the yous?" Olivia asked. "What does that mean?"

The look on the lady's face- as well as the faces of many other Fathoms- was that of frustration. Not at her though. More like frustration at themselves for not being able to accurately articulate what it meant to say.

Olivia thought about it. The creature was built from bad dreams, from nightmares. So, when it said that it had seen her through itself in Literals, that must mean that it had seen *her* in the nightmares of others. Why would she be in the nightmares of-?

Oh.

"That wasn't me," she said. "The person you saw in those nightmares, it wasn't me. Her name was Ophelia, and she was a-" she struggled to find the right word- "corrupted version of me from another universe. She killed and hurt many people not that long ago- which is why people are still having nightmares about her." *Including me.* "But I am different from her. Separate."

The host of possessed Fathoms considered this. "Yoouu, aannd not yoou." The old lady pointed an arthritic finger into the crowd. "Meee, aaand not mee."

"It's not really comparable," Olivia crossed her arms. She noticed that its speech was becoming a little less strained. "You're possessing people. People who should be allowed their own thoughts and will. You don't have to take people over. That version of you- the scout- that tried to take me. It had taken the form of a Script Angel, but hadn't taken over one of the Script's bodies."

"Eeasier ttoo taakke than to maake."

The fox had said something like that. "But the angels are all connected to each other, so they would have noticed if you infected one of them," she inferred.

"Noot strooonng eennoough tooo taakke Naattiivves. Yett."

Olivia was getting antsy. She wanted to get to the point. "Why are you doing this? What are you even doing? Making more of yourself? Taking over the Paracosm? To what end?"

"Ieeee waannt. Iee amm meee."

"That's it? You're doing what you were made to do? A pretty simple motive. Some might even say uninspired."

The Reaver took a few seconds before forcing its words through the old lady's lips. One of her curlers fell out. "Myy… straaay… itt believvves Iee amm a sicckneess. Does illnesss haave… motiiive?"

"So you're a disease? Fine. I've heard worse reasons to take over the universe." Olivia stood up straight. "Wait. Your 'stray'? What does that mean? The angels, they called the fox a stray. Is that what you mean? What is he to you?"

"A mis-take."

She shook her head. "I don't understand."

But the creature changed the subject. "You neevver foounnd yoour looost frieend."

Olivia furrowed her brow. "Yeah, we did. Alibaster and Penelope. We found them both."

"Sheee dooees not knoow," it said, almost to itself. "The laasst frriend wass hiddeen. Byy uss-mee. Aaand nooott byy uuss. Weee suppoose that it dooes noot matterr. Yoou haave mooore pressing matters to attteend tooo."

"More pressing? What are you-?"

Olivia stopped. She had planned to keep the creature distracted, but what if the reverse had been true? She bolted back inside, none of the dream-folk taking any moves to stop her, and flew up the steps once more, taking two or three at a time. She called her friends' names as she climbed, but got no response. When she finally reached the top floor, there was no one but the fox. The covering over the vent was still in place. It hadn't been moved. The rest of the floor was completely wrecked, though. Furniture turned over and slashed through, vases and lamps smashed.

"Look out!" the fox yelled before she could take it all in. He jumped on her, knocking her to the ground. If she had had any wind left over from the climb, it would have been knocked out of her. For a split second she thought he was attacking her and she fought against him. Then, something pounced, flying over them and landing a few feet away, and she found the real danger the fox had just saved her from.

A panther. An actual panther. Sleek, black fur, sharp claws tearing up the hardwood floors. Circling them with fluid, confident motions.

Sure, why not?

Chapter 21: Things Just Won't Stop Happening

Olivia froze. "Where the hell did that thing come from?" she asked in a panicked whisper.

"They're gone," the fox said. "They're all gone." Olivia looked at him closely. He was shaking, and covered in small cuts. Bits of fur had been torn, and a deep dark slash covered what was left of his left eye.

"What?" she asked. "What do you mea-"

The panther made a deep growl from its throat, shutting Olivia up. Did this thing kill her friends? If it had, wouldn't their bodies be… about? But there was no sign of them. She hoped that was a good thing.

Then the panther opened its jaw further than a normal- a Literal- panther should have been able to. Like a python's, it unhinged wide enough to fit inside the average Olivia. What happened next was a little harder to explain.

Its mouth, then its head, then its entire body seemed to shift and shimmer into a vortex of light. It did this, while somehow still retaining the basic shape of a large death cat. The vortex spun, and small pieces of debris- broken chair legs, small bits of shattered lamps, and the like- all started being pulled into the vortex.

"Get away from it!" the fox said, running awkwardly over to her (was one of his legs hurt?) and pulling on her pant leg with his teeth, trying to motivate her to move away.

"What is it?" Olivia asked, as they found the door to the closet she had hidden in earlier. She hung on. The fox dug his claws into the floor. The pull was getting increasingly more powerful.

"Anima maelstrom!" the fox said quickly. "Changling creature. Living portals. Very rare. Took the others."

"But not you?"

"Doesn't want me."

"Where did it come from?"

"Kitchen. Apparently there was a cat in a bread box."

"That was this thing?!" Olivia grabbed the fox and pulled them both into the closet, just barely getting the door closed behind them. Through the keyhole, she saw the vortex cease. The colors and swirling closed back into itself until the head was that of a sleek feline once more. It sniffed, and started licking a paw.

"You knew this creature was here?" the fox asked accusingly.

"Oh, sorry for not assuming the napping cat was a shape shifting wormhole!" she whisper-yelled back. "I was being chased by a nightmare dressed as an angel at the time. I didn't have the opportunity to mull it all over." She looked back through the keyhole, and saw the panther's eyes.

Black with copper slits.

She remembered the Reaver's scout, the one who had chased her. Before it had flown into her trap in the attic, it had stopped in the kitchen. It must have infected the cat. She relayed the conclusion to the fox.

"That makes sense," he said. "Anima maelstroms usually keep to themselves. They almost never attack outright. They much prefer to stay hidden, for no one to know what they truly are. But now, it's one on the collective. A pet for the beast."

"And it's taken my friends," Olivia said.

The fox looked a little ashamed. "It happened so quickly. There was no time for anyone to react. When I did, sustaining these injuries in the process, it was too late. They had been swallowed."

She had just gotten Alibaster and Penelope back. And now she had lost them again. Along with Koz. Dammit, she thought she had been clever, but all she had done had just led her into the Reaver's own trap. It had wanted them all to come up there. It had only pretended it hadn't because it knew they would. Reverse psychology 101. She had urged her friends to go on without her, and now they were…

"Where does the portal lead?" she asked.

The fox shook his head. "No one knows but the creature itself."

"Would it have taken them all to the same place?"

"Most probably."

"We need to go after them."

"Which is just what the beast wants us to do."

He was right. She hated it, but he was right. And she was not going to march right into the *actual* jaws of danger without some sort of plan. So they needed time to think.

"Ok, back to the original plan," she said. "Get into the vent. Get away from all aspects of the Reaver, come up with a daring idea to save my friends and all Paracosmers- Paracosmites?- everywhere. I just don't know how we're getting past that death machine. But once I figure that out, we're golden."

"The bread box," the fox said. "All anima maelstroms are formed with cages or means of containment. It can be trapped back in the box."

"I don't think that hundred pound thing is going to fit in that small wooden box anymore."

The fox shook his head. "Literals. Trust me, it will work."

And even though she had many questions for the fox and his connection to the Reaver- questions she *would* get answers to- she did trust him. Maybe she was naive. Maybe he was the Reaver's agent, and all this had been his fault. Maybe his injuries at the hand (or claws) of the panther were just for show. But for the moment, she needed him. If he was some sort of double agent or not, she couldn't do this alone. So she would play along until she knew the truth.

"Fine," she said. "You want to be on bread box duty or distraction duty?"

"Seeing as I do not have thumbs..." The sentence died away.

"Are you sure you can keep out of its reach?" Olivia asked.

"Just be quick."

She nodded. "Ok, on three." Her hand gripped the doorknob. "One… two… three!" She swung the door open, and they both bolted in opposite directions.

Olivia headed to the kitchen area; the fox pounced towards the panther. The creature- the anima maelstrom (or the animaelstrom)- bucked and shook as the fox dug his claws into the flesh of its front shoulder blades. The fox growled with more ferocity than he probably felt. The panther crashed into a wall, pinning the fox.

"In your own time," the fox wheezed to Olivia. It was the first time he had attempted sarcasm. She was slightly amused, but also realized she had been mesmerized by the battle, which was only taking place to give her time.

The kitchen was a mess. Indeterminable food stuff littered the ground and counters; containers busted and crushed edibles scattered. She heard more growling and crashing from behind her as she searched the wreckage. Part of her wondered why the animaelstrom wasn't trying to suck the fox into its portal. Maybe it was difficult to concentrate with claws in its back. Maybe it had only been instructed to take her and her friends, and not the fox. What did that imply about his connection to the Reaver? Were they secret brothers or something? Ones that just chose different career paths?

But it wasn't as if the panther wasn't holding back either. It was still fighting against the fox the best it could. Just without its more frustrating abilities. Though claws, teeth, and a hunter's instinct were all pretty frustrating…

She forced her mind back to the task at hand. She didn't see the box anywhere in the debris. Just torn bags, tossed silverware, and pieces of wood...

Ah.

"The box is busted!" she shouted to the preoccupied fox.

More sounds of furniture rearrangements came from the living room. "Then put it back together!"

"I'm not very good at puzzles," Olivia said, picking up two of the larger pieces. "And I don't know where the wood glue is."

"That is not a-" there was a pause and a pained howl- "that is not a Literal bread box. It has the strength to contain one of the most intrinsically powerful creatures in the Paracosm. Just get the pieces in the same place."

"Ok." She started picking up pieces and putting them on the counter. There was silence from the living room. "Are you still alive?"

"Just catching our breath," the fox said raggedly. "This is a fight that could go on forever. Neither of us can kill the other. But we can each do a lot of damage to the other's form."

That was an interesting bit of information, which Olivia tucked away for later.

That was when the old lady who owned the house, curlers still in and robe still on, walked out of the stairwell and into view.

"What is all that awful commotion?" she asked, speaking like a person and not as though her vocal cords were being plucked like a harp.

"What?" Olivia asked herself, completely taken aback. She took three quick strides out of the kitchen towards the lady. Her eyes were no longer those of the Reaver. Her irises were flecked with gray and hazel.

"Who are you? What are you doing in my house?" she asked Olivia. Before Olivia had a chance to form any sort of acceptable answer, the lady forgot about her and turned to the animals. The fox looked ragged and awful, as if the only thing holding him up at this point were invisible strings, and if they were cut he would surely drop dead. The panther had taken a few good licks itself, but it was still a fleking panther.

"Nestor, just what have you done?" the lady asked the giant cat. She picked up a dented spray bottle from the floor and spritzed the creature with unyielding resolve. "You bad bad cat, you. Bringing home strays, destroying all my things." She scolded the apex predator, even throwing in a "tsk tsk" for good measure.

The hundred pound death beast sat there and took the unrelenting spritzing, looking to the floor and whining ashamedly.

Olivia and the fox took this unorthodox- but not unwelcome- reprieve, to shuffle back into the kitchen. "Want to explain that?" Olivia asked as they continued shifting through debris to find even the tiniest splinters of the bread box.

"The beast must have let the dream-folk go," the fox said, sweeping the mess away with his tail. "They had done their task. Distracted you, and forced us up here. It needs to conserve its energy, and besides, even if controlled, Fathoms still can't leave their realms without being erased."

"That's all very interesting, but I was kind of talking about that lady not noticing her cat's growth spurt."

"Fathoms are odd before they're fully autonomous. They can easily change their limited perspectives to fit into a shifting reality. Like how the ones in this village don't easily notice people who 'shouldn't' be here. She probably just sees her cat as she always does, chasing a squirrel or something through the house. She seems to have forgotten about us already, at any rate. Let's hurry up."

"Do we even still need to fix the box?" Olivia asked. "The maelstrom seems pretty pacified."

"For now. It's more difficult for the beast to control animals. Their instinctual nature and straightforward minds leave any task of manipulation challenging. The anima maelstrom was shocked by the arrival of its 'owner', reverting back into the character of the narrative it crafted for itself. It is obviously not a house pet, but such creatures forge cover stories for themselves to hide in."

"They're like full method actors."

"Indeed. It may be calm now, but it might be a temporary measure. It's better we solve this problem, so we have one less thing to worry about."

"It ate all my friends!"

"Yes. As I said..."

Eventually they found all the pieces to the box. Well, the big pieces at least. There were still several slivers missing after the pieces fell back together like a self-solving puzzle, or rewound footage of a box collapsing. Olivia found a box of toothpicks though, and several were used as substitutes for the smaller gaps.

"It will have to do," the fox said.

The pair left the kitchen- the box under Olivia's arm- and crept over to the vent in the floor. They needed to get it open beforehand so they weren't negotiating that and a domesticated jungle cat at the same time. And as the fox had previously articulated, he didn't have any hands, so he would be useless in opening the vent if it came to that.

Olivia went to the old lady (who probably had a name, but at this point she would always be "the old lady" to Olivia) as the fox (same thing) crept behind the panther, to try and herd it the right way if it attempted to scarper or attack. The fox looked barely able to stand; a corpse that just hadn't realized it was dead. Olivia had been chased by zombies that looked more alive than the poor creature at this point, but he was still willing to do battle once more if it came to that. Olivia admired the determination, but her mind still itched to find out just exactly what he was in relation to the Reaver.

She pushed it back, and swiped the spray bottle out of the old lady's hand. She had been spritzing the creature for an absurdly long time. Most people just did it once or twice before letting the recalcitrant animals think on what they had done. The panther was soaking; water dripping from its fur and whiskers as if standing in a storm. The lady didn't notice the bottle was now out of her hand, and she continued curling her finger as if it was. She seemed to have fallen into a sort of loop. It was like she was a broken record playing the same three lines. Or a glitching videogame character, walking into a wall over and over. Man, Fathoms were weird.

Olivia awkwardly shook her with the hand holding the bottle. The glaze came out of her eyes and she blinked. "Who are you?" the old lady asked dreamily.

Olivia opened the lid of the breadbox, and shoved it into her hands. "No time. Hold this please."

"Oh," the lady looked down, seeing the box. "Ok."

The panther was starting to stretch and shake the water off. Any second now it would remember what it truly was, and the orders programmed into it by the Reaver would take hold once more. Olivia was not about to allow that to happen. She held out the squirt bottle, and not for the first time in her life, realized just how ridiculous the action she was about to attempt was.

She pressed down, and a fine layer of mist flew out of the nozzle, and surrounded the big cat's big head. "Bad," she said, more meekly than she intended to. *No, you have to mean it.* She cleared her throat, and summoned a sterner voice that held more authority than she had any right to feel while scolding a deadly predator that was also a living vortex.

"Bad cat," she said with another spritz. "Bad- uh…" She looked to the old lady, who seemed to be teetering between the wakefulness of true autonomy and the dream state of her programmed routine.

"Bealzigar," she said as if hypnotized.

Olivia gave an aggravated sigh. "No, not your name- wait. Really? That's your name?" She had expected Gertrude or Beatrice; a normal old lady name. Certainly not Bealzigar. It sounded like the lead character in a comic book about the teenaged heir to the underworld. Penelope would read a story like that. Anyway. "The cat's name," Olivia urged to the old lady (who was previously stated to be the "old lady" to Olivia forever, despite her totally awesome name).

"Nestor," said the lady.

She turned back to the cat. "Bad Nestor!" Spritz. "You naughty cat, boy, baby, cat…" She was losing the thread of this. She had never had to scold an animal before. And even given the life-or-deathness of it all, it still felt rather silly. She needed to move it along. "Back into the box with you. In you go." *Please turn back to regular cat size. Please turn back to regular cat size.*

The last thing she needed was for this to turn even more absurd by having a six foot long beast try and hop into a breadbox. It would just injure the lady, and break the box again.

For half an instant the eyes of the cat flickered back into those of the Reaver, and the creature snarled and bared as many of its deadly teeth as it could. But before Olivia could determine a sane course of action to take to deal with these events, she squirted the bottle once more. Nestor recoiled and its own natural feline eyes took hold once more. A look of anguish seemed to pass over its face.

The fox had been right. It was more difficult for the Reaver to inhabit animals, and the panther was fighting back. It shook its head vigorously towards the floor, and pawed at its head as if trying to get water out of its ear (which it probably was). It took a protective stance, and it was obviously about to bolt. It was going to try and run away from whatever was inside it, before it took hold again.

It was a big old metaphor that was getting a little too literal for Olivia's liking. She knelt down slowly, and put the squirt bottle down. She got to eye level with the beast, and could feel its hot breath on her face. It smelled like ozone, wet cat food, and the orchestrated chaos of being able to fold two or more points of space to touch each other (which smelled a lot like old eggs left in the sun).

"It's ok," Olivia said, not feeling ok. "It's ok. You're fighting it. That's good. You don't have to do anything you don't want to. So when I ask you to get back in the box, think of it less as an order and more as a very polite, very firm suggestion."

Could it understand her? It was hard to say. But it made no move to attack or suck her into god-knew-where, so she was taking it as a positive. The fox was looking at her from behind the cat like she was crazy. His stance said that he was reluctant but ready to pounce whenever this experiment went sideways. Luckily, the final showdown never arrived, because the oblivious old lady spoke.

"Nestor, time for din din."

Nestor looked up, and studied the bread box she held. It seemed to come to some sort of conclusion, nodded its head in a way that cats didn't do, and was suddenly no larger than a scruffy black kitten. The lady didn't notice anything was different, and she put the box on the floor for her cat to climb into. It was over. Just like that.

It was a very surreal ten seconds.

Once the cat was inside, Olivia shut the lid, did the latch, and picked it up. She and the fox hurried to the vent before the lady's AI or whatever could register.

She had kicked this lady out her house, let her be taken over by a malicious entity, had the entire top floor wrecked during the battle between the animaelstrom and the fox, and now she was stealing her cat in the hopes that she could get her friends back.

"Sorry," Olivia said simply, before following the fox into the vent.

Chapter 22: Sorry, My Mind Went Blank

From the time she was nine to twelve years old, Olivia was considered pretty tall for her age. She was taller than all of her friends, which meant she often got picked first for teams at recess. To the minds of ten year olds, it was impeccable logic that there must have been a ratio of positive correlation between height and athletic proficiency. Nobody seemed to notice Olivia's detest for running, or that her coordination skills were that of a drunken Cyclops. The only time she ever actually managed to kick a ball was on accident. Any victory granted her was due to a well intentioned trip.

Olivia was tall though, that was the point.

And because she was tall, that meant that whenever she went to an amusement park, her friends were forced to live vicariously through her. She could ride all the rides that they could not; reporting back to them the wonders and exhilarations of the rollercoasters, like a double agent relaying back well guarded secrets of enemy plans. Her friends were enamored with her tales, taking mental notes as she explained every heart stopping incline, head pounding corkscrew, and vomit inducing loop; dreaming of the day when they could experience the manufactured terror themselves. Nobody ever asked her if she actually *wanted* to ride all these well funded death traps by herself (she did not), always falling victim to the incessant pleas and vague threats of prepubescent peer pressure.

One of such days, when a friend's parents had taken a few of them to a water park, Olivia foolishly thought that this outing would be different. All of her friends were old enough to swim, and pretty much all the rides involved inner tubes and could be ridden at any age with the accompaniment of an adult. She had of course forgotten about the Big One. It probably had another name, but that was what everyone called it.

A water slide that- to the ten year old mind- was roughly twenty thousand feet high and was a straight drop down. There were many a tale of people going on it, and speeding up so fast that they caught fire like a meteor falling to Earth, only to be extinguished by the pool at the bottom. Other stories told of people falling so hard that the pool didn't even cushion the fall, they simply hit the water like concrete. Splat.

Naturally, these rumors needed to be put to the test, and Olivia was just the guinea pig over forty-eight inches to test them. To try and persuade her, one of the "friends" had told her that if she did it and survived, everyone would think she was a total badass. Unfortunately, the friend's mom heard her, and made her sit by the towels the rest of the day for swearing. The rest of the group followed Olivia to the behemoth of a slide.

She had been surprised after climbing the many stairs to the top of the slide that she didn't have to sign a waiver of some sort. She had ridden every rollercoaster her peers had thrown at her, but she had never known a fear like this. There were no straps or harnesses. Nothing to keep her arms and feet inside at all times. No thin illusion of safety in the form of a small metal cab to shield her. It was just her versus the unyielding pull of gravity.

Now, over ten years later, in a dimension of sleep and stories, Olivia Jones was once again falling, and reminded of that day in her childhood.

For the first fifty feet or so, the walls they fell past were metallic; the kind of walls one would expect to find in a ventilation shaft. They started out at an easy- almost fun- forty-five degree angle. No worse than an average slide. It soon became apparent that they were speeding up though, and that the incline was becoming steeper.

And as she and the fox gained speed, the metal walls soon fell away to walls of dirt, grass, and roots. She felt like Alice falling down the rabbit hole. Maybe it was more of a foxhole, given the circumstances. The loose earth and roots scratched and scraped at her back as she continued falling, but only for a moment. The angle of descent was waxing further away from the nice and safe acute angle it had started with, and was now dangerously near the straight drop of ninety degrees.

And as Olivia fell, clutching the breadbox as she went, her mind was drawn back to that fateful day at the water park; the instant where her back left the slide entirely and for a split second she was just falling. Her mind had frozen in that instant. She couldn't even comprehend her own terror at what had just occurred. That wasn't supposed to happen, some small part of her had screamed. People weren't supposed to be able to just drift away from the slide like a child gently releasing a balloon. But before she had even begun to wrap her head around the absolute probability that she was going to die, her back hit the slide once more, and she skipped like a stone into the pool below.

Since then, Olivia had been in much more dangerous scenarios, but even in a crashing spaceship there was always the small chance that the craft could right itself at the last second. They were made for falling, after all. But as her back rose up against the hole she was tumbling down, she knew with certainty that in a competition between a squishy sack of flesh and bone and the ground that was undoubtedly coming up to reach her, there was really no contest at all. Even if the sack of flesh and bone she currently inhabited was of the figurative variety. There would be no pool of water at the bottom to catch her.

The rabbit hole faded, being replaced with a tunnel of sky. Blue and bright with wisps of clouds on all sides. As if her fear couldn't increase, she was now skydiving without a parachute. The fox might have been yelling something to her, but he might as well have been on another planet. Her heart was racing, and she could feel it in every part of her body. Then she remembered hearing somewhere that skydivers that had died hadn't actually died from impact, they had died from being so terrified that heart attacks had been induced. And even though a stray brain cell or two wondered how anyone could possibly know that, Olivia did everything she could to calm her racing heart that was like a rocket chained to a launch pad.

Nestor the animaelstrom was screeching from inside its box. Or it might have just been the high velocity wind screeching past Olivia's ears.

Then even the sky did away, and the tunnel shifted too fast for her to get accustomed to each new change. They were in the rainbow of a wyrmhole. They were falling through the darkness of space. They were plummeting through pink and wrinkled flesh. They were descending through the hollow of a tree.

An empty elevator shaft.

Possibly a chimney.

A giant blue twisty straw.

The connecting honeycombs of a giant beehive.

A billion stacked shoe boxes.

Fast and faster, through so many tunnel shifts Olivia lost count. They might have been falling for days; there was no way to tell. Time was such an immeasurable construct in the Paracosm, there really was no difference between seven seconds and two weeks. Olivia's immediate fear for the end of the fall started to dissolve, as it was replaced with a fear of falling forever.

After a time, it didn't even feel like she was falling. It felt as if the endless shifting tunnels were just moving past her, and she herself was stationary; fixed to one point in space while this weird world rocketed past her. She closed her eyes, trying to feel if she really was still descending or not. It was hard to tell, she had gotten so used to the sensation, she couldn't differentiate against it. Like driving a long stretch of road for so long at one speed, the force of the movement couldn't even be felt anymore. It simply became a part of the driver until the car eventually had to stop.

Olivia opened her eyes, and could say with complete certainty that she was not falling anymore.

"Oh," she said simply at her surroundings. Or rather, her lack of surroundings.

The tunnels were gone, which was something. But so was everything else, which was not. There was ground, if it could be called that. She was definitely standing on something. It just wasn't much of something. Actually, she was more standing *in* it than on it. It felt like she was up to her ankles in some kind of liquid thinner than water. It almost felt like nail polish. But the substance- whatever it was- couldn't be seen. It was like her feet were simply gone, though she could still feel them under her.

The world around the fox and herself was empty. It kind of reminded her of the Nothing, but on the opposite end of some unknown spectrum. Where the Nothing was mostly the darkness before the light, this place was like light that had never known darkness. There was not anything in any direction but stark white, devoid of any color or shape whatsoever. It was impossible to say how far it went on; there was no sense of distance or depth. The horizon could go on for miles, or it could end at Olivia's nose. There was no way to tell.

"Welcome to the Blank," the fox said. "It was lucky that you finally decided to close your eyes. It's against the rules to witness your own entrance to this place. I was trying to tell you as we fell."

Olivia was going to explain that she hadn't heard him, but another part of what he said hooked into her thoughts a bit more. "Against whose rules?"

The fox shrugged. "The universe's I suppose." His own paws had disappeared too. Under whatever this strange gunk was. The injuries sustained from his fight with Nestor looked marginally better. The gash across his eye was definitely less horrific to look at, and several clumps of fur that had been torn out had new patches of red-orange growing.

"So what's the Blank?" Olivia asked, hazarding a step forward. Her foot reappeared without a trace of having stepped in anything, before returning once more into absence. Luckily, the world did not seem to end at her nose. The box under her shoulder was starting to get uncomfortable, so after a quick peak to make sure the animaelstrom was alright, she set it down. Half of the bread box faded out of sight, and she quickly ran a hand along the inside of the box to make sure none of the strange invisible liquid was getting through. The cat just stared at her as if it really were just an innocent kitten. When she was sure Nestor wouldn't drown, she closed the lid. "You said that the vents in the Paracosm led to behind."

"Yes, well I refuse to call it 'the Behind'. Not very magisterial." The fox looked uncomfortable. "Not much is known about this place. No one born from the Paracosm can be here for long without risk of being… redrafted."

"Redrafted?"

The fox struggled to find the words to express. "The Blank is kind of the... seed from which the Paracosm grows. The foundation, the base code, what have you. It is the empty page before the story- every story- is written upon it. Hence the name. What we're standing in, there isn't an exact translation that Literals would understand. The closest analogy might be amniotic fluid. Primordial soup. The stuff which instigates life on most Literal planets. But instead of being filled with sugars and amino acids, the substance we're in now is made of unrefined ideas. It connects Literals like a collective unconscious. They dream and create, and the stories are given form and shape here, before being born into the Paracosm proper.

"But once born, you cannot return back to the womb. If any inhabitants of the fifth dimension come here again, they risk being overwritten by new ideas and stories, which can completely transform them. Because in the Literal universe, tales change constantly as they are retold. If a Native dies, then there is no choice but for their essence to be brought back here and reshaped like clay, but nobody tends to come here voluntarily before such a time."

Olivia pictured a game of telephone, where a word was spread from one person to another until the word was different altogether. The first person might start with "banana" and by the time it got to the last person it might have been "bandana" or "Montana". Whenever Olivia played it as a kid, there was always some boy in the middle who thought he was funny by changing the word purposefully. The new words were always something super original like "fart" or "shiitake" (always emphasizing the first syllable of the latter).

Stories were just like games of telephone, only passed down through generations. Alterations and amendments were bound to happen. A character that started off as a villain the first time the tale was told might have been made into a hero by the thousandth. How strange it must be for the Natives of the Paracosm, to know they could be reborn when they die, but not necessarily as themselves. Or, more technically, as new versions of themselves that might seem alien to the previous iteration.

Olivia looked at the box full of cat that she had set down. The fox followed her gaze. "It'll be fine," he said. "Anima maelstroms are not born of the Paracosm, they simply sought refuge here. No one knows from what, or where they really came from."

Another mystery for another time, Olivia supposed. "What about you?" she asked the fox. "Will you be redrafted?"

The fox seemed distracted. "I was not born into the Paracosm in the conventional sense, so I'm not sure how many of its rules apply to me. But the sooner we leave here, the better."

"What does that mean?" Olivia asked.

"Some other time. We need to focus on-"

"No," Olivia stopped him. "We have time. Time means nothing here, remember? And it's time you told me just who or what you are. You say you brought my friends and me here to help, but that could be a lie. We've been led into traps before. And you seem to be connected to the Reaver somehow. You could easily be its spy or accomplice or something."

"I assure you I am neither."

"Then what? Because I've really been trusting you since I've been here, and I'd like to know if that trust is warranted."

"Your friends-"

"Will be fine. They're smart and resourceful and I will find them as soon as I can. But I refuse to take one more step until you tell me just who you are and why I should keep listening to you."

The fox danced around nervously. This obviously wasn't what he planned. He had wanted to delay this conversation for as long as possible. He probably hoped they would all be kept so busy with fighting the Reaver that his identity would never come up. But the time had come, and he could see he didn't have a choice. Even Nestor stopped his pitiful whining from inside his box.

"Fine," the fox said. "Of course you have every right to know." He paused for as long as he dared before continuing. "I am connected to the beast, but not in any collaborative or conspiratorial capacity. I am neither a Fathom nor a Native, because I was not thought up by any Literal. You heard the Script Angels refer to me as a stray. They weren't wrong. I am a stray in several senses of the word. I am a stray thought, an idea made tangible by an imprisoned monster. I am the first and only of my kind, because I am the only thing ever born by a dream and not a dreamer. Or perhaps it is more apt to say, I was born of a nightmare."

Olivia absorbed that, before taking a step back. "The Reaver created you."

Chapter 23: Recent Reaver Reveal

Olivia didn't know what to think. "So what? You're like its son or something?"

"I am an experiment gone wrong," the fox explained. "The beast was lonely, locked inside the mind of that poor farmer for so many eons. It wanted companionship. More than that, it wanted something else. Being alone for so long, it was sick of its own thoughts. Bored of them. It wanted to experience itself in a new way. For that to occur, it figured it needed something to debate; a foil to its own drives and desires. It created me to be its superego, acting as its moral conscience. I was there to try and explain to it the things it did not understand."

"Did it work? Did it learn anything?"

"I… cannot say. All I do know is that once it- we- were freed, and found our way back to the Paracosm, it banished me from itself. It had no further use for me. After all, it's pretty hard to harvest and corrupt the souls of innocents when you understand the concept of morality." He paused. "I drifted for a time, incorporeal; a ghost watching and learning of this larger universe I had not been privy to for so long. Studying through dreams and the Paracosm until I came upon you and your friends. You made quite the story yourselves. Battling ancient gods, avenging the deaths of fathers, even fighting your own worst thoughts and instincts, actualized through the lens of another universe.

"I needed help. I was nothing but a notion. I could not stand up to the beast that spawned me. So I went to you in your dreams. And because you were the first person I ever made tangible contact with, I imprinted on you in a way, and you were able to grant me this form." He motioned to his battered canine body. "I was hoping for a more useful shape, but I am grateful nonetheless."

Olivia was trying to remain critical, but his story made a lot of sense. Well, it didn't make any sense, but neither did anything else having to do with this realm. But it all made sense within the nonsensical walls of the Paracosm. If the fox was originally part of the Reaver, then that would explain how he could manipulate her sleeping self into changing their ship's flight path to Illetica. "So you could've been anything else? A palm tree, an aardvark, an amoeba, anything?"

"If I had reached out to someone else, yes."

"Why choose me?"

"I just explained-"

Olivia shook her head. "No. Yes, I know why you came to us for help, I mean me specifically. Why not Alibaster or Penelope?"

"Because you know what it's like to face a dark aspect of yourself."

She remembered when she had first seen the fox, in her recurring nightmare of killing Ophelia. He had helped her get past it.

"Is that your plan?" Olivia asked. "Do you want to kill the Reaver?"

"How does one kill a nightmare?" the fox asked. "During the first war with the beast, the best option was to imprison it. This is what must happen again."

"Yeah, ok. I guess that makes sense." It did seem like the best and only option. But according to the tale the fox had told, it took the combined might of every inhabitant of the Paracosm to battle the Reaver the first time. And even then they only barely succeeded. The fox had said that he didn't want to risk another war with the creature, and Olivia was inclined to agree. But that would mean it was just them. How could two Earthlings, two Illeticans, and the cricket thrown from the Reaver's shoulder possibly hope to stop it before it infected every slumbering mind in the cosmos?

And there was something else… It pulled and nagged at Olivia's mind like a child tugging at her shirt sleeve, but she didn't know what it was.

There was also *another* something else, which she had just remembered. (There were just too many things to stay on top of. She should really start carrying a notepad to write all her queries down like a grocery list.) "When I was talking to the Reaver- when it had taken over those Fathoms- it mentioned a lost friend. Someone it thought was connected to me who it had hidden for some reason."

"Well, *it* took all of your friends," the fox said, nodding to the bread box.

Olivia shook her head. "No. I don't think that's what it meant. I think there is someone else out there. Someone we have to find. They're trapped because the Reaver thinks they have something to do with me or my friends."

"To be used as leverage, perhaps?" The fox considered. "If true, that's troubling. The beast has never been clever in its brutality in the past. It had never any need for strategy. It might not be the creature of pure instinct that it once was. It may be evolving. Learning."

"Maybe you taught it something after all," Olivia said, before coming to wonder how her foot had entered her mouth without her knowing. "Sorry."

The fox shook it off. "Whatever I tried to teach it, it would always come to the wrong conclusion. It would always miss the point."

"So if you had told it something like 'work smarter, not harder'…" Olivia said.

"Exactly."

Olivia considered all the things that needed doing. "I need to get my friends back. And we should find this mystery person the Reaver's hidden away. Maybe they have something to do with us, maybe not. But either way, knowing they are out there- imprisoned to blackmail us or whatever- we need to find them."

"Agreed," the fox said. "If the beast thinks it has some sort of strategic advantage because of this person, I would very much like to know who they are, and get them as far away from it as possible."

"So should we split up? Cover more ground and whatnot?"

The fox inclined his head. "I hate to divide our forces further…" Olivia almost laughed. What a sorry bunch of "forces" the pair of them made. The fox continued. "But I can move quicker on my own. I can hide and tread places you cannot. I will get back to the primary Paracosm and scout around. See if I can learn anything about this prisoner, and what the beast has planned. I always assumed its plan would be just to attack everything in sight like a caged… well, beast. But I now fear its thinking has become more nuanced. I would like to gather more intelligence before deciding on how to proceed."

"Ok," Olivia said. "Then I guess I'm going after my friends." She looked to the bread box, bent down, and opened the lid. The kitten that wasn't a kitten was sleeping. It purred softly and stirred as Olivia poked its belly. "Ok you crazy freak of nature you, time to spit out all the people you ate."

Nestor pawed at its face. It gave a tiny yawn, then mewed.

"It said it can't," the fox translated. "Your friends are no longer where its vortex dropped them."

"You got all that from a meow?" Olivia asked.

"It's not an exact translation," the fox said. "Context clues and inflection are more important when speaking to anima maelstroms."

Nestor bit its own tail.

"It wants to thank us for bringing it along," the fox said. "Our interference has helped it cut loose from the beast's influence, and it is grateful. But it still cannot do anything to retrieve the others."

Olivia bit her lip. "Then I guess I'm going in after them. There's always a way out. And if we can't get back out through the cat's maelstrom, then we'll find another way." She addressed the cat. "Do you at least know where you dumped them? What I'm going to be walking into?"

The cat rolled onto its back and pawed at the air.

"Oh, great," the fox said in a tone that implied it was not. "They're in the Infinite Elevator."

In her journeys, Olivia had been to the planet of the dead, the Nothing at the center of creation, the core of chaos that sat within the first planet, faced dragons in the Chasm, and a whole lot more. When she heard the words "Infinite Elevator", she got the sense that it wasn't great, but it honestly didn't sound as bad as "the hell dimension" or "the Land of the Lasting". It sounded more tedious than dangerous. The fox might as well have said "the Infinite Line at the DMV", or "the Infinite Having to Sneeze but it Just Won't Happen".

"The Infinite Elevator is a nexus, connecting a number of places in the Paracosm," the fox said. "If you don't know how to navigate it- which many do not - it is very easy to get lost. Especially since the concept of physical space is so fluid here to begin with."

"So Alibaster, Penelope, and Koz…" Olivia drifted off.

"Could literally be anywhere in the fifth dimension."

One step forward, eight steps back. She sighed and closed her eyes for a second. "Fine. That's not great news, but it doesn't change anything. I'm still going after them. Will you be able to find me again once you're done with your recon mission?"

The fox obviously didn't like her going to this elevator alone, but kept his reservations to himself. "Yes. You've been in the Paracosm long enough that I can track your aura through the connection that's been forged between us."

Whatever that means. "Great. Good luck." Olivia picked the kitten up out of the box, and set it gently in the imagination soup, or whatever it was. The tiny thing's legs disappeared entirely, and a bit of its belly too. Cats generally didn't like getting wet, but after that old lady and her spray bottle, this pool of dormant ideas barely fazed Nestor. Also, the fox said it was a shape shifter, so who knew what its true form was.

"Ok cat," Olivia said. "Your cover's been blown. As they say in movies, you've been compromised. You can't go back to the shrunken town to live with that lady. You'll have to start fresh, find some new dream or story to settle down in. Somewhere you can keep out of the Reaver's way until all this- hopefully- blows over."

Nestor purred and rubbed itself against Olivia's leg. She guessed it was a thank you of sorts. Either that or it was just feeling around for a scratching post.

"But before you do that, I need a favor: Eat me."

The cat stopped, looked up at her with adorable cartoonish eyes, before emitting a sound one might expect would summon the Kraken. As the sound grew, so did Nestor (which probably wasn't this mysterious and powerful creature's real name, now that she thought about it), returning to its panther form. It circled Olivia twice, as if trying to decide whether to eat her like it had eaten her friends, or to actually eat her and mail the bones back to her parents.

Then it stopped, and unhinged its jaw in that grotesque python manner. A vortex of light and noise filled Olivia's vision. She gave one last look to the fox, who was a good distance away. He nodded at her somberly, before turning around and disappearing as easily as smoke.

He was gone.

She felt her feet lift off the ground of their own volition, flew into the whirlpool in the feline's mouth, and she was gone too.

Chapter 24: Alone in the Elevator

The sensation of being pulled from one point to another via cheats of nature was not wholly alien to Olivia. She had gone through wormholes, and more recently wyrmholes. And as it was with the former, she couldn't recall much of the experience caused by the animaelstrom swallowing her. A blinding flash of colors, an unintelligible screeching that's frequency pitch increased and decreased spontaneously- possibly due to some odd Doppler effect (it might have been her own screams, but there was no way to know for sure)- and the feeling of being the last bit of toothpaste forcibly squeezed from the tube.

At the end of the ride, she tumbled out of the vortex and fell front first onto something that should not be fallen on front first.

"Ugh," she said, with her face pressed against cool metal. She stood up with only one or two stumbles, and turned around just in time to see where she had fallen from. It looked like a scrape or cut, hanging in the air a couple feet above her. It swirled with blues and all the colors of fire, and gave off such an odd and hurt sensation, it seemed like reality itself had skinned its knee. Then it closed itself right back up, like someone had pulled a zipper up from the other side, leaving Olivia to her new surroundings.

Well, it sure was an elevator. That much could be said with any certainty (though it was very little certainty). As for infinite…

That was yet to be seen.

The space was large. Maybe the size of Alibaster's ship hangar back on Kertsraw. And packed tightly in rows, one on top of the other, were hundreds of elevator doors. On the walls, the ceiling, and the floor, in a number of styles and designs. Olivia was standing on one of them now. There was gentle light which came from the small space in between one door and the next. If she had been in the Literal universe, Olivia might have said that it was some sort of bioluminescent paint. Was that a thing? Olivia wondered. She'd have to look it up. There was also a small amount of light which came from the slits where each half of the elevator doors met in the middle.

"Hello!" she called into the open space. "Alibaster! Penelope! Koz!" Her voice echoed than died, and she strained her ears to hear a response, but none came. She walked around for a bit but still saw no sign of anyone. They must have gone through one of the doors. *Figures.* "Why wait for me?" Olivia asked herself. "Yeah, sure, totally. Just wander away. Don't even assume I'll come looking for you. And if by some miracle I do, why make it easy on me? There's nothing more I would like than to spend the rest of my life searching through endless doors while I wait for a gestalt entity made of ACTUAL NIGHTMARES to come and… Well, I don't know for sure. But I'm sure it'll be horrible. Eat my eyeballs with soup ladles or some shype." She sighed. "With friends like these…"

Olivia stopped walking, and bent down to try and pry open the nearest door. She had to start looking somewhere, after all. But it was no use. The door didn't budge. She tried another, wondering if perhaps some doors were heavier than others. But no matter how many she tried (she stopped after eight), she couldn't move any so much as an inch.

What use was a room full of doors that didn't open?

When was a door not ajar?

No, if this was supposed to be an elevator, there had to be some way to access certain areas of wherever the doors led. Even in the Paracosm, there had to be some amount of sense, right? Some point to the place. Where was the panel with brightly lit numbered buttons?

On the wall to her left, about halfway up, sitting slap right in the middle of all the doors, was an empty square. It was a dark color- perhaps purple- and as wide on each side as Olivia was tall. It was the only free space in the whole massive arena of lift doors. That had to mean something, surely. She should try and reach it, see if it yielded any answers. But how?

She walked across several doors to where the floor met the wall, and stared up. It was probably three storys up. "And me without my climbing gear," Olivia mumbled. Why was nothing ever easy? "There must be some way…"

She tried pressing herself against the nearest door on the wall, then jumping up to try and hook her fingers around the top of the frame. It worked. *Now what?* Olivia wondered as she hanged (or was it hung?) She didn't wonder for long, as… something happened.

"Uff." The wind was knocked out of her suddenly. It felt like she had fallen a very short distance. Now she was pressed against the door she was gripping, but in a different way. In the way that gravity pressed one against things.

"What the…?" She let go of the doorframe, and she didn't fall back to the ground, she stayed firmly pressed against the closed door. She tried to get up, and found that she could now stand on the wall she had been trying to climb. There was the empty space, straight ahead of her, and where she came from was now a wall behind her. Gravity had reoriented itself around her, so it seemed.

"Huh," she said, making her way towards the space.

When she reached it, she saw that it was in fact purple. Purple carpet. The scratchy kind that was used at movie theaters because it was short and easier to clean. Looking closer, it had some sort of pattern on it in a slightly darker hue, which could have either meant something extremely important, or was just decorative. It was a number of squares inside more squares, but each proceeding square was turned on its axis about fifteen degrees. It almost looked like a spiral of right angles.

She stepped into the center of it, and the glow-in-the-dark paint that surrounded the carpet glowed brighter, and started expanding upwards, over and around Olivia like an oblong dome of light. Reaching her hand out to touch it, she found it didn't pass through. Some kind of force field?

She kept watching as the light separated, and bits of it darkened and solidified in front of her. Soon enough, there were about thirty rows, consisting of eleven strange symbols each. After a moment of trying to decipher what they were, she realized they must have been the buttons she was looking for. Each of these symbols- or pattern of symbols- must correspond to one of the doors. But how to know which one her friends had chosen? Hopefully they had decided to stay together. This was going to take long enough without having to search for them all separately.

As a test just to see what would happen, she pressed the very first symbol. A pleasant ding sounded from nearby; the kind that might go off to signify that people should stand away from the doors because they were closing, and the last thing this hotel needed was another lawsuit because some idiot got themselves caught in a gently closing door.

Olivia heard the sound of massive gears start to shift and click. Then, through her strange little bubble, she watched as the whole world rearranged around her. Every door on every wall/floor/ceiling was moving; rising and falling, or moving laterally and diagonally. As they moved it was revealed that the doors were attached to elevator cabs as well. It was as if some giant invisible hands were manipulating them. After a minute, Olivia had to close her eyes. Watching all the cabs move about like this was giving her motion sickness.

Soon enough, the noise and the vibrations stopped, and another ding sounded. This one was of a slightly higher- possibly friendlier- tone. It was the sort of ding that signified that it was now time to get the heck off, and please don't forget any luggage or children, or someone else was bound to come by and sell them to the nearest pawnshop.

She opened her eyes, and saw that a hole now stood in her force field, just to the left of the rows of symbols. In the hole was an elevator cab, with the doors facing her. It was golden, with artwork delicately chiseled into the doors of what might have been two Hy-Dragons. A startling thought washed over her as the doors started to open.

"Please don't open into the Chasm. Please don't open into the Chasm."

Taking a step back just in case one of the limbless beasts (unless retractable wings of fire counted as limbs) waited for her on the other side, she watched as a new world came into view.

Inside the cab- or wherever the cab looked into- a harsh crimson snow was falling. The sky was awash with pinks and oranges. And what must have been several hundred miles away, mountains sat. The cold was bitter and immediate as it all seemed to want to escape into the portal at once. It might have been a part of the Chasm, or perhaps some fictionalized version of it. Olivia couldn't say for sure, she had only been there once, and she hadn't gone sightseeing. She hugged herself, and part of her wondered if she should step in and search for her friends. But no. If she tried to call out to them, her voice would be lost instantly in the harsh biting winds. And she would without a doubt become lost as well. She just couldn't see her friends choosing to go there.

The door closed again, trapping the chill once more inside its rightful world, dream, or story. But the cab didn't move. It stayed right where it was, waiting for Olivia to try something else. So she pressed the next button on the light pad.

The same thing happened as before. Gears shifted, elevator cabs found new spots to settle, the golden cab left, only to be replaced by a new one with a ding. This one had goop like strawberry jelly dripping down the doors in congealed groups. They opened into a dark and damp house. Olivia stuck her head through to look around, and found she could see her breath again, even though she wasn't cold. Old wood creaked and snapped somewhere on the landing above her.

"Hello?" she whispered. "Guys? Anyone?"

There was no immediate reply other than the hiss and ticks of a weathered house settling. She looked back down, and as her eyes started to adjust to the dark, a shape was able to be made out some feet in front of her. It was roughly the shape of a person. But there was something about it…

It seemed to be a woman; skin as gray as trees in winter. She looked slightly sad, but also slightly translucent. *Oh, crap.* The woman took one step forward, impossibly closing the gap between herself and Olivia instantly. Their noses were almost touching.

"Flek!" Olivia stumbled backwards, and scrambled to press another button.

As the doors shut and the cab left to be replaced by another, she realized that the dripping substance might not have- strictly speaking- been strawberry jelly.

Chapter 25: Olivia's Not in this Story

And so it went. She spent the next chunk of time trying out a number of elevator cabs, only to be scared away or deciding the climate was too harsh for her friends to survive. There didn't seem to be any consistency or pattern to where the doors led. One opened up into a sunken pirate ship with tap-dancing eels, another inside an office building full of cannibals and rabid things that might have been considered dogs. There were three different magical forests with differing levels of outward hostility (Olivia quickly learned to never follow a fairy down a darkened glen, and to never trust anything that asked for a lock of her hair). There was a nail salon filled with either some species of dinosaur, or just aliens she had never encountered. Their nails were more like talons, which were more like butcher knives. It took whole cans of paint to cover each one, and they looked sharp enough to slice molecules back into atoms.

Sometimes Olivia would forget which symbols she had pressed- they all started to blend together after a while- and would press the same ones multiple times. It was getting very frustrating. She was on the third row of light buttons, and no closer to finding her friends. *One more,* she told herself, *before I reconsider my tactics.* "Tactics" was a kind word for "randomly pressing buttons, hoping for something good to happen".

The last button on the third row brought forth yet another cab. It looked old-timey. Like the kind they had in big cities on Earth in the nineteen-twenties. The doors were made of a nice, dark, polished wood, and when they opened, there was a gold gate beneath. Olivia pulled the gate to the side and found herself in what must have been a desert.

The sky was open and filled with dark blues and lavenders. The ground was covered with dunes of obsidian sand that rose and fell like still waves. As she stepped through the door and into yet another new world, she found a slight chill in the air, yet not an uncomfortable one. The black sand felt cool between her tired feet, and she dug into it with her toes as she looked around to see if she could find any footprints or signs of life.

She had learned with her previous attempts that yelling "Hello", or "Is anyone there?" was not always the safest approach. Things might respond, and those things had a habit of not been her friends. So instead she decided to walk a couple dozen yards, and climbed up a taller dune for a better vantage point across the sea of sand. The elevator door still stood behind her, where it had opened into this world. It stood completely out of place, a rectangular hole in the world. She had found that they always stayed open while she was inside whatever habitat they housed. That was nice of them, seeing as she would have no idea how to get back if they closed.

She had also learned that no creature residing within any elevator landscape could even see the doors. It was no wonder most of them had treated her with hostility. To them, it was like she simply appeared out of nowhere; an intruder just casually appearing into their homes, shouting random names.

She scanned the horizon, but- to her complete lack of surprise- there was no sign of her people. She was about to turn back around, when she caught a glimpse of something in the corner of her eye. She turned her neck so fast she almost got whiplash, and saw- maybe a quarter mile away- someone running down a steep dune.

Olivia scrambled down her own dune and ran as well as she could through the loose sands. As she got closer she noticed a second figure behind the first. They were not running with the first, instead gently meandering down the slope, following the first's footfalls.

Olivia was close enough to see that neither of them were who she was looking for. Her heart sank, and she crouched down low behind a small hill before either figure saw her.

The first was smaller; a child of indeterminate species wrapped in shawls and wearing goggles, but humanoid enough. He laughed as he ran down the hill, letting the angle of descent and gravity increase his speed. It was impressive he didn't fall down. He shouted and whooped as he climbed halfway back up the dune, before lying on his back and rolling down.

The second figure was more feminine in appearance, and had more intricate shawls drawn around her. Possibly the child's mother or sister, Olivia guessed. The woman had dark hair down to her waist, covering her eyes and face so that only the nose could really be seen. The child never looked at her; never said "Watch me", or "Did you see that?" as children tended to do. He just kept climbing up each new hill, only to tumble down in a variety of fun ways. Cartwheels, somersaults, or even just sliding down on his bottom. The feminine figure followed slowly, but never strayed from the child.

As Olivia watched, she couldn't help thinking that this all looked familiar. This exact scenario. The déjà vu was tickling her brain. Had she seen a painting of this scene somewhere? "The child on the hill and the veiled menace lurking behind." The words came to her, but she couldn't remember where they had come from. Was it a quote? A chapter title? If the Paracosm was a land of stories, then she was bound to come across one she had read at some point or another.

Try as she might, she couldn't remember where she had read this story, but she suddenly remembered that the dark haired woman was not a woman at all. It was some sort of-

"Foul beast!" came a shout falling from the sky.

Oh, thought Olivia, *right.*

The owner of the voice fell like a star and landed several yards away from Olivia with all the stealth and tact of a cannonball tied to fireworks. Sand was displaced as a small crater formed to accommodate the landing. As the dust fell, the figure was revealed, a figure that might have inhabited the dust jackets of Mrs. Jones' romance novels in scantily clad coverings, had he not already been on the covers of a number of his own books all over the universe.

Plexerious: Hero of the Twin Goddess.

He was roughly seven feet tall, with long, luscious locks of hair that blew without need of wind. His eyes were deep amber, which looked intelligent, alert, and ever so slightly mischievous. He was built as if sculpted; every muscle, contour, and curvature carefully mulled over and precisely fashioned. Of his four incredibly powerful arms, two held sleek and menacing weapons, and one held a shield. The fourth was held out to the child who was on the ground with no idea he was in danger, looking bewildered, but not afraid. He helped the kid to his feet.

"Stay behind me, my boy," Plexerious said. His voice was deep but jovial, and he gave the kid a quick smile and wink as reassurance. Both his eyes and his teeth seemed to sparkle. He turned to the dark figure that had been following the boy, and the smiled dropped. He puffed out his chest. "Leave this place, creature of twilight. For I know what you are, and I know how you may be slain. You will not take this child."

But, being a monster in a story, the woman who was not a woman did what all storybook monsters did. They attacked the hero. She transformed into something like an oyster on spider legs, ripping through the false body like a hyena from a wet paper bag, and it and Plexerious pounced at each other. The boy hid behind a hill not far from where Olivia was hiding.

As they traded blows, she tried to remember what she knew about the great hero.

Olivia had read a few of his books (well, she had skimmed them). They were often considered biographies, depending on who was asked. Some only considered them parables. She tried to recall any information she could about him.

He had been a real person, thousands of relative years ago. From a planet called Apex. He had done a number of memorable things, accomplishing many impossible tasks and challenges. He was kind of like an outer space Hercules. A lot of people saw him as the perfect hero archetype. He had even been folded into a few religions somewhere down the line. And watching him now, Olivia couldn't say she blamed them.

Plexerious moved with grace and fluidity, but also with precision and meaning. No move was a mistake as he dodged a blow or struck his sword against the creature.

This was the story of The Underground Dwellers of Bloosh. Olivia finally remembered. She had read about it in the libraries on Kertsraw. The planet Bloosh had a great many dangers lurking on or just beneath its surface, such as the walking clam trying to snap the great hero in half. To survive against such creatures, the people of the planet decided to colonize the vast tunnel systems which sat further underground than any of the creatures could reach. There they were safe. But every once in a while, the young and curious would want to see the sky, not scared by these conceptual horrors described to them, and they would sneak to the surface. And so, venturing forth- and having fun he should not have been having- a monster strikes, to the surprise of no one but the child. But of course, in this particular instance, the hero saves the stray kid from the big bad monster, and the boy goes home with a new found respect for his peoples' rules.

Had this really happened? Perhaps. Olivia had no fleking clue herself. Maybe something like it happened once, but time had twisted it into an allegory about listening to adults, or curiosity killing the cat or something.

The fight was finishing up, and while Plexerious had taken a few hits, they were negligible compared to what he had inflicted upon the arachnid/crustacean hybrid. It fell, having had most of its legs cut out from beneath it, and died with a pitiful deflating sort of sound as it bled out from the stumps where its legs used to be. (This part wasn't usually mentioned with much detail in the stories.)

"Why do they never heed my warnings?" Plexerious asked himself with a sigh. He looked almost sorrowful, like he was saddened by having to kill the creature. Olivia found this an oddly refreshing stance to take for someone renowned for fighting monsters his whole life. He found the child, who had been watching the spectacle without blinking. It was probably the most exciting thing that had ever happened to him, and he wasn't even entirely sure what *had* happened. He stood up, and craned his neck to look at Plexerious' face.

"The danger has passed," said the hero. "Return home, lad. Lest we stay here and wait for deadlier foes to arrive." He gave that smile again. "I would welcome any challenge of course, but I would rather not fight needlessly."

The boy nodded, and ran off the way he had come, carefully sidestepping the bleeding carcass as he went.

"I am ready to get back on course," Plex (Olivia decided to call him Plex) said to no one. A large, vaguely heart-shaped mass descended from the sky (cartoon heart, not actual). Lights shined down on him as it lowered itself, displacing more sand and dust. Olivia shielded her face. This must have been his ship. One of them, anyway. He had had so many; one per epic it seemed. He wasn't exactly a guy to pick one, call it the Argonaut, and be able to keep it in one piece long enough for more than two daring adventures.

Olivia remembered that this story, the one she had stepped into, wasn't the main plotline. Plexerious was on his way to topple some evil empire in the name of some fair maiden, and this- the boy and the monster- had just been a side quest. He had just been passing by, and his ship's long range scanners had picked up a rare humanoid heat signature to find on the surface of Bloosh. And anticipating trouble for the wandering child, he naturally jumped out of his spaceship from low orbit. Because that's what heroes did, apparently.

Well, this had all been very interesting, but Olivia really needed to get back to the elevator and figure out how she was going to find-

What was that?

Something had moved to her right. There, it moved again. It was displacing sand, but in a different way than the spaceship. It was if something was tunneling just below the surface, leaving a trail. It seemed to be heading towards…

Olivia jumped from her hiding place, ignoring all the sand that had found itself in unfortunate places. "Plexerious!" she yelled over the ship's engines.

The hero turned around. "Eh? Who goes there?" He saw Olivia. That was good at least. She had half worried that he would adhere to the rules of the Fathoms, and not acknowledge her because she wasn't a part of this story. But he was probably more of a Native, right? Or was that just for stories that were never true? Plex had been real- Literal- at some point. What did that make him here? Just some construct? An amalgamation of the tales told about him? How different was he from the Literal version that had lived centuries ago?

It was like Jack the Ripper, in a way. No one knew who he was, but there were still scores of fictionalizations about him, influencing the way people thought he must have been. Maybe that's what this Plexerious was. As the fox had said: there was a collective unconscious which informed the reality of the Paracosm.

Olivia thought all this in the time it took a giant barbed appendage- like a scorpion tail- to reach out from the ground and strike at Space Hercules. Before she could yell for him to look out, he had unsheathed his great sword and slashed the barb right off. It fell to the ground heavily, twitching and oozing a sizzling green liquid. The appendage it was attached to writhed and fell back into the sand.

Plex smiled that knight-in-shining-armor smile, and looked back at Olivia. "Fear not, beauteous stranger, for I have-"

Before Olivia could be both flattered and inwardly cringe at being called a "beauteous stranger", another appendage rose up from behind Plexerious, and impaled him through his mightily toned chest.

Chapter 26: Shock Value Death

"Gah!" Olivia fell backwards, as the thing lifted Plex into the air- the hero struggling and gurgling- and flung him to the ground mere feet from Olivia. She fumbled towards him to gauge just how bad his wound was. There were many tales of his legendary healing abilities. He could heal from almost any gash or broken bone within a few hours. Whether those abilities had been true or exaggerated in regards to the Literal Plexerious were moot, because people believed them to be true. After a fashion, the Paracosm and its inhabitants were shaped by belief, which meant that this version of him must have had those abilities.

But looking at the wound in his chest now, where a great deal of innards and bits of spine should have been…

Well, a stack of paper couldn't heal from being hole punched.

Maybe that was where the phrase of getting one's ticket punched came from. Olivia would have wondered about it more, but she was a little preoccupied.

"You're ok, it's ok," Olivia lied as soothingly as she could with her shaking voice. She might have thrown up at the sight of the gore, only there wasn't any. There was no blood or organs or other such things that would do well to stay where she couldn't see them, thanks very much. Inside the wound that had effectively turned the universe's most iconic hero into a donut, there was nothing. Just a weird, mostly solid goop the color of Plex's skin. It was like he was made of clay. Ideas weren't made of flesh and bone, it seemed.

"The creature…" Plexerious struggled to say. "What in the bedeviled quasar is a… a *Sun-Setter* doing here?"

The name sounded familiar to Olivia. She looked around, and saw the appendage that had impaled the hero had slithered back into the ground. Others were now carving their own paths under her feet. At least six that she could count were now circling them with menace, but with no real sense of urgency.

If she remembered rightly, Sun-Setters were from the Chasm. They kept to the outer fringes of the sub-dimension, to keep out of the way of other top predators; mainly the Hy-Dragons. They were big and ugly and had any number of extremities to trap their prey like fish on a line. The larger and stronger the Sun-Setter, the more extremities it grew. Since the body that should have been attached to the extremities couldn't be seen, that only meant the whole beast must have buried itself in the sand; perhaps waiting for some unlucky hero to spring the trap. Plex was correct in his astonishment. This creature definitely should not be there with them now.

Because this hadn't happened. This wasn't part of the story. Plex was supposed to make a pit stop to save a wandering child, and then resume his quest, having adventures in spades along the way. He was not- by any stretch of the imagination- supposed to have been fatally wounded by a creature from another plane of existence.

"We're going to get you out of here," Olivia said as she kept one eye on the many protuberances writhing under the sands.

"We?" Plex asked with a cough. "You travel this desert with comrades? They must be very skilled at obscuring themselves from view."

"It's… It's just a figure of speech," Olivia said. Truth be told, she had said it on accident. A force of habit. She had grown used to her friends being right next to her the past few months. *"I'm going to get you out of here."*

"How courageous of you, beauteous stranger… Though I must confess, I feel I am not long for these worlds."

"Nonsense. You think a tiny scratch like that will be enough to stop the Hero of the Twin Goddess?" She gave the most reassuring smile she could. "That'd be like…" she tried to string together an amusing analogy. "That'd be like felling a tree with a blunted butter knife."

"Hah," he tried to chuckle, then winced.

"And enough of the 'beauteous stranger'," she said. "My name's Olivia. Olivia Jones."

"Well then Olivia Jones, I think it prudent you take your leave of me. I cannot be healed, and I cannot be moved. You must go. Go before that incongruous creature decides you are a threat, and strikes again."

He had a point. She was surprised the Sun-Setter hadn't attacked her already. Maybe it didn't care about her, only Plexerious. But why? And how had it gotten there in the first place? Had it hopped stories? Could inhabitants of the Paracosm do that? She knew Natives like the Script Angels could. So the monster below her feet must have been a Native, right? She recalled the first cab she had called forth in the Infinite Elevator, how she was worried it opened unto the Chasm, but was relieved when it had seemed desolate and empty. That relief was now gone, as she imagined who-knew how many beasts escaping their enclosure through the Elevator into any number of other worlds within the fifth dimension.

Worry about all that later, she told herself. It was rude to be distracted while someone was dying right next to her.

"I-I don't want to leave you," she said.

Plex smiled weakly. "You are kind, and brave. That much is obvious, Miss Jones. But you must flee." His voice was steadily dying away. Barely a whisper. And though it would have been rude to say aloud, Olivia thought it was taking him quite a long time to die with a hole that sized torn through him. Even with no blood or anything. Maybe it was that healing thing he had, trying its best to hold on. Or maybe it just took longer to kill a symbolic or iconic person than it did to kill a Literal. It took more effort to kill an idea of a person than to kill a person.

And you would know, a voice flitted through her head. *Shut up*, she told herself.

"We'll meet again," Plex said. "In the next life. But I do hope your next life isn't as soon as my own. Take my sword. Just in case you need to fight your way out of this desert. It is a trustworthy blade. Its edges are so thin and so sharp; they can cut through the very fog itself. And slice an errant thought clean from a man's head."

How poetic. But there were several flaws in that plan. The first being that the longsword which had fallen from his grasp was about as big as Olivia in both length and width. She did not see herself wielding it to battle beasts any time soon. The second was that even if she could hold it, she wouldn't know how to use it.

"I don't like weapons," she said instead of outwardly rejecting the gesture.

"An admirable quality. Though not always a practical one." He paused, as if to catch his breath. Olivia tried not to wonder how that worked since he didn't seem to have lungs, and if he had, they were now somewhere on the other side of that dune. He continued. "Then my shield. Take my shield."

Now that, she could do.

She went where it laid, and picked it up. It was disc shaped, roughly the size of a sled Olivia had as a child. The metal was smooth, polished, thin and surprisingly light. The face was inlayed with a simple design; a rose wrapped around a battle axe. The crest of Plexerious. There was debate over what it meant. Some thought it was meant to show how passionate he was about battle. That war was almost itself like a lover to him. Others believed it was to show the duality of the man; his warring, brutal side versus his kinder, gentler side. A yin/yang type thing.

It had a couple straps where an arm could be fitted through, and a longer strap which would help the wearer carry it on their back when not in use. Thanks to her many hours spent forced watching medieval era documentaries at her grandparents' house during her formative years, she knew this strap to be called a guige.

She fitted the shield to her back, adjusting the straps to fit an Earth girl instead of a seven foot tall, four armed demigod. Only feeling a little like an upright turtle, she turned back to Plexerious.

"It suits you," he said. "Now go." He breathed out once more, and he was gone. Not just dead: gone. Like a phantom disappearing from view. The only remnants he ever existed at all were his shield and the indent his body had left in the sand.

Just like that, the story had been rewritten. Olivia wondered how this was possible, and what the implications would be.

"Sorry," she whispered, but not really sure why. Then she turned and set off back towards the elevator door, even using the shield as the sled it so closely resembled to descend more quickly down the larger sand dunes.

The Sun-Setter didn't bother her, didn't try and stop her. That only secured her fears further. It wasn't just random coincidence; an animal escaping its habitation. It had purposefully come here. It had targeted Plexerious specifically. This had been planned. There was intelligence behind it.

Just as she reached the door, she turned and gave the landscape one last look over. There was a new dune rising up the way she had come from. No… it wasn't a dune. It was the Sun-Setter. It was emerging from the ground. As truckloads of sand fell away from it, more of it became visible. Its body was like a giant, ugly jack-o-lantern that had been left in the sun a few days beyond its use-by date. All its appendages were attached to where the stem of the pumpkin might be. They writhed and squirmed like the snakes of Medusa's hair.

As the two stared at each other, Olivia was not at all surprised to find that its eyes were black as pitch, with tiny pinpricks of copper in the center.

"Soon…" the beast's voice echoed. It sounded clunky and pained; an unintelligent creature forced to speak.

"Yeah," said Olivia. She turned away with more courage than she felt, and walked back into the Infinite Elevator, letting the doors close between them.

Chapter 27: Alibaster, Star Destroyer

Once more she was back within the confines of the oblong force field, the rows of buttons lining a section in solid light. Olivia took a moment to absorb everything that had just happened. She looked down at the ground; at the pattern of askew concentric squares.

"Wait…" she said, with a spark of realization flashing through her mind like a sudden static shock. She turned around to face all the buttons. She had seen it, she knew she had. Seen, but not noticed. Too focused on trying all the other possibilities. She scanned each one until…

There. Fifth row down, seventh across. This button had the same pattern as the floor did. Surely, it couldn't be that easy. Olivia pressed the button, and the Infinite Elevator did its thing with a ding. The door to the incongruous pumpkin monster in the desert was now falling back into the sea of other cabs; all of them shifting and churning and rearranging like an elaborate card shuffle. A new cab appeared at the hole in the force field. It was fairly nondescript, though there were hints of rust around the edges. Another ding signified its arrival, and the doors creaked obnoxiously as they strained to open themselves.

Olivia braced herself, not wanting to get her hopes up, and not knowing what fresh new hell this cab might lead her into. Poking her head in, she saw probably the last thing she expected to see after the slew of mystical places she had been visiting lately.

A tavern. The place looked old; built of weathered- almost rotting- wood, with candles on the tables and walls instead of any kind of electrical setup. There was no ceiling. Instead there was just an open night sky with thousands of stars which looked close enough to touch.

No, wait…

It was odd. As she walked forward, her perception changed. It seemed less like there was no ceiling, and more like the sky *was* the ceiling. A curtain of darkness and stars blanketing the top of the old building. She actually might be able to touch them if she got up on a table.

And there, sitting at the bar along the far wall were Penelope and Alibaster. Koz was behind the bar, mixing and dispensing several beverages not suitable for those under a certain age.

Olivia didn't say anything as she made her way across the tavern, and sat down on the stool to the right of Alibaster. He nodded at her and stirred his drink. A small glass with brown liquid inside. "You found us then," he said.

"I found you then," Olivia agreed. She looked on the other side of him to Penelope. Her head was on the counter, and she was clutching her stomach and shivering. She looked between Alibaster and Koz for explanation.

"She doesn't seem to be coping with the Paracosm any better," Koz said, wiping down a glass. "I don't really understand her biology or abilities, but the aura of timelessness this place exudes clearly isn't good for her."

Alibaster tapped his teeth. "Her being can't get used to it, because it refuses to accept it. It goes against her very nature as a temporal responsive."

"It's just going to get worse," Koz said.

Penelope forced a chuckle but it turned into a gag. She spoke without lifting her head. "Me? Oh I'm just dandy. Barkeep? I'll take a scotch with water, hold the scotch. I also wouldn't say no to some wine. White, preferably." Her voice was feeble, and to say the phrase "shaking like a leaf" would be disrespectful to leaves, which looked like body builders in comparison to Penelope at the moment.

"I didn't know you liked wine," Olivia said. Koz filled a glass with water, dropped in a fun swirly straw, and slid it in front of Penelope.

"Not to drink," Penelope said, concentrating very hard on her shoes as she spoke. "I like to smell it. The bubbles tickle my nose."

"Oh," said Olivia. Because how else could she respond to that?

Alibaster took the tiniest pipette-like sip of his own drink, and puckered his face. "Well *that* will burn the hair right out of your nose. I have no clue why my dad liked this stuff." He pushed the drink away.

"Where are we?" Olivia asked, motioning to the ceiling.

"Another dream, presumably," Koz said.

"No, I don't think so," Alibaster said. He scrunched up his face in thought. "I think I remember reading something a while back. An old Oob-Loobian myth. Something called the 'Tavern of Titans'. A place where the gods of that world sit outside the universe; drinking and watching creation like a movie."

"How do you know that?" Koz asked.

Alibaster shrugged. "I have a lot of interests."

"Such as?"

"Anything interesting." He played at nonchalance, but Olivia knew he loved it when people were impressed by his obscure knowledge. "Some gods- the less benevolent ones- play with the universe; or so the tales go. They would make bets on who could do the most damage, like normal people would bet on a card game." He climbed onto the bar, licked his thumb and forefinger, reached them up to the expanse, and squeezed the nearest star between them, extinguishing it like a candle. He got back down. "See?"

"Hopefully nobody needed that star," Olivia said. The Paracosm might not be the Literal plane, but there were still who-knew how many creatures and people living there. She had no idea how all of them lived, or where they might reside. It wasn't out of the realm of possibility that there could be a planet- or several- that had relied on that star. Alibaster might have just inadvertently committed genocide.

"No kidding," Koz said. They picked up the nearest candle, got up on the counter themself, and reached the flame right into the empty space Alibaster had created. The little flame left the candle, and stuck to the sky as easily as a fly on tape. The flame condensed into a pearl-like ball of white light, and Koz got down. "We really shouldn't mess with that. Just in case."

"Sorry," said Alibaster in a rare state of repentance.

Olivia looked around, making sure they were alone. "Where are these gods or titans or whatever?"

None of her friends had an answer.

"Where's the fox?" Koz asked.

"Reconnaissance," Olivia said. She then elaborated, telling them all she had been through since they became separated; the animaelstrom, the Blank, and the Infinite Elevator.

"You spent all that time searching for us in the Elevator?" Alibaster asked. "What about that giant clue we left for you? We found this place, thought it a decent enough spot to wait, then drew the symbol on the ground to lead you here."

All Olivia could say to defend herself was, "Yeah, well…"

"You must have been gone for quite some time from your perspective," Koz said. "We've only been here a few minutes."

"Hrk," said Penelope, sounding like she was going to retch.

Olivia gave a pitying glance towards her friend before continuing. "I also met Plexerious."

At this Alibaster scoffed. "And I'm the Tenth Duchess of Krelm."

Olivia pulled the shield from her back and set it on the bar.

Alibaster's eyes lit up. "No fleking way. Where was he? Where *is* he?"

"Dead," she said a little too casually. "Courtesy of the Dream Reaver."

"Are we really calling it that?" Penelope asked, mostly to herself.

"What happened?" Koz asked Olivia.

She told them. How she had unknowingly fallen right in the middle of a Plexerious adventure, before that adventure was given a new draft due to an unexpected cameo from a Chasm Sun-Setter.

"It all must be part of the Reaver's plan," Olivia said. "I think it drained the version of the Chasm that exists here of its creatures, and is using them to rewrite stories to fit its own ends."

"It might not just be the Chasm," Alibaster said. "It could be monsters from a number of legends."

"And it's doing what, exactly?" Koz asked. "Just letting them run loose in the Paracosm?"

"I don't know," Olivia admitted. "I'm just telling you what happened. Maybe it's just a step in a larger plan we can't see, or maybe it just found where I was and killed Plexerious to frighten me off."

"That's another thing," Alibaster said. "Why hasn't it killed any of us? It's had ample opportunity. That big cat thing, whatever you called it- an anima maelstrom? It could have easily torn us to shreds, but instead it just 'ported us to the Elevator. A hindrance, but not actually threatening."

"Bad guys always need us for something," Penelope said with a groan from her near fetal position.

They all considered that. "Maybe it's because of the fox," Olivia said. "The two can't kill each other. That's what the fox said. Maybe the Reaver can't kill us because we're helping the fox." Even as she said it she knew it was quite a tenuous leap of logic. But anything seemed possible when it came to this dimension. Besides, half the fun of theorizing was throwing as many ideas at the wall as it could hold before crumbling.

Her friends all looked at her, confused. Even Penelope briefly flicked her eyes in Olivia's direction. "Oh," Olivia said. "I forgot to tell you. The fox is part of the Reaver." Looking at all their faces, she sighed. "Probably should have led with that."

Chapter 28: Time Heals Penelope's Wounds

"So, just to recap-" started Alibaster after Olivia had told them what she had learned- "the very thing that brought us here is actually an aspect of the monster it enlisted us to fight against."

"I think it's a little more nuanced than that," Olivia said. "But yeah. Basically."

"You do realize the fox could be in cahoots with the Reaver, right? That this could be a trap set for us?"

Olivia gave him a look that told him not to treat her like an idiot. "It did cross my mind, yeah. And did you really just say 'cahoots'?"

Koz poured a drink for themself, and leaned against the counter. Their eyes looked up at Olivia and Alibaster over the large blue rimmed glasses. "I think you guys overestimate your importance."

Alibaster and Olivia looked blankly at each other and then back at Koz.

They laughed. "All this? A trap just for you three? What circuitous lengths to go to. For what? To what end? For what purpose? We've already established that the Reaver- or whatever you want to call it- doesn't want you dead. At least for now. Maybe Penelope's right and it wants to use you for something. The three of you do seem to have some kind of power a storybook villain might be drawn towards. (I still don't know how you did that power blast back in the village.) But even if that's true, there would be easier ways to get you to the Paracosm without having a double agent dressed as an Earth animal sent to collect you. Something like the Reaver… From what we've seen, it really doesn't need to trick you. It's has power, and is gaining more all the time. What use does power have for tricks? It can just do and take what it likes. It doesn't need a 'man on the inside' to gain your trust. What would be the point?"

They all considered that while Koz sipped their drink.

Penelope was the one who broke through the silence of contemplation. "For the story."

Everyone looked at her. She had broken out in a cold sweat, and her skin was pale as a sheet. Under normal circumstances it might look like she had the flu.

"I believe she may be onto something," said a voice from the tavern's door. It's real door, not the one from the Elevator. It was one of those swinging ones that cowboys liked to walk through dramatically in Westerns. And walking right under it into the tavern was the fox.

Koz and Alibaster straightened up as they saw him. Like two kids who had been badmouthing the teacher as he came around passing out tests. Olivia was nonplussed, and Penelope barely even registered the new arrival.

The fox padded his way over to them, not put out in the least by the nature of their discussion. All the injuries inflicted upon him by Nestor the animaelstrom were completely gone. This either meant the fox had extraordinary healing capabilities, or from his perspective he had been separated from them for such a long time that he had time to heal at a normal speed. Olivia tried not to wonder about it too hard. The fox continued. "I don't blame you for being wary of me. As I told Olivia, it was the main reason I waited so long to reveal my true origins."

"How'd you find us?" Alibaster asked. "You didn't go through the Elevator."

The fox looked up. "I know more about the Paracosm's nature than any Literal could ever hope. Besides, we still have a link connecting us." He looked towards Olivia.

"Lost animals are always following you home," Penelope tried to joke. "Well you can't keep him. You'll have to find his proper owners, and hopefully earn a sizable reward to pay for my funeral."

"Can you help her?" Olivia asked the fox. She really didn't feel like rehashing the whole discussion of trustworthiness. It always just led in circles. Olivia was prepared to trust the fox until he gave her reason not to. "You brought us all here, but Penelope isn't going to be able to help anyone the way she is now."

Penelope almost laughed. "Ask not what you can do for Penelope, but what Penelope can do for you."

The fox studied her. "She is a child of Time in a place where its structure is unwieldy at best. The most I can do is shield her from feeling too much of the effects. If I can concentrate the little amount of Time the Paracosm has and focus it around her, it could be enough for a reprieve from her misery. I have no idea how long such a shield will hold, though. It will be like finding a fish in the middle of a desert, and dropping it into a bowl filled with water. It can keep the fish safe for a while, but eventually the water in the bowl will evaporate."

"Time shield. I dig it," said Penelope, struggling off her bar stool. Olivia and Alibaster hurried to each of her sides to help steady her. "Let's do it."

"Alright," started the fox. "Time may be irrelevant in the Paracosm, but it still exists. The building blocks are still here, they just have not been fathomed into arrangement. Individual bricks scattered around the land, instead of the house that can be built from them. What you need to do is use your abilities- difficult though that may be right now- and pull the bricks towards you. Focus your temporal sensitivity outwards in every direction, and find the pockets of then and now that are near. Pull them to you. Use them to craft a barrier."

Penelope nodded and took a breath. She started to focus, and her face looked immediately pained. Trying to use her powers must have been like trying to light a match at the bottom of a lake. Or like a fly attempting to escape a spider's web. But she was Penelope Brownstein-McClain. She was strong and stubborn, and not only the most willful eighteen year old Olivia had come across (which was a feat amongst itself), but one of the most willful people she had ever met, period.

Penelope had denied the destiny that had been set up for her, she had raged against the god who tried to possess her, and exiled what was left of him back into the Nothing. She had spent multiple lifetimes trapped in the Temporal universe, until she finally broke free and rescued Olivia and Alibaster. She helped save the multiverse from Olivia's dark doppelganger, and has helped hundreds of people since. She could also make a pretty mean tiramisu if the mood hit her.

There was nothing Penelope couldn't do once she decided something needed doing.

With her face looking like the halfway mark between deadlifting a school bus and having been constipated for a month, a light behind her eyes flickered to life, and they finally started to glow that wonderful blue. With a clenched jaw she told her friends to stand back. Olivia and Alibaster let go of her, and she stumbled a bit before catching herself.

Penelope reached out her arms in front of her, and displayed her hands in such a dramatic way, Olivia felt as though Penelope should've been holding a skull and reciting Shakespeare. (Or at the very least been wearing a long red cloak.)

Then from all directions, bubbles appeared from out of thin air. They varied in size and color, and they were all opaque, with the vague air of a stopped clock emanating off of them. They drew around Penelope, swirling around her as if they were thunder clouds and she was the eye of the storm. As they swirled faster and faster, they began to pop, leaving only trails of colored mist, which encapsulated Penelope like a cocoon of shimmering rainbow particles.

The blue died from her eyes, and she put her arms down. "Wow," she said, standing up straight, "that is so much better."

Alibaster, Koz, and Olivia all looked at each other and then back at Penelope.

Alibaster sighed, and rubbed his eyes. "This place is so fleking weird."

"Now onto business," the fox said as they all sat back down. "We need to discuss the beast, and what it is planning."

It was clear from the cagey look on his face that Alibaster didn't quite trust the fox, but this wasn't surprising. Alibaster didn't trust anybody other than himself and Olivia. At times he was still on the fence about Penelope. But the 'time shield' trick had won Penelope over, it seemed. And Koz was cautiously optimistic that the presence of the fox wasn't some sort of elaborate trap. Maybe they were right, and the Key of Three did think too much of themselves. For now, they all just listened.

"Did you find anything out?" Olivia asked.

"Indeed I did," the fox said gravely. "I've been following the beast's trail of destruction, and I've noticed something different; something that was not there during its previous attempts of chaos."

"What's that?" Alibaster asked.

"A pattern." He paused before continuing. "It has never had a plan before; never needed one. It would simply tear through dreams and stories like a twister, unprejudiced in the carnage it wrought. Now though, it seems to be going after specific residents of the Paracosm. Perhaps this is due to its weakened state; at being locked away and starved for so long. Maybe it has just evolved from the mindless creature of instinct it once was. I cannot say for certain. But the fact remains the same.

"I believe you were wondering where all the gods who frequented this tavern had gone. Would any of you like to hazard a guess?"

The four all looked at one another. Koz was the first to speak. "Are they… dead?"

"Either dead or deep in hiding," the fox said. "I could find no trace of any of the primary sixty-eight thousand five-hundred twelve Oob-Loobian deities. And there are others from numerous planets and mythologies that have disappeared from their legends as well."

"Well you said Natives could travel to different places in the Paracosm," Olivia said. "They could just be… out."

"That is true. But millions of them at once? And even if they all did decide to partake in some merriment at the Swan and Swine, they would all return home eventually. There would be some hint of them. But there is none. The Oob-Loobians, the Crestfallen, the Racknovitians… Even several of the ancient Illetican and Earthling gods of legend have gone missing."

An image of Zeus and Odin sipping martinis and reading old magazines in an underground bunker almost made Olivia smile.

"So the Reaver is taking out the competition," Penelope said. "Trying to secure a place at the top of the pyramid."

"Probably dealing with them individually so that they can't rally forces against it," Alibaster added thoughtfully.

"I am afraid that is just the beginning," the fox said. "Because it isn't just the deities that the beast is going after." He looked to Olivia. "As you know firsthand."

Olivia raised an eyebrow, before catching his meaning. "Plexerious. He wasn't a god."

"No he wasn't," the fox agreed.

"So the Reaver is taking out heroes too?" Koz asked. "Its plan is what exactly? Wipe out all the good guys?"

"That is an arbitrary term," the fox said. "Even here in the Paracosm, where things are more easily… I believe the term is 'wrapped up', or categorized. The idea of 'good' and 'bad' is often dependant on perspective."

"So what would you call what the Reaver is doing?" Alibaster asked. "Who exactly is it going after?"

"Protagonists," the fox said. "Everyone is the hero of their own story, but some are heroes to others. Because of this, Literals can become legend, like your friend Plexerious. The beast has taken up the task of wiping the Paracosm's slate clean of first: any with combined power to oppose it, and second: any legend of such symbolic significance that without them the Literal plane- and its collective consciousness- would suffer. Quite simply, the beast is rewriting stories, and aims to put itself at the center of them."

Koz was leaning on the counter, and put their head in their hands. "That's crazy. This is just so… *absurd*." They looked up at the Three. "You guys seriously deal with this kind of heinous nonsense on a regular basis?"

Alibaster shrugged. Olivia nodded. Penelope said, "And we don't even get paid."

"And what about us?" Alibaster asked. "What does the Reaver want with us?"

The fox considered. "If I understand how the beast's mind works- and I should, since I used to be part of it- then I would say that what it wants from you is spectacle."

"What does that mean?" Koz asked.

Olivia then remembered what the possessed Sun-Setter had said to her as she was walking back to the Elevator. "Soon," it had said.

"Oh," she said.

"Quite," the fox said, as if reading her mind. (And he might have been, depending on how that link between them worked.)

"What?" Penelope asked.

"The Reaver isn't keeping us alive," Olivia said. "It's just keeping us alive *for now*." Her friends stared blankly at her. "Don't you see? Once it's done with all the other myths and legends, then it'll kill us; probably the only Literals to ever try and fight against it. We're its grand finally."

"Why?" Alibaster asked. "What for?"

The fox answered. "It is as Penelope said earlier: for the story."

They all took that in, not knowing quite what to make of it. After a minute the fox spoke again, this time his voice taking on a slightly lighter tone. "By the way, I looked into that missing person that the beast mentioned to you, Olivia."

The change in topic was abrupt, but welcome. "Oh," she said. "And?"

"I heard a name whispered upon winds which were possessed by the beast," the fox said, then winked. "An informant of mine."

"How can this wind be your informant if it's possessed?" Penelope asked.

"Nothing can truly direct the wind but itself. Anyways, its words were mostly incoherent, but I heard a couple clearly. Does the name 'Musscivite' mean anything to any of you?"

Musty, Olivia thought.

“Musty?” Alibaster said.

“Musty!” Koz said at the same time.

The two looked at each other in astonishment. “Wait, what?” they asked one another in unison.

Chapter 30: Holding Hermanos Hostage

"How do you know Musty?" Alibaster asked Koz.

"How do *you* know Musty?" Koz asked Alibaster.

"He's my brother."

"He's my boyfriend."

"Oh!" Olivia chimed in. "When I met you at the Swan and Swine, it was Musty you were waiting for." *What a small universe.*

"Yeah," said Koz. "But he never showed up."

"And that didn't worry you?" Penelope asked.

Koz shook their head. "He has a hard time finding his way into the Paracosm sometimes, even though he's been invited. His mind is very straight forward. This place isn't always easy for him to maneuver through. Sometimes he makes it in, sometimes he doesn't."

"He never mentioned me?" Alibaster asked.

"He mentioned a surrogate brother that he hadn't seen in years. But he's never said your name." Alibaster looked hurt.

"Guys," Olivia said, "we have bigger things to worry about."

"Yeah," agreed Penelope. "Like where the heck is he?"

"And why did the Reaver take him in the first place?" Koz asked.

"And how are we going to rescue him?" Alibaster added.

"The beast must have known this 'Musty' was known to all of you," the fox said. "And since he was already trying to enter the Paracosm, it would have been easy for it to grab him at the border between his dreams and this dimension. It's just another way to slow you down or distract you from your fight with it."

"Right," Penelope said, swirling her glass of water in her hand. "While we go on a rescue mission, the Reaver can keep on keeping on, getting rid of the gods and heroes, and releasing more monsters from their proper dreams or stories. Keeping us occupied so that we won't get to it before it's ready for us."

"But it's not like we have a choice," Koz said. "We have to save him, wherever he is."

"I agree," said Alibaster.

"I'm going to be the bad guy for a second-" Penelope started.

"How out of character," Alibaster interrupted with a mumble.

Penelope inhaled calmly, and continued. "But why do we need to save him? He's probably safer than we are right now. The Reaver would want to keep him alive and unharmed as incentive for us to go after him. And not to be a broken record, but it's probably just a big trap for us. If we do somehow manage to rescue Musty and make it out… Well, we still have to deal with the Reaver. We still have to have our boss battle. Only now *your* brother and *your* boyfriend is right in the middle of that danger with us. Out of the frying pan, into the nightmare."

Koz and Alibaster considered that. They didn't like the idea of leaving Musty, but Penelope-callous though she could be- was right. They would just be saving Musty to put him back in danger. It was a pretty lateral move. Even the fox couldn't weigh in on what the best tactic was.

Olivia was the one to break the silence. "This is our fight." She motioned to herself, Alibaster, and Penelope. "We were brought here. This is the life we chose to lead. Or maybe this is the life that chose us." She looked to the bespectacled Illetican behind the bar. "Koz, you were only here for a date. You didn't ask to be brought into all of this. You were just trying to help me, and that's put you in danger. I say we rescue Musty, and then you two get out of here. Go somewhere safe. Wake up. Live your lives, and leave the monsters under the bed to us."

Alibaster gave a shallow nod of approval. Penelope stirred her water some more. The fox looked agitated, but said nothing.

"I don't really want to leave you all yet," Koz said slowly. "You didn't pull me into anything. I chose to come along all this way. Part of me wants to stay and see what happens. But you may be right. It's probably better for me to get Musty out of here. I really don't want either of us to be in the path of destruction that seems to be barreling down at you three."

"Cheers," Penelope mumbled.

"Understandable," Alibaster said. "I don't really care for it either. But as Olivia said, this is our life. These are the cards we've been dealt. It's our job to play whatever hand we're given to the best of our abilities."

"I'm not really sure if that analogy tracks," Penelope said. "Comparing fighting monsters and killers to a card game. Now if you had said roller derby…"

Alibaster was about to say something snarky in rebuttal, but Olivia had seen this show too many times before. If the two of them got going, they'd argue indefinitely. Alibaster and Penelope were too similar; each constantly trying to prove their cleverness, and their nonchalance at their cleverness. Always needing to get the last word in. They could have been the best of friends if they could get over themselves. Not that they'd ever see it that way. Olivia had four younger siblings; she was well versed in being the household peacekeeper. She cut Alibaster off before the fighting started.

"So where's Musty?" she asked the fox. Whatever Alibaster was about to say died in his throat, as his attention was pulled back to saving his childhood friend.

"From what I could gather from the corrupted wind," the fox began, "your friend needed to be kept somewhere difficult for Literal minds to get out of. The beast's choice was in the Wasteland of Efivabh."

"Oh! I know this one," Koz said. "Some old religious folktale from the Tornadic nebula. It once was a paradise, but it was devastated by some great catastrophe. Some suggest a nuclear war. It was hallowed ground, believed divine in many ways. So when it was destroyed, the very air itself became cursed. The once benevolent spirits which resided there had their hearts hardened and fled. It's more barren than the driest desert, and to wander it is to wander eternal. The only person to ever do it was some spiritual figure who was said to have survived three hundred ninety-nine terrestrial years there, achieving spiritual enlightenment and personal peace in the isolation."

"And probably radiation poisoning," Penelope murmured.

They all stared at Koz.

"What?" they asked. "I read."

"Three hundred ninety-nine years?" Alibaster asked. "Couldn't make the last push to an even four hundred?"

"So that's where Musty is?" Olivia asked. "This wasteland?" She wasn't looking forward to another desert. After her experience with Plexerious, she had hoped to be done with deserts for a while.

"Yes," said the fox. "Within the islands of the lost which encapsulate the Paracosm, sits the Wastelands of Efivabh, where those who are trapped carry their prisons with them."

There was a short pause as they all tried to wrap their heads around this. "I think my headache's coming back," Penelope sighed.

Chapter 31: Getting too Handsy

The Wasteland of Efivabh could not be entered by four Literals as easily as it could by something like the fox. A more circuitous route was needed. The plains were one of the many islands of fiction which surrounded the Paracosm's circumference; creating somewhat of a border- a buffer zone- between the minds of dreamers and the fifth dimension. This meant that the space around it was less defined, and more mutable. Like the outer limits of a videogame city that didn't render past a certain point. Sometimes uninvited dreamers would go for a walkabout outside of their minds and end up ttrapped in these buffer zones. They would become lost, unable to find their way back to their proper dreams and minds. Only by being invited could a Literal forgo this firewall and enter the Paracosm properly.

This is what the fox explained to the quartet as they walked through an underground cave system which had acted as the setting for a recurring nightmare of some poor creature with taphophobia, cleithrophobia, and claustrophobia. (The fear of being buried alive, the fear of being trapped, and the fear of small spaces, respectively.) Olivia hadn't known that there was a specific word for so many fears, but she was starting to understand the fear itself quite a bit. The tunnel was low and narrow, everyone- save the fox- having to crouch and side shuffle at different intervals to try and weave through the rock and dirt. Phosphorescent stones were imbedded in the walls, which glowed just enough for someone to see their next step.

Apparently, dreams themselves didn't enter the Paracosm unless the dreamer has died. And even then, they had to have died in their sleep. As they drift away towards whatever came next, whatever they had been dreaming about drifts unto the Paracosm's shores. It was a little sad that this meant a person's nightmares might be all that's left to remember them by. But at least they become immortalized in some way, through these little pieces of who they were.

She could have done without the zombie hands coming out of the walls, floor, and ceiling every few seconds, grabbing so lazily at her and her friends, one might mistake it for a rough-skinned caress. It seemed that the dreamer had also been necrophobic. But they hadn't been as scared of dead things as they were caves and tunnels, so this fear was put on the backburner. Serving as more of an annoyance than an actual danger to any who needed to go through what was left of their mind.

Olivia swatted a decayed hand that was trying to pull its yellowed and cracked fingernails through her hair.

They moved in a line. The fox led of course. Then behind him were Alibaster, Penelope, then Koz, with Olivia at the rear. They hadn't drawn straws or anything; it had just ended up that way. Not that Olivia minded. As she positioned her body into a loose question mark to pass through the next chunk of jutting limestone, she tried to strike up conversation with Koz to keep the mood light.

"So how'd- ow!- you and- dammit!- Musty meet?"

Koz took a moment before answering, and Olivia was wondering if they hadn't heard her or if they were just ignoring the question. "About a year ago I was in the hospital," Koz finally said. "I was… I had to stay there for a while. The first couple weeks were very… dull. But then I saw this boy. He came in to clean up, change sheets, whatever. He was a volunteer." They paused to maneuver through another narrow gap in the tunnel. "He smiled politely at me as he worked, and said that my glasses matched his hair. And… I don't know. He was the first person I had seen working there who wasn't ancient or apathetic. And he was so gorgeous. Not just outwardly, but as a person. I'd never met someone who cared as much as he did. He was so filled with passion, but he was still so reserved and contemplative.

"We hit it off, and he came back to visit me whenever he could. He would even stay after his shift to talk, so that it didn't get in the way of his work." Koz laughed, remembering something. "After- oh it must have been about a month- he wanted to do something nice for me I suppose. He brought me flowers. But he didn't just want to get flowers from the gift shop. He wanted them to be special. But unfortunately the only things in bloom that time of year are these terrible things called 'yard pests'. Who knows how long he spent picking several of the least offensive ones he could find. Then he presented a bundle to me, and his face got so red when I laughed. I told him I wasn't laughing at him- even though I sort of was- and I took the flowers. I loved them, I told him. And from then on, it became our flower. These weedy little things. That must sound silly."

"Not at all," Olivia said, remembering the flower Koz had behind their ear when they first met.

Koz went on. "We got to know each other better. We talked about anything we could think to talk about. How he wanted to be a doctor, but he was too young. He had to wait until he was thirty-six to go to medical school. Two more years."

Olivia raised an internal eyebrow at that for a second, before she remembered that Illetican's aged half as fast as Earthlings. All those years ago when she had met Musty, he had looked about fifteen, but was actually around thirty.

Koz went on. "Even though he wasn't properly taught or trained, he seemed to know more about things than a lot of the doctors. He said he grew up with a pathologist, and had studied extensively on his own. At the hospital he would sometimes casually suggest something- like this medication instead of that one for this patient- and sometimes the doctors or nurses would agree. He said that he couldn't be forceful or insistent, or else they wouldn't listen. His suggestions had to come off nonchalant, like it didn't matter if he was listened to. 'People don't listen to you if they aren't shown the respect they think they deserve,' he had told me. 'Even if you're right.'" Olivia could practically hear Koz smile at the memory. "He said he'd learned it from watching his brother, who was himself filled to the brim with disrespect."

"Ha," Olivia said. "I can vouch for that. Alibaster doesn't suffer fools- or anyone he deems a fool- gladly. I have never met someone who rebels against authority so eagerly. I watch his blood pressure rise every time we have to go to Kertsraw."

"He doesn't," Koz said in disbelief. "He's rude to the Fate Makers?"

"That's one word for it." She hoped Alibaster was far enough ahead so that he couldn't hear them talking about him. Even so, Olivia dropped her voice. "I've lost my temper with them once or twice as well. And Penelope."

"What?" Koz was taken aback. "How are you all not in prison? Or even still alive?"

"I ask myself that every morning when I wake up."

Another pause. "Hopefully we all get to wake up this time."

If the tunnel hadn't been so awkward, Olivia might have put a hand on Koz's shoulder. "We will. We'll rescue Musty, and find a way to stop the Reaver."

"I hope so; I'd really hate to lose this place."

A few yards ahead, Alibaster and Penelope were arguing about something that was without a doubt trivial. Olivia sighed as she kicked another zombie hand that was grasping at her ankle. *Let them work it out for themselves for once,* she thought. There wasn't any room down here to throw punches, so she didn't think it would escalate to violence unless they were really determined. Why did her two best friends in the universe have to be so contrary? Didn't it get tiring having to be right all the time? Having to always have the last word? She knew they were both under the strain of this place. Penelope with the timelessness, and Alibaster with the illogic of the realm which did not leave him a firm place to stand. He hated not being able to science his way out of a problem. Arguing with each other was familiar; something for the two of them to hold on to. But Olivia could only be so sympathetic.

She did her best to ignore it and continued with Koz. "How did you first get here?" she asked. "To the Paracosm, I mean."

"I don't really know," they said. "I've been able to come here as far back as I can remember. I don't know who invited me. If I did know, I've forgotten. Maybe it was a Native who was watching my dreams and found me interesting. I'm not sure."

"Wait," Olivia would have stopped in her tracks if she were not currently positioned like an abstract sculpture. "The Natives can watch our dreams?"

Koz might have shrugged. "I mean they *can*. They don't tend to."

"But that's still kind of creepy, don't you think? Like… an invasion of privacy."

"True. But we read their stories. We can just find whatever books they're in and learn about their lives and struggles and causes and motivations and inner thoughts. Is that an invasion of privacy?"

"But a lot of them are just characters… They aren't…" Olivia stopped herself, but Koz finished the thought for her.

"Real?"

Olivia folded her lips.

"It's ok," said Koz. "But you're right. It is kind of creepy."

Olivia thought about how sometimes, she would fall into a restless sleep due to the distinct feeling of eyes on her. It was like someone was watching her while she slept. Now, she knew that wasn't the case at all. Nobody was watching her sleep, they were watching her dream.

Koz continued. "This place has always been a sanctuary for me. I came here alone every night. I thought I liked it that way, but I realized that there is a thin line between being alone and being lonely. One is by choice, and the other is not. After a few months of knowing Musty, I took the plunge, and invited him into my haven. Invited Literals have the ability to invite one other, and I chose him."

"Why only one?" Olivia asked.

"So the place isn't overrun with us. This isn't our proper realm. We can visit, but we can't live here. Imagine what would happen to the Paracosm if every single Literal mind in the universe could come here. This is a place of the figurative and vague. If pushed out by an overwhelming force of Literals, it would change the very nature of this place, and the universe as a whole. So, the rule of one exists. And anyone brought in by someone who was themselves invited, does not get to invite someone else. So Musty can't invite anyone for himself."

"Still, I'm surprised this place isn't well known. There should be people in the waking world vying to get here, but as far as I know, no one's ever heard of it."

"The door to this place is through dreams," Koz explained. "Do you remember all your dreams?"

"So what are you saying? That no Literals who come here ever remember the experience upon waking up?"

"Most don't. Musty doesn't. I do. Honestly, I'm the only Literal I've ever met that's able to remember the Paracosm once I wake up, so the ability has to be super rare. Maybe because I was admitted at such a young age, I was able to shape my consciousness around it easier. Like how little kids can learn new languages quicker than adults."

Olivia pondered that. "So chances are none of us will remember this? Me, Alibaster, Penelope… Everything we've seen and done here, just forgotten?"

"I can't say for sure. Your admittance is a peculiar one. Maybe that counts for something. Or maybe you're all as special as you say you are, and that'll let you keep your memories."

Olivia was about to protest about being "special", but she let it go. She was more worried about the prospect of not being able to recall any of the things she had seen or done in the fifth dimension, and not leaving it alive to not be able to recall them.

They walked on for a while longer; ducking and weaving and shooing away the gentle caresses of undead hands. Finally, from up ahead, came a light. They all found themselves in the cave's mouth. Everyone stretched, once again having the elbow room to do so. Yes, they were finally out! Except…

"This is the way we entered," Alibaster said. "We've just gone in a circle! But how? We didn't turn around at any point."

Penelope nudged him. "Dream logic, genius."

"Well what was the point?" Alibaster sounded tired, and the tiniest bit whiney. "Why did we come here at all if we're just going out the same way?"

"It is what was needed," the fox said, licking at a small trickle of water flowing down the cave wall. "For Literals to find any of the vague islands which surround this creation, first they must be lost. You must exit from somewhere which has no exit. The nightmarish maze of a frightened man seemed an acceptable choice."

"I swear he's making half this stuff up," Alibaster said under his breath. "We're just blindfolded children being led around the playground."

"It's actually pretty logical if you think about it," the fox said. "All the islands of dream and stories which border this realm, they are those of weary travelers and lost souls. It follows that to get there, you too must be lost. Nobody wants to end up there on purpose."

"We do," Penelope said.

"Yes, well, I am doing what I can with the script I was given." He inclined his head to the entrance. "Come on."

Chapter 32: Can't We Call a Cab?

They all had to shield their eyes from the harsh oppressive light which covered the landscape with the heat and intensity of multiple stage lights all directed on one person. It was a light that was so prevalent it could almost be heard, like a constant high pitch note.

"This is the Wasteland of Efivabh?" Alibaster asked doubtfully.

"No," said the fox. "It is one of the other islands of the lost; some representation of not being able to orientate yourself from the position of the sun, due to it hanging at its zenith."

Everyone's hearts sank. The fox tried to put a spin on the situation. "We're close though. We just need to keep moving, and not become separated."

"Well that's pretty much jinxed us," Penelope said. "Now we're bound to be separated."

"Not if we're quick, and keep our wits about us," the fox said. "The borders of the Paracosm are where souls go once a spirit has given up and a mind has gone. Staying here too long voluntarily could have unforeseen consequences on all of you."

"Good pep talk," Alibaster grumbled. "Now let's get going. Lead the way."

"Of course," the fox said, though did not move.

"Is there a problem?" Olivia asked.

"No, not at all. Though I was wondering… if you might accompany me for a few moments, Kozmoklor."

"Me?" Koz asked.

Through her squinting eyes, Olivia could see that their glasses had tinted into becoming sunglasses. And they were wearing clothes that one might wear on a summer hike. How did they do that so easily? It must have been because they had been a part of the Paracosm for so long; they had picked up ways of manipulating little things to their favor. Olivia wished she had some of that mojo. She was still in her childhood pJs, barefoot, with a few dried spots of obstinate angel sick covering some ducks on her shirt. And Penelope was still in her customer service uniform: shirt tucked into khakis, nametag, and all.

"There is a matter I wish to discuss with you," the fox said. The implication being that he preferred this conversation to be alone.

Koz looked at Olivia, who in turned just shrugged.

"Sure," Koz said with a trace of trepidation, walking to the fox.

"Splendid," said the fox. "Let's be off." He padded away with Koz by his side, leaving the Key of Three sharing confused squints. They all followed before they lost sight of their guide completely.

It was amazing how much of any given adventure was just spent travelling. Sure, there were fights with robots, and death defying escapes, and being imprisoned for inciting another revolution… But as far as time spent, all of that probably only amounted to twenty percent of the trio's average week. Most of the time was just this: getting to the next destination. And of course Olivia would rather walk than teleport, but still.

Was it too late to call the angels back?

And so they walked some more, having traded the dark enclosure of the cave of phobias for the bright flat landscape of wherever they were now. The three did their best to keep the fox and Koz within their line of sight- which was a pretty slim line to begin with- without losing either of them. Maybe Penelope was right, and the fox had jinxed them.

"What do you think they're talking about?" Penelope asked.

"Where best for them to go once we save Musty?" Olivia guessed.

"That wouldn't need to be a private conversation," Alibaster said.

"If the Reaver can read minds, or take them over, then yes it does," Olivia rebutted. "If Koz and Musty get away and go hide somewhere, it's better if we don't know where. If we go up against the Reaver, depending on how powerful it will have grown by the time we get to it, it could just reach into our minds, find where our friends our and capture them again."

"And on that cheery note-" Penelope started- "we should probably have a plan for when we actually have to face off against the king of all nightmares."

"If it can read our minds, then what's the point?" Alibaster asked.

"Hey, I was just throwing out possibilities," Olivia said defensively. "I'm just as in the dark as this thing's true power set as you are."

"The fox said he didn't want another war with the Reaver," Penelope said thoughtfully.

"I'm inclined to agree," Olivia said. The less people risking their lives (regardless of if those lives are figurative or Literal), the better.

"But it *took* a war to cow it the last time," Penelope argued. "It took the combined might of probably every story and dream in this place. So what I'm saying is-"

"How do we fight this thing without an army?" Alibaster finished the thought. "How do we even fight it at all?"

"And it's killing everyone who stood against it before," Penelope continued. "It's rewriting stories- retconning all of fiction- so that it can stand unopposed and crown itself as the one true hero or whatever. So it's not like we could have a draft, even if we intended to brute force this."

They all went on for a while; trying to come up with strategies against the Reaver that could be fought with just the three of them. But it was a difficult task. None of them understood the Paracosm very well. They didn't know the terrain or many of the rules. Before, with Krah, he had been imprisoned in the Nothing at the center of creation. And even then, the portal to the Nothing was held within the Land of the Lasting on Kertsraw. Both were designed to keep their prisoner in check. And when they fought Ophelia, she was from another universe altogether. (Not that these things made it much easier to deal with either of them.)

But the monster definitely had the home field advantage this time.

Most of the ideas they floated involved use of their Key powers. But given the demonstration that had occurred while they were trying to close the circuit with statue Penelope, the ideas were all tenuous. They had no clue how their abilities were affected here, or if they could be relied upon within any plan they might put together. It was another unknown variable.

As they went on, the shapes of what might have been people passed into and out of view. They flitted away so quickly, at first Olivia couldn't tell if they were mirages or not. But soon enough, one of the creatures spotted them as well, and hurried towards them in a kind of hobbling hurry.

"Please…" the poor creature started as it- no he- got closer. They all took a reflexive step back, but that seemed to hurt his feelings. "I- I mean you no harm."

His visage was not a pretty one. He might have been human once, or at least humanoid. Now he wore ancient and tattered robes, with a large hood covering most of his face. But even under the hood, his visage could still be seen to be scarred and burned beyond recognition. Possibly from the never setting sun of this island. His voice was harsh and strained. It gave out in random places, where he tried to swallow but could not. It was clear he had neither anything to drink nor anyone to talk to for quite some time.

"I was with my… my crew," he said. "I don't know… Where am I? I've been here for so long. Longer than me. Longer than I should have ever lived. Why am I still here? Am I being punished?" If there had been any fluid to spare within this man's frail body, he would have been crying. Before any of them could respond, his demeanor changed, and his voice grew louder (yet still fragile). "Are you my captors? Dragging me here to torture me? Do you find amusement in my torment? Are you even real? Am I? Was I ever?"

Alibaster was the one to respond, but it was clear even he didn't know how. "Those are… big questions."

Olivia was about to elbow him, but the before she could, the burned man fell away before their eyes. He was quite literally dust in the wind.

The three stared at the empty space for a second before starting their trek once more. They caught up to the fox and Koz, who had apparently finished their discussion and were ready to rejoin the group.

"Phantoms," the fox said after Olivia had described their accosting. "Memories of those who have been… misplaced. The lost lands are full of them. Usually they keep to themselves; gone wandering in their own minds as well as out here."

"Are they stories or Literals?" Olivia wondered. The fox didn't answer.

There was a dense fog up ahead. So dense it could be seen despite the harsh star above. It was like a thick curtain of gray. "Stay near one another," the fox warned as they approached. As a precaution, the four humanoids huddled a step closer to each other as the fox led them on.

"So what'd you two talk about?" Alibaster asked Koz as they went. This time Olivia did elbow him in the ribs.

It was difficult to read their expression in the oppressive light, but Koz's voice seemed a little too calm and casual. "Oh, the fox and I were discussing certain possibilities as to what I should do once we save Musty."

"Take him and run like hell out of the Paracosm," Alibaster said. "Problem solved."

Olivia was going to have another talk with him about his manners. There was a reason he only had two friends.

Soon enough, the wall of fog was right in front of them. The fox turned around to address them all. "We are about to cross into another domain for the disoriented, and the passages between them can be difficult to negotiate. They are made to keep the inhabitants of each island where they're supposed to be, which means they are designed to lead you astray."

Penelope gave a short chuckle. "So these places want to keep people lost, but lost where they are meant to be. Can't have them getting turned around in the wrong patch of grass, can we? And just to make sure they don't, there's a security measure that- let me make sure I have this right- makes them *more* lost." She shook her head. "This freaking place."

The fox ignored her. "I suggest you keep your minds occupied as we traverse the fog. Recite poetry or songs in your head. Work out complicated equations. Keep focused on something. It will make it easier to get through."

They all took a moment to think about what to think about. Penelope started half mumbling half humming the lyrics to some hip hop song from the 1990's (explicit version) which Olivia recognized but couldn't remember the name to. Alibaster's lips started moving and his eyes started darting, like he was reading lines from an invisible blackboard in front of him. Koz did nothing as far as Olivia could see. And Olivia herself…

She instinctively took her friends' hands in her own, and made sure Penelope took Koz's. She didn't really know what to expect, but getting separated from her friends *again*- in mind altering fog no less- wasn't something she felt like dealing with. The fox nodded, and turned back around, disappearing instantly in the compacted clouds.

Hand in hand, Olivia and company took their own steps forward. As they passed through the curtain which walled off lost stories, she started singing quietly to herself, and thought of her dad.

"Hello my baby, hello my honey, hello my ragtime gal…"

Chapter 33: The Shortest Distance Between Two Points Is a Lie

The intense light from the forever noon sun was gone in an instant. This was the good news. It was probably the only good news. Because as Olivia and the others blinked some sight back into their eyes, they realized that it hardly mattered if the sun was gone, because the fog which closed around them now would not allow them to see more than three steps ahead.

The fox spoke in a hush. "Stay behind me, be swift, don't wander off, and don't let your minds wander either."

Olivia continued her song in her head as she gripped her friends' hands tighter. As in the desert and the cave, they walked. She was really getting her step count in today. And without shoes, too. She was going to wake up with some blisters tomorrow. If she made it to tomorrow… If she woke up…

Send me a kiss by wire…

What was that? Up ahead. It looked like…

No. It was just a shadow. The fog making shapes.

Baby my heart's on fire…

She looked at her friends to see if they had noticed the shape. But they were all preoccupied with their own distractions, and not tripping over unseen debris. Why was she so jumpy? Walking through fog? Ha. Not even remotely dangerous compared to the life she'd led.

If you refuse me…

She heard a voice. A familiar voice. It wasn't coming from any of her friends, or the surefooted fox. Was it coming from her? She tried to touch her tongue to her lips, only to find that her mouth was closed. Nope. Not her.

Honey you'll lose me…

Oh! The shadow! It had been that shadow! She could see the shape again. It started out rather undefined, but became more vivid with each step taken towards it. It was speaking. And since only Olivia seemed able to hear it, it must be speaking to her. What was it saying? And why did the voice sound so familiar? It almost sounded like it was in trouble… In pain.

Then you'll be left alone…

The shape roared in agony. Something was happening to it. It needed help. Olivia ran towards the cry, leaving her friends behind in their own distracted haze.

She made it to the creature. It was scarred and blistered and mangled, just like the man that had come up to them a few moment ago (had it been a few moments ago?) had been. This person must have been one of those the fox had warned them about. People who were on a certain island, and then entered the fog and got super extra lost. They were hunched over on their knees, clutching their stomach and groaning. They might have been about to throw up.

Oh baby, telephone me and tell me…

"It's ok," Olivia said. "Are you…" she almost asked if they were lost, before stopping herself. Duh. Of course they were. "Are you hurt?" she asked instead, still feeling that the answer was pretty obvious.

"Thanks… to you…" the poor thing rasped. It looked up at her with hateful eyes; the only part of their body that seemed unscathed.

"What…?" Olivia asked. She looked closer, into the eyes; eyes which had looked back at her from mirrors her whole life. She gasped.

I'm your own…

"Ophelia?"

Who had said that? Had it been her, or the disfigured creature on the ground? Wait. No. She was the disfigured creature on the ground, looking up on the unmarred face of her executioner. She scrambled away like a wounded animal. *Mustn't let her near. Can't let her hurt me anymore. How does she keep finding me? Even in death I can never be free of her. Why must she haunt me? Why must she hunt me?*

"No!" Olivia yelled. "No, not again." She was suddenly back in her own body, staring at the scared and scarred form in front of her. She was not Ophelia. She was not. This was just like what happened in that mental prison where they had found Alibaster. "You can't trick me the same way twice," she called out to… whatever it was that was trying to trick her. The fog? The Paracosm? Her own mind?

"I am not you," she repeated out loud. "No more than two twins are the same person. We each were given autonomy- free will. You chose you're life. You chose to hurt people in the name of a greater good. And I chose to stop you. We are separate."

"Does that… help?" the strained voice of Ophelia's memory asked. "Help… ease the burden? Yet you killed me for this… greater good. Was your choice different than mine?"

"Yes," Olivia said bluntly. She was done playing around with this. She was done with the guilt and the nightmares. This wasn't a TV show. Sometimes morality had shades of gray. But not this time.

"But we both-"

"No," Olivia interrupted. "Don't start with that crap. I know just what you're about to say. 'You killing me makes you just like me.' Is that it? Well, no it doesn't. And no I'm not. You had killed entire universes. Whole creations popped like bubbles, their innards sent tumbling into the Nowhere. All to create your precious little omniverse. You told yourself that chaos would breed utopia, and you so desperately wanted your image of utopia to be fulfilled. But that was just a lie. You lied to yourself, and you used that lie to get from A to B. Used it to justify any of your actions. Someone had to stop you or you would have just kept going."

The phantom in front of her looked at Olivia's face searchingly. It was probably trying to find a new approach. "If you do not regret your actions, then why do you dream of me?"

Olivia had asked herself this question so many times. "Because I'm not like you. I didn't enjoy it. I took no pleasure in ending your life. It went against everything I am, everything I strive to be. It felt wrong. Deeply and truly. Right down to my core. When I think about it I want to throw up. And I know- I *know*- that the memory of you will haunt me and plague my dreams for the rest of my life. But that is a consequence I am prepared to accept, because you are gone, and my universe- and all the others- are safe from you.

"I do not regret the act of taking your life; I regret that I had to in the first place. I regret not finding another way to stop you. But if I had to make the choice again, I would. Because even with all that Fate Maker knowledge rattling around my head, I could not see any alternatives which would last.

You were sly and clever. You had caused incalculable damage to the fabric of everything, and had too many tricks from too many universes up your sleeve. Any prison or trap we put you in, you would have escaped from somehow. And as heartless or callous as it sounds: no one escapes death."

The phantom sneered. "You did."

Olivia said nothing.

The corpse-like figure before her continued. "But I think a part of you did not. A small part of your soul is gone for good. Lost to the aether beyond the veil."

"Maybe," Olivia admitted. "Maybe not. Frankly, I don't really care. I destroyed you by willing myself to die. I was prepared to sacrifice us both if it meant an end to your madness. I got incredibly lucky and was able to return mostly unscathed. So if a small piece of me stayed lost because of my actions, then that's a consequence I'll just have to live with."

Olivia crossed her arms. She was ready to wrap this up. "Quit trying to manipulate me; to prey on my guilt and disappointment in myself. What are you hoping to accomplish? Do you honestly think you could ever tell me anything I haven't told myself a thousand times? Did you think you'd just play evil armchair psychologist, and I'd crumble to the ground? That I'd give up if you told me how unforgivable I am? Well, sorry to disappoint. I'm not giving up. Not ever. Not while people still need help, and I have the means to give it. And maybe that's arrogant of me. Maybe I'm overstating my own importance. I don't know. What I do know is that I'm done letting the memory of the worst day of my life dictate all my days to come. While I know that choice will stay with me forever, I will not be dragged down by it or you any longer." She gave a shooing gesture. "So just get out of here."

The deep brown eyes glared at Olivia. The ghost knew it was beaten. In an unprecedented turn of events, Olivia had found herself in the fog of the lost. The form started to flicker and dissolve, like smoke released from a popped bubble. Before Ophelia dissipated completely, she said one more thing.

"We may be separate, but we are still mirrors of one another. So if a part of you did indeed stay dead that day, maybe a part of me survived. Food for thought."

And she was gone.

Olivia deflated. The "bad guys" were always trying to manipulate her or her friends. She was used to the monologuing, and the endeavors to break her spirit. They were all the same, in the end. Just transparent attempts to get her to question herself. But it was different this time. Sure she talked a tough game, but that was the job. How eerie it was to shake off such attempts when it could very well have been some projection of her own mind trying to break her down.

She closed her eyes. Even though Literals didn't need rest in the Paracosm, she still felt very tired. When she opened her eyes once more, she found herself back beside her friends, hand in hand. They were all still walking, and the fog appeared to be thinning. Penelope and Alibaster had glazed looks in their eyes. Whatever had just happened to Olivia, it seemed something similar was happening to them. Koz was leading them, their hand still in Penelope's, not affected in the least.

The fox, a few steps ahead of the rest, was speaking. "-almost there. Without the fog's influence, they should find their ways back to themselves."

Koz grunted distractedly.

Neither had noticed that Olivia had found her own way back to herself.

"Our companions assume a trap," the fox continued. "With the beast's heightened cognitive abilities, it is not an unwarranted fear. But somehow, I don't think so. It wants us distracted and out of the way until it's ready to deal with us properly. But hopefully by then, it will be too late. And it will have fallen into *our* trap."

"Yeah, right," Koz said with uncertainty.

What does that mean? Olivia wondered. Have the two of them been conspiring? If they had a plan, that was great. Why not share it?

Koz voiced Olivia's question themself. "Are you sure we can't tell them about it?" They nodded back at the three trailing them. Olivia did her best to make her eyes look unfocused and distant, but Koz barely even glanced at her before returning their gaze back to the front.

"Our friends will have their part to play," the fox said with care. "I wouldn't have called them here if they were not needed. But I fear they will… dislike certain aspects of the plan. They would disapprove of your part in things to come. We don't need to be at odds with our allies; our enemies are more than enough."

Olivia didn't like the sound of this.

"And you're sure there is no other way?" Koz asked.

The fox seemed genuinely apologetic. "I am sorry. Are you having second thoughts?"

"Well of course I am. But I'll still do it. Of course I will. And hey, not many people have died in service of the whole universe. Maybe they'll name a couple star systems after me." They sighed. "Not that any Literals will ever even know."

Died? Did they just say "died"? What was going on? What were the two of them planning?

Olivia was struggling to decide if she should let go of her façade of still being under whatever hypnotism the fog put her through. Should she just ask outright what the fox and Koz were going to do? Before she could come to a decision though, they all stepped out of the fog.

Before them was a scene that could only be described as desolate and dreadful.

Penelope and Alibaster blinked, coming out of their induced disassociation, muttering confused syllables as if jolted from sleep. They looked around.

"Welcome my friends," the fox said, "to the Wasteland of Efivabh."

Chapter 34: Meeting Lizard

The use of the term "wasteland" was apt. There was a persistent and immediate chill in the air, and a gentle but constant wind whistled in everyone's ears. There wasn't much light. As much as there would be before a very bad thunder storm, maybe. The sky above swirled with pregnant clouds, which threatened to open up at any moment. The little light that was allowed through was a slime green hue, giving everything a sickly feeling.

What once might have been buildings were strewn around the landscape. Original shapes and designs could now only be guessed at, as they were now little more than ruins and rubble.

The ground was dry and cracked, with something like black sand sprinkled here and there. Bones stripped of all skin and muscle littered the ground. They too were cracked and brittle, meaning they must have been there quite some time. In short, the place looked like an abandoned battlefield.

Had this place been real- Literal- once? Had there truly once been a holy land in the Tornadic nebula which had been decimated? Its very memory so obliterated that nobody even remembered where it once stood? Or was this place just constructed to be a parable? Did it even matter?

Figures could be seen darting behind the dilapidated structures. "I thought you said nothing could live here," Olivia whispered to Koz.

"No," Koz corrected. "I said that to wander here is to wander eternal."

"Can't we just go back the way we came?" Alibaster asked. "Once we find Musty, obviously."

"I'm afraid that's easier said than done," the fox said. "These places- the islands of the lost- they don't like to give people back once they've entered. They will do everything in their power to keep us here. Their very purpose is to lead people astray. That is why we have been granted entrance without much issue. After all, it's much simpler to become lost than to be found."

"So how do we get back out?" Penelope asked.

"I'm working on it," the fox said. "But for now, we must focus on your friend."

Penelope crossed her arms. "That's reassuring."

And for the eight millionth time, they started walking.

Eyes poked up from behind the broken walls as they went.

"Do we have to worry about them?" Olivia asked.

"They won't bother us if we don't bother them," the fox said.

"But we kind of need to bother them," Alibaster said. "They might have seen Musty."

"You can try and interrogate one if you wish," the fox said. He said it in the same way in which a subpar parent might dare a child who won't stay away from a lit candle to touch the flame. A "go on, see what happens" kind of tone.

And like the child, it wasn't surprising when Alibaster spitefully took the bait. He marched right over to the nearest of the hiding people; a five foot reptile with webbed feet and hands, crouching behind what might have once been a bookshelf, eating what might have once been a rat.

"Hi, how's it going?" Alibaster asked. The creature jumped with shock, but didn't move away. It looked at Alibaster with piercing yellow eyes. Alibaster continued. "Don't suppose you've seen a friend of mine? About yea high. Blue hair. Lots of pockets. Mammalian."

The lizard person seemed to consider, then put down the carcass of the rodent it had been gnawing at, and grabbed Alibaster by the lapels of his jacket.

"She grows weary in the harsh light," it said conspiratorially. Its voice was that of an iguana with strep throat. "It burns the bearer to not beware the burdens of the boastful. How can you breathe? How can you stop? How can you take your own life, when it is yours in the first place? One cannot steal what is already their own. We can only give up what we own. Will you give your life, my creature? To seed the stars? To become the dust you came from? Hope springs eternal, but eternity does not. It will all fall into the black. It will all become naught. Only when all the lights are gone for good will she grow beautiful once more." It was all spoken quickly, with such urgency that the poor thing couldn't seem to get the words out fast enough. Alibaster gently removed its hands from his coat.

"You don't say?" he said. He backed away from the reptile, who went back to its hovel, hunching over its rat as if nothing had happened.

"Well that was enlightening," Alibaster said once back with the group.

"I warned you," the fox said.

"Yeah, yeah, I get it. Islands of the lost. Fine. Now what?"

"Tread lightly. Keep your eyes open. Your friends could be any one of these wanderers. But I would not advise approaching any more of them unless you are absolutely sure it is him."

"How big is this particular island?" Penelope asked. "And don't say that space has no meaning in the Paracosm, or whatever. If you don't know, just say so."

Their four legged guide took a breath, as if about to speak, then reconsidered and said something else. "I… do not know. As large as it needs to be."

"Yeah, well so am I, but saying so doesn't really help us."

"So we need to cover a lot of ground pretty fast," Alibaster said. "Any ideas?"

All of them looked at each other knowingly.

"Besides splitting up?" Alibaster added.

Their gazes all fell.

"Ugh," he groaned. "Fine."

"Travel in pairs," the fox said. "I can search alone, but you all would do well to have another for support in this Waste. As long as you have companionship, you can never become truly lost."

"You know, I think I've read that exact fortune cookie," Penelope said.

Olivia really wanted to be paired with Koz in this buddy system. She wanted to question them about whatever they and the fox were planning, and why they didn't feel it necessary to tell her, Penelope, or Alibaster. But the thought of Alibaster and Penelope paired alone together…

Olivia often thought of locking those two in a room together and not letting them out until they worked out the crap between them and became proper friends, so this would have been an excellent opportunity to do something similar. But there was too much going on, and having them at each other's throats would not help anyone (specifically Musty).

"Penelope and I will go that way," Olivia pointed. "Alibaster and Koz-"

"We'll go that way?" Koz finished for her, pointing in the opposite direction.

Olivia nodded. "Fox, you go wherever you feel like, I guess."

"I always do," the fox assured her. "It is the nature of the form you granted me."

"If any of us find Musty, then we'll all meet back up-" she scanned the area until she found the tallest bit of ruin she could see- "there."

Everyone nodded their agreement.

"What if he's been… lost?" Koz asked. "Like the others here?"

"As his friends, you can hopefully act as the lighthouse to guide him back to himself," the fox said. He looked to the sky, at the green clouds that were fit to burst. "We must move swiftly. The weather here… well, I'm sure I don't need to tell you that an atmosphere can alter quite fundamentally due to enough manmade disaster. Who knows what those clouds are filled with, and what will rain down upon us when they decide to open."

And on that cheery note, they all set off.

Chapter 35: Don't Let This Place Get to You

"Nickel for your thoughts?" Penelope asked Olivia once they had searched the nearest patch of ruins, with no sign of Musty.

"Why a nickel?" Olivia asked.

Penelope sighed. "Because my dads called me Penny, so they had a joke when I was a kid that was like, 'A nickel for your thoughts? I'd ask for a penny, but this particular Penny has thoughts worth more than one cent.'"

"So… they're worth five?" Olivia wondered.

"So it seems. But hey, that's four more than everyone else's."

"That's kind of cute."

"So…" Penelope prompted.

"Let's see this nickel first," Olivia said

Penelope turned out her khaki pockets to show they were empty. "Funnily enough, I didn't bring any with me through my dreamscape. I'll write you an IOU."

Olivia scoffed. "Like you have an IOU on you either."

"Dude," Penelope said, seriously, "what's going on? You've been… I don't know. Distant. The whole time we've been here."

A mangy animal with a pitiful look in its eye darted across their field of vision. Olivia watched it until her eyes could no longer make it out. Then she spoke. "Do you remember what we talked about before all this? When we were on our way to Illetica?"

Penelope nodded. "Your nightmares."

"Since we've been here- in the Paracosm- I've encountered Ophelia a couple of times. Some memory or projection of her. The first time, I… I switched places with her. Briefly. When we were trying to find Alibaster in that prison. She was in a cell, and then I was in the cell as her. And then when we went through the fog, she showed up again. She was disfigured to such a degree that no one would have recognized her but me."

"And what happened?" Penelope asked. "What'd she say to you?"

"Oh the usual stuff. Mustache twirling villain crap. 'We are not so different, you and I'. All that. And it's like, yeah. No duh. But that doesn't mean we're the same either. Why do bad guys never understand the nuances of life? I told her off, and said that I wouldn't let the one action I had to take to stop her dictate how I live my life."

"Well that's good. So what's the problem?"

"I'm trying to figure out if I lied."

Penelope didn't know how to answer, and as they reached the next outcrop of fallen buildings, they searched the area in silence. The only beings who had taken refuge there were four crystalline creatures, with deep and prominent cracks lining their diamond skulls. Each was a few inches shorter than the last, and they stood side by side in order of height. They moved in delayed unison, like they were all mirroring one another, but the mirrors were a second slow. Olivia thought she had read about this species before, in Alibaster's files aboard the ship. These beings were all part of the same central mind, and it could be seen by their abrupt and tormented body language that they were all supposed to be moving perfectly in perfect sync with one another, and were angered that they could not. It was as if each body was a finger on a hand, but none of the fingers could properly coordinate with one another. They left the Earthlings alone, distracted by their own discontinuity, as Penelope and Olivia took a second to watch them.

"I saw us," Penelope said without taking her eyes off the creatures. "In the fog, I mean. I saw us. You, me, him. As we were as the Triad Fate. As we would have become if we had stayed like that."

"Do you miss it?" Olivia asked. When she had done what she did, she had kind of made the decision for all of them. First to become the Fate in the first place, and then to have it recalled. She never really gave Alibaster or Penelope a say in the matter.

"We've talked about this before," Penelope said. "I don't miss the power. Power corrupts or enables, and too much power is just plain paralyzing. I just miss having the answers. Having the proper pieces fit in the right places. That sense of unity of self. All my life I've been trying to force different parts of myself together. My humanity and my inhumanity, I suppose. Like trying to shove the triangular block into the round hole. And when we were that, all of my shapes became fluid and entwined with each other naturally, and then melded with you and him. It was the only time I ever felt like my soul wasn't screaming at me. Does that make any sense?"

"A little," Olivia said; which was what she usually said when Penelope tried to explain herself like this.

"Don't *you* miss it?"

Olivia almost said "A little" again, but stopped herself. "I don't know. I don't really think about it. It was kind of just something that we had to do. A means to an end."

They left the ruins- and the poor four part creature- behind and started heading in the direction of a ditch or crater that could be made out a little ways off.

"And now there's this place," Penelope said after walking in silence for several yards, as if having a conversation in her head and suddenly deciding to vocalize it. "My extrasensory stuff- my Time instincts or whatever are more cut off and confused than they've ever been. Like a part of me is in sensory deprivation. And this suit of small time helps a bit, but it feels like I'm confined in a hamster ball or something. I can't interact properly with the Paracosm. I don't think I was ever meant to be here, the same way nobody but me is supposed to go to the universe of Time."

"Hopefully we'll be done soon," Olivia said, "and we can get you back to the Literal universe."

"Soon has no meaning here," Penelope said tiredly. "It's a vague approximation that could mean anything from three seconds to a hundred million years."

They were kicking up dust as they walked, which was starting to tickle Olivia's throat. "Well I don't think we'll be here for a hundred million-"

"But don't you see?" Penelope asked urgently. "We could have been already. Like in the Land of the Lasting. The universe could have passed us by while we've been here, and we'd never know. Our Literal bodies could be dust, and we're just remnants of memories with illusions of sentience."

Olivia had been a step ahead of her, but now she stopped and turned around. "What are you-?"

But Penelope cut her off again. "Like Fathoms, we have no real autonomy. Just the parameters of motivations dictated to us by some random dreamer. Some little kid in Idaho, maybe. Or a sleeping sun a billion light years away. We aren't really here. We aren't really existing. We can't stop the nightmares because we're living in it. Insomuch as we are alive in the first place."

"Penelope-"

She looked at Olivia with the same wild fury and sorrow and confusion that had been on the face of the reptilian Alibaster had spoken to. "We are just thoughts here. Just notions. How does a dream keep time? How does a story? They can't. It's absurd. This is just a prison. And I know just who's keeping us here. That bastard, Krah. We never escaped. The last three years of my life have not been my own. I'm still stranded in the sea of Time in which he tried to drown me. I thought I escaped. I thought I was free." There were tears in her eyes now. Olivia couldn't remember ever seeing Penelope cry. "But it was just the illusion of freedom. Just another torment. And it worked. He trapped me in a life I would love, keeping me placid and content for months, and then manipulated the scenario into the worst thing imaginable for someone with my sensitivities. He played the long game, getting me as happy as I'd ever been just to rip it all away by bringing me here. How clever. The easiest way to break someone is by giving them something that can be broken. I'll never be free of him. Never. You stupid, stupid girl." She was hitting her head with the sides of her fists.

Olivia stepped forward and grabbed her wrists. "Hey, hey. Penelope. Penelope! Look at me."

The younger girl struggled against Olivia, but Olivia held her firmly, until Penelope had no choice but to stop and look at her.

"It's ok," Olivia said. "It's going to be ok. Listen to me. This isn't Krah." Penelope started to argue, but Olivia shook her head and kept speaking. "It isn't. We beat him. We did. You did. He's gone. I swear to you, he is gone. This- where we are, what we are doing now- has nothing to do with Krah. The last three years have not been a lie. He has not been manipulating you. All your choices have been your own. I am real. This timeline is yours. Not one of your possibilities, but *yours*. I need you to believe me. I need you with me. It's this place. Honey, this place feeds on your thoughts. Twists you all around. Islands of the lost, remember? I know the Paracosm is hard for you. I wish I could do something to help, but I can't. So I need you to be strong. I need you to see the truth of this place, and stay with me. Can you do that?"

Penelope sniffed and wiped away her tears. She didn't respond for a few beats, but eventually she nodded her head shallowly.

"Good." Olivia took Penelope's hand, and they continued on.

They passed one or two more dilapidated buildings with one or two more equally dilapidated individuals, before making it to the lip of the crater. Olivia couldn't have said why she had gone there. It just seemed like a good place to go. Like there was some unknown force drawing her there. It felt as if it were some sort of epicenter. As if whatever happened to make this place a wasteland started there and moved outward in one large ripple.

At the top of the lip, Olivia and Penelope looked down. The crater was just a pit of gray dust and ash, which had maybe a half mile diameter, and went down for probably half of that. And it was difficult to see in the insubstantial green light, but Olivia could have sworn she saw something move at the bottom.

"Come on," she said to Penelope. "We need to get down there."

They slid down the rim awkwardly, like a child trying to stand while going down a slide at the playground. The ground beneath them was loose and shifty, meaning there was very little traction. It was going to be a hell of a time climbing back up. But one thing at a time.

"Why are we doing this?" Penelope asked.

"Call it a hunch," Olivia said. She felt Penelope stare at her. "Just trust me. You get your instincts and feelings about all the Timey stuff; I have a feeling about this."

Penelope didn't argue.

They made it to the bottom, half burying themselves along the way as the various gray and black particles clung to their legs and feet like those of Father Christmas after a few rounds of chimney diving. They tried dusting themselves off, but there was really no point.

Thunder rolled from above like the sky was taking a deep breath that was about to be let loose. The atmosphere was suddenly charged and the air smelled like ozone and sweat. The Earth girls bristled at an unexpected chill, as if someone had walked over their graves. The heavy clouds were roiling and darkening; fit to burst any minute.

"What do you think the odds are that it's just rain in those clouds?" Penelope asked, looking to the pale green sky.

Olivia wondered if that would matter. What if it was just rain? How much? Would this crater fill up? Would they drown? She kept those thoughts to herself. "Come on," she said instead. "I saw something this way."

What she was looking for found them before they found it. It spotted them coming towards it, and barreled down at them like a bear protecting its cub. Both Olivia and Penelope lurched out of its path as the shape flew past them, and then it stopped when they were no longer in its immediate line of sight. It stood still, as if nothing had happened. It was covered in a hood and ragged clothes, like so many others of the lost islands were.

"What was that about?" Penelope asked in a whisper.

Olivia shrugged. "Short attention span?"

They tiptoed over to it, and slowly peered under its hood. Olivia's suspicions were confirmed as- from the side- she looked at the blank face and glazed eyes.

"Musty."

Chapter 36: Needling Questions

Penelope almost stepped in front of him.

"No, don't!" Olivia said quickly. "Don't get in his line of sight."

"Why not?"

Olivia swallowed drily. "Hang on. Let me try something." She slowly reached her hand right in front of the Illetican's face, and Musty started snarling. Actually snarling. Like a wild boar or something. Olivia quickly retracted her hand, and the noise died in his throat.

"I think he's lost," Olivia said. "But like, in a hostile way. Protecting what he sees as his home, or nest or whatever."

"Maybe something the Reaver did," Penelope said. "To stop us from getting him out. We can't rescue someone who we can't even get close to."

"Possibly," Olivia said. "Probably." Without entering his vision fully, she tried speaking to him. "Musty? Musty, can you hear me? It's Olivia. Olivia Jones. We met once, a few years ago. I'm a friend of Alibaster's. I was at Cal Cyte's Final Goodbye. Do you remember me?"

He didn't react at all.

"He must be pretty far inside himself," Penelope said. "He can't seem to hear us. He only notices outside stimuli when it's right in front of his face, and then forgets about it when it's not." She gave a short chuckle. "He literally can't see past the end of his nose."

Maybe the fox would know what to do. Or maybe Koz could help him, like they had helped Alibaster pull himself back together from the imprisoned smoke. The tough part would be getting Musty out of this pit without letting him see either of them. Maybe they could blindfold him. Then what? Shove him up the slope of the crater? Climbing back up on their own would be difficult, let alone while carrying the dead weight of a lost soul.

"What's that?" Penelope asked, interrupting Olivia's worried thoughts.

She looked to where Penelope was pointing: Musty's right hand. At first Olivia didn't know what she meant, but then she saw a faint shine of light reflect off the young man's palm. Slowly, and still while remaining on the fringes of his peripheral vision, she took his wrist and lifted his hand up, turning it over to show- what was that? A needle? A sewing needle. Planted right in the center of his palm like a metal splinter.

Olivia and Penelope looked at each other in utter confusion. They couldn't even think of any question to ask, because the discovery was just so bizarre, they didn't really know how to process it.

"Maybe we should try pulling it out?" Olivia suggested.

Penelope shrugged, but gave a by-all-means kind of gesture.

"Gee, thanks," Olivia mumbled. With Musty's wrist in one hand, she positioned her other over the needle with her thumb and forefinger in a claw shape. She touched the needle, but before she could even start to pull, Musty let out a shocked gasp, as if he had just pinched a nerve.

"Sorry, sorry," Olivia said reflexively. But she found that she was talking to the air. Both Musty and Penelope were gone. She spun around. Where could they have gone so quickly from inside a crater? But it became immediately clear that she was no longer in the crater at all.

The space around her now was anything but a wasteland. It was lush and vast and green. The grass beneath her was thick and came to her waist. There were trees scattered about, each one at least the size of a moderate skyscraper and easily as wide. Flowers of varying bombastic colors and stylized petals grew anywhere and everywhere, the smallest of which were as tall as Olivia.

The sky was still green, at least. But not the faded, defeated green that it was before. Now the sky was a seafoam shade, and wispy clouds flowed along in a way which made the sky seem more like an ocean at low tide, lazily moving with the currents. The two suns that sat a short distance apart were warm, but not oppressive.

Oh, and also there was the giant face of Penelope.

It was fixed in the sky like a tear in the world. Gigantic eyes peered down at Olivia, making her feel very much like the last bug left in an ant farm. It looked like Penelope was trying to say something. Her mouth was moving, but no sound came out.

"What?" Olivia asked, yelling as loud as she could for the giant to hear.

"I said-" Penelope said, suddenly Penelope sized and by Olivia's side- "that I think you just travelled through the eye of the needle."

"Oh," Olivia said. "Huh."

"You touched the thing, and then just vanished."

"And now you're here too," Olivia said.

"Yeah, I touched the thing."

"Which means we're both stuck here."

"It looks that way, yeah."

"Awesome."

The tear in the sky which Penelope had been peering through mere seconds ago was now… well, it wasn't gone, but it was less obvious. Less defined. It stood out as a discolored spot, like a bruise in the sky of a sicklier green. Penelope looked around. "What do you suppose this place is?"

Olivia shook her head. Wherever they were, they needed to get back to the Wasteland, and get Musty back to the others.

Penelope- while facing the opposite direction- tapped her knuckles softly against Olivia's arm. "Hey, you know that old hypothetical about how many angels can dance on the head of a pin?"

"No," Olivia admitted.

"Oh, well it's a thing."

"Ok."

"So I don't know the answer to that one…" Penelope turned Olivia around, and found several very angry looking creatures with red eyes, horns, and sharp teeth coming towards them. "But give me a second, and I think I could figure out how many demons can hide in the eye of a needle."

Now, that might not have been too fair. They had both seen many numerous beings of alien species, and it was never smart to judge a book by its cover. But, yeah, Olivia had to admit it; the group of creatures about to mow them down definitely looked like they belonged to the cover art of a dark fantasy videogame. These "demons" rode on semi-equine creatures that were categorically not horses. They looked like skeletal, four legged, single-toed, furry velociraptors, and galloped at considerable speed. So neither Olivia nor Penelope thought it particularly prudent to try and run.

The demon creatures and the monsters they rode reached the girls, and circled around them, so any remaining hope of escape was quickly quashed. They wore heavy armor with spikes, and each had a weapon strapped to their backs. Some brandished maces, some broadswords, and some had spears. One held a flag or standard. It hung from a vertical bar attacked to a longer pole, was the same color of the sky, and in the center sat the symbol of a tree with intricate root work.

"Hold," one of them- probably the leader or general- said. His voice was gruff, but kind of awkward with all those large imposing teeth jutting out of his mouth. It kind of sounded like he was speaking with too much bubblegum in his mouth.

The others pulled the reins on their steeds, which made a number of half whinny half growling noises, and stopped with the Earth girls completely surrounded.

Olivia pulled Plexerious' shield off of her back (it was so light, she had almost forgotten she carried it) and pulled it in front of herself and Penelope. Not that it would do much good, since the demons were on all sides, but it made her feel a little better.

"There will be no need for that, milady," the head honcho said with a snarl that might have been interpreted as a chuckle. "You two are visitors. We so rarely receive visitors, but when we do, they are treated as honored guests."

"Oh," said Penelope, visibly relaxing the tiniest degree, "that's… nice."

"Where exactly is 'here'?" Olivia asked.

The commander nodded to the one with the flag. This demon, the smallest of the bunch, got down from his mount, and planted the flag firmly in the ground. The others moved out of the way as quickly as if he had just planted an explosive, and Olivia readied the shield. What happened next happened almost too fast for Olivia to properly perceive. The flag was there, waving lightly with the breeze, and then it wasn't there, and in its place, several miles off, stood the large imposing tree which had been the flag's icon. And all around the tree stood buildings. Buildings that hadn't been there an eye blink ago. Buildings with absurd yet beautiful architecture which no description could do justice. The city beyond almost seemed to twinkle in its own glory, like a solid mirage. It looked like what one might consider paradise.

"Welcome, dear friends," said the leader, gesturing to the city beyond, "to Efivabh."

Chapter 37: One for the Price of Four

They were now riding towards the city on the backs of the dinosaur horses. Both Olivia and Penelope gripped the soldiers who were guiding the steeds they rode. The beasts ran swiftly and deftly, easily traversing any shift in terrain or elevation. As they went, the General (who had identified himself as Diobtiel) explained away several of the questions Olivia and Penelope would have asked had they not been negotiating the carnivorous mounts under their legs.

"The Unprecedented Catastrophe occurred," Diobtiel said through the whistling winds and his many large teeth. "Efivabh was thought lost. Our structures decimated, our gardens burned, our people displaced or dead. The land which once was perfect was now tainted. The city now a blemish where it once was a blessing." He took a moment before continuing, his blood red eyes moistening in the corners. "Then there was this place… A single seed survived where the rest of the forest was incinerated. This haven, this bolt hole hidden away from an otherwise unforgiving universe, is all that remains of the glory of our paradise. The one tiny shard of glass left over from a mirror which has fallen and splintered."

"How?" Penelope asked. "How did that happen? How does this place exist?"

"We do not know for sure," Diobtiel admitted. "Perhaps it was the saving grace of the Creator. Her guiding hand shepherding the few survivors of the Catastrophe through the Eye, and into a place so well hidden, that Her flock and the children which came from it could never be hurt again. Perhaps not. We are just grateful it does exist."

As wonderful as all this was, Olivia's mind was preoccupied. The further they rode away from the tear- or what the General had called the Eye- the further away they were getting from their friends. And she still had no idea how to get Musty out of that crater, or why the needle which led to this splintered Efivabh was stuck in his hand. It felt like she was reading a book out of order, and that there was something she should understand, but just couldn't fit together the little pieces of context she had.

The closer they got to the city, the more that large tree stood out. Sure the other trees they had passed had been big, but this one- the one which had been the symbol on the soldiers' flag- was mountainous. It blocked out the suns as they reached its shadow. She shivered at the sudden temperature drop. Olivia had never felt more like an ant. One falling leaf would be enough to crush them all. If she looked straight on, the bark of the trunk created a wall around the horizon. And the buildings- all the structures which sprouted up beneath and around it- they seemed to somehow be part of the tree itself. Like they were each grown from the gigantic seeds which could have dropped from the branches; twisting and rising into those absurd and beautiful shapes. It was obvious that this tree was holy to those who lived in Efivabh.

Many cultures throughout the universe had some legend about an original spark which gave the rest of the universe life. This spark often came in the form of a tree. But to actually see an interpretation of the Tree of Life up close…

Olivia had travelled the universe, and seen infinity first hand. She had battled gods and monsters with powers and abilities almost beyond comprehension. But she had never felt so small or insignificant as she did right now, under the shadow of Efivabh's great tree.

Penelope summed it up rather quaintly. "Nice tree."

Olivia almost burst out laughing at the criminal understatement. This drew her out of her head and away from her humbled mindset.

"You should have seen it in all its original glory," said the soldier Penelope rode with. "None of us have, we are too young. But our ancestors were all nurtured by the tree's predecessor, before the calamity."

Olivia could only imagine. If this was indeed just a splinter, then the original must have been the size of a planet.

"Where are we going?" she asked once they reached the city proper. Large beams of sunlight shot down through the holes in the leaves and branches, shining down on various buildings like heavenly spotlights.

Diobtiel pointed a large clawed finger towards the tallest building. It had three spiraling towers all connecting to a center castle-esque structure which had a domed glass roof. The bricks and materials which made the four buildings were the soft color of peach ice cream. Blue, gold, and lavender flowers the size of minivans grew like ivy upon the stones and bricks. "Our queens will want to meet you. And I imagine you would like to see our other guest."

Before Olivia had a chance to ask who the other guest was, Penelope broke in with a quick mutter to her. "What kind of utopia has a ruling class?"

The kind in storybooks, Olivia thought but didn't say.

They dismounted once they reached the primary structure. The girls' chaperones led them inside, where they were all immediately greeted by the most impressive greenhouse garden Olivia had ever seen. All the plants there were more subtly sized, but it was still stupendous. It was like an inside forest. There was even a slight mist emanating from hidden sources. The light that came in from the glass ceiling reflected and refracted at multiple points, using the mist to create several small rainbows.

They walked along a path of the softest grass Olivia had ever felt. The green tickled her bare feet like feather vanes. A complicated looking butterfly with four wings of shifting hues fluttered by her face. A number of alien insects and birds trilled and buzzed from their hidings spots within the flora.

"Even inside, one should never be apart from the gift of nature," said a voice.

Olivia and Penelope turned towards the voice, and saw a figure sitting under what was presumably the Efivabh equivalent of a willow tree. Its trunk was a fine silver and had leaves and flowers the color of coral and magenta. Sitting beneath the foliage was a delicate looking woman. Her skin was pale, her eyes were milky white, and her toffee colored hair was thin and wispy, reaching down to her waist. Dead twigs, dried leaves, and wilting flowers were situated throughout the locks. She sat cross-legged, with bare feet caked in mud up to the ankles. Her clothes were stark white and loose fitting; flowing with the slightest suggestion of a breeze.

She looked human enough, which was not what Olivia had expected. She would have thought that this person all the soldiers were now bowing to would look a little more like their fire-and-brimstone selves. Olivia and Penelope both bowed their heads politely, but did not fall to the ground in prostration like the others. They had been in a number of these situations. They wanted to be polite and respectful, but still show that they were not the subjects of this realm.

The woman raised a sculpted hand upon a dainty wrist, urging all the soldiers to rise. "You may leave us," she said. The soldiers obliged the request. Once Olivia and Penelope were alone with the woman, she spoke again.

"Welcome to our haven," she said to the visitors. "We are the queens here. You may call this iteration Autumn."

Both Olivia and Penelope tried to look around casually, but saw no others.

Autumn politely ignored the confused looks. "I believe this is the point in the conversation where you introduce yourselves."

"Oh, right. Sorry. My name's Olivia," said Olivia.

"Penelope," said Penelope.

"And how do you find yourselves here Olivia, and Penelope?"

Oh boy, this is going to take a minute, Olivia thought.

But once again, before she could say anything, Penelope spoke. "We were looking for a friend who had gotten lost in the Wasteland. We found the needle thing stuck in his hand. It brought us here."

Autumn nodded an almost imperceptible nod. "Our shelter has chosen a new protector. He came to us some while ago. The 'needle thing'- as you call it- seemed to have fixed itself to his person."

"That explains why he attacked us," Olivia said. "He was protecting this place."

Penelope crossed her arms. "But we still got here fairly easily."

The queen considered the two before her. "He must have believed instinctively that you were not a true threat to us or our people."

"He didn't look too capable of thinking or believing anything," Penelope said. "He was just a mindless attack dog out in the Wasteland. Did you do that to him?"

Ok, now we're bordering on impertinence, Olivia thought. *Penelope's specialty.* Hopefully the queen didn't take offense and throw them in a dungeon or something. What would the dungeon of a proverbial paradise look like? Olivia imagined a rather middle lane motel room. The kind that didn't have little soaps or free wi-fi.

If the queen took umbrage with Penelope's tone, it didn't show. But in the sort of way where leaders and royalty were taught not to give anything away, and to keep their emotions in check. Behind the nonplussed face, an obvious fire could be seen kindling in Autumn's eyes.

Olivia averted her own eyes from the queen's gaze, trying to keep a semblance of respect intact. They still needed information, and the last thing they should be doing is treating this audience like an interrogation.

The queen spoke. "For his service to us, your friend has been granted the benefit of residing here in Efivabh."

Olivia lifted her head, immediately forgetting why she had lowered it a second ago. "He's here? Musty's here? How? What do you mean?"

Queen Autumn seemed to ponder her explanation. "Everyone is a sum of parts. They have multitudes; layers, which- if one is careful- can be peeled back and separated. What you saw in the Waste was the outer shell; a physical force to throw at any who would mean this place harm. His other self is here as our honored guest."

Olivia glanced Penelope trying to hide a look of disgust. She knew exactly what her friend was thinking about. Several months ago, when Ophelia had attacked the Fate Makers, Chairman Mawteze had escaped, and had manipulated Penelope and the timeline to his own ends so that he could be rescued. In doing so, he had to nullify that nasty free will business, so that he could take control and allow the proper events to occur to lead to his salvation. He chucked Penelope's soul into a ravaged universe of Time, basically leaving her for dead while he used her body to save himself. If Fate Makers could be killed, there was little doubt in Olivia's mind that Penelope would have done away with the slug for what he had put her through.

The queen must have noticed the expression. "You may think it odd or unfair to do such a thing, but I assure you there was no ill intent in the split. It was simply the only way to proceed. To make sure one does not lose their mind in the Wasteland, the mind must be placed elsewhere."

This calmed Penelope a little bit, but she still didn't trust herself to speak.

"Can we see him?" Olivia asked.

"By all means," said Autumn. "Another of us will take you too him presently. Forgive me for not going myself, but I am more a stationary queen, than one of hustle and bustle."

Before Olivia could begin to wonder how the term "hustle and bustle" could have possibly found its way to a splinter of an alien story within the fifth dimension, the form of the queen changed before their eyes.

The woman before them now had dark skin, thick and curly snow white hair, wore clothes made of animal hide and comfortable furs, and was not frail or sickly looking as Autumn had been. The only thing similar between the two was the eyes. But where Autumn's had been milky white, these new ones held a colder, more calculating stare.

"You may call this iteration Winter," she said.

Olivia *ahh*-ed to herself. Now she got it. There were multiple queens, but they all shared one body. Many forms in a single host.

Winter stood up, towering a good foot above Olivia (and a good foot and a half above Penelope). They both felt the icy white gaze of the new queen, and this time even Penelope averted her eyes. "Your companion is near," Winter said. "Let us go to him."

Olivia and Penelope nodded their agreements, too frightened and awed to speak.

They moved away from the willow, and followed Winter deeper into the indoor forest. They were both amazed at all the alien flora and fauna which surrounded them. Even Penelope, who hated nature and claimed that there should be such a thing as "outdoor air conditioning", was impressed by the splendor of this Efivabhian castle. A muskrat-adjacent creature with long twig-like antennae and spider eyes even rubbed the side of its head against Penelope's ankle and she didn't shoo it away. The Christmas miracles had started early this year, it seemed.

They tried not to stand right behind Winter as they went, as their seemed to be a chill radiating from the queen's person. A few flakes of snow fell from her as she walked. (Assuming it *was* snow, and not royal dandruff.) And wherever she stepped left a thin layer of frost on the grass underfoot. Olivia resisted the urge to make a bad dad joke about Winter's literal cold shoulders.

At last they came to a clearing; a flat space devoid of anything but the soft grass.

"Your friend is here," the queen said, indicating the field. It was the first time she had spoken in several minutes and the unexpectedness of her voice was jarring and matter of fact.

Both Olivia and Penelope looked around. There was no Musty. Was he invisible? Had he somehow been transformed into turf? Olivia had heard the phrase "All flesh is grass", but this was-

Wait. There. Something shimmered in the sunlight.

"Look," she said to Penelope, pointing at what she saw. They headed to about the center of the field, and found a single flower among all the grass. Well, supposing it could actually be called a flower. It looked more like a fancy weed. It had drooping puce petals and a withering center stalk.

"A yard pest," Olivia said. Penelope shook her head. "An Illetican wildflower," Olivia explained, remembering what Koz had told her. But there was something different about this one. It reflected sunlight. What kind of flower…?

They looked closer, and found that the whole thing was incased in some sort of crystal. Like a protective shield perfectly molded to the yard pest's shape, cocooning it from the outside world. But why? What for? And what was this random thing from Illetica doing there?

"Oh," Olivia said. It seemed her flesh to grass theory hadn't been that far off course.

"You don't think…" Penelope wondered.

"I do. Unfortunately."

"As you can see, your friend's mind is perfectly safe from harm," Queen Winter said. "And here it will remain; safe of being lost and corrupted. Forever."

Chapter 38: This Flower's Kind of Musty

They were not in the Literal universe. The Paracosm didn't follow exact structures or rules. Everything in the fifth dimension was metaphorical. So when someone said they'd separated someone else's mind from their body, of course there wasn't just going to be a brain in a jar and a body on a slab. It would have to be a little more symbolic than that.

"To become one with this garden, one's spirit must be transformed into a plant which is meaningful to that person," Queen Winter explained.

"The yard pest is Musty and Koz's flower," Olivia told Penelope.

"Interesting," Penelope said, not very interested. "How do we get this thing back to his body in the Wasteland?"

"You do not," Winter said, with an accompanying chill that made the girls shiver. An aura of ice emanated outwards, covering a circle of grass under her with an aggressive layer of frost. "I brought you here to say your farewells. The Eye of Efivabh has chosen your companion as its champion and protector. It is his duty to defend our shard of paradise from harm until he falls."

"Yeah," said Penelope, all respect gone from her voice, "that's not going to happen." She reached for the crystal encased flower.

"No," the queen said, motioning a hand towards Penelope. Penelope froze. Like, she actually froze. Her body was suddenly encased in a thin layer of ice, mirroring the flower incased in its crystalline chrysalis. She was stuck in the position of reaching down to pluck the flower. For the second time in a single adventure, Penelope had been turned into an effigy of herself.

Olivia froze too, though not in the same way. She just didn't know how to respond. It all happened so fast. Did Penelope just die? Or was she just incapacitated? Olivia's mind was whirring, but her body and mouth refused to move.

"You are not a threat to this place," Winter was saying, as if she hadn't just frozen one of Olivia's best friends alive. "That much is obvious, or you would not have been allowed passage through the Eye. But you must understand, that your friend is-"

She stopped. There was a cracking sound which interrupted the queen's speech. It came from Penelope. Or rather, it came from the ice around Penelope. A fracture was split down the frost from her torso down her left leg. Another crack sounded, as another split appeared. And another. And one more. Lines of water dripped down the ice, as if it were melting. More and more appeared, watering the grass like chilled rain. It *was* melting! Quite quickly, too.

In no time at all, all the ice melted or evaporated from Penelope's body, as if she had been placed over a hot stove. She stood up from her bent position and gasped for breath.

Olivia rushed to help her. She was dripping wet from head to toe, but she was alive.

"How did you…?" Queen Winter started.

Penelope gave her a glare. One of her glowing-blue-eyed glares which told people they had not even the tiniest conception of who see was or what she was capable of. The queen went tight lipped with awesome speed. "The suit of small time the fox put around me," Penelope said to Olivia. "I wasn't sure if I could manipulate it. I wasn't going to try, just in case. But needs must when you're freezing to death."

Olivia kind of understood. "You fast forwarded the ice so it would melt faster?"

"Yeah, that's the good news." Penelope pushed a hand against the side of her head. The glow of her eyes dimmed. "The bad news is that some of the shield is gone. Whatever illness this place was giving me is coming back. Not much yet. It's like a brain freeze, funnily enough. But I don't think I should try and use the shield anymore. If I wear it out completely, I'll be as incapacitated as I was before."

Olivia touched Penelope's elbow reassuringly. "We'll worry about it later."

"One thing at a time?" Penelope asked with a pained smile.

"Exactly." She was still worried about her friend, though. Who knew what she could handle in her weakened condition? And who knew what else they'd have to go through? Olivia sighed. *And miles to go before I wake,* she thought. She took Plexerious' shield from her back and handed it to Penelope. "Hang on to this for me."

Penelope took the giant dinner plate and studied it. She gave an *"Are you sure?"* look, and Olivia nodded. "Not worried about me, are you?" Penelope asked, sliding the strap on and placing the shield on her back. It made her look a bit like a turtle. *Is that how I looked this whole time?* Olivia wondered. *A turtle in pajamas?*

"Incredibly," Olivia said truthfully. *Now, for the matter at hand.*

They both turned back to face the queen, only to find a new woman in the place of Winter. She was thin, had dark skin as well, and had a head of champagne colored hair, pulled back in a tight afro bun. She wore a slimming suit of gentle pastels and floral print, and high heels which gave Olivia vertigo just to look at. Her white eyes looked like the light of a moon.

"Spring, I presume?" Penelope asked, trying to bluster through her headache.

"You should never presume anything in the company of the Queen of Seasons," the woman said. Her voice was soft and melodic, but still held authority in the undertone. "But you are correct. I am Spring, the renewal of life. The beginning of the circle of rebirth."

"I don't suppose you'll let us take our friend here, and be on our way?"

The third queen (or was she the first?) didn't answer straight away. Instead she walked effortlessly on her towering heels to the nearest tree, and plucked a fruit from its branches. It looked like a blistered kumquat. She broke the fruit in half, perfectly splitting it down the center, picked a small seed from inside, and dropped it on the ground. In no time at all, a sprout appeared.

Spring walked back over to her guests, and handed them each a half of the fruit. "Eat, and learn the truth. Then we will discuss the fate of you friend."

Olivia and Penelope were both wary enough to sense a trick of some kind. After all, Spring's predecessor had just tried to freeze Penelope alive, and they had turned Musty's mind into a flower. So there really wasn't a lot of trust to spare when it came to this four-in-one queen.

But they really needed to move this along. They needed to get back to the Wasteland and their other friends, and they couldn't go back without Musty. So if this would somehow expedite the situation, then whatever. If this was a trap, then bring it on. The sooner they fell in, the sooner they could escape and get on with their own crap.

Olivia and Penelope bit into their fruit halves, and saw the story of Efivabh unfold around them.

Chapter 39: Bored of Paradise

The green world of Efivabh fell away, leaving Olivia and Penelope staring at a darkness of only each other. Then there was an explosion and a millions tiny lights flew past them.

"Once upon a time there was a universe," said a voice, which might have been that of Spring. "A big, wonderful, terrible, complicated universe which never gave reprieve or respite to those who lived within its sphere." An undefined figure appeared. One which was larger than planets, made of smoke and stardust, and watched intently as the stars passed by. "The Great Onlooker, who had witnessed the first embers of creation unfold into the endless blaze, decided that this universe was too chaotic and unjust. There must be some sort of break in the constant cacophony. Somewhere in which a chosen few could exist and be free from the rest of the cosmos.

"Thus the Great Onlooker became the Great Creator. She took the unfettered chaos and fashioned order and peace; sowing these seeds into a great tapestry of land which would be called Efivabh. This land would be a paradise for those who lived there, and it would all center around the First Tree. The Tree was a majestic, powerful display of nature in a free yet lawful form. The Tree would spread out its roots and touch all living things within Efivabh, and all would live, learn, and thrive from the fruit which grew from its many limbs."

Olivia and Penelope watched all this occur as it was being narrated, like a time-lapse documentary.

"All would find haven here, so long as they ate the fruit. For eating from the First Tree was to open one's mind. Life depends on curiosity; on the eternal quest of knowledge and understanding. We must grow and change and evolve just as nature intended. Stagnation is poison, and contentedness is death. The Creator knew that a paradise could only be eternal if its inhabitants were forever reaching. For a time it worked. All was well. We learned, grew, and with each day became more than we were yesterday.

"But after several centuries, the Creator's worst fear came to pass. People stopped eating the fruit. The inhabitants were becoming too satisfied with what they already knew and could accomplish. Taking a rest was one thing, but so many of Efivabh's people were no longer searching, no longer questioning, no longer striving. 'What was the point of this endless quest for betterment,' they would wonder, 'if we are already in paradise?' And perhaps you can guess what happened next."

The girls watched as the planet sized tree started to wither before their eyes. "The Tree needed its fruit to be eaten. Its knowledge needed to be absorbed. It needed curious minds to water its roots. After all, what is the point of a question that is never asked?"

The Great Tree didn't die like a normal tree. It seemed more like it was coming undone. Growing in reverse. Shrinking from its gargantuan size, getting smaller and smaller like a grape shriveling into a raisin. As it shrank, all the other plants of Efivabh started to dry out and die as well. In no time at all, only the familiar Wasteland was left. All that remained of the Tree was its seed the size of a meteor. Then that too shrank down, folding in on itself until nothing remained but a sewing needle and the hole in which the seed had been originally planted.

Koz had been wrong, Olivia thought. The Great Catastrophe hadn't been a nuclear war like many believed. It had just been people who had given up on bettering themselves.

The narrator spoke again. "The Great Creator either left Efivabh, ashamed of Her subjects, or died off with the Tree. None know for certain. All that remains is the Wasteland, where wanderers and nomads fear to tread. And our splinter of original paradise, left to the few true servants and their descendants by the last breath of the dead Tree."

The images or illusions disappeared, and they were all back in the garden with Musty's frozen flower.

Chapter 40: Protector to Defector

"Do you understand now?" Spring asked, standing before them once more. "Do you understand why your friend is needed? We need a protector. Our haven's last light is fragile and needs to be guarded from extinguishing. The Eye of Efivabh chose this boy."

See, that just wasn't sitting right with Olivia. "But did it?" she asked. The moonlight eyes were on her. Olivia swallowed and continued. "Ok, I get that this place needs security measures of some sort. A pocket dimension inside a sewing needle can't be the safest place to live. I would understand if the 'Eye' as you call it had chosen, say, Plexerious-" *if he were still alive-* "or some other person of considerable power. But Musty? He's just a kid. He wants to be a doctor, and I doubt he's ever been in a fight in his life. He's a good guy, but if something came to extinguish this place, I really don't think there's much he could do about it."

The queen seemed nonplussed. "It is not for us to question the ways or choices of the Eye."

"But what if the Eye didn't choose him?" Olivia asked. "What if something else chose Musty?"

"What 'something'? For what purpose?"

"To trap him, and keep my friends and me occupied."

"The Reaver?" Penelope asked quietly.

Olivia shrugged. "We already knew it had thrown Musty in the Wasteland. It's not a big leap in logic to say it might do a little more to keep us busy while it goes around sweeping away stories." She looked back at the queen. "How isolated are you and your people? Do you know what's going on out there?" She pointed upwards.

"In the Wasteland?" The Queen scoffed. "Nothing ever happens-"

"Not in the Wasteland. The Paracosm. You do know where you are, right? Where Efivabh is?"

The queen bristled. "We know that our home had been... relocated in a higher dimension. One of ideals and symbolism. Though we have no other contact with this dimension's inhabitants."

Olivia wondered if that was true; if Efivabh had been Literal once, but was granted sanctuary in the Paracosm when the splinter was created. Or maybe it was all just part of the story, and the Paradise had always resided in the fifth dimension.

"Ok, fine," she continued. "Have you ever heard of a creature of nightmares? One that- when at full power- can take over the Natives and Fathoms of the Paracosm, and create an army of itself?"

Spring cocked her head. "What of it?"

"Have you not heard?" Olivia asked. "It's escaped its prison. It's here, in the Paracosm."

The queen looked frightened. Genuinely, properly scared. So scared, the iteration of Spring ceased to be entirely, leaving in her place the incarnation that could only be Summer.

The fourth and final queen was the tallest of them, but just by an inch or two. She had a very well sculpted face; all high cheekbones and symmetrical angles. Her hair was a strawberry blond, and cut in a bob just at the neck. She had freckles spattering her nose, cheeks, and bare arms like haphazard constellations. She wore a dark sundress and fancy sandals with elaborate looking straps that wound their way up to her knees. Behind pentagonal sunglasses, a light was dimmed. Olivia got the feeling that, in contrast to her immediate predecessor, Summer's eyes were the white at the hearts of stars. Those eyes would definitely rival Penelope's own piercing blue gaze.

"We do not speak of that… abomination here," the new queen said. "There is no place for the devil in paradise."

"You can't ignore it," Penelope said. "Since this creature- we've been calling it the Dream Reaver, but don't ask me why- has escaped, it's been growing in power."

"Killing heroes and gods," Olivia added. "Attacking anyone who could pose a threat to it."

"Efivabh poses no threat to that… thing," Summer said coolly. "Efivabh poses no threat to anyone. Our military is little more than a royal guard. We are hidden, we keep to ourselves. It would serve the creature no purpose to assail me or my people."

"None that we can see," Olivia said. "We have no clue what's going on in that thing's head."

Penelope nodded. "And if it really is the one who planted the needle on Musty, then it definitely knows of your hidden little slice of heaven."

"This only proves that we need a champion now more than ever," the queen argued.

"One that the Reaver itself picked?" Olivia asked.

"So what would you have me do? Leave my world unprotected?"

"I expect you to release the mind of that poor boy- who is most definitely here against his will- and find a new protector."

"What happened to the one before Musty?" Penelope wondered. "Couldn't you just- I don't know- rehire the last person to get their hand stuck on the needle?"

The queen's face furled into a tight frown. "Being the champion of Efivabh can be… taxing to the soul. Your friend's predecessors are no longer viable."

"Well that's worryingly ominous," Penelope said.

"They all went mad, to be blunt," the queen said. "The Eye- the needle- is the last surviving piece of the original Tree. A life from which more life sprung. To keep in constant contact with such a powerful presence can prove mentally jarring. Eventually the protectors break down and try to destroy the needle; try to silence the constant thoughts and information being poured into their heads. At which point they are relieved of their duty, and a new host for the needle is found." She motioned to the frozen flower. "That is why we implemented this new process. If the mind is separated from the host, it cannot be broken by the suffocating knowledge and will of the Tree."

Olivia and Penelope shared knowing looks. They looked back at Summer. "The Wasteland isn't what drove those people crazy, is it?" Olivia asked. "All those broken creatures we saw, they were all your past protectors. You just dump them in the Wasteland when you have no more use for them."

The queen looked scandalized. "What else could we do? Keep all those tainted souls here, in the heart of utopia?" She shook her head. "I think not. The Wasteland is the only safe place to put them. It resides within the lost isles already. What are a few more wayward spirits to such a place?"

"That's terrible," Penelope said. "Why are those who claim to be the most enlightened always the most terrible?" she asked under her breath.

"Give us our friend back," Olivia said. She was suddenly feeling very anxious to leave Efivabh. "Please. We need to get him out of here, then out of the Wasteland, and back to his Literal self. After that- after everything- we will find a way to help all those people, and find you a willing champion."

"Those are not insignificant promises." The queen crossed her arms.

Olivia hardened her gaze. "They're hollow promises if the Reaver isn't stopped. If it's allowed to gain full strength-"

"If it hasn't already," Penelope interjected.

Olivia sighed. "Yes. Thank you," she whispered quickly. She blinked, turned back towards the queen, and tried to find the gaze she had held a second before. But for some reason she just couldn't summon the intensity. Hopefully her words would hold enough authority. "If it gets to full power and isn't stopped, it will ravage all of the Paracosm, which in turn will affect the collective unconsciousness of the Literal plane. It will be able to manipulate dreams, stories, and even belief itself to rewrite the universe and turn everything towards its own image. Nowhere will be safe. Not even Efivabh."

"So you might as well give us the flower," Penelope added, "because no protector you've ever had could stand up to that."

"But you can?" Summer asked, patronizingly.

"Us and our friends…" Olivia thought about how best to explain, fighting the urge to say that this wasn't their first rodeo.

The queen stepped closer, and the light behind her sunglasses seemed to burn brighter, and reach into their minds. Olivia felt the same itching in her frontal lobe which she felt whenever encountering telepaths. But this felt slightly different. Like it wasn't her mind the Queen of Seasons was reading, more like her heart, via her mind. She was reading intent, purpose, and truthfulness.

After an eternal moment of looking between Olivia and Penelope and back again, the queen stepped back, pursing her lips in thought. "Perhaps you are correct. Perhaps your friend- or even the Eye itself- let you pass into this splinter because they knew you could do what others cannot. That you can help when all seems helpless."

"We should put that on business cards," Penelope muttered to Olivia. Olivia shushed her.

"Very well," Queen Summer continued. "You may take the flower and return it to the empty shell in the Wasteland."

Olivia bowed slightly. "Thank you." She bent down, and gently plucked the encapsulated weed from the ground. Even through the crystal tomb, it felt warm and alive. It was an odd sensation. She had never held a metaphorical representation of a living mind before.

"How are we supposed to get back to the Eye?" Penelope asked. "I'd really like to never ride one of those prehistoric looking ponies again."

"The Eye is everywhere," said a familiar voice which was no longer Summer. The frail figure of Queen Autumn was sitting down where the previous queen had been standing. She pointed a near skeletal finger upwards, towards the glass dome ceiling. Behind the fragmented rainbows and the sea of green sky, a tear opened up. Or perhaps it had always been there, and was just once more visible. "Reach towards it," Autumn said. "Let it take you."

Olivia and Penelope did as instructed. For a moment nothing happened, and they both started to feel a little silly. But then, as they looked up, arms outstretched, they saw that the light at the fringes of the Eye were snaking their way down. Ribbons of green touched the tips of their fingers, then grabbed hold fast, like Chinese finger traps.

And they were pulled out of the hidden city of Efivabh with all the grace of being dragged upwards by bungee cords.

Chapter 41: He Must Really Hate Sewing

"Ahh!" was the first thing Olivia heard once she and Penelope were back in the Wasteland crater. In conjunction with the exclamation she also heard a cry of, "Shype!"

The first sound had come from Kozmoklor, and the expletive had been emitted by Alibaster. They both jumped back as Olivia and Penelope appeared out of nowhere on either side of the rag-clothed Musscivite.

After the initial jump scare, the two Illeticans recognized the two Earthers, and started bombarding them with sounds and syllables which were curtailed with question marks, but gave no actual indication of meaning.

"Huh?" said Alibaster.

"What the…? Where the…?" wondered Koz.

"But you…" Alibaster jumped in.

Eventually the fragments grew into actual sentences.

"Where have you been?" Alibaster asked.

"The fox found us, and said that he couldn't detect your-" Olivia's- "mind in the Wasteland anymore," said Koz. "He found us and brought us here. The last place he felt your presence."

"We found Musty," Alibaster continued. "What's left of him. What the hell's been happening?"

Olivia was about to answer all their questions (which was a nice change of pace as far as she was concerned; doing the answering instead of asking), but before she could speak she noticed her hands. She noticed they were empty.

Oh no, the flower.

Had she dropped it as they were leaving Efivabh? Was it back on the other side of the needle's eye? Did it plummet back to the ground and shatter like glass? Oh, god. Had she just effectively killed Musty?

She looked around the dust and sand at her feet frantically, hoping she just dropped it upon reentry. As she looked- letting Penelope explain the situation to the others- her eyes met the fox's. He stood behind Alibaster and Koz, and his blank eyes locked with hers for a moment. He nodded to her, and it took her a second to realize he was actually inclining his head; using it to point behind her.

Musty.

She turned to face him. He was blinking the hard, long, dazed blinks of someone who had just been woken up by a punch to the head.

"Guys," Olivia said with a flutter of a hand behind her. They all stopped talking, and Musty suddenly became very wobbly. He looked as disoriented as a child who had spent his entire afternoon at the playground roundabout. Olivia caught him, really hoping he wasn't about to throw up. She wasn't stoked at the idea of having to wash off more vomit from her person.

Alibaster and Koz both flew to Musty's aid, and Olivia gave them all some breathing room.

"Musty! Hey buddy," said Alibaster. "You're ok. Take it easy."

"What happened? Are you hurt?" Koz asked.

As they both fussed over him only like chosen family would, Musty looked confused as he stared back and forth between his childhood friend and his significant other.

"Ali? Koz?" he asked with the clunky and slurred speech of the inebriated or the numb tongued. "What are you both…? I was… something. I… hm."

He looked past them, his eyes still fighting off the glaze that had covered them. He saw Olivia. "Hey. I know you."

Olivia gave a small smile and a slight wave.

Musty looked at Penelope. "I don't know you."

"I'm Penelope," she said. "Nice to… meet you. I guess."

"Mm," Musty agreed.

"Your nickname is really dumb."

"Mm," Musty repeated. "What's been… happening?" he asked everyone at once and no one in particular.

Penelope shook her head at Olivia. "You do it this time. I hate giving the exposition."

Olivia acquiesced. First, she explained to Musty just where they all were and what had happened up to the point where they all decided to rescue him. Alibaster or Koz jumped in at various intervals to give their own commentary. Afterwards, Olivia explained to everyone what had happened to Penelope and herself since the group separated. She gave as abridged a version as she could, hitting the main plot points of Efivabh still being alive to a degree inside the needle on Musty's hand, and how they had to save his mind from imprisonment there because he had been deemed protector over the pocket dimension.

At the end of her rather rushed tale, no one but Musty looked any the wiser.

"I remember," he said. He had regained most of his faculties during the retelling, and could now stand without assistance. He looked at his palm. The needle stuck out of it like the thorn from the paw of Androcles' lion. Musty continued. "While I was trapped, I was fed information about Efivabh. I learned what it was, how it was destroyed, and what the duty as protector entailed. And I learned other things. Things about what happened to my predecessors, and how they went mad by the words this needle spoke to them. The words the last spark of the Great Tree imparted. The Tree which founded the fabled city… Which had spent eons granting its inhabitants knowledge and wisdom. They had separated me from myself so that I couldn't act upon the wisdom being given to me. Because the citizens of Efivabh had been wrong. The words hadn't driven the other protectors mad like they thought. The Queen of Seasons just refused to understand. She just banished them all to this Wasteland, where they did eventually lose themselves. The Queen had refused to listen. Refused to learn." The young Illetican suddenly had a very dire look in his eye. "Which is against everything that Efivabh is supposed to stand for."

He plucked the needle from his skin, his face twitching slightly at the discomfort.

Then he took it in both hands.

And he snapped it in two.

Chapter 42: Wasteland, Maybe!

Musty dropped the two halves of the needle to the ground, and for several heartbeats everyone just stared at him in varying degrees of shock and horror. Well, it would have been several heartbeats if Olivia hadn't felt like her heart had just stopped in her chest. Even the fox looked distraught.

"What… did you just do?" somebody asked. It may have been Olivia, she wasn't entirely sure. *Did he just destroy the last remnants of Efivabh?* she wondered; her mind racing to come up with any other- less terrible- possibilities. *Or had he just closed the portal to enter the splinter city? Or is it something else entirel-*

Before she could finish her thoughts, the world exploded around them. Or more accurately, it exploded from under them.

From the ground, things clawed their way to the surface with awesome speed, shooting skywards from every inch of the dust and ash. It happened so fast and so simultaneously, for several seconds none in the group could discern just what was going on. Everyone was just grabbing on to one another as the world shook, and looking around for some spot to find shelter or safety.

But they were at the bottom of a rather steep crater. There was really nowhere to escape to.

"Come on!" Musty said over the all consuming rumbling. He ran- as much as one could run on top of vibrating sand- towards the edge of the crater floor, scrambling up the wall a few steps until he found a foothold.

The others followed suit, not knowing what else to do. They dodged large stalks of something, as more and more shot forth into the sky. It was like running through a minefield, except the minefield wanted to shish kabob them instead of shish ka-boom them. They all dodged and weaved, and weaved and dodged, which was pretty difficult to do considering they had no idea where the next stalk would be coming from. Luckily, no one was impaled (which was not a sentiment Olivia believed she had ever had to be grateful for before) and they made it to Musty's side unscathed.

And they all watched as dozens of stalks rose and rose and kept rising some more. They looked like they might topple under their own height, but before they could, something amazing happened.

The stalks all started to wind around one another, twisting and pulling themselves taut into a larger, steadier, more unified thing. It was like hundreds of strands of twine coming together to form a rope. And as they all joined and solidified into one, everyone started to realize just what was rising from the ashes. Rising from its own ashes.

"The Tree!" Olivia said.

"How can-" Penelope started.

Musty cut her thought short. "All of you! Do what I do when I do it! Or else the trunk will crush us into the wall of this hole as it grows."

Since beginning her travels, Olivia had started making a mental list of sorts: *All the ways I do not want to die.* Up until that sentence, she had one hundred seventy-three items on that list. Now there were one hundred seventy-four. (It might be worth noting that items one hundred sixty-six onwards were all added during her time in the Paracosm. This really wasn't helping her warm to the place.)

The circumference of the Tree's trunk- along with the rest of it- was growing exponentially. It would indeed be upon them any second.

"Now!" Musty yelled. He leaned forward, arms outstretched, and grabbed the nearest of the combining stalks. It kept growing, unhindered by the Illetican now attached to it, and lifted Musty higher and higher into the air.

"Musty!" Koz yelled.

"No time!" Alibaster yelled back. "Everyone, go!"

Before Olivia could talk herself out of it, she did exactly as Musty had done. After grabbing the nearest stalk and holding on for dear life, she too was hoisted up and away. Despite the roar of growth, she heard short gasps and shocked utterances of the others grabbing hold from somewhere beneath her.

There was no time to make sure everyone had made it, because from above her- through the wind and displaced dust kicked into her eyes- she saw Musty let go of his own perch, kicking off from the trunk like a swimmer kicking off from the wall of the pool.

She realized what he was doing. He had let the tree pull him out of the crater, but now he- and by extension everyone else- had to jump for it, or else they'd just keep going up and up with the Tree for who knew how long. A fanciful thought flitted through Olivia's mind briefly as she watched Musty hit the ground rolling. The thought involved her and her friends living out the rest of their lives in the Tree of Efivabh. Surviving high above the world in house sized foliage, subsisting off the fruit the Tree provided, and living a life secluded from any monsters or bad guys. It was a nice- if not entirely selfish- thought, which only lasted about a quarter of a second, before she too had been raised over the lip of the crater, and needed to jump free.

Don't land on Musty, don't land on Musty. The thought looped in her head as she fell. *And also don't die.* From what height had she jumped? It was definitely higher up than when she had wrestled free of the Reaver entity that had been disguised as a Script Angel. She hoped it wasn't more than fifty feet. She once heard of someone- a pilot or something- who had needed to abandon his plane without a parachute, and survived a fall of several thousand feet. For some reason the thought didn't comfort her as much as she felt it should have.

She didn't need to add "falling to my death" to her list of ways she didn't want to die. There were already at least two dozen variations of the same fearful idea within said list. But still, after all she had done and still needed- still wanted- to do, a death now would really be unfortunate. Not to mention anticlimactic.

Luckily she did not die. Nor did she hit Musty, though she did get uncomfortably close to kicking his head. She hit the ground and rolled as many times as she felt adequate. She didn't know if kinetic energy worked the same way in the Paracosm as it did the rest of the universe, but it made her feel better to dissipate it at any rate.

She got up and turned around just in time to see the rest of the gang jump as well. Alibaster's limbs flailed as he fell. Koz fell gracefully, like they had just jumped from a diving board. Penelope jumped in a rather devil-may-care way, like a comic book character. Olivia wouldn't have been surprised if she had landed with a bent knee and a fist to the ground.

Even without the accoutrements privy to the average humanoid life form, the fox seemed to be doing just fine. He scaled the side of the increasingly immense trunk- presumably with claws and cunning- and jumped free at the allotted time with the others.

None of them seemed especially hurt by their landings.

This was the positive.

The negative was that Musty was correct in his previous prediction. The Tree was still growing. And not just up, but out. Past the edges of the crater. The crater had only meant to be the hole to fit the seed, after all. Bark and roots and everything else came spilling forth like dough overflowing from a popped can. The ground kept shaking, as mounds of dust were shifted and shoved.

"Run," was all Musty said now.

None of them had to be told twice.

They all turned and ran as quickly as they could in the opposite direction of the Tree.

Huh, Olivia thought. *I've never had to outrun a plant before.* She made a mental note to start another list, this one of all the things she had ever had to flee from. She also pondered how ironic their deaths would all be if it came at the hands of the Tree of Life.

The team just barely kept ahead of the growing mass. Olivia was sure everyone was wondering the same thing she was: What had Musty done? Why had he done this? What was he hoping to achieve?

If they survived to ask him, the answer had better be pretty damn good. Olivia didn't know Musty too well, but she was getting an urge to throttle some sense into him. But more than likely she would have to stop Penelope from doing just that before she got her own chance. Or even possibly Alibaster or Koz. Everyone seemed pretty miffed at the boy.

Instinctively, they headed towards the nearest batch of ruins. None knew if the decaying buildings would provide any sanctuary from the ballooning mass of bark, branches, and roots, but it was better for the morale to run with a destination in mind.

They all reached a cluster of walls which were half torn down (or half built up, if one considered themselves an optimist) and each threw themselves toward some illusion of cover. Someone might have yelled something like "Hold on!" but if they did, the roar of the Tree quaking the earth beneath them coupled with Olivia's own fragmented prayers of *Let us live let us live let us live* screaming in her head rather drowned out any external warnings.

The roots which had been spreading towards them had reached the now stationary targets. On some level, Olivia knew that the Tree was probably not purposely targeting them. So to label them as "targets" might not have been too accurate. They were simply in its path as it grew (as was everything else in the Wasteland). But right then, as the world under their feet shook and cracked and broke- threatening to reach up and drag them down into hell below, like the limbs of wooden zombies- it felt pretty fleking personal.

The thick brick wall- behind which Olivia, the fox, and Koz were taking refuge- shook like delicate china. It had been the corner of a building- still attached to a half circle of concrete flooring- which meant the right angle which they hoped might protect them was quickly becoming acute as the quaking threatened what was left of its structural integrity. A bit of spreading root quickly lifted out of the ground under the fox, who had strayed a foot or so away from the solid floor; lifting him a few feet into the air before he could yelp with shock and jump down. He retreated back to the wall, and the root dove back into the dust in a dolphin-like arch.

Several yards away, Alibaster, Penelope, and Musty were all crowded into a sturdy looking alcove. They were crouched and covering themselves like they might for an earthquake. Olivia glanced at them to make sure they were ok, before realizing that they were getting closer.

At once, Olivia and her party understood what was happening, and pressed themselves into the wall as much as their bodies would allow without merging with the structure altogether. The trunk of the Tree had reached them, and it was sweeping aside everything in its path. As they were pushed forward in their own little angle of false safety, they watched as other- less substantial- bits of scenery got demolished along the way. But they were less worried about that than they were about smashing into their other friends at alarming speed.

Both groups of three had thick walls behind them, and no one was very eager to see how snuggly those walls fit together with them in the middle. An image flashed through Olivia's mind of her brother Tracey. He used to empty small bags of potato chips onto his open sandwiches, then crush them between the two pieces of bread before eating them. She imagined a similar experience awaited her and her friends within a few seconds.

None of them could jump off the ride without risking either A: the other crumbling ruins falling down on top of them, or B: random stalks of Tree shooting out and getting lucky.

How's the rescue mission going? a part of Olivia asked as the whites of the eyes belonging to her friends in the alcove became clearer and clearer.

Oh, you know, another part of her said. *Can't complain. Could be worse.*

You're only lying to yourself, the first part said.

She wondered what death would be like. This was not the first time she ever wondered this. This wasn't even her first time wondering this today (or whatever passed for days in the Paracosm). One might be forgiven for assuming that Olivia was probably the only person in the universe who knew what death would be like, seeing how she had died and gone to an afterlife of sorts. But that place where she had sat in her nursery with Neddy-K had been her death as a Fate Maker. She worried her death as a mortal wouldn't be nearly as lucrative.

As they were swept within arm's reach of the others, her thoughts turned to that of her sister Patrice, and how she would always force her dolls together to kiss. It was always really forceful. She would just smash the two dolls faces together repeatedly; almost violently.

What a weird way to go, Olivia thought. She thought it sad, but not very surprising, that she only really thought about her family in these moments, a hairsbreadth from the end.

But just as they reached the alcove… As the two semi-structures were about to connect like the fingers of Adam reaching towards those of God…

They stopped.

Everything stopped.

The wall in which Olivia's team stood shaking. The immense prescence of the Tree, only a few meters behind them. The roots, the stalks, the shuddering ground…

All stopped.

All that could be heard or felt was the combined heat of the ragged, trembling breath the six of them were currently producing in their exceedingly close quarters.

Olivia herself was intimately close to Penelope, who stood across from her. Had she done this? Olivia wondered. Had she used her shield of small time to stop the world?

But no. On some deep level, she knew even Penelope would have no power over the Tree of Efivabh. It did what it liked, when it liked, and did not bow to any rules of Time or reason.

"It's over," Koz breathed with relief.

"No," said Musty, "not over. It's all just beginning." He smiled. The smile quickly died when he saw the looks of quiet rage on everybody's faces. "I had a good reason," he argued. "I promise. Ali, give me a boost up."

The alcove and the two walls were currently situated in such a way that none of them could see what was going on outside of their little closet. Like two hands cupped together after scooping up a bug. Which meant they couldn't get out without climbing over. Alibaster made his hands into a stirrup, and helped his friend scale the bricks. Musty sat on top, and swung his legs over onto the other side. As he looked down towards the others, his smile returned. "You're all really going to want to see this."

Chapter 43: He Speaks for the Tree

All six of them sat atop what moments ago was just their refuge. What they saw was no longer a Wasteland. From the gigantic Tree, spreading outwards in all direction was… green.

From the dead ash, grass grew. From the grass came flowers, bushes, and trees of all shapes and hues. From the barren buildings, vines and moss stretched upwards. From atop the Great Tree, miles above them all, they saw millions of leaves and buds grow from the many numerous branches. Even the sickly color of the sky seemed to change and brighten. The other inhabitants of the Wasteland were coming out of their own hiding spots, laughing or cheering or straight up jumping for joy.

They were all, in this moment, baring witness to life.

And as they all watched, their anger at Musty fell away. They could not begrudge someone who had just breathed life back into the lifeless.

Well, *they* couldn't. But the Queen of Seasons could.

"What have you done?" she asked, in her Winter incarnation. Several of her demonic guards flanked either side of her. Where they had appeared from was unclear. It seemed like they had just stepped into being out of nothing. She looked up at them in their perch. Her snowy eyes were blazing with cold fury at Musty.

"I freed you," Musty said, either ignoring her rage or being too swept up in all the new growth to notice. "The needle was the last remnants of the Tree's seed. It had been screaming at each protector to be planted once more. But you wouldn't let them."

"You had no right."

Musty pshawed. "I had all the right I needed."

"Where we were…" the Queen started. "Inside the Eye, we were safe."

"You were trapped," Musty rebutted. "You were hiding. You were so scared that Efivabh would fall as it had before, that you wouldn't even let it grow again. For a utopia which prides itself on enlightenment and growth, that isn't a very progressive mindset." Now he looked to the soldiers. "Personally, I'm a guy of science. I don't believe in much that I can't feel or study for myself. But you, all of you… The Tree, and maybe this Creator which you claim to worship, was giving you hope; giving you another chance. But you were too afraid to take it. You refused to take that leap of faith. You eat the fruit of the Tree, and you gain knowledge and perhaps wisdom. But what use is knowledge if you're hidden away? What is the point of wisdom if it isn't shared? Small minded people often say that knowledge is power, and it is, just not in the way they think. Because knowledge is more powerful shared than hoarded. And now you have a chance. Efivabh is restored to its proper glory for the first time in generations. Instead of fearing it will fall again, use this gift to share the story and the wisdom. Teach everyone and anyone about what your world has to offer. If you do, then it can never fall to the tides of stagnation again."

"Enough of this," Winter said. "Arrest him. Arrest them all."

The soldiers made no move. They looked at each other.

"Well?" Winter blazed.

"He is right, myladies," the ranking man Diobtiel said. "It is time for our world to bloom once more. You can stunt its growth no longer. Nature must rebound. You should understand that more than anyone."

In the briefest of moments, in less time than it took to blink, the Queen of Seasons flashed through all four of her iterations, before settling back into Winter. It was if they had all conferred with each other in that instant. Going through their own cycle of life in less time than it takes to inhale. She still did not seem happy. But she was outnumbered by her soldiers. She was tight lipped, and for an endless minute just stared down at her men. But finally, she gave the tiniest, most imperceptible nod, acquiescing to those around her.

All the soldiers bowed, showing deference even in their disobedience. Without another word, she turned and stalked off, her men following in her wake. Before they all disappeared from view entirely, the faintest shift in the Queen's figure could be seen, and Winter turned to Spring.

"So what now?" Penelope wondered.

"Efivabh keeps growing," the fox said. "When this place is restored to its former glory, it will break away from the chain of lost islands, and find its way into the Paracosm proper. All the poor wretches of the Wasteland should recover their faculties, and start anew here or elsewhere."

"You did it," Koz said to Musty in disbelief. "You saved all these people. You saved this whole world." They squeezed his hand tight. Musty suddenly looked very bashful, and all the authority he had just demonstrated to the Queen was gone. He said nothing, but squeezed Koz's hand back.

Alibaster clapped him on the back. "Good job, brother."

"Well this is lovely and all," Penelope said. "But I meant what do *we* do now? How do we get out of here?"

The fox smirked. "I might have some idea as to that."

As if on cue, a shadow passed from overhead. They all looked up to see the cause, and as a shape descended, Olivia could have sworn the thing flying towards them looked just like a ship.

Not a spaceship.

A ship as in a boat. A *ship* ship. A wooden sailing vessel, just flying through the air. And with it came an eerie, constant gust of wind.

"You recall my informant?" the fox asked as the ship landed close- but not too close- to them. "The sentient wind which found where the young Illetican was imprisoned? Well, while we were all separated, I contacted it again to ask for assistance. It seems to have procured a vessel for us."

The five humanoids stared in amazement as sails blew, and wood creaked and groaned from the strain of landing. A rope ladder fell over the side of the hull. Something else swept down to greet them. It was small, mostly green, squawked, and had a single eye set in the center of its face above its beak.

"Ah!" Penelope swatted it away, as it flew towards her. It squawked again, and flew back to the ship, offended.

A parrot. An actual parrot.

The fox jumped down from the wall, and the smile widened a degree. "All aboard."

Chapter 44: How the Story Must End

They had all boarded the great ship. It was obvious that some of the team (primarily Alibaster and Penelope) were dubious of the saving grace that literally fell out of the sky, but they were too eager to leave Efivabh to protest.

Besides the parrot (which spent its time flying from one mast to another and making noises like it was trying to cough up a tire) the ship was completely empty. There was no one at the helm, or dealing with the sails, or manning the mizzenmast, or whatever crews on sea vessels actually did besides drinking swill, saying "arrg", and guffawing in unison at the plights of others.

And yet, the sails still adjusted, the wheel still turned (and presumably so did the rudder), and the ship still flew. And at all times, there was that same eerie breeze. The fox's informant, it seemed, could man the craft easily enough by itself. Had it owned a ship? Sails needed wind, but it was hard to believe the opposite was true. More than likely it had found or stolen the vehicle upon the fox's request. Some poor storybook pirates were probably waking up from a hearty night of plunder only to find themselves suddenly landlocked.

At least, Olivia assumed it was a pirate ship, due to all the skull-and-crossbones insignias on the sails. The skulls only had one eyehole in the center of the foreheads. Cyclops pirates. Well, that explained the one eyed parrot. *How fun. Let's hope none of them have the means to come looking for their ship,* Olivia thought as she watched the fog of the lost islands recede. Even the Tree and its quality of unreachable height, like Jack's beanstalk, fell away from view. Now they just traveled through a sea of sky. Space and stars heaved like an ocean below them in an impossible and beautiful display.

After they all spent some time exploring the ship, the fox called them all back together. "We'll be taken somewhere we can decide our next plan of attack against the beast," he said. "I fear what the creature has accomplished since we've been… preoccupied." He deliberately did not look at Musty as he said it, Olivia noticed. "But there is still hope," the fox continued. "The destruction can be reversed, and the monster stopped." That time he did not look at Koz. Olivia wondered what that implied.

"Well our first priority should be getting Musty out of here," Alibaster said, leaning against a mast with his arms crossed. "That was the whole point of the rescue. To get him out of this dimension, and back to the Literal realm. Away from the danger."

At this Musty shook his head defiantly. "Nuh-uh. No way. I'm here to help. I was tasked to protect Efivabh, and even if this Reaver creature only did it as a trick, I still have a duty. Efivabh has just been replanted. If this nightmare creature is half as bad as you all say, then I can't just abandon the people there, or anywhere else in the Paracosm."

Olivia had never considered Musty courageous. She had hardly ever considered him at all. But in that display, she became quickly impressed. Even if she wasn't too pumped about putting someone else in danger, she had to admit that they could use all the help they could get.

Alibaster- it was instantly clear- did not agree. He had a look on his face which he rarely ever had. Anger mixed with concern. It was the look an older sibling gave the younger when the younger wanted to do something the older considered really stupid.

"Oh yeah?" he asked. "And what makes you suddenly so qualified to battle monsters?"

"What makes you?" Musty shot back. He looked from Alibaster to the other two thirds of the Key of Three. "What makes any of you qualified to deal with this?"

"A good deal of prior experience," Penelope muttered.

Alibaster shot her a look.

"What's that supposed to mean?" Musty asked.

Musty did not know that Alibaster had been imprisoned by the Fate Makers, or that he had taken up what some referred to as "the good fight" against evil in the universe. More than likely he was sparing his brother, so that Musty wouldn't worry about him. It was also possible that Alibaster kept the illusion of "travelling Kertsrawian exceptional" going because it was the last lie of normalcy his life held. The last piece of him from before his father died.

Before Alibaster could decide how to answer, Koz chimed in.

"He's right," they told Musty. They hadn't left his side since they all got on the boat.

Musty gave Koz a confused- almost betrayed- look. "What?"

"The whole point of saving you from the Wasteland was to get you away from danger," Koz argued, "not throw you into more."

Alibaster nodded agreement at his newfound ally's words.

Musty threw his hands up dramatically. "Well then we should all leave!"

Koz shook their head. "Not with the Reaver still loose."

"So you get to help, but I don't?" Musty was obviously affronted. "You get to chuck yourself at the monster, and I have to watch you from the sidelines? How is that fair? I don't want to watch people I love fight for their lives, but I am damn sure not going to let them do it without me."

It was hard for any of them to argue the point. The only thing worse than letting your friends walk into hell was letting them walk alone.

Olivia touched Alibaster's shoulder. They locked eyes and had a very brief conversation of facial expressions. Alibaster sighed, all the frustration falling from his face, leaving only weariness and perhaps a little anguish. He shoved his hands into his pockets and walked over to Musty.

"Come on," he said, motioning to the front of the ship (which Olivia was ninety percent sure was called the bow). "We need to talk."

Musty was taken aback by this sudden change of tone. He followed Alibaster wordlessly.

The rest of them stared at each other for a silent moment.

"I'm… sure I have something to do," the fox said, trotting away from the awkwardness as quickly as his little legs would carry him.

"Ditto," said Penelope. "And that something is finding a hammock to lie down in. Can you actually fall asleep here? Ah, I guess I'll figure that out." She wandered off towards the crew quarters.

Koz hugged themself in the wind. They looked deeply sad. It was an anxious sort of sad, like they were dreading something yet to come

Something was going on with them; it had been for a while. And Olivia was very tired of being kept in the dark.

"Come with me," Olivia said. "We need to talk too."

With the guys needing privacy at the ship's bow, Olivia decided to take their conversation to the rear. For a moment, both she and Koz leaned over the edge, and watched the liquid night ripple and bubble beneath them. It was almost like the whole boat was upside-down in an ocean. Conceptually it was both amazing and puzzling. It didn't help matters that Olivia was pretty sure she saw the colony squid drifting just beneath the surface, now only the size of her hand, instead of that of a moon.

Even though she had instigated the need to converse, she waited for Koz to speak first. Eventually they did.

"I love it here," Koz started. "In the Paracosm. I love being here more than the Literal realm. Before Musty, the physical universe just seemed so unbearable. So without imagination or magic. But this place… This place *is* imagination. It's creation, and belief, and soul. I would stay here all the time if I could." Tears started to well in the corners of their eyes. They took off their glasses and wiped them away. "That's why I was in the hospital… Before. I tried… I thought if I was asleep… I took these pills… It didn't work. Obviously. And now, I'm glad it didn't. But I still feel more alive- more real- here than I do there."

Olivia did not speak. What could she possible have said?

"I would do anything for this place," Koz continued. "Anything. That's why I stayed with you all in the first place. If I could help save the Paracosm- save my haven- I would. And now… it turns out I can."

When it was clear that they wouldn't give any more information on their own, Olivia spoke. "What are you going to do? What do you and the fox have planned?"

"The fox doesn't want me to tell you," Koz said. "He thinks you'll try and stop me. But you'll find out sooner or later, and I'd rather tell you now than have you find out in the thick of it."

"Koz?" Olivia was now getting worried.

"That farmer, the one in the story the fox told us. The farmer from Illetica who was chosen to fly into the Abyssmal and trap the Reaver within his mind. He had a very rare and very special connection to the Paracosm. Before, the fox told us that the man was chosen at random. But he wasn't. He was chosen due to his deep rooted connection to this dimension. And that…" Koz suddenly got choked up, and they had to grab the side of the ship to keep from falling over. They took a moment to collect themself. "That connection, it passed down to the daughter he never met. Then that daughter passed it down to her child. And so on and so on. Until…"

Olivia's eyes widened. "You? You're his descendant?"

Koz nodded, and spoke without lifting their eyes from the watery night. "It was this mysterious connection which the Natives were able to manipulate and use as a prison for the Reaver. It wasn't serendipity which caused us to meet at the Swan and Swine. It was that connection, drawing you to me like a spiritual instinct. It was making sure I got to you and the fox, so that… so that when the time comes I can…"

"Do what the farmer did," Olivia said. She felt like she was going to be sick. Then she realized that as an empath Koz was probably feeling her own anguish mixed in with their own. She tried to wrangle her emotions. "You're going to sacrifice yourself. Kill yourself, so that the Reaver can be contained again."

"I'm the only one who can do it," Koz said. "The fox explained it. I'm the only one who can hold the nightmare back. We need to weaken the Reaver like before. Then it can be corralled, and backed into a corner of my mind. Then I'll leave the Paracosm, wake up on Illetica, steal a coffin, and head to the Abysmal. It won't be easy; fighting that… *thing* off that whole time. But if my forefather could, then I suppose I have to be strong enough as well."

Olivia didn't believe what she was hearing. "No. No way. I won't allow it. This isn't going to happen."

Koz almost laughed. "It's not much of a choice. Me versus the rest of reality? What would you do in my position?"

Koz thought they were asking a hypothetical, not knowing that Olivia knew exactly what she would do in their position, because she *had* done it. She had sacrificed herself for the greater good. So she knew just how hypocritical she was being by telling her friend not to do the same, but she didn't care. "There has to be another way," she argued. "There has to be."

"I'm all ears," Koz said with a mirthless smile. "But face it, the Reaver can't be killed. You can't kill concepts. The most you can do is keep them from spreading. So it has to be contained somewhere it can't infect anyone."

Olivia locked eyes with Koz and dropped her voice to a conspiratorial whisper. "We will find another way. We will. We're going to beat it, and no one is going to die."

This time Koz did laugh; a humorless thing that died in their throat and threatened to free new tears. "Yeah, sure. Good luck with that." They were both silent for a while. Shivering together as the ceaseless breeze assailed them both.

They both looked across the ship and saw Musty and Alibaster coming their way. "Do me a favor," Koz said. "Don't tell Musty. I want him safe, and if he hears what I'm planning to do he'll never agree to go back home. I was going to go back with him, before I found out about… everything."

Olivia said nothing to confirm or deny the request. Instead she addressed the boys as they reached them.

"Good talk?" she asked.

"Enlightening," Musty said. His face was a mess of frustration and worry. The same face Alibaster had had for him. It was safe to assume that Alibaster had finally spilled the beans that were his life to his childhood friend, and Musty was going to need some time to come to terms with it all.

"So now that I assume everything's out in the open, you'll be going back to Illetica?" Olivia asked Musty. "How does that work? Do we have to find the place you were dreaming before you entered the Paracosm? Or-"

"I'm not leaving," Musty said. "I'm with you. All of you. Until the end of this."

Olivia didn't have to be an empath to see the dread Koz felt at this.

"You-" Koz started then stopped. They looked at Alibaster. "You're allowing this?"

Alibaster shrugged. "What do you suggest I do to stop him? I'm not stoked about it either. But if he wants to help, then we let him help."

"Why are you two acting like my parents?" Musty asked. "My parents never even acted like my parents. We're all in this together now. End of discussion."

"I-" Koz started then stopped again. They turned back towards the sea. Olivia sympathized. Nobody wanted their loved ones to see them in pain; to see them die. To see them sacrifice themselves. What was coming next, Koz had hoped to spare Musty, but they didn't have it in them to argue anymore.

"Fine," they said, though it was very clearly not.

Chapter 45: Sinking Feelings (and Ships)

Having decided that Musty would come along, the fox eventually had them all regroup once more to discuss their next course of action. The way he looked at Olivia as they all ambled over…

He knows, Olivia knew. He knew that she knew about his plan to sacrifice Koz. She didn't know if it was due to whatever weird connection they had, or if she was just really bad at hiding her rage towards him. She struggled to control her face, deciding instead that the wooden planks on which she stood were suddenly very interesting and deserving of study.

The fox ignored her anger, feeling it more important to get on with the matter at hand. "From what I could gather from my intangible informant, we lost quite a bit of footing during our excursion to Efivabh." He hopped up on the ledge, and motioned for them all to look down into the starry seas. Several rippling images appeared as if the liquid on which they rode had become a viewing screen. It showed pictures of a number of places: forests, cities, ships, microscopic views of blades of grass, and impossible structures within the hearts of stars. They all varied in so many ways, save one.

They were all empty. No living creature could be seen in any of the shifting images.

The fox continued. "It seems that the beast has not stopped or slowed in the slightest. The nightmares have been gaining ground. And with each creature it has assimilated or killed, the larger its foothold grows."

Alibaster mumbled something about the law of exponential growth.

The fox nodded. "Most of the Paracosm has become quiet. Worlds of Fathoms have been absorbed or slain, not having the ability to flee their homes. Any Natives who escaped are refugees, hiding from the insidious threat which has taken over their homelands."

"So you're saying we already lost," Penelope said. "That the Reaver did what it set out to do. That it's over."

The images on the ocean surface faded, and fox paced the ledge with the grace of a hunter anticipating his next meal to come to him of its own accord. "The beast will use its victories to its advantage, editing every tale ever told until it is in the center of it all. The consequences will reach the waking world in no time. There is still time to halt the process though, and for the Paracosm to heal the injuries inflicted upon it. Our only hope is to use its weaknesses to drive it back into a single form for capture."

"It has weaknesses?" Alibaster asked, the tiniest spark of optimism hiding behind his eyes.

"If it didn't, it could never have lost the first battle waged against it," the fox said.

"I remember you saying that battle took quite a long time," Penelope said. "Even by Paracosm standards."

"That was back when nobody truly knew what they were dealing with," the fox rebutted. "All they knew was that the creature infecting their home had to be stopped. They never truly knew what the beast was capable of. Or what its limits were. In short, they didn't have me."

"Well don't keep us in suspense," Musty said. "What are these limits?"

"First you have to understand what goes on when the beast takes a person over. It isn't mind control in the conventional sense. It simply… imparts a piece of itself into the targeted creature. This piece then takes over the host, like a computer virus. It rewrites the host into following the commands written within the shard of the beast's self. These commands are already within the shard when contact is made. 'Obey. Go forth. Spread. Assimilate.' Things of that nature. Simple instructions, which the host's mind is trusted to interpret as they will. When you face someone who has been corrupted by the beast, you are not facing the beast itself. Not in a very straightforward way. Yes, the creature can often speak through the mouths of those absorbed, but that is really just a parlor trick. It is more like fighting a civilian who has fallen victim to particularly aggressive propaganda and rhetoric."

"So it's more like really thorough brainwashing than possession," Koz said.

"So they can fight back," Olivia said. "Those who are being controlled, they can break free."

"If the will and instinct to fight against exploitation is fierce enough, then yes," the fox said. "We saw this in Nestor, the anima maelstrom. That is why the beast is killing as well as gathering. Some wills are too strong for it to impart itself. The trouble lies with those who do not believe they can rise against their new master. It is easier for many to just do as they're told than to fight back against something with such widespread influence and power."

"So how do we do it?" Alibaster asked. "How do we break the hold this thing has on half of the Paracosm? How do we get the Reaver down to a single form?"

"I have a plan," the fox said matter-of-factly.

"Where do we start?" Musty asked.

The fox turned back to the water, and a new image appeared. An image which made a circle of sea look like it had been displaced from reality, leaving a stark white spot in its place. "The Blank," he said simply.

A question started to form on Musty's lips. Presumably the question would have been something like "What in Qlarn's name is the Blank?" But before the first syllable could leave his tongue, the ship started to heave. The structure creaked as everything started to tilt, even though the waves were no worse than they had been. Then the bow of the ship started to descend. The fox jumped down from the ledge. "I suggest you all find something to hang onto."

The ship tipped forward at such an angle, gallons of star filled liquid poured onto the deck. The humanoids struggled to get clear of it, to make their way to the rear of the ship. But the angle at which the vessel was at now was too high, and they couldn't climb up to the back.

The ship's sinking, Olivia thought as they all scrambled away from the rising water.

No, she corrected herself. *It's diving.*

But diving where? Into the Blank? But how? She thought only vents led to the base code of the Paracosm. They all took the fox's advice, and held fast to anything nailed down. The ship plunged, the liquid hit, and Olivia instinctively took a breath to hold. The last thing she heard before going completely under was the parrot screaming bloody murder from somewhere above.

If she hadn't shed every conception she once had about the fifth dimension, she might have said they were in outer space. But the way all the stars shimmered and rippled, and the fact that she could hold the lights in her hand if she reached out… It all kind of reminded her more of what she had referred to as "shimmeries" within the universe of Time.

It felt as if wet washcloths were wrapped around her whole body. Not really pleasant, but not the frigid cold of the deep ocean or outer space.

"You don't need to hold your breath," the fox said. His voice sounded muffled, as if speaking to her through a wall. She thought he was talking to her, but in that moment she saw the rest of the party exhale, and realized they had all had the same instincts as her.

Down, down, down. Deeper and deeper. They passed entire universes as small as a thumb, and single celled organisms the size of galaxies. People made of song, and auras forged by complex mathematical formulae.

It obviously couldn't be said how long they descended. Olivia had once read that within the first few years of life, a child's mind makes hundreds- if not thousands- of new neural connections every second. That was what this felt like. As if they were seeing and experiencing hundreds of things within a single instant, yet spread out enough for them to comprehend. One eternal second.

They finally reached the seafloor. Or the floor to whatever this non-ocean actually was.

Oh, Olivia realized as she saw what they were heading towards. She had been right, it seemed. One could only reach the Blank through vents.

And what sat at the bottom of oceans?

A vortex of bubbles, heat, and absurdity flew out of the hydrothermal vent. And the stolen Cyclops pirate ship flew right into it.

Chapter 46: Their Commandeered Ship Gets Commandeered

Now they were all truly falling. The entire ship was falling through corridor after corridor of nonsense, just like Olivia had her first time trying to enter the foundation of the fifth dimension. Everyone still clung to the vessel, not wanting to fly away and be lost forever.

"Close your eyes!" Olivia yelled as they passed through the inside of a giant penne noodle. "Everyone! We can't witness our entrance into the Blank!"

"Why not?" Alibaster asked.

"Hell if I know! Just do it!"

It took a few seconds, but the falling ceased, and everyone crashed to the deck like so many sacks of potatoes.

They all spent a private moment groaning, cursing, and collecting themselves.

"Everyone still alive?" Alibaster asked once everyone had calmed down.

"No," said Penelope with all the strength of crumpled tissue paper in a wood chipper.

"Good," said Alibaster, ignoring her. "Musty?"

"Give me a minute," the blue haired boy said, grabbing an overturned barrel to right himself. "Not all of us are used to crash landing on a regular basis."

"It's not really something you get used to," Olivia assured him. She looked around. "Where's Koz? And the fox?"

"Over here," Koz's voice called from the front of the ship. The fox was sitting- rather masterfully- upon the long pole which extended from the bow. What was that called? A bowsprit?

Once they reached each other, they all looked over the edge of the ship, to find it now sailing on a sea of shifting invisibility and an endless sky of porcelain white. The fox explained quickly where they were and what the Blank was.

"This is where we make our final stand against the beast," he said, studying the empty potential beyond.

"I thought you said the Reaver couldn't survive here," Olivia recalled.

"It has gained enough influence that it can now send foot soldiers here without irreparable harm," the fox said. "After all, it has bodies to spare now."

"How do you know it will come here at all?" Musty asked.

"It will come. It has to. It intends to rewrite everything. This is the only place it can go to edit its new draft of the universal story."

"You said you had a plan," Alibaster said. "I know we're all just dying to hear it."

"Preferably before we actually die," Penelope added.

Koz winced at that. Olivia and Musty both noticed, but only Olivia interpreted correctly what the wince was about. Still, Musty laced his fingers into Koz's as reassurance.

The fox went on. "Well the first part of the plan includes falling into a trap."

"A trap?" Alibaster asked.

"An ambush, more accurately."

"Not sure I like this plan," Penelope said.

"What ambush?" Olivia asked, suddenly feeling a stone drop into her stomach.

"You all know my informant, the sentient wind?" the fox asked. "It procured this lovely ship?"

They all nodded.

"Well, it seems I was incorrect in my assumption that wind could not be controlled." He spoke in a way which implied that he was not in the least bit surprised by this. "We have a spy in the camp. A double agent. The traitorous breeze has dropped us right into the beast's lap."

Gooseflesh spread across Olivia's skin as the current of air blew colder and harder.

"And, oh dear," the fox continued (even though everyone really wished he wouldn't), "I've just alerted the spy to my knowledge of its disloyalty. I wonder what will happen now." It was obvious to everyone that the fox probably had a pretty good idea of just what was about to happen now.

Stillness befell everything. Everyone held their breath once more, no one daring to be the first to break the silence. No one wanted to set off whatever hair triggered event was about to transpire.

They all saw movement as they looked over the edge of the ship. The color lacking amniotic fluid of all unwritten dreams and stories was bubbling. The void that was the sky rumbled.

Olivia couldn't help herself. She had to ask. "What's happening?"

The fox stared ahead. "The first wave. Everyone prepare."

"Prepare for what?" Musty asked frantically. "How?"

Shapes started dropping from the sky and rising from the unseen depths.

"I think we're going to have to fight," Alibaster said, his eyes shifting to catch each new movement.

"Fight what?" The shapes were getting nearer, becoming more defined.

"Natives," Koz guessed.

"Everything," Olivia said. "Every being the Reaver has collected or rewritten. Everything is coming for us. Right now."

Penelope sighed. "Right. Of course. This is going to be interesting."

They all collected at the center of the main deck and formed a circle, facing outward. No weapons, no reinforcements, no plan whatsoever.

Business as usual, Olivia thought despondently as the ship was boarded.

Each shape was foreign to Olivia. Aliens she had never encountered of fictions she had never read. The only thing similar between one form and the next were the black and copper eyes indicating that they were indeed all under the same malign influence. The first who made it on the ship's deck seemed to be a quadrupedal manatee carved completely of amber. The still form of preserved insects and small animals were visible within its body. It had no mouth, but it did speak.

"Weelllcome, to yoouur fiinaal chaappteer."

Chapter 47: Not Actually the Final Chapter

In Team Dumb Luck's experience, usually bad guys- the sort of bad guys who wanted to do something malicious which involved the whole universe- liked to hear themselves talk. God, did they like the sound of their own voices. Even when they said they weren't like others the team had faced, and that they weren't going to reveal their grand plan, they still did. It's like they couldn't help it. The grandstanding. The delusions of grandeur. The shouting to the heavens that everything was about to change.

As much as Olivia hated to put up with all of that, she did admit to its usefulness. It was a good way to learn what the enemy was all about; motivations, that sort of thing. The monologuing was also good if the team was in a particularly precarious position and needed time to think themselves out of it.

So the fact that the Dream Reaver didn't take this moment to gloat- conveniently giving the new and improved Team Dumb Luck the time they needed to think- and instead had its lackeys come at them on all sides…

It really bummed Olivia out.

So many thoughts raced through her head as a dozen possessed creatures surrounded them. How were they going to win? How were they even going to survive? Why had the fox purposefully led them into this trap? Had Alibaster been correct in his distrust? Had the fox really been on the Reaver's side all along? Or did he truly have a plan to help? Did he really believe that they could somehow defeat these creatures?

The beings closed in on their own small circle. Many hunters stalking the same prey. Each one of them wanting another to try first. (Because surely this sad group of humanoids couldn't pose as little threat as they appeared to. Surely they had something up their sleeves.) Olivia imagined that from above, it might have looked like part of an insidious synchronized swimming routine.

The first one finally lost its patience and made its move. It was made of vines, had a head full of snapping, drooling Venus flytraps, and wherever it stepped six leaf clovers grew spontaneously from the cracks of the ship's floorboards.

It lunged at Penelope. In one swift motion, she swung the shield from her back, and swatted the plant man with the brunt of the crest. A crack sounded, not unlike that of a baseball bat snapping after hitting an impressive homerun. The flora fella flew a good several feet, and fell to the ground. Several small whimpers could be heard from the flytraps, and the creature did not get back up.

Olivia and the three Illeticans looked at Penelope in astonishment.

"Wow," Penelope said, looking impressed with herself. She was kind enough not to say the cliché about not knowing her own strength.

The shield is one of legend, Olivia thought. *It must have strength of its own.* She suddenly really wished she had accepted the sword.

"We're supposed to be helping them, not hurting them," Koz said.

"Tell them that," Penelope argued.

At seeing their fallen comrade, the other creatures all stopped in their tracks. They studied their prey with a tense look; assessing the new information with their darkened eyes. They wouldn't be wary for long though. It would take no time at all for them to realize that they should all attack at once instead of one at a time.

So Olivia and company needed to take this brief reprieve to come up with a strategy- any strategy- to survive the next five minutes.

She saw the fox still on his perch at the tip of the bowsprit, watching the action unfold intently. *Thanks for the help,* she thought bitterly. She looked up, and saw the parrot staring down at them from the top of the shortest mast. It cocked its head at her, as if it were watching an intriguing movie and was wondering what was going to happen next.

Ok, think, she ordered her brain. *Maybe if they-*

Before she could even finish the idea, let alone dismiss it for being stupid and reckless (as most of their plans tended to be), she saw a new figure. It climbed over the edge of the ship from out of the figurative primordial soup. The other creatures looked over to the new arrival. Almost as if they hadn't expected anyone else to storm the ship at this juncture. This made Olivia wondered just how much or how little the Reaver's influence connected them all.

Anyone with any sense would have taken this new arrival as a godsend. It provided the team just the distraction they might have needed to slip away. But slip away to where? And besides, the new figure distracted them as well.

There was something familiar about him…

As he walked over towards them with confidence and purpose, Olivia racked her brain to try and fit a name to that face.

He looked like an alien had a baby with an ancient Roman. He wore one of those bronze helmets that legionaries used to wear. It had an impressive purple plume mohawking from the top. His armor matched the helmet, looking battered and frayed, but still sturdy. His skin was the color of sculpting clay, and it was covered in scars. He had four hairy, muscular arms, and in three of them he held worn but impressive weapons. One of which was a chainsaw, of all things. His eyes were of course black with copper pupils, and his whole beaten yet chiseled face wore five o'clock shadow and a permanent sneer.

It was on the tip of Olivia's brain. She knew this guy. Didn't she? That wasn't a silhouette one would forget easily.

Just as the plant man, he walked straight towards Penelope. Man, Olivia thought she had been protecting her friend by giving her the shield, not making her more of a target.

Wait… The shield! Olivia's heart deflated. *Oh, duh Jones.*

The man reached the group. He towered over them all; a mountain of a person. When he spoke, his eyes did not leave the shield which Penelope held in front of the organs she felt most important.

"Thaaatt dooooeessss noooott beeelooong toooo youuu."

Penelope and the others looked perplexed, but Olivia understood.

"Plexerious," she said. "Plexerious, it's me."

His gaze shot to her, but the rest of him stayed still. He showed no indication of recognizing her.

"Oh, God," Olivia said. "What happened to you?"

He looked completely different than he had when she met him. The shining knight of legend now struck the figure of a one man army. He had died, she had seen him die. Nobody survived a hole punched through the solar plexus. But they were in the Paracosm. Normal rules didn't apply.

So what happened to stories when they died? Of course. Their essence came back to the Blank to await reconstitution. But why was he so different? What had the fox said? That the Blank connected all Literals? Meaning what? Olivia considered.

Maybe the collective unconsciousness of all who knew of Plexerious had shifted. Stories changed little by little with each retelling. The game of telephone. Perhaps nowadays, most people thought of the mighty hero as a gritty, battle weary warrior.

When Olivia and Penelope had left Earth six months ago, they had each packed several creature comforts to remind them of home. One of the things Penelope had brought was a milk crate full of comic books from the 1990s. The covers included gruff, bloody men with mullets and completely over the top weapons. Penelope had explained that during this time, readers were tired of the, quote, "cookie cutter, right and wrong heroes of the previous generation". They wanted something they considered "more realistic"; protagonists who lived in the gray of morality. Antiheroes instead of superheroes.

And so it seemed something similar had happened upon Plexerious' rebirth. The Warrior of the twin goddess had been rebooted into something much more dangerous. And this more dangerous version was now under the control of the Reaver.

This also explained why the Reaver bothered killing people it couldn't control. It wasn't just to get them out of the way. The souls of the figurative people would come back to the Blank, where it could grab control of their new selves before they were fully reconstituted.

Great. It never rains, but it pours.

His eyes flicked back to Penelope. "Givvve meee myyy shieeelldd."

Penelope ducked behind the shield even more. "Ummm, pass." Even though the words were defiant, her voice still squeaked.

Plexerious lifted his chainsaw, which turned on without as much as a pull to the starter rope.

"Shype," Alibaster said over the grinding roar of the weapon, "never meet your heroes."

The great hero brought the saw down, crashing against his own shield. The noise which followed was pained and uncomfortable. It was the sound of an unstoppable force meeting an immoveable object. The chainsaw sputtered and protested, as the metal of the shield threatened to give.

Olivia broke rank before her friends- or her brain- could ask her just what in the actual hell she thought she was doing, and grabbed Plexerious' free hand. With futility she tried to pull the wall of muscle away from Penelope.

"Plex, stop!" she yelled. "You're being controlled! This isn't you! Please, stop!" The other creatures aboard the ship watched in confusion and amusement, none of them stepping in to ruin the show. Or perhaps they were all frightened of Plexerious, and were waiting for the great legend to swat the foolish girl away like a half acknowledged fly.

And to her- and everyone else's- surprise, Plexerious did stop. His chainsaw wielding arm fell to his side, and his entire body drooped a bit. Like a robot that's been deactivated. Olivia let him go, and everyone took a wary step away. Then his head lifted, and he blinked. He looked first at his hands and the weapons he held, then to the insignia on the shield before him, before finally turning to see Olivia. His eyes were tired, but once more their original amber hue.

"Olivia Jones," he said. His voice was no longer strained and awkward, though he sounded like a serial chain smoker. "I remember you. I remember me. Who I am. What I have been. What I am now."

His sentences were clipped, his words no longer boisterous and larger than life. "I remember that creature killing my previous self. It then interrupted my renewal. It took control."

"You're not the only one," Olivia said, motioning to those around her. The creatures still possessed were starting to get twitchy. "Are you ok?"

"What you are really asking is if I am prepared for battle," Plex said.

Olivia didn't answer.

"The answer to that question, no matter who I become, will always be yes." Plexerious gave a crooked smile; extenuating a nose that had been broken so many times it could no longer be set properly. He gave one last look to Penelope, who had still not lowered the shield. "Keep it," he said. "It will only slow me down." He looked towards his many foes who had only a second ago been his allies. "Get somewhere safe," he ordered Olivia and her friends.

"No problem," Alibaster said.

Plexerious lifted all his weapons, and squeezed his free hand into a fist the size of a small boulder. With a battle cry he charged at the rest of the Reaver's forces.

Chapter 48: Hidden Huddle

"Is it just me or was that really easy?" Musty asked. "Plexerious- and I still can't even believe that *was* Plexerious- just snapping out of the dark conditioning like that."

They had all climbed up to a higher deck (Olivia's knowledge of correct nautical terms was very limited), and hid behind a bunch of overturned crates, leaving Plexerious to battle the hordes on the main deck. They had all forgotten about Team Dumb Luck for the moment, completely engrossed in their rather one-sided battle with the warrior. (Though not one-sided in the way they probably hoped.)

Olivia wanted to help him, but like the shield, she was afraid she'd just be in the way.

"I try not to question it when things are easy," Alibaster said. "It'll only jinx everything."

"He is one of the universe's most well known heroes," Olivia said. "His will, or at least what people believe his will to be, must be on a whole other level."

"No, Musty's right," Koz said. "I felt Plexerious' mental state before and after. While he was being controlled, it was just that static lack of emotions I got from those possessed Fathoms in the village. But the second Olivia made contact with him, it was like a switch was flipped in his head, and he was back to normal. If angst and bottled rage are qualities of his typical mindset. But there was no struggle at all. No fight against the Reaver's influence in a battle of wills. It was simply gone."

"So it was something Olivia did," Penelope said while peeking over the crates to watch the battle. More and more beings of dream and story were scaling the sides of the ship to join the fray. Plex was holding his own as well as could be expected from such an indestructible legend. Watching him fight was like watching a freight train composed of blades. But for all his newfound fury and unhinged combat skills, eventually even he would fall to the sheer number of bodies being thrown at him.

"Something I did?" Olivia asked.

"You heard Koz. Something must have happened either when you spoke to him or grabbed him," Penelope reasoned. "You holding out on us? Some secret powers of your own?"

"It is not just Olivia," the fox said. He came into view, trotting low to make himself a harder target to hit.

"What is going on?" Alibaster asked, at his wits end. "What did you do? Why did you leave?"

"I couldn't reveal my plan until the beast's forces were otherwise occupied. We can't risk it overhearing."

"So you just threw us into the deep end of monsters in the meantime," Musty said. "Gee, thanks."

"What do you mean it's not just Olivia?" Koz asked. "What's not?"

"Within all of you, is held the truth," the fox said. "Courtesy of our trip to Efivabh."

Several raised eyebrows spontaneously materialized into being.

"Explain," Penelope demanded. "Now."

"The Tree," the fox started, speaking quickly, leaving no room for questions. "You have all been touched by it. Some of you have even bitten its fruit. The Tree of Efivabh, for all of its splendor, is but a piece of a larger whole. There are legends of the Tree of Life all throughout creation. The Host Stump of Glacicon, the World Tree of Earth myth, the Final Seed of Thought from the Pli clusters. All of these:

millions of variations of the same idea. A first life. A beginning to all knowledge and sentient thought. And the greatest wisdom it can impart is the sense of self, of the individual, at thinking for oneself through the employ of critical thought. In return for freeing one of the pieces of the collective, the symbol of the Tree has granted you all a gift. A gift which can only be used in the Paracosm. A gift to set the possessed and manipulated free of the beast's control. With a single touch, you can help them all see the truth."

They all took a moment to absorb this while the clashing and grunting of battle came from below them. Olivia guessed it made just as much sense of anything else that had been going on. Ok, so that was kind of a plan. Wait for Plex to knock everyone out (and hopefully not kill them) and then just give the bodies a poke, and boom. The Reaver's gone from their minds.

But this was an incredible help. Why would the Reaver have trapped Musty in the Wasteland in the first place if there was a possibility of them all coming out of it with this newfound power of knowledge? It must have been incredibly dim, or incredibly overconfident in its own abilities…

Unless.

"You planned this," Olivia said to the fox. "It was you who threw Musty into the Wasteland. You knew we'd go after him. You knew the Tree was trapped in the needle. You knew we'd free Musty, and Musty would free the tree."

The others looked towards Olivia at the accusation, then towards the fox.

"Yes, I did," the animal said. "I knew the beast could never be beaten by brute force alone, and I could not free the Tree myself, because it would look into my heart and find my motivation for doing so selfish. Then it would not grant me the power I sought for the beast's defeat. I needed you all, because I knew you would do the right thing without prompt or incentive."

When Olivia had tried speaking to the Reaver back in that village, it had said that her lost friend had been taken by it, but not it. She hadn't understood at the time, but that obviously meant the fox, the Reaver's discarded conscience. *Some conscience.*

Now she knew why her mind had chosen to give the entity the form of a creature depicted to be cunning and self-serving. Considering past experience, she was surprised she hadn't chosen the form of a bald slug.

"So just so we're clear," Alibaster said to everyone, "we're angry about this. Correct? We're all mad about this?" He asked like someone needing feedback on his workout playlist.

"Furious," Penelope said. She reached out and grabbed the fox by the scruff of the neck, standing up and holding him at arm's length. A static cling filled the air and her eyes were that familiar intimidating glowing blue. Musty, who had never seen this display, stared wide-eyed. The fox kicked and wriggled against her, but she held him firm. "I do not like being manipulated. I do not like being used. I am on the record as saying as much. I am very vehement about my distaste of Machiavellian machinations. Especially when my friends or I are on the receiving end. You will not lie to us anymore. Am I clear?"

The fox nodded. "I have no need to lie to you anymore."

"Let's hope *that's* not a lie," Alibaster muttered.

Olivia thought about the irony of both those statements. Because the fox and Koz were both still lying- or at least withholding information- regarding another part of the "plan". *And I suppose now I am too,* she thought. Koz seemed to read Olivia's guilt, and shook their head pleadingly.

Penelope considered the creature for a moment more, before dropping him unceremoniously and dimming the brightness of her eyes. Hopefully that display of intimidation hadn't burned away too much of her suit of small time.

"So now what?" Musty asked.

"Now we go help," Olivia said. "Be careful, stay low and hidden when possible. It looks like Plex has taken down quite a lot of them. Go to those you're sure are down for the count, and-"

"Place hands on them?" Penelope rolled her eyes. "Hopefully none of the Fathoms from the village hear about this. If they find out I can exorcise demons by touch, they'll never stop worshiping me as their goddess."

"They what?" Musty asked incredulously.

"Never mind," Olivia snapped. "Come on. We have work to do."

Alibaster sighed. "Go team."

Chapter 49: The Real Heroes Stay on the Sidelines

This was how things went down during the next chunk of time.

First, Team Dumb Luck separated from one another. It would be extremely easy for any of the Reaver's forces to spot a five headed target, walking side by side like a herd of sheep. So while it was a risk for them to each go on individually, it lessened their chances of having any unwanted attention drawn to them.

Second, while keeping low and remaining as close to the edges of the main deck (and as far away from the actual fighting) as they could, each member of the team scoped out any creatures that Plexerious had already felled. None of the opponents looked dead, which was a relief considering Plex's new persona, but none of them looked like they'd survive another bout with the beastly space Hercules. No heartfelt cry could rally these broken troops. One of the Earthlings or Illeticans would then do an awkward crouching run to the sides of these fallen stories-turned-soldiers, and use the gift imparted upon them by the Tree of Life to give each of the Reaver's drones the wisdom and knowledge to look inside themselves, find their strength of character, and fight their master's programming.

As the black and copper left their eyes, they would often give a weak "thank you", or just give cries of agony now that they could feel whatever terribly creative pain the universe's greatest hero had inflicted upon them. Olivia half wondered if there was some kind of hospital in the Paracosm, or if they would heal on their own. If they were returned to the sea of ideas upon which the ship floated, perhaps that would help. But she didn't like the image of tossing these poor people overboard.

While this was going on, Plexerious kept fighting. He moved completely differently than his earlier iteration had. This one flew from one opponent to the next with ferocity, and attacked with only the barest hint of mercy. He was truly an army of one. His armor did what it could to shield him from the many blows of appendage and weapons, but it couldn't stop every strike. He was receiving new injuries every second. And though it was clear that Plexerious would not stop fighting as long as he could still stand (and probably even after that), the hordes of possessed still kept coming.

One new wave after another, and somehow the ship never seemed any more crowded. As if it was expanding to accommodate all the new "passengers".

Plexerious could not hold out forever. It was only a matter of time before either someone got a lucky shot in, or the Reaver stopped throwing cannon fodder into the ring and sent in its A-Team, facing Plex with a foe even he could not defeat.

The fox watched anxiously from higher ground. No one paid him any mind. He could not enter this fight, nor could he be fought. A fight between the Reaver and the fox would bear no fruit. Since neither one could fatally harm the other, it would be a fight without end.

From on high, amidst the cries of battle and the clank of weapons, the parrot flew in circles and screamed. Olivia would have felt sorry for the thing, if its constant screeching wasn't giving her an unyielding urge to wring its neck. After a moment it abandoned its perch, flying away from the fighting as quickly as its wings would carry it. Soon it fell completely from view, and its screams died away as it disappeared into the Blank.

They were doing pretty well, all things considered. Some combatants weren't wounded too badly by Plexerious, so when Olivia or her friends helped purge the Reaver from their systems, they actually got back up to help fight. The help was greatly appreciated by them, though it couldn't be said whether Plexerious even noticed his new allies on the battlefield. And these new allies were few and far between. Maybe one in every twenty was left fit enough for the possibility of a second wind.

But even with the steadily growing help, it was still slow goings. The ship had become a theatre of war, and their opponent had an endless reserve of fighters. The five of them helping each individual individually… It would take forever. There had to be a quicker way; a more efficient way. Some way to help multiple possessed at once.

She was in the middle of helping some kind of cybernetic kelp creature back to its feet (tendrils), when one of the infected finally caught on to what they were doing. It was something like an octopus and a tarantula, which made it half slimy, half hairy, all *ew*. It broke away from the twenty on one fight with Plexerious and made its way towards Alibaster, who was the nearest of the five. Olivia saw this and tried to yell at Alibaster to watch out, but she couldn't be heard over the noise of battle. Alibaster hadn't noticed the creature, occupied with helping one of the fallen.

With his back to the creature, the octo-pider raised one of its tentacles and squirted what looked like ink out of a suction cup, right at Alibaster's head. Right as that happened, Penelope came from nowhere and shoved the creature aside with the full weight of her body against her shield.

Because of this, the shot of ink went wide, landing on the deck instead of Alibaster's skull. The deck under the black splotch sizzled and the wood disintegrated. *Acid ink. Nasty.*

Alibaster turned around, saw the creature, and quickly placed a hand on the octo-pider's ten-eyed head. Olivia watched from afar as all the eyes turned from black to… What was that? Magenta?

Either way, the creature was free. She watched it shuffle uncomfortable on its many legs, no doubt trying to form an apology. Alibaster said something, shook his head, and then pointed to the seafaring combat zone. The creature nodded, and set off to help in the skirmish.

He and Penelope spoke for a moment, before Penelope moved off to help wounded on the other side of the ship. Olivia didn't know what was said, but she'd bet anything the interaction had been awkward as flek. Those two were terrible at sincerity. They were also terrible at acting like they didn't hate each other. But that didn't mean they wouldn't be there for one another in an instant whenever the world was against them. As long as they all had each other, they could weather any storm.

That thought must have jinxed her, because just then the whole ship trembled, rocking from side to side like a herd of stampeding buffalo had tried to mow it down. It was almost like a thunder strike, low and insidious. The empty sky of the Blank grumbled and darkened, and from the smoky horizon, new figures emerged. The fighting stopped, as everyone looked to see the new arrivals.

At first only silhouettes could be seen. Giant, towering shadows, larger than any creatures Olivia had ever seen.

"What now?" Koz asked despondently from somewhere.

Plexerious leaned on one of his swords like a cane, and was breathing in sharp ragged inhales. "At a guess," he said with a matching lack of enthusiasm, "monsters. Gods. Titans. Under the creature's influence, more than likely."

Even with all the people and creatures they had freed from the Reaver's influence, they couldn't fight what was coming. They couldn't. There was no chance.

Olivia turned to the fox with her last milligram of hope. He must have a plan. He must have anticipated for this eventuality. She didn't even care if it was another secret plan he had hidden from them, as long as he *had* a plan.

But the look he gave her scattered her last grains of optimism to the wind.

They all turned to face what was coming; Literal and figurative, friend and foe, possessed and free. For an eternal moment they looked up, some holding onto the ship as it rocked with each thundering footfall. And together they waited. Waited as some of the oldest, most powerful stories in the universe came to end their own stories once and for all.

Olivia had no need to add to her list of ways she didn't want to die. "Angry gods" was one of the first things she'd ever cataloged.

Chapter 50: Throwing Bodies at a Problem

This was it. Team Dumb Luck was no longer dumb lucky. The well of fortuitous accidents had run dry at last. They had failed. They would die there, in this hidden dimension. The nightmare creature would spread its influence and rewrite everything, until the collective unconsciousness connecting every thinking thing in creation shifted and everyone became twisted, disparate versions of themselves. The Reaver would ascend to where it thought it belonged; ruling every sentient thought from the dark, holding everyone hostage within their own minds.

Would anyone be able to fight back? No one would even know what was happening. They'd all be overwritten; taught to believe the new big lie of the universe. Made to believe whatever the creature in the shadows of their heads whispered to them.

Olivia had just about resigned herself to the fact of her death, when she heard a noise. A noise distinct from the footfalls of ancient legends. A noise like a strangled screech.

Oh great, she thought as she turned to find the source of the screech, *the cavalry*. She expected to see a tiny, one-eyed parrot fluttering back to its perch, completely oblivious to the new danger coming its way. What she saw instead could not have been more different.

The creature making its way towards the ship now was larger and serpentine, with green feathers the size of elephant leaves covering its length, and a beak that was almost a muzzle. It also had brilliant bat-like wings beating against the air with considerable power, and six leering red eyes, three on each side of its face. The only things which made Olivia sure of the magnificent beast's identity were two things: the nails-on-chalkboard screech, and the hues which made up its body.

It seemed the parrot was now (somehow) a dragon.

Huh.

And it was not alone.

The ship's mascot reached its perch above the tallest mast and circled it in an ouroboros-esque motion. Everyone aboard the ship, and perhaps even the deities beyond, stopped and watched the latest developments. Because deep in the mists ahead, straight in the direction the dragon had just come from, came new noises. Well, familiar noises, but coming from a new direction.

The noises were vibrations, and the vibrations rocked everyone to their very core, just as the footfalls of the gods opposite had.

Oh, Olivia thought. It seemed the once-bird had brought the cavalry after all. Because making their way towards them all now were more giants, more legends of force and nature. More gods. And these deities didn't have black and copper eyes. They reached a spot about fifty yards away from the ship, mirroring where their counterparts had stopped. They all held still, stared at the titan opposite them, and held a line.

How had this happened? How had all these beings known to come here?

And in an "Ask and you shall receive," kind of way- which tended to happen when one was in close proximity to numerous pantheons of deities- the answers were inexplicitly present within Olivia and her friends' minds.

These were all the deities that had been able to defend their minds against the Reaver. Those who were able to hide from the terrible influence until called upon to help rise against it. Most of these beings were also somehow connected to the various Tree of Life stories. (The presence of Efivabh's Creator could be felt trying not to step back into Her long lived isolation.) This meant that within each of them was the same gift of outward and inward evaluation that the Tree had bestowed upon the once named Team Dumb Luck, and the newly named "Team Quick Somebody Buy a Lottery Ticket and Let's go Swimming with Sharks During a Lightning Storm". This meant that they could help free all the minds of the infected.

And they had all been brought there in the moment of need by something that was neither a parrot nor a dragon, but something rather more mysterious. Something capable of creating whirlpools within the reality of the Paracosm and transporting beings across the infinity of ideas. Something like…

Nestor? Olivia wondered, looking up at the creature. The anima maelstrom howled as if in confirmation. Olivia liked the cat look better, but she was glad of the shape shifter's help.

For a moment, she was excited; elated even. They had backup! They wouldn't have to fight this battle alone. They might not even have to die.

But it was the looks on her friends' faces, scattered around the deck as they were, that made her realize how incredibly stupid she was being. The gods had all grown to their full mountainous heights. They were charged with all the power of belief they had accumulated over the eons, and were about to do battle there in the blank space of which stories were told. Maybe those touched by the Reaver would win, or maybe those who were still themselves would be victorious. But either way…

Neither side looked like they particularly cared about the boat filled with combatants drifting in the center of them. It might as well have been a rubber duck for the amount of attention they paid to it.

So her elation deflated, as she came to the conclusion that they were all twice as royally fleked as they had been two seconds ago.

In the tense calm, as the titans of both sides unsheathed their weapons or called forth their power, Olivia and the rest made their way back to each other. The others on the ship- both infected and not- did not resume their battle, as everything had just been put into colossal perspective. They were all filled with pure, unfiltered dread. Especially the fox.

"This war can't take place," he said when the team had regrouped. "Not here. Not in the most malleable, influential point of the Paracosm. The ripples of consequence could be monumentally disastrous, no matter which side walks away victorious."

"But when the Paracosm fought the Reaver before-" Penelope started.

"It was within the walls of stories," the fox interrupted. "Stories which no longer exist. The first war purged even the memory of the tales from creation. They were destroyed so completely, that they could never be reborn. Imagine what might happen to the Blank."

"I'd rather not," Alibaster said, pinching the bridge of his nose.

The gods were all ready, all waiting. The air around them was charged, and thick with anticipation. Each side was just waiting for the other to make the first move. The instant one side grew more impatient than the other, it was all over.

Koz looked like they were ready to barf. No doubt receiving all the empathic backlash from everyone in the Blank.

Musty held them steady. "There has to be something we can d-"

And then four fissures opened up in the sky, just above where Nestor the dragon was circling. *Great,* Olivia thought, *because we don't have enough things to worry about.* What was it now? How much more could the universe possibly pile onto their plate?

The fissures were like the points of a square, and swirled with all the colors of the visible spectrum. They may have also swirled with colors on the invisible spectrum, but there was really no way to know that, nor did it matter. Everyone but Musty sighed collectively. Wyrmholes. And where there were wyrmholes there were bound to be...

"Put your fears aside, for the Script Angels have come," the beautiful condescending voice of one of the four siblings flew out of one of the holes, followed immediately by the beautiful tattoo covered, winged bodies of the four Scripts; each descending from their holes like long awaited messiahs.

Everyone onboard the ship looked up in confusion. The angels obviously mistook this for awe at their glorious forms. "We have come to help turn the tide in this battle," one of them said. "The nightmare beast tried to pose as one of us, and that sin cannot be forgiven."

Another took up the helm of monologue. "So we bring forces to fight against this egregious abomination."

As they all floated in the air, each one next to their respective wyrmholes, bodies started plummeting out of the holes. Bodies of all shapes and sizes. Hundreds of them falling onto the ship like boxes of ragdolls being emptied off a building. And somehow the ship compensated to fit them all.

The angels were still talking. They were still. Fleking. Talking. "Those of sound mind, and wills of great fortitude were chosen by my others and me to partake in this, greatest of all battles."

As bodies hit the deck, they just as quickly stood up. They brandished weapons and snarls, but no black and copper eyes. They were all completely ignorant to how irrelevant the fight they had just dropped into had become; totally oblivious to the god-tier battle seconds away from wiping them all off the face of creation.

"Is no one going to thank us?" an angel asked, offended at everyone's lack of appreciation.

Penelope threw her shield as hard as she could, like a discus, striking the nearest Script in the temple. Both he and the shield clattered to the ground. The other three looked at the spectacle in puzzled outrage as Penelope collected the shield, and fought the urge to curb stomp the fallen angel.

"You morons," she said. "You fleking morons! How is this helping?"

Before the angels could answer, the first god fired a shot. A ball of fire and electricity volleyed, arching across the sky like a shooting star. It hit the god opposite square in the chest. He roared in pain. He fell. And then came the war cries of an infinitude of deities. They started to close the distance between one another.

This got the attention of the new combatants on the ship. Some stared in awe, as they finally gained perspective. Many from either side refused to be deterred by such things- what went on between such powers had nothing to do with them- and kept advancing on their enemies.

The angels fled through their wyrmholes, leaving their fallen brother behind.

"Yeah, that seems about right," Olivia said as they watched the Scripts go.

They had seconds left. Seconds before a full out war. A war that they had wanted to prevent. A war which would alter or destroy every story in the universe, and pave the way for the nightmares to finally and definitively come out on top. There would be no chance then. No hope in such a reality.

There would only be fear, confusion, and hatred, which would spread out across everything like ink spilling onto paper.

Olivia took Alibaster's hand, and she closed her eyes.

Chapter 51: Penelope, the Living Deus ex Machina

Olivia waited for the end.

And she waited.

And she waited some more.

And she kept not dying.

She opened her eyes.

The world had stopped. Everyone- everything- save for her, her four friends, the fox, and the animaelstrom overhead was locked in a frozen stance. The ship was like a statue garden depicting the beginning of a great battle. From the gods beyond, power and energy could be seen coursing through and around them, but the vessels which housed the power stood still.

The only sound which could be heard was a struggling gurgle from Penelope's throat that she was straining to keep at bay. She stood apart from the rest of them, arms outstretched and shaking, as if attempting to hold apart two great walls that were trying to crush her. She was sweating, and her knees looked like they were about to buckle. Her glowing blue eyes stared at nothing; glazed over. As if any energy spent looking at anything would be enough to break her.

Olivia took a step towards her. Alibaster held Olivia back, and the fox leapt in between her and Penelope.

"I wouldn't do that," the fox said quietly. "Any distraction, any draw away from her focus, might be enough to break the spell."

"But she's in pain," Olivia said. "She's never pushed herself like this before. Never used her power like this. And doing it here, where her powers are weakest…"

"Yes," the fox agreed. "She has brought forth the aura of small time I placed around her, manipulating it to freeze everyone in the Blank in a single instant. But that time is very limited. There is a very real possibility that the expenditure could cause her irreparable damage."

"I'm so confused," Musty said.

Koz nudged him. There was quite literally no time for explanations.

"So we need to think of a plan," said Alibaster, "fast."

"If we free all the infected from the Reaver's grasp, then there would be no need for a battle," Koz said. "They'd all just go home."

"We can't just keep going around touching everyone," Alibaster said. "It just isn't pragmatic. Penelope's stubborn and strong willed, but it might actually take us forever and a day to get to everyone here. She can't last that long."

"That wasn't what I meant," Koz said. They looked nervous. "Penelope is giving everything she has to give us this chance. I think we need to take it."

"What do you mean?" Musty asked.

Koz looked at Olivia and Alibaster. "You remember how we saved Alibaster from that prison? How we brought him back together from that smoke state?"

Olivia nodded. Alibaster shook his head.

Koz continued. "I used your emotions, Olivia. I used your determination, your resolve. I funneled them through my own mind and we broke him free of the fog."

"So?" Alibaster asked. "What are you suggesting? You do the same thing, but for every infected soul in the Paracosm?"

"Yes," Koz said in all seriousness.

"Tiny bit of an ask," Alibaster said.

Koz bit their lip for a second, before glancing at the fox, whose own face was controlled and unreadable. They continued. "It's recently come to light that I am not just an empath. I am also connected to the Paracosm in ways no one else is. My spirit has been woven into the tapestry of the fifth dimension, and it turns out there are more to my abilities than I might have once thought."

Alibaster and Musty looked at each other, then back at Koz. "What?" they asked in unison.

Olivia understood though. "Penelope is the child of the fourth dimension. Koz is the child of the fifth. The descendant of the farmer who locked himself and the Reaver inside the Abysmal the first time around."

The boys were too dumbfounded to form any recognizable syllables.

Olivia spoke to Koz. "And you think you can use these newly unlocked power boosts to get rid of the Reaver's influence in everyone in the Blank?"

"I couldn't before," Koz admitted. "But how everyone is now; frozen, their minds locked in stasis. There's no bombardment of emotions. No wailing static of it all swirling together. Everything is much less chaotic. I'm pretty sure… Well, I at least have to try. My own abilities mixed with the gift the Tree gave us, it should be enough."

"It could work," the fox conceded. "And since the Blank is the touchstone of the Paracosm, then if there are any infected beings that are not here- though I find that hard to believe considering I can't whip my tail without hitting someone- Koz's countering influence should spread out to all corners of the dimension, freeing all from the beast."

"But that would kill the thing," Alibaster said. "And you said that it couldn't be killed."

"Once it is banished from all its hosts, what is left of its consciousness will rush to find another vessel. Enough to sustain it. But fighting one foe is a much better alternative to the madness around us."

"And then?" Olivia asked accusatorially, knowing full well what Koz and the fox had planned.

"Then we do what needs to be done," the fox said with sympathy but not regret. "We hope it finds a… convenient vessel. We trap it. We save creation from its nightmares."

Olivia was about to protest. There was another way. There had to be. She wouldn't let Koz sacrifice themself. But before she could speak, she saw one of the combatants' fingers twitch before freezing again. Beads of sweat were falling down Penelope's straining face, and… Was that blood trickling down her ears and nose? She had a minute- maybe two- left before…

"Fine," Olivia said. "Let's try it. What do you need from us?"

"I need altitude," Koz said. "To reach those gods, I'm going to need to be closer to them."

"Done." Olivia cupped her hands to her mouth and yelled upwards. "Nestor!"

The animaelstrom recognized its name (or at least the name that old lady had called him) and dove down to the deck. Olivia wondered why he hadn't been frozen with everyone else. Obviously Penelope had enough control to save the core group from her time stopping, but Olivia doubted she had chosen to spare the shape shifting vortex. The fox had said that no one knew where anima maelstroms came from; their histories were clouded in mystery. And Nestor had fought off the Reaver's control on his own. Who knew what the species could do or what powers they were immune to?

The dragon that was once a bird that was once a cat lowered its head, and beckoned Koz to climb its neck.

"I'm going with you," Musty said.

"Me too," Olivia said. They both said this, but how they might help, neither knew.

Koz considered. "Part of me wants to be the brave hero and say something like, 'This is something I need to do on my own'. But I'm pretty fleking scared right now, so it might be better if you were there with me to pull me out if I stretch myself too thin."

Musty pulled Koz close and gave them a kiss on the forehead. "It'll be ok. You'll do great."

Olivia nodded her agreement. Koz tried to give a courageous smile.

"What should I do?" Alibaster asked. Olivia realized this was probably the first time he had ever asked this. He was so used to having a plan of his own, but now he was feeling superfluous.

It was the fox who answered. "You and I, my Illetican friend, will stand guard over Penelope. If her power starts waning- when it starts waning- we will be here to fend off any combatants who slip through the time freeze. We will keep her safe for as long as we can, so she in turn can focus on her own task and give our other friends as much time as she can."

Alibaster didn't seem happy about this, but he picked up Plexerious' shield, and plucked the hero's sword from his frozen hand. The weight made it fall to the ground, but Alibaster soon got the mighty weapon under control. "Sure. Because when people see my limp noodle physique, their first thought is: 'Oh boy, look at that off duty warrior go. Math and massacres, he really does it all.'"

Olivia touched his shoulder the way she did when he was nervous and rambling. He stopped talking, looked at her, and swallowed. "Right. Yep. Ok. Let's do this. Let's stop the bad guy, and wrap up this super duper meta adventure."

Koz, Musty, and Olivia all climbed aboard the serpent's back, and held onto handfuls of feathers in lieu of reins. As Nestor's mighty wings started to flap, raising them into the air, Olivia saw one of Penelope's knees buckle. She was now kneeling, as if about to give the most painful marriage proposal ever. But her hands were still outstretched and shaking, and her face gave no hint of recognizing any outside stimuli. She was still holding back the flood, but she was weakening by the second.

Alibaster took up a post in front of her, and the fox took the back, taking a hunter's stance. Hopefully they wouldn't have to fight at all, but who knew how all these people would react to being frozen? Once free, would they be angry enough to go after the girl responsible? There was also the possibility that the battle would just pick up once more, and Penelope was smack dab in the middle of the scene, unable to protect herself from crossfire.

The dragon rose, with Koz, Musty, and Olivia along for the ride. They left the ship and their friends below as they ascended towards the rows of black eyed juggernauts.

A moment later, Nestor paused in front of the first behemoth. Its wings flapped, but its body was still as it stared down the nearest god with its six red eyes. It might have been just a trick of the light (or whatever passed for light there), but it almost seemed as if the copper in the mountain's eyes were looking at them. Like the eyes of paintings in museums.

Olivia really hoped it was a trick of the light.

"Ok," Koz said with forced ease. "Let's get started."

Chapter 52: Resolve

It did no good describing each individual god. First of all, there were just so many of them. The rows filed them back and back, deeper into the fog of the Blank than could be seen. Secondly, they weren't very… vivid. Their forms… They didn't quite shift, so much as blurred. Like a charcoal picture that someone had wiped with their hand. A basic shape could always be seen underneath, but the rest- the colors, the garments, the skin tones, the demeanors, the details- were never the same from one instant to the next. Even frozen in time as they were, the millions of conflicting beliefs which shaped them flitted and fought for dominance.

It was much more disorienting looking at them at close range than it was on the ship.

Olivia chose to focus on Koz instead.

Only the side of their face could be seen positioned how they were, but it seemed tense and unsure. Koz's hands were gripping Nestor's hide tighter than a second ago, their white knuckles betraying whatever false bravado they might have had.

Like Penelope, they seemed to be concentrating heavily. But it was a different breed of concentration. Penelope was forcing her will outwards, into the world around. Koz was pulling the world into themself; pooling in all the snapshot emotions and mental states into their own mind, like Nestor's vortex would drag things into his maw. What Koz was doing could be felt by Olivia and Musty, for they were being affected too, like a current tugging at their minds. A current of calm and rationality. A current which told them to know their true selves, to not be swayed by promises of grandeur and lies of power. Things which Olivia and Musty already knew. But these thoughts weren't being aimed at them; they were simply in too close proximity to the ground zero where the feelings were coming from.

As far as the frozen titans were concerned, nothing was happening. Koz might have been a gnat trying to topple a tank. They pushed harder.

Know yourself, the voice said (which wasn't a voice, so much as an instinct or feeling). *Look deep inside your hearts and minds. Deeper than the darkness can touch. Deeper than you may even know is there. Seek both the parts of yourself that you hide from view, as well as the parts which you wish to improve. The things you wish to work towards, the ways you want to better yourself. It may seem like a dream come true to just accept this "gift" which the nightmare has handed you. But it is just an excuse. It is just the easy way out. Giving up your own free will, for a life in which no consequences are your own, because the monster you follow says it's alright. The beast does not need you, it does not care for you; it is simply using you to extend its own reach.*

If you want to be better- if you want to make your life, your story, better- then you must break free. You must decide what that means for yourself, and not bow to the dark simply because you cannot see the light. The light is there. It is always there. It is your job to find it, no matter how long it takes or how hard the task may seem. Accept the difficult truth, and not the convenient lie. Find the light. Find yourself. Find your own story. Find a better story.

The impulse went forth, rippling through the Blank and the infinite realms of the Paracosm beyond. Perhaps even going past the fifth dimension, and touching the minds of all the Literals dreaming at that very moment. Beseeching every being it touched not to fall victim to the manipulations of the Dream Reaver.

And for a moment it even seemed to work. Several black/copper eyes- the only constant in the forms of the fluctuating deities- started to dissipate; becoming once more a variety of whatever colors all the believers thought their gods' eyes should be.

The strain on Koz was obvious, but didn't seem as drastic as the exertion Penelope must have been feeling. (If she could still feel anything in her disassociated state.) Because while Koz was reaching out to touch the minds of countless figuratives and Literals, they weren't forcing anything upon them. They were only… How would Olivia's mom have put it? "Strongly suggesting"? Koz was asking everyone to look inside themselves, but they were still only asking. Penelope was twisting her immediate reality by sheer force of will. Two different beasts entirely.

Trusting in the better nature of the universe was truly a gift. One which Olivia envied Koz of a bit. Maybe she, Alibaster, and Penelope were becoming jaded in her travels. Koz was taking a big risk here; giving everyone a chance to do the right thing, and cast out the bad dream. Such optimism was… rare. If even one person refused, if a single soul decided they were better off with the Reaver inside them, it was over.

Since time had little meaning in the Blank (even less so now that most folks were temporarily temporally transfixed) it really couldn't be said how long they waited; Koz with their eyes closed, muttering their plea into the minds of the universe, with Musty and Olivia sitting behind them, feeling about as useful as oblong wheels.

Through the pep-talk Koz was cycling through her head, Olivia worried about her friends below. Every now and again, one of the gods would shift position before locking up once more like rusted robots. If they were starting to move, then that meant that all the creatures on the ship might start unfreezing too. The fighting would begin again, and now Penelope, Alibaster, and the fox were right in the center of it all. Plexerious had been on his last leg three legs ago. There was no one to protect them.

"Resolve," Koz said, loud enough for her to hear.

"What?" Olivia asked.

Koz didn't open their eyes or turn around. "Your negativity is interfering. You need resolve. Both of you. You need to be my anchors. My tethers as I stretch myself to the limits of the collective unconscious. You have to believe we can do this. That's all this place is. Belief shapes reality. So believe we can do this. Believe in me. In our friends. Believe we will win. Believe we'll survive. You need resolve."

Olivia nodded. Musty took a breath.

Koz was right. They had to trust that they would win. Because they had always won, Olivia and her friends. And it was no different this time. Because it wasn't the Fate Makers, or the Key of Three, or any of that crap. It was them. Just them. They fought the battles no one else could. And they would do it again. And again. Until it killed them.

But that wouldn't be today.

Because today they would rise above the nightmares. They would hold back the war of stories. They would stave off the corrupted, and free possessed gods. And they would rid every mind of the Dream Reaver, and put it back in its prison so that it could never infect anyone again.

It would all be so. They would make it so.

"It's working," Musty said in astonishment.

Olivia returned her attention to the living mountains of power in front of them and saw more and more of their eyes returning to normal. As far back as she could see, and even further back afterwards. She could feel it. It was the smallest shift in the atmosphere, but it was there. Like lying on one's back in the stillest water, only to suddenly feel the tiniest ripple. Like the gentlest chime going off right at the front of her mind; an acupuncture needle placed between the eyebrows.

It had worked. Koz did it. They fleking did it!

Everyone. Everywhere. The Reaver had been cast out. All the Fathoms, all the Natives, and any wayward dreamers. Free. Their minds their own.

The gods started moving again, suddenly, like pressing play on a show that had been paused. It took them all aback, and Nestor flew backwards a few dozen yards.

The gods paid them no attention (as were gods' wont), and spoke amongst themselves in what seemed to be incomprehensibly beautiful and thunderous confusion.

So this is either really good or really bad, Olivia figured. Either Penelope had sensed the same calm Olivia had, knew the "infection" was gone, and freed the gods of the time stop of her own volition.

Or…

Before she could ponder any of the negative implications of what might have happened to her friend below, Koz coughed and inhaled hard. Then they turned back, gave Olivia and Musty the weakest, most thoroughly drained smile anyone had ever seen.

Then their eyes rolled back, their grip on Nestor loosened, and they slipped off the dragon's back, plummeting towards the floor of the Blank.

Chapter 53: Flip the Script

"Koz!" Musty yelled.

"Hold on!" Olivia yelled to him, as she quickly scooted up the dragon's neck and reapplied her grip. "Nestor, go!"

The animaelstrom obeyed, and shot down towards the ground at a ninety degree angle. It reminded Olivia of that one waterslide. The Big One. There was even liquid- of a sort- at the bottom. Would that be enough to cushion Koz's fall? They were pretty high up…

No, stop it! Olivia scolded herself as wind whipped past her face and blurred her vision.

They were catching up to the freefalling hero of the Paracosm. Olivia tried to keep her balance as she reached a hand out past Nestor's head. If she could only grab onto them… But Koz was just barely out of reach. *Come on… Come on…*

The dragon was giving it all he had. His wings beat mightily to try and bridge the gap. But no matter how much closer they got, Koz was always just out of reach. It was like there was some force keeping them apart. Almost as if Koz was willing themself to fall faster.

Oh, no.

Just before their body hit the invisible amniotic fluid of ideas, several hundred yards away from the ship, Koz looked up at Olivia and Musty with a face that was not their own.

With eyes that were copper and black.

And they went under. Nestor swooped up at the last instant, and circled the area of Koz's impact.

"No… No…" Musty kept repeating.

"Did you see that?" Olivia asked. "Just before-"

The liquid below bubbled. Then steamed. Then exploded like a geyser.

Then, strangely, it all settled down again.

"What just happened?" Musty asked.

Olivia didn't answer. Instead she hopped down from the anima maelstrom. The jump was only a couple feet. Her feet hit the liquid, and she was shocked that it only came up to her knees. Her calves and feet could no longer be seen, as they disappeared into the invisible ink.

"What are you doing?" Musty asked, starting to climb off.

Olivia put a hand up to stop him. "No, stay with Nestor."

"But-" Musty started to object.

"I need Nestor to round up all the gods and send them home with his vortex." The last thing they needed were confused gods trampling everyone. She directed her attention towards the dragon himself. "Presumably you can do that, seeing as you brought half of them here to begin with."

Nestor might have nodded. She took that as a yes.

Olivia looked back at Musty. "And I need you to get the others. Tell them what's happening."

"What *is* happening?" Musty looked miserable. He wasn't used to this life and death stuff. All things considered, he was handling it rather well.

"Just get them here," Olivia snapped. She calmed down at once, and added, "Please. I know you don't know me that well, but I need you to trust me."

"And Koz?"

"I'll find them. I promise. Now go."

Before Musty could offer any more uncertainties, Nestor set off. As they flew away, headed towards the nearest giant, the anima maelstrom was opening its giant maw, and a vortex of light spewed forth.

Now then...

"They're gone," Olivia said. "Show yourself. It's just you and me."

Koz rose from the ink a few feet in front of her. First the top of their head became visible. Then their face. Then came torso and arms and legs. They rose like a dais was lifting them to the surface. They looked both rigid and corpselike. Their movements were just the slightest bit unnatural. Like those of a marionette.

They studied Olivia with soulless eyes.

"I get it," Olivia said, struggling to seem more confident than she felt. "God, that was actually pretty clever. Of course you would go to Koz. Their will was weakened from stretching their mind so thin. And since they were touching everything and everyone you were infecting, it must have been like a million pathways suddenly converging. The most obvious place to flee once you were cast out."

The Dream Reaver manipulated Koz's vocal cords in a horrific facsimile of a laugh. "Who said we were cast out?"

This took Olivia off guard, but only momentarily. It was trying to tell her it had chosen to leave all its other hosts; that all this was part of some sort of plan. But Olivia didn't believe it. It didn't make any sense. This was just a weak attempt at manipulation. The Reaver was just scrambling for some sort of purchase over the situation. It had to be.

"Admit it," she continued. "You lost. The war you wanted to reenact, the power you craved, it's all gone. You have nothing left." Usually it was beneath her to mock the villains, but she needed to keep the Reaver occupied until she could figure out how to get it out of Koz. Using the gift of the Tree was probably out of the question, considering Koz had it too, and the Reaver had still been able to slip past it.

The Reaver flicked a wrist. "You know nothing of what I want. Your problem is that you still believe this to be your story."

Olivia noticed something then, and kicked herself for not noticing it a second ago. "Your voice," she said, "your speech, it's not-"

"Not slow and jumbled and ambling?" the Reaver finished for her.

Olivia nodded. This was not the first time she had seen a friend possessed, but the experience didn't get any easier with added quantity. It did, however, help her sketch out an educated guess as to what was happening.

"It's Koz, isn't it?" she asked. "They're like your perfect vessel, somehow. Maybe because you were trapped inside their ancestor for so long. Or maybe it's due to their empathic abilities or connection to the Paracosm."

The Reaver adjusted Koz's glasses. "Or maybe it's just easier to control one form than it is to control several hundred million, and perhaps I simply chose your friend out of convenience, or some form of posthumous revenge on my former prison host."

Olivia considered. That seemed like a probability too. Honestly, the why's of it didn't matter. What mattered was getting the Reaver out of Koz, and containing its essence somehow. The question was whether it could be contained without a host of some sort. No one else needed to sacrifice themselves for this thing's imprisonment. Least of all Koz, who just saved like every-freaking-body from it.

The beast changed topics. It was suddenly chattier, now that speaking wasn't such a chore for it. "Why did you send the boy away? Was it something to do with their... affections towards each other?"

There was no point lying. "Yes," she said. "I knew seeing Koz like this- like *you*- would be hard for Musty."

"You hoped to spare him pain?"

"Yes."

"You hope to spare my host body pain as well?"

Where is this going? "Yes."

"As well as all the others? Symbolic and Literal alike? Would you spare them all pain?"

Olivia hesitated. "If I can."

"What would you do? Ask yourself. To protect them from me- from my 'infection' as you all call it- what would you do?"

She stood her ground. "Whatever I can."

The Reaver motioned to Koz's body. "Would you take this one's place?"

Olivia's blood froze. "What?"

There was the barest hint of a smile. "Oh, I know all about the plan concocted with the help of my stray conscience. The same plan the elder Natives enacted upon me so very long ago. But with the descendant of my original captor. How poetic. How just. It might even work. There is still time for you to give a rousing speech to your friend, and get them to fight against my terrible influence. Dear Kozmoklor might come around, exerting enough will power to take control of their faculties while still holding me within. Time enough to leave the Paracosm, return to the Literal realm, and launch us both back into the abyss in space. The universe would sleep safe once more." It inclined its head and stuck out a pouty lip. "But..."

"But Koz would be dead," Olivia finished. "Yeah. I know."

"And you..." the Reaver started circling her, with hands behind Koz's back, making Olivia feel a little like she was about to be rapped on the knuckles with a ruler. "I can sense an acute offness about you. You stink of one who has managed to climb back on the mortal coil. You've died before."

Olivia didn't answer.

"So my question is a simple one." It stopped circling. "Would you do it again? To save the universe? To save your friend? Would you take their place, and be damned to an eternal sleep in a dead nebula? Your only company an endless torrent of nightmarish visions pouring into your corpse mind for all time?"

She didn't feel like making a joke about how that was more than one question. But she considered. If the Reaver was actually offering to let Olivia take Koz's place, to sacrifice its freedom just for the sake of some odd experiment in personal morality, then she had to accept. Right?

The Reaver did not seem gleeful by its proposition or Olivia's hesitation. Instead it seemed genuinely curious as to what she would choose. Like it almost couldn't comprehend why someone would even consider trading their life for another, and it wanted to understand.

"So Miss Jones," it said after not giving her nearly enough time to mull it over, "just how quick are you to fall on your sword?"

Chapter 54: Olivia's Worst Idea Ever

"Don't do it!" a voice called from behind her.

Olivia turned around as much as she dared while still keeping the Reaver in her peripherals. Coming towards them was a small rowboat- presumably a lifeboat from the Cyclops pirate ship- holding Alibaster and the fox. A rope was tied to the front which was being pulled by the Script Angel that had been left behind.

The boat reached Olivia and what once was Koz, and the angel stopped pulling. He floated several inches above the liquid of the Blank, and Olivia wasn't sure whether it was because he didn't want to touch it, or if he just needed to constantly look down on everyone.

"Don't do it," Alibaster said again as he clamored out of the boat. "We saw you all fall from the sky. The fox guessed what probably happened."

Olivia didn't respond. Instead she noticed how tense the fox was. His fur was standing on end, and he was keeping to the far end of the boat, as if he couldn't back away enough. His eyes never left that of Koz's infected form.

The Reaver smirked. "If it isn't my severed morality. The nagging voice, which I set adrift. Cut away like a gangrenous limb. I see you found a form- an identity- of your own. How novel."

A growl was forming at the base of the fox's throat.

Olivia snapped her fingers between them, diverting his attention. "Where's Penelope?"

The fox calmed a few degrees, and looked down. Olivia walked the few paces to the edge of the boat and looked down herself. Penelope was lying on the floor of the craft. Her eyes were closed, and her whole body was shaking as if frigid. She also had- what were those? Cuts? They were scattered all over her body. They varied in size and depth, but from them came not blood, but light. The same blue light that often fell from her eyes. The light of capital "T" Time. And as Olivia stared at them, it almost looked as if they were closing. Like her body was repairing itself on its own accord. And inch by inch, the lights receded, as the skin mended.

"What?" Olivia asked quietly, to no one in particular.

"Expending all that power in such a way," the fox said, "it has never been done before. By all accounts she should be dead. Disbursing that much energy in such a fashion for such an extended length... Well as you can see. It should have ripped her body apart."

"Why didn't it?" Olivia wondered, though not ungrateful.

It was Alibaster who answered, keeping Plex's sword trained on Koz as he spoke. "Our working theory is the power of belief. She is a goddess, after all. Sort of."

The Shrunken Village. Of course. All those Fathoms who saw Penelope erupt from the ground after escaping her own dreams, and turn to stone before their eyes. They must have more autonomy than previously thought. Or perhaps Penelope had become a fixture of that place; cementing herself in its psyche. Either way, the people remembered her. And even though Penelope was a Literal, they were still in the Paracosm, and the reality of the Paracosm was forged by belief. Maybe their belief was healing her. Making her into the immortal goddess they thought her to be.

"Like she needed any more of an ego boost," Alibaster muttered.

Olivia looked to the angel. "And you're here because…"

The Script had his arms crossed, and studied a tattoo on his bicep. "Penance, for the… impulsive actions of myself and my others. We thought we were helping."

"You dumped an army onto a ship and tried to run away," Olivia said. She stroked one of his wings with the tips of her fingers, before plucking one of the feathers in either spite or pettiness. The angel flinched, and backed away a few levitating paces.

"Yes, well. Perhaps that was not the most… prudent course of action. I called my others back, and they are cleaning up the ship of all we-" he cleared his throat- "'dumped' there."

That was something at least. And since her friends had made their way to her of their own accord, she suddenly felt bad about sending Musty off with the dragon. They usually didn't have so many people helping. It was a bit of a surplus to requirements. Not that she was complaining.

"So now what?" Alibaster asked.

"Yes," cooed the Reaver. "Now what, Olivia Jones?"

"Now we put you back where you belong," said the fox with a snarl. "And we're all finally rid of you."

Olivia studied the feather she plucked as she contemplated the situation around her. Like wyrmholes, it shimmered with every color of the spectrum. Something the Reaver had said was niggling at her. It had called the fox a severed limb. As if certain impulses could just be removed from a mind. And that reminded her of something else. Something she had seen when she first got to the Paracosm. Back at the Swan and Swine. And now, in the Blank… The way it had reshaped Plexerious…

"Dammit," she sighed. She might have the makings of a plan. But it was not one she really cared for. She doubted it would work. But if it was between a tenuous idea or letting Koz die in the Abysmal, then there wasn't much of a choice.

She gripped the feather in one hand, and the other she positioned in front of her possessed friend for a handshake. Shady deals always involved handshakes.

"Ok," she said. "I'll do it. I'll trade places with Koz."

In the corner of her eye, she saw an appalled look on Alibaster's face. She shook her head at him, silently pleading with him not to protest, to trust her. And while she couldn't see the fox behind her, she hoped whatever link or connection was between them was still on and working. Hopefully he could sense what she was doing. He had to act when the time was right. They both did.

The Reaver looked neither pleased nor disappointed by her choice. It had simply been curious as to what she would decide. For the creature itself, it was a pretty lateral move to switch from one host to another. No doubt it would try and go back on its word somehow. It would infect her, maybe muck around in her mind for a bit. Try to drive her mad, all that fun stuff. Then it would leave her for dead, her mind and spirit broken, and return back to Koz: the perfect vessel for an entity of the Paracosm.

So Olivia had to act quicker than it could.

Quicker than treachery.

Quicker than thought.

This'll be fun, she thought dryly.

The Reaver took her outstretched hand, and the fog swept through Olivia's mind.

Chapter 55: Welcome to the Nightmare in My Head

Within an instant it became abundantly clear that the Reaver was not trying to recruit her like it had with all the others it had possessed. It was not whispering sweet nothings of comfort, safety, or power into her psyche. No propaganda telling her to "believe in the nightmare" or whatever crap it had been spewing. Maybe this was due to the Tree, maybe it was Olivia's own strength of character.

Either way, it was just digging.

Digging for all her secrets and lies. Everything she kept from others as well as herself. Everything it could use to turn her against herself.

And she could feel it as it burrowed through her neural pathways. For some reason it reminded her of when she was little, and her grandma would try and brush knots and tangles out of her hair. It was so aggressive, and she pulled so hard. Her grandma would simply tell her to stop squirming while she made Olivia's hair "manageable". That was what the Reaver was trying to do now. Trying to find every Achilles heel it could slice. To make sure she was no longer a threat. To make her manageable.

She could still see the outside world. But it was different now. It was like she was looking out of two pairs of eyes. One set in front of another. She saw Koz, kneeling and blinking. And Alibaster shouting something. (Presumably, "Get out of her, you bastard.") But he seemed far away. Like she was watching him on a movie screen. As if she was sitting in the back row of her own mind.

With the Reaver poking around her synapses, that meant that it wasn't overly interested with what her body was doing at the moment. All she had to do was one simple motion… Lift her hand to her mouth. She hoped that was enough.

It was easier said than done, though. She had to do it inconspicuously, without the Reaver noticing what she was doing while it riffled through her memories. And the process was clunky; like trying to move an avatar in a virtual reality game when something wasn't synchronized properly. Olivia would try and lift her arm, but it would just spasm at her body's side.

The Reaver had just activated a memory. When Olivia peed her pants in second grade because the substitute teacher was too scary to ask to go to the restroom.

Huh, ok. Didn't know I remembered that.

She shook off the embarrassment, and tried again.

This time she got her arm to a ninety degree angle before it fell back to her side. Olivia got excited, then angry, then forced herself to calm down in case the nightmare was monitoring her emotions.

It was difficult to stay focused, as she kept being bombarded by unwanted memories. It was like the Reaver was skimming through the filing cabinet of her life, and tossing random papers on the floor of her head. Once it had enough ammunition, it would start with all that fun spirit breaking that bad guys loved so much. It would take all the things she was self conscious about, all the things she disliked about herself, all the bad choices she'd made, all her failures, and it would regurgitate them all right back at her. It would take the emotions all those instances elicited and concentrated them down into distilled despair. A despair so deep she would never be able to crawl back out. Then the Reaver would have full control, and it would no longer be a matter of two wills fighting for control of one body.

And the one memory that it was dissecting the most- playing it over and over again, studying it like a coach studying a past game- was the most obvious. The memory she had been haunted by every time she closed her eyes for the past half year. The one which had cropped up to meet her there in the Paracosm as well.

Killing Ophelia.

And on another day, perhaps reliving that horrible moment might have been enough to deal Olivia the final blow. But since her journey in the hidden dimension began, she had confronted her greatest regret. Owned it. And while she would never allow herself to be totally liberated from it, she would no longer bow to the grief it caused her.

While the Reaver thought it was adding fuel to the flames of desolation, it was actually stoking the fire of Olivia's motivation.

Because she had gotten it wrong then, she refused to choose the same path now. Neither she, Koz, nor anyone else would ever have to sacrifice their lives to keep the monster contained. That wasn't how this story was supposed to go. And as she gave one last mental command to her distant arm, the Reaver finally took notice in what was happening.

What are you doing? it asked, swimming up her neurons toward the corner of her head where it had swept her out of its way.

Outside, in the Blank, Olivia's arm bent. Her hand reached her mouth. She uncupped her hand, and shoved the angel feather behind her teeth, hoping it would be enough to do what she needed it to. The feather melted to liquid and slid down her throat with the taste of lemon zest and petrichor.

Inside the theater of her mind, she smiled. *I'm writing a better ending.*

Chapter 56: You Can't Disown Your Mistakes

The experience of what happened next wasn't painful, but it didn't feel great either. The Reaver was forced out of Olivia like a petulant weed being torn out by the roots. The creature exploded out of the back of her head with the feeling of a bursting balloon mixed with a violent sneeze. Olivia's mind and body were once more her own.

What made up the thing of nightmares hung like a dark cloud over and slightly behind her now. This might have been the first time that the Reaver was ever seen without a host body. Its true form revealed at last. But since it was an amalgamation of all dark thoughts and fears in the universe, its form wasn't what one might call "stable". It sat above them all in an almost bubble. It consisted of a black and gray mass of thick liquid the consistency of hot tar. The tar writhed on all sides, giving way to shapes and forms which would half appear before being pushed back down and drowned by new shapes. It bubbled and oozed as it fought against the sudden restraint, as well as itself. It wasn't terrifying at all. It was actually kind of pathetic.

"What just happened?" Alibaster asked as they all stared at the thing.

Koz answered before Olivia could. "Drift Back," they said with a chuckle. "You used Drift Back to eject the creature from your head. Amazing."

They quickly explained to Alibaster what Drift Back was, while the Script Angel couldn't seem to decide whether to be offended at Olivia for getting a free sample, or impressed with himself because obviously this meant he had helped.

"It will not last long though," the Script said. "The way you ingested it was not Drift Back in its distilled form. It is not concentrated enough. You have but a minute before the effect dissolves and that monster is plunged back into your mind." He paused. "Though I can offer you Drift Back of a much more lucrative quality. Stuff that will last. It will only cost you the small price of-"

"No," Olivia cut him off. "No soul selling for me today, thanks." She looked at Alibaster. "You have Plex's sword. He told me once that it could cut the thoughts from a person's head. When I give the word, I need you to cut the invisible string connecting the Reaver to me."

"What?" Alibaster asked. "That's your plan? That's a terrible plan. Not just the logistics of how that would even work, or the leaps of logic of how you came to the conclusion that it would. But even if it did, then what? The thing would just fly into someone else, and we'd start the whole thing over."

Olivia pointed to the boat. "The fox."

The fox shuffled nervously. "Me?" He already knew what she had in mind, she knew he did.

Olivia nodded. "You can be the Reaver's vessel. You're the only one who can. You are the conscience it cast away, but you can reclaim the creature. You are made from it; you are two pieces of the same puzzle. Yin and yang, and all that. Please. In the state it's in now, it's weak. You can become the dominant part of the consciousness. You can keep a lid on it within your own mind. And that way, no one else will get hurt because of it."

"When I was in the beast's mind, it nearly drowned me," the fox argued. "I was glad to be released from its hold."

"You can't run from your demons forever," Alibaster said.

"It's just like you told us when we were trying to pull Alibaster out of that prison," Koz said. "When you try to escape who you are, people end up hurt. Especially yourself. Think about all you've gone through because of the nightmare. All the pain and struggle you and others have dealt with due to it. No, you can't outrun it. The best way forward is to own it. Change it. Claim the Reaver and do everything you can to change its nature from the inside. Teach it your perspective. Help it be better. Help yourself."

"And if that doesn't work?" the fox asked.

Olivia shrugged. "We're in the Paracosm. Belief is a powerful thing. And I believe you can do it. You can help the Reaver grow into something better. Something more. You can make up for the havoc it has caused."

The fox still looked unsure, but he put on a brave face. "Ok. Ok, I will try."

"You have seconds left," the Script Angel said.

Olivia nodded to the fox. "Be ready." Then she looked at Alibaster.

With a strained grunt, he raised Plexerious' sword over his head, and sliced right through the empty air between Olivia and the Drifting Reaver.

Olivia took an experimental step away, and the bubble of tar didn't follow her like a trailing balloon. It had worked. But the Reaver was boiling. It churned and twisted upon itself angrily. This was the first time in a long time it had truly been on its own, within its own mind. No host minds to hide in and distract itself. No conscience to talk to. It was finally forced to see itself for what it was.

And it was abundantly clear that it didn't care for the experience. Within an instant it would escape from the lingering effects of the Drift and be free to find new vessels again.

Olivia, Alibaster, Koz, and the angel all looked at the fox. "Go!" Olivia said.

"Yes," said the fox, his eyes not leaving the Reaver. "Yes. Of course. It's just- well it seems silly. I can't seem to feel my legs. Perhaps if I-"

Just then, Penelope sat up in the boat, opened her eyes, grabbed the fox by the scruff, and tossed the animal straight into the floating black mass.

Chapter 57: No Animals Were Harmed in the Writing of This Chapter

In the hero business, this action would have been classified as "a bit of a dick move".

The bubble of Drift Back that was containing the Reaver's essence popped, and all that was the nightmare creature instantly clung to the fox as he passed through it, like an oil slick with abandonment issues. It absolutely needed a host, and one had literally just been thrown its way. It must have been instinctual, an innate primal need, because there was no way the Reaver would willingly choose to bind itself once more to the very part of itself it severed.

The fox passed through the popped bubble, and landed in the Blank's liquid completely enveloped, as if he were now nothing but a shadow given depth. He had an attacking stance, each spider colored hair on his body standing on edge as if electrified, and a low growl was trying to claw its way to the surface. One of his eyes was the familiar black/copper. The other remained his usual pupilless white.

"Fox…?" Olivia asked.

No response.

Alibaster still had Plexerious' sword at the ready. "Should something be happening?"

"He's fighting," Koz said. "I can feel it. So far I haven't been able to sense the fox's emotions. But this is so strong. Both of them. They're both fighting for control. Two parts of a single mind warring against each other."

By now, Penelope had gotten out of the boat. All but the tiniest of cuts had disappeared. She was still wobbly, and looked like she might pass out again at any moment. She shrugged off any attempt to help steady her. "How do we help?"

"Full emersion might work," the Script Angel said. "Completely under the liquid which has rewritten so many before. Though it would help if the hybrid creature were dead. Then the dominant side would take over upon resurrection. No need for all this inner conflict."

"And if the fox isn't the dominant side?" Alibaster asked rhetorically. "Not willing to test that."

"Also- and I shouldn't have to say this- but no killing," Olivia said.

Something of what they were saying must have made its way to the fox's understanding. Because suddenly, the animal fell through the liquid entirely, as if a trap door opened up under him.

It was then that Musty and Nestor came back into the fold. Musty climbed awkwardly down from the dragon next to Koz. "Koz! Are you ok?" He looked them over as Koz assured Musty they were fine. Then Musty continued. "We just got done sweeping up the last of the gods. Well, this guy did most of the work." He pointed a thumb at the animaelstrom. "I swear, I've never seen an animal's jaw unhinge like that. It was insane. And I went to the ship but you were all gone-" He stopped himself as he looked around the group. "I take it I've missed something?"

Olivia gave him the bullet points. "The Reaver is in the fox, who are both underwater. Not water. Whatever. We're hoping that the fox can take control of the Reaver since they are kind of sort of the same being."

"Ok," Musty said with a face which said that really didn't clear much up at all.

They all watched the spot where the fox had sunk. There was no telling how long he would stay under or what he might become once emerged.

"Everyone, circle up around where the fox went under," Olivia said. "If they come back up and the Reaver's in control, we can't let it escape." Though what any of them could do to stop it, she had absolutely no clue. "Nestor and angel guy, cover the air. If things go sideways, one of you needs to use your portals to get us out of here."

"Or throw the Reaver into the most incredible black hole anyone's ever dreamed of," Alibaster suggested.

"*If* things go sideways?" Penelope scoffed. "Our whole life is a perpetual state of quarter turns, right after the other. We've gone sideways so many times; we're right side up tenfold." She groaned. "Sorry. Tired. Head swimming. Ignore me." She yanked Plexerious' shield from Alibaster's hand. "Give me that."

Together they waited.

Olivia's heart was beating hard with anxious anticipation. She counted thirteen *thu-thumps* before something happened. It started as a dot, like a droplet of ink, appearing right in the center of the circle they had formed. Right on top of the still fluid of the Blank. Then the droplet grew, spreading outwards like food coloring squirted into water. Soon the stain would reach them. Then it would go past them, and infect the entirety of the Blank, and the Reaver would be all powerful once more.

This was really a one step forward two steps back kind of day.

To prove the point, the five of them took a couple steps back to get away from the spreading darkness.

The Blank liquid was no longer invisible. Wherever the Reaver's influence touched, shapes could be seen forming upon the not-water's surface. Horrific, groaning masks of faces. Monstrous or spindly shapes of things half remembered from long forgotten nightmares. Clawed or disfigured hands emerging from watery graves only to fall back in on themselves. These forms weren't substantial yet, but they would be. The Reaver was winning its fight with the fox. It was pushing him back with the only tool in its arsenal: fear.

"Come on fox," Olivia said. "Fight back."

"You can't give in," Koz added. "The Reaver is you. You are it. But you don't have to be controlled by it. You can save yourself. You're its conscience. Its soul. Take the reins."

The infection hit the circumference of their circle, and they all flinched, expecting to be taken over. But something odd happened. The spread stopped. As if a dome had been placed right where they all stood. The inside of the circle was completely blacked out and still writing with half formed monsters, but it didn't go any further.

Step forward, a voice rang out. It was instantly recognizable as the fox's.

"Did you guys all just-" Musty started. Everyone nodded. "Oh, good. Glad it's not just me."

They all took a step forward. The area of the darkness retreated so that it still fit inside the slightly shrunken circle.

"Interesting," Alibaster said.

"Are we doing this?" Penelope asked. "How are we doing this?"

"The power of belief?" Koz suggested.

Alibaster and Penelope cringed. "A little on the nose, don't you think?" Alibaster asked.

"The Tree of Life," Musty said. "We still have the power it gave us. We can still push the influence back."

Olivia supposed that was a possibility. The Reaver had only been able to infect Koz in a moment of mental fatigue, and Olivia after being invited in. If they still had the power granted them, they could push the Reaver back. Shove it back down, and help the fox take control.

"Let's take another step," she said. They did, and once more the splotch shrunk.

They kept stepping closer, closing the gap between each other. As they did, the manifestations within the infected area of liquid became more violent. They thrashed and spewed and screamed, like crazed animals trying to fight their way out of a tar pit. But in the end, it became abundantly clear that there was no real threat. When it came right down to it, the Reaver- just like all power hungry monsters- had no real power at all.

And in that moment, as they closed the circle completely, Olivia pondered something. She thought about how there were five of them, and how there were five dimensions, and how the universe always had a cruel sense of coincidence. Because the Paracosm was forged by symbolism. And right there and then, each of them might have represented a different dimension.

Musty as the first. The still point. The most knowable and consistant, yet still so brilliant and fundamental.

Alibaster as the second. The moving line; forever flying from one point to another. Never stopping, never slowing, never knowing where he'll be next.

Olivia herself as the third. The one which helped add purpose and physicality to the all the moving lines which her friend created.

Penelope as the fourth. The child of Time, who could see so much potential in a universe she never quite felt at home in.

And Kozmoklor as the fifth. The legacy of the secret dimension. The empath who helped rid countless minds of an intruding terror.

All of them, coming together to banish the dark. As if every level of the universe was telling the Reaver that it would not be manipulated by fear and the prospects of empty promises. It would not be controlled by the dark. No longer influenced by its nightmares. Just as Koz had said, it would always shine a light to reveal the truth and strive for something better.

It wasn't just the gift of the Tree doing this. It was them. All by themselves.

The Reaver roared, using its last bit of strength to form a hideous creation from what was left of its power. It swirled up like clay being worked, towering over them with several gnashing mouths and vengeful eyes.

Nestor flapped out of the way and hissed at it. The angel swore as he dodged out of its path as well, and then immediately repented.

From the mouths of the monstrosity came a number of voices. All sounded different. Distorted. All speaking in unison. "I am what waits; suffocating the light! I am what fuels the thoughts of the night!"

"Oh God," said Penelope with an eye roll. "Now it's rhyming."

The Reaver continued. "I am what sits in your head and feeds fright! I am the Nightmare. You will fall to my might!"

"You done?" Alibaster asked.

"It's done," Musty confirmed. He pressed his hand into the monstrous mass, and the others followed suit.

It felt like seaweed and clammy skin, and it recoiled at each touch. It screamed and thrashed and melted back into the liquid of the Blank until it could no longer be seen at all.

Chapter 58: Wrapping Things Up

Ten breathes and some awkward staring before the fox surfaced. He looked different, though. He no longer had the body of a typical red fox, which Olivia had subconsciously designed for him. His features all looked slightly different, and his fur was now gray. His eyes were still the same white, but now they had rings of copper acting as pupils.

"Thank you," he said. He sounded the same, but different. Olivia couldn't put her finger on it. "Thank you all. I knew my choice in champions was well founded. As well as my choice for companions. I hope in time you can learn to forgive me for all I've done. All I've put you through. From this point on I will begin my existence anew, and do all I can to redeem myself in the eyes of those in the Paracosm."

"What do you mean?" Musty asked. "Why are you apologizing for the Reaver's actions?"

"I am one entity once more," the fox said. "The Reaver's actions are my actions. And in some way, the Reaver no longer exists at all. But I must still make things right."

"Everyone in the Paracosm will be after your head," Alibaster said.

"If I must stand trial or be imprisoned, then that is what I will do. We all must be held responsible for our actions." The fox's head perked up. "But you all will be remembered here. The Paracosm will know of who you are and what you did to save it. I will make sure of it. A great testimony. The story told to stories. "

The five looked at each other. "Please don't do that," Olivia said. "The last thing we need is celebrity status, and our images leaking into the minds of Literals."

"It's easier to do our job if we stay somewhat anonymous." Alibaster added.

"And I don't handle paparazzi that well," Penelope admitted. "Still have about eight lawsuits pending against me from some rather insistent photographers of grateful planets."

"Two of them weren't even trying to take her picture," Alibaster said. "They just pointed their cameras in her general direction and she started swinging."

"So what now?" Olivia asked.

The fox considered. "There is much to do. The state of the Paracosm is in disarray."

"How can you tell?" Alibaster muttered.

The fox continued. "There are still those who I killed and have not yet… respawned. We must leave the Blank as soon as possible to let it do its work. There is also the matter of the monsters and creatures I set loose on stories which they were not native too. I should start my penance by doing what I can to round them all back up and put them where they belong."

"I will assist you in this venture," the Script Angel said. "I will call on my others to do the same. Perhaps we too can repent for our time spent astray from our original purpose."

The fox nodded appreciatively.

Nestor screeched, drawing attention to himself.

Olivia winced. "Sorry buddy, it seems you'll have to find another new home."

It couldn't be said how the animaelstrom thought about this. It simply twisted in the air, and made its way back towards the ship. As it got closer, the ship seemed to move further away. No, that wasn't it. The ship was shrinking. It got smaller and smaller until…

You have got to be kidding me, Olivia thought. The pirate ship which had expanded to encompass oh-so many figuratives, was now but a small breadbox floating upon the surface. And the lifeboat which her friends had used to reach her was now only a toothpick sized splinter. Nestor gripped the breadbox between his teeth, and flew to find his next story or dream.

"What about me?" Penelope asked once the dragon was out of sight. "Am I still going to have these goddess-y powers? How does the power of belief in the Paracosm affect the Literal universe?"

"Miss Brownstein-McClain, I am afraid that you were never meant to be in the fifth dimension at all." The fox looked repentant. "I brought you here because I needed your help, and I put that over your own needs. Look what this realm has done to you. I might as well have dropped you in a radioactive wasteland. Once you return, all will be as it was. But you must never come here again. You might not be so lucky in your survival if you do."

Penelope really didn't look too bothered by this news. "Go on. Twist my arm about it." She dropped her shield. "Give that back to Plex for me."

Alibaster laid down his sword. They each floated atop the liquid as if they weighed nothing. "This as well."

The fox nodded.

"So that's it?" Olivia asked. "We all leave the Paracosm?"

"You've all earned some rest," the fox said. "I can send you back to your points of entry, and from there you can slip back into your dreams. I wish you many pleasant ones. From there you will wake in your proper places."

"And what?" Olivia asked. "Forget this ever happened?"

The fox smiled. "Is anything ever truly forgotten?"

The world fell away.

Chapter 59: To be Read after Chapter 5 for the Full Confusion Experience

Olivia opened her eyes. What had happened? Had she fallen asleep? Where was she? She looked around and found herself in her co-pilot's chair. Strapped in. Why was she strapped in? Alibaster and Penelope were in their own chairs to the right of her. They were strapped in too. The ship didn't seem to be moving.

She tapped the release mechanism on her chair's arm, and all the safety harnesses retracted back into the chair. She did the same for her friends, and shook them awake. "Guys?"

Alibaster and Penelope both groaned and Olivia checked the instruments on the control console to see where they were. But all she really had to do was look outside and see the large fields of orange grass which the ship now sat.

Illetica. That was right. They had been going to Illetica. And the ship just failed. Everything had failed. And they had all passed out. But somehow it seemed the ship had started functioning again, and had landed itself. Well, that was nice. And lucky. Unless luck had nothing to do with it, and their freefall had been planned. Designed.

Perhaps by Olivia herself. Maybe when she had set the coordinates for Illetica in her sleep, she had also tampered with the landing controls, so that when certain systems were activated the whole ship would experience a complete system failure. But then what? After they had all passed out, the ship just rebooted itself in time to perform an auto-landing? What for? None of this made any sense. She needed answers.

"Agreed," Alibaster said after he had gotten his bearings and Olivia had articulated her worries to him. "But if any of what's happening has to do with Illetica, then the first thing we need to do is make sure Musty's ok."

Olivia nodded. "So where is he?"

Using one of the ship's terrestrial vehicles, Alibaster, Penelope, and Olivia all took a drive to the nearest city. They found the hospital Musty worked at, and Alibaster pestered the administration desk until they contacted him. Musty was on-call and had been taking a nap in one of the staff dormitories until a few minutes ago. Now though, he was in the cafeteria.

After getting confusing directions, and getting turned around multiple times, they all found the cafeteria. Musty was sitting at a table across from a cute bald guy with blue octagonal glasses, a flannel with the sleeves rolled up, and formfitting jeans. Neither had food in front of them.

They both smiled when they saw Alibaster, Penelope, and Olivia.

"Hey Ali," Musty said. "Olivia. Penelope."

"Have we met?" Penelope asked.

Musty and the boy snickered, as if thinking about some inside joke.

The boy with the glasses stood up and hugged Olivia tightly. "It's so good to see you."

"Um," Olivia said.

"Aren't you wondering why we're here?" Alibaster asked his brother.

Musty shook his head. "No. I know why." He nodded to the boy. "Koz helped me remember."

The boy's name was Koz. That was one blank filled in. Now as to why he just tried to squeeze the stuffing out of Olivia…

"I keep discovering more abilities," Koz said. "It's like second nature almost. But it's a nature which has layers upon layers. And I don't know if I'll hit the final layer. Is that what it's like for you? With your Time stuff?" He directed the questions at Penelope.

Penelope stared.

"Man, their confusion is palpable," Koz said.

"You don't have to be an empath to feel that," Musty responded. "Come on. We can't keep them in the dark. It's just being mean."

"Fine, you're right." And like that, a wave of memories bombarded Olivia's head. And by the looks her friends had, it was hitting them too.

And within a second, they all remembered everything. The fox, the Dream Reaver, the Paracosm.

"Oh," said Olivia. And then she smiled, and laughed, and flung her arms around Koz, squeezing them just as tightly as they had squeezed her. "Hi."

Koz laughed back. "Hi."

Epilogue:

It was three weeks later. Three weeks since they fought the nightmare and saved the Paracosm. Yesterday they just got done dealing with those future ghosts they had originally planned on helping out with. It took longer than expected, and they were all tired. All they wanted to do was sleep. But Olivia didn't want to reschedule their appointments. Their lives were always going to be busy, so they had to commit, or else they would always just keep cancelling or rescheduling.

They had had to fly all night through hyperspace to make it on time. But made it they did. Alibaster and Penelope were still a little cool to the idea, but Olivia had made her case and voiced her strong opinions. And in the end they conceded that she was right. As they sat in the waiting room Alibaster fidgeted and squirmed, while Penelope had her head leaning back with her eyes closed. Olivia had a compact tablet from the ship and was writing a letter to send to her family. News was just announced that some tiny planet called Earth would soon be getting limited Withive capabilities, so she could keep in touch with them easier now.

Right now they were on some colony outpost on the fringes of some quasar or another. The name was hard to remember and had a bunch of numbers and slashes. The idea for this venture came inadvertently from Koz. After seeing how they helped first Alibaster in that desert prison, and then all the infected creatures of the Paracosm, it became clear that people with their abilities could help in ways other people could not. They could understand someone's mindset and help that person understand themself better than before. Especially if the empath was taught and trained a certain way. That was when the idea hit Olivia.

Empathic therapist.

That had to be a thing, surely. In a universe this big, everything was somewhere. And after hours of searching on the Withive, she at last found someone. She had asked a certain robotic Fate Maker to do a background check (one can never be too careful). And the results came back clean. He wasn't well known, but he was highly rated by those with atypical traumas.

And the things Olivia and her friends had been through definitely fit under the umbrella of atypical. It wasn't healthy to keep going how they went without actually dealing with the things they went through. It just hindered their abilities to help themselves as well as others.

A head poked into the door of the waiting room, and Olivia put down her tablet. "Who's first?" The head asked. "Or would you like to go together?"

Olivia and her friends had already talked about this. "One on one to start with," she answered. "And we'll see how it goes from there." She stood up. "I guess I'll go first."

The doctor- whose name also had a lot of numbers and was hard to remember- smiled softly. "Wonderful. Come on in."